SAVAGE EMBRACE

Abbey shrieked; the water was cooler than she'd first thought.

Hearing her scream, Kwan spun with alarm. He shook his head when he saw her neck-deep in water, shivering. "You wake the forest with your cry." He came toward the water, his intent clear.

Abbey froze, staring. "What are you doing?"

Kwan smiled. "It is night. I cannot see you." He was lying. He could see her—a hint of white flesh just below the lake's surface. And he felt a definite urge to touch this slave.

Kwan dove into the dark water, surfacing several feet away from Abbey, rising from the lake like some glistening pagan god. There was a look in his eyes that frightened her . . . and thrilled her. Dear God, she thought, what is wrong with me?

"Ab-bey." His voice was low, hoarse. Abbey gasped, suddenly conscious of the sleek moist heat of his powerful body . . . the tantalizing smell of wood smoke. Drawn by his hypnotic gaze, Abbey felt herself leaning toward him, her face raised upward, her lips slightly parted. Kwan bent his head and kissed her . . .

WATCH FOR THESE ZEBRA REGENCIES

LADY STEPHANIE   (0-8217-5341-X, $4.50)
by Jeanne Savery
Lady Stephanie Morris has only one true love: the family estate she has
managed ever since her mother died. But then Lord Anthony Rider
arrives on her estate, claiming he has plans for both the land and the
woman. Stephanie soon realizes she's fallen in love with a man whose
sensual caresses will plunge her into a world of peril and intrigue . . .
a man as dangerous as he is irresistible.

BRIGHTON BEAUTY   (0-8217-5340-1, $4.50)
by Marilyn Clay
Chelsea Grant, pretty and poor, naively takes school friend Alayna
Marchmont's place and spends a month in the country. The devastating
man had sailed from Honduras to claim his promised bride, Miss
Marchmont. An affair of the heart may lead to disaster . . . unless a
resourceful Brighton beauty finds a way to stop a masquerade and keep
a lord's love.

LORD DIABLO'S DEMISE   (0-8217-5338-X, $4.50)
by Meg-Lynn Roberts
The sinfully handsome Lord Harry Glendower was a gambler and the
black sheep of his family. About to be forced into a marriage of con-
venience, the devilish fellow engineered his own demise, never having
dreamed that faking his death would lead him to the heavenly refuge
of spirited heiress Gwyn Morgan, the daughter of a physician.

A PERILOUS ATTRACTION   (0-8217-5339-8, $4.50)
by Dawn Aldridge Poore
Alissa Morgan is stunned when a frantic passenger thrusts her baby into
Alissa's arms and flees, having heard rumors that a notorious highwayman posed a threat to their coach. Handsome stranger Hugh Sebastian
secretly possesses the treasured necklace the highwayman seeks and
volunteers to pose as Alissa's husband to save her reputation. With a
lost baby and missing necklace in their care, the couple embarks on a
journey into peril—and passion.

*Available wherever paperbacks are sold, or order direct from the
Publisher. Send cover price plus 50¢ per copy for mailing and
handling to Penguin USA, P.O. Box 999, c/o Dept. 17109, Ber-
genfield, NJ 07621. Residents of New York and Tennessee must
include sales tax. DO NOT SEND CASH.*

CANDACE McCARTHY
WARRIOR'S CARESS

ZEBRA BOOKS
KENSINGTON PUBLISHING CORP.

ZEBRA BOOKS

are published by

Kensington Publishing Corp.
850 Third Avenue
New York, NY 10022

First printing: September, 1992

Printed in the United States of America

10 9 8 7 6 5 4 3 2

For Roberta and Gerard, my in-laws, who welcomed me into their family and gave me the greatest gift of love . . . their son.

And for Judy and Colleen, who were there when I needed support and who taught me to appreciate the Woodland Indians of North America.

Chapter 1

Fort Michaels; Summer, 1737

Abbey didn't know what woke her. She sat up, listening, her breath lodged in her throat, as she glanced about the strange bedchamber. Moonlight spilled in through a single window, creating an eerie glow about the room. She could hear the tall case clock in the downstairs hall, a timepiece she had noticed upon her arrival late that afternoon. But other than the clock's soft *tick-tick-tick* that mirrored the steady thumping of her beating heart, the night was peacefully quiet.

She lay back against the feather tick, staring at the ceiling. She was here at Fort Michaels, deep in the New York wilderness, far from her home in England. Colonel William Breckingridge, the fort commander whom Abbey had come to see, was currently away on assignment with the English army. Abbey was waiting for the colonel to return so that she could implore him to find her brother Jamie.

Except for Jamie, Abbey was alone in the world. Both of Abbey's parents were dead; her physician father's death six months past ended for him a year and a half of grief and guilt over not being able to save his wife.

"Oh, Jamie," she whispered into the night. "I need you so."

Months ago, she had stood alone at their father's grave in Kent, holding her mother's ruby brooch, her only legacy of her dead parents' love. And she had mourned for both herself and Jamie. Then she'd dried her eyes and sold the brooch to finance the journey to be reunited with Jamie.

Abbey's eyes drifted shut as she recalled the long ocean voyage to the New World. Her quarters had been cramped, crowded, and musty, and there had been days when she'd wondered if she'd been better off in her grandparents' cold, unloving household. She'd managed to endure the rough seas by thinking of Jamie, and remembering the lovely word pictures he'd painted in his only letter home.

"The sky is so blue and the land has an aura of lush green magnificence, Abbe," he'd written about the Colonies. He had then gone on in terms of eloquent description of the sights he'd seen and the people he'd met, but mostly of his friend Walt and Walt's uncle, the boys' employer, a silversmith in Philadelphia. He'd promised to send for her and their father when he'd earned enough funds for their passage to the New World.

Abbey frowned into the darkness, her eyes open. *Jamie doesn't know about Father's death.* In Philadelphia, she had found her last letter to her brother

8

at the silversmith's unopened, unread. Jamie was missing, captured along with his friend Walt by Indians while he was delivering a silver consignment to a family deep in the Pennsylvania wilds.

He must have disappeared right after he'd written her, she realized.

Would she ever see Jamie again?

Her chest constricted painfully. Her brother in the hands of savages! She had to find him, rescue him from the heathens.

She shuddered, envisioning Jamie being tortured . . . *murdered*. Were the bloodthirsty tales she'd heard in England true?

Colonel Breckingridge was expected back at the fort in three days. Abbey was afraid that he'd be furious with her when he learned that she'd deceived his servants by allowing them to believe that she was the niece he'd been expecting from England.

She hadn't intended to be dishonest, but she'd used the last of her funds to make the journey from Philadelphia, across Pennsylvania, to the fort. Without money, she'd felt desperate. The guide she'd hired had seen her to the fort gate and then promptly left for Philadelphia, where Abbey had contracted his services.

The natural assumption on the head housekeeper's part that she was Susie Portsmouth, the colonel's niece, had seemed a heaven-scent solution to Abbey's dilemma. What other choice did she have but to seek shelter in the man's household? Surely, the man would understand that she needed a place to stay while she waited for his return! And Abbey was convinced that if the household servants knew her true identity, vulnerable or not, she'd be turned away.

Abbey sat up, staring straight ahead. She simply had to see Colonel Breckingridge! He was a man with a well-known reputation for rescuing white captives from the Indians; he was her only hope at finding Jamie.

But will I be able to convince him to help me, she wondered. *Or will he be too angry with my deception?*

He would understand! she told herself firmly. You haven't lived your life as a physician's daughter and often his helper without learning something about man's nature . . . how to deal with anger or fear . . .

With that knowledge to reassure her, Abbey allowed herself to relax back against her pillow. Her eyes drifted shut as she felt a wave of exhaustion overtake her. It was a quiet, pleasant night. The window to her room was open, and the summer night sounds were soothing, lulling her gently to sleep . . .

Suddenly, a shrill scream rent the air, shattering the night. Abbey sprung up in bed, startled. Her eyes widened as her gaze fastened on the open window. A naked savage was on the balcony outside her bedchamber!

Heart racing, she jumped from the bed, her gaze searching wildly for a weapon as the fierce-looking warrior climbed from the balcony over the sill. Grabbing the candlestick from the night stand beside her bed, she wielded it before her to fend him off.

"What do you want?" Abbey gasped as the Indian came toward her, wearing only a thin cloth covering his loins. "Stay away from me," she warned, swinging her only weapon. "Don't come any closer!"

Eyes glinting in the shadowed room, the Indian babbled in his own tongue; Abbey couldn't understand him. He was a hideous creature with angular features. His face was painted with war colors; he was bald but for a small dark tuft at the crown of his head.

"Come any closer, and I'll kill you," she threatened.

The Indian laughed. *"Wa thoon wix sus!"* he sneered.

Abbey went numb with fear. She was trapped!

The brave stalked her about the room, his eyes gleaming, his muscles coiled in readiness to attack. Too frightened to scream, Abbey retreated with each step he took, waving her candlestick threateningly.

Suddenly, the warrior lunged for her. Abbey gasped, swinging the candlestick high to smash it against his head. The savage caught her hand, wrenching away her weapon to send it crashing against the wooden floorboards.

Abbey refused to cower as he squeezed the flesh of her upper arm. She struggled wildly, but was stunned into submission when he backhanded her across the face.

Blinded by tears, Abbey gaped at him. The savage cocked his head to the side, a look of surprise crossing his features when she didn't cry out or whimper for mercy.

His chest glistened in the moonlight. His copper skin looked shiny, greased. His face appeared darker, almost black, in the shadows. He stared at her, his eyes pinning her where she stood, two bright evil orbs glowing in the darkness. She saw herself as he

11

must see her . . . her fair hair a tangle about her face and shoulders, her blue eyes bright with hostility, her womanly curves embarrassingly evident beneath her thin garment.

Muttering in a harsh, guttural language, the Indian dragged Abbey out the door, into the hall. She heard the screams of Breckingridge's servants. The house was full of Indians. Propelled by his strong arm, Abbey stumbled along in his wake.

The house echoed with the raiding Indians' fierce war cries as Abbey's captor shoved her roughly down the stairs to the front entrance. She tripped on her nightgown and slipped to her knees. His fist tangling in her flaxen hair, the Indian hauled her upright.

Outside in the yard, he gestured toward an area in the compound where women and children were being herded together like animals. *"E yoh te an ti,"* he growled.

Abbey planted her feet solidly on the ground, refusing to move.

"E yoh te an ti!" her Indian captor barked, enraged, propelling her forward with his cruel grip on her arm. He flung her into the line of captives and went back into the house.

Several Indians guarded their prisoners, so that no one could escape. The women captives sobbed, some grieving over lost loved ones, others whimpering with fright. They were a picture of vulnerability, clad only in their nightclothes, their unbound tresses in wild disarray. Young children cried and clung to their mothers while others appeared too shocked by the commotion to utter a sound.

There were English soldiers—those left to guard the fort. Young soldiers lying dead or wounded. Wizened old-timers felled by hatchets or spears, lying in dark crimson pools of blood.

The gruesome sight chilled Abbey to the bone. *Please let this be just a nightmare!* But the spot on her arm bruised by the warrior's hold and the lingering, vile odor of his greased body confirmed that this wasn't a dream from which she could escape. She was in the hands of savages!

The noxious odor of burning wood filled the yard. A wild male scream rent the air, and Abbey gasped, closed her eyes against seeing a warrior torturing a young English soldier. Tears filled her eyes while she steeled herself against the next blood-curdling howl of pain as the Indian drew his knife across his victim's bared chest. My God, she thought. They're monsters!

Oh, God, Jamie! Abbey swallowed hard. *Did you suffer so?* Would she ever escape to find out?

She must! She must not panic. Her life depended on it. *"Use your head, girl, when you meet trouble,"* her father had once told her. *"Think! And in the end, you will triumph."*

Only by remaining rational would she be able to think of and plan her escape . . . if only to return to the Indians and see them pay for their brutality.

A toddler wandered into the yard, bawling for her mother, stumbling, blinded by her tears. Without thought, Abbey broke from the line, scooped up the tousled-haired child, and holding the girl to her breast, soothed and comforted her. A warrior leapt forward, yanking the child from Abbey's arms.

13

Stubbornly, Abbey held on to the screaming baby. Angered, the Indian went into a wild tirade and cuffed her against the side of the head.

Her temple throbbing from the assault, she snarled at the savage, refusing to be intimidated. "I'm not afraid of you!" she said. Inside, Abbey quaked with fear. But she would not give up the baby.

She met him fierce stare for stare until he stepped back. The Indian was clearly taken aback by her boldness. He appeared uncertain and then he abandoned the struggle to confer with one of his tribesmen. Abbey hid her triumph as she returned to the line of captives.

Why, he's just a boy! Abbey thought. She shuddered. The stories she'd heard in England about the Indians were true. They were indeed savages to teach their youngsters such wild, animalistic behavior.

Abbey felt satisfaction that she'd held her fear in check, stood her ground. The feeling faded when her gaze met the dark fierce eyes of the savage who had climbed through her bedchamber window. She swallowed hard and clutched the weeping child tighter to her chest.

Her own eyes were dry. *I won't let you break me,* she vowed silently.

Iroquois! Abbey gasped and felt renewed terror as she glanced back at the woman behind her in line. *Man-eaters!*

"Are you sure?" She glanced at Rachel Votteger, the mother of the golden-haired toddler Abbey had refused to surrender to the Indians.

Abbey shuddered when her new friend nodded.

"Mohawks and Onondagas," Rachel whispered, her eyes mirroring Abbey's fear. The big German woman glanced about quickly, checking to see if they were being watched. "I heard one of our soldiers"— she inhaled sharply—"before they killed him."

A shiver raced down Abbey's spine as she spied a savage staring at her. He was carrying a musket, picked up from a dead British soldier; and she wondered briefly if he knew how to use it. In England, she'd heard stories of the dreaded Iroquois tribes. There were a number of nations besides the Mohawks and Onondagas, but how many she had no idea.

She forced her gaze forward, on the older woman directly ahead of her. The poor creature's gait had slowed considerably in the two hours of their arduous journey through the woods. Abbey felt instant sympathy for the woman. Abbey's own bare feet were cut and bleeding from the trek. Her only garment was a thin night rail which had torn on forest brush and was little protection from the night air and the savages' evil stares.

Where are they taking us? she wondered, shivering, hugging herself. What are they going to do to us when we arrive?

The woman before her stumbled and fell. A warrior was instantly at the woman's side, muttering in his Indian tongue, kicking and prodding her with a musket.

Enraged, Abbey rushed forward to help the woman rise, and the Indian swung the muzzle of the musket against Abbey's shoulder. She cried out at the impact;

pain radiated across her back and down her left arm. Suddenly, there were three Indians above Abbey and the fallen woman, arguing wildly in Iroquois.

One savage raised his fist in readiness to strike. The other woman cried out, begging for mercy. She was wrenched to her feet and hit by two braves, and she stumbled, falling a second time. The third Indian snorted, spitting at the ground near the woman's feet, clearly disgusted with the woman's cowering behavior. He raised his war club with the intent to punish.

Abbey threw caution to the wind and shoved the nearest Indian aside to aid the older woman. "Leave her alone, you brutes!" she shouted.

The Indians moved, gaping.

Abbey gently helped the woman to rise, cradling the woman's thin shoulders within her arms. "For God's sake, have you no mercy?"

The woman's forehead bled where an Indian had struck her. "She's hurt!" Abbey accused, glaring at the captors.

"*Ka jeeh kwa!*" The Indian with the war club raised his weapon high into the air, his eyes narrowing. "*Ka jeeh kwa!*" he bellowed.

"Abbey," Rachel whispered from behind, "he's going to strike you!"

Abbey barely flashed Rachel a glance. "Go on, savage! Hit me! I dare you. Hit me!" She was already a mass of bruised, throbbing flesh.

"No, Abbey!" hissed the older woman by her side. She seemed to gain strength as she pulled from Abbey's grasp. "Don't anger them. Not if you want to live!"

16

The light of anger faded from Abbey's blue gaze. "Are you all right?" She saw the woman nod, heard her swallow.

The woman's right, Abbey thought. Jamie was out there waiting to be rescued. She mustn't do anything that would jeopardize her own chance for escape! And what if these Indians knew Jamie's whereabouts? The thought calmed Abbey, as she realized it would be to her advantage to act more submissive.

She released the woman—whose name was Mary, Abbey learned—and fell back into line to continue the trek.

Fortunately for all concerned, the Indians accepted her decision without further punishment . . . and the long journey through the woods continued.

*Somewhere along the shore
of Lake Ontario . . .*

"Kwan Kahaiska," Silver Fox murmured as he touched his son's shoulder, "our runner has returned with news. Our braves have left the white men's fort. They come even as we speak."

Great Arrow nodded, and Silver Fox saw a subtle easing of the Indian's tense broad shoulders.

It was hard, this waiting, Silver Fox thought. For two years, the Iroquois had waited for their moment of revenge, two years since that terrible day when Colonel Breckingridge and his English army had attacked and killed a peaceful band of Onondagas, including women and children . . . among them Great Arrow's promised wife.

17

Vengeance was the Iroquois way. As an Iroquois sachem or chief, Great Arrow would do his duty; revenge would be exacted no matter how long it took. Time didn't have meaning for the Indians in such matters. The Iroquois were a patient people . . . as long as in the end they had their revenge.

Silver Fox frowned as he studied his son. A breeze off the lake tossed the unbound strands of the sachem's golden-streaked brown hair. As Great Arrow continued to stare across the water, his father recognized the tension in him, in the line of his square jaw, in the taut muscles of the younger man's lithe warrior's form. He knew that Great Arrow would find no joy in the final moment of retaliation, for revenge would not bring back dead loved ones. It would not bring Morning Flower back to life.

"What of the white man . . . Breck-ing-ridge?" Great Arrow said, turning to gaze at his father through bright silver-colored eyes.

The old man's gaze clouded. "I am sorry, my son. He was gone from the village. They bring back only his niece."

"So be it," Great Arrow said quietly. He looked across the water. "It is written then. The niece will pay for Breck-ing-ridge's wicked deed. She will pay for she who was taken from among us to the Afterworld." His eyes narrowed against the sun's glare. "Soon," he continued, "it will be over."

Silver Fox agreed. "Vengeance will be ours."

Chapter 2

The captives were in poor condition as they neared the Indian village along the shores of Lake Ontario. They had traveled through the night and several hours past sunup.

Trudging through the thicket, Abbey stared ahead. She must not falter. The Indians, she'd learned, were intolerant of any signs of weakness. They'd been quick to punish their prisoners when they slowed or stumbled along the way. Those that fell were ordered to their feet; if they didn't comply, they were dealt with severely.

Abbey was hungry, achy, and exhausted, but she was aware that she'd fared better than the other captives. Her night rail was practically in shreds; her feet were cut and blistered, her arms bleeding. But she was alive. Alive! And she was thankful.

She shuddered, recalling some who were not so fortunate. One young woman—Abbey recognized the Breckingridge household maid—had tripped. Unable to rise, she'd sobbed, pleading for mercy, and had been beaten by not one but four Indians. When the savages were done with her, the woman lay in her own blood, her brown eyes open in a blank, death stare, her limbs twisted at odd angles.

Remembering, Abbey blinked back tears. During the trek when she'd felt too exhausted to go on, when her muscles cramped and she wanted to cry from the agony, it was the remembered horror of the woman's death that kept Abbey going, that gave her strength.

She would live, damn it! She wouldn't suffer the same death as the maid. The savages wouldn't get the best of her! The image of the maid's death would haunt her forever. Abbey hated these Indians.

The day continued like a nightmare for her. Hours later, her body was bone-weary as she continued the trek. Would it never end? she wondered.

Dusk fell across the land. An owl hooted in the distance, and to Abbey's surprise, an Iroquois brave answered it.

A signal, Abbey thought, her eyes widening when Indians suddenly appeared from the surrounding woods. The newcomers were tribesmen of her captors. Onondagas, she decided, now recognizing the difference in the way they wore their hair, the Mohawks in a cock's crest, the Onondagas in short little tufts at the head's crown. Abbey watched as they greeted one another, and she realized with a sinking heart that they must be near their final destination.

She had the discomfiting sensation of being stared at by a group of the warriors who'd just joined them, one of whom approached her. The Indian grabbed a lock of her hair, yanking it until tears burned Abbey's eyes.

"A-nik-ha o-non-kwi-eh!" the Iroquois murmured, leering. He gave her a wicked smile as he fingered the long, silky strands. He seemed fascinated with her hair's golden color.

She shuddered at his nearness, wrinkling her nose at his smell. The Indian turned around and said something to his friends that made the warriors cackle with delight. Angered at his tone and the implication of his look, Abbey slapped his hand away, and he released her as if stung.

The others within the group howled with laughter at her show of spirit, but the brave didn't find it amusing. Glaring, he caught her arm, squeezing it until she winced. His eyes held the promise of retribution as he scolded her fiercely in Onondaga. Then he spun from her and stalked away.

Man-eaters! Surely it isn't true that these people eat men! she thought. Chills raised the hairs at Abbey's nape as the line of captives began to move again. She wondered what the future held for her and the others.

It wasn't long afterward that Abbey spied a clearing through a break in the line of trees. The travelers had reached the end of their journey. There, ahead, lay a village or hamlet surrounded by a stockade fence. Abbey heard dogs barking.

As the captives were led toward the compound, the child in Rachel's arms began to cry in earnest, perhaps sensing her mother's renewed fear.

Rachel tried to calm her child, but the toddler only cried louder.

"Is she all right?" Abbey whispered, flashing the pair a quick glance.

Rachel gave Abbey a crooked smile. She was a big,

21

strong woman, but her captivity had taken a toll on her. "She's afraid."

The two women exchanged a look that mirrored little Anna's fear.

"I'll take her," Abbey offered, holding out her arms.

The German woman looked ready to fall. She had carried her baby for miles, and the effort had cost her dearly. But as she had several times during the journey, Rachel declined Abbey's offer. "Anna needs her *mutter,*" she said softly. She smiled with gratitude. "I am all right."

Abbey nodded, but was skeptical.

The mingled scent of smoke and roasting meat was heavy in the air as Abbey and the other captives were led into a large clearing at the center of the village. Human meat? Abbey wondered about the smell with a feeling of sick horror. Venison, she decided with relief at the familiar odor.

Her gaze swept her surroundings, noting the huge long structures made of logs and tree-bark that had been built along the perimeter of the village, surrounding the dirt yard. The air was dusty from the activity of the children and dogs. There were no cook fires to be seen . . . just a large empty space. One building stood by itself, away from the others. It was built similarly but on a much smaller scale. It was obviously big enough to house one or two persons. The chief's? she wondered. And perhaps his bride?

The warriors had burst into the village, hooting and howling, shouting cries of victory. The dogs, running about freely within the compound, went into a frenzy, howling and yelping. The English children, frightened by the noise, began to whimper, clinging to their mothers in their fear.

The Indian women had come from their cook fires and long houses to inspect the captives. Abbey flushed, startled by their dress, for they wore no covering above the waist; their bare breasts hung like copper melons in all sizes. And the young Iroquois children—both male and female—wore no clothing at all.

Encircling the group, the squaws chattered loudly among themselves, their manner jeering as they plucked at the prisoners' clothing. They pulled hair, spat in the captives' faces, snatched crying children from their mothers' arms. And the white mothers reacted . . . some with the ferocity of mother lionesses protecting their cubs . . . others whimpering and sobbing for their babies to be returned to them.

Abbey stared, horrified, as the Indian women clearly enjoyed the sport in tormenting the helpless prisoners.

One squaw tore the baby from Rachel's arms. "No!" the German woman wailed. "My Anna! My baby!"

Abbey started to reach for her friend's child, but she was hauled from the screaming Anna when a squaw caught her by the hair, yanking her back roughly. Fighting the Indian's hold, Abbey swung her arms about wildly, until someone hit her hard between the shoulder blades.

Abbey was stunned by the blow. She fell to her knees as pain quivered down her spine, making it difficult for her to breathe. She struggled to her feet as the fierce pain subsided.

"Abbey!" Mary cried, and Abbey felt a second strike to her right shoulder.

She gasped with the impact. A third strike to her head. Stars danced before Abbey's eyes. She fought to stay conscious. A squaw with one blind eye raised her arm to hit again. Abbey closed her eyes in anticipation of the strike, envisioning the one white orb of the woman's gaze.

The blow never came. Amazed, Abbey opened her eyes. A hush had settled over the gathering of Indian women. All gazes were on an old Iroquois woman, who had come to inspect the prisoners.

The Indian matron wavered in Abbey's vision, but Abbey felt the power of this woman's presence. Even in her weakened state, she sensed a new attitude in the air, one of respect for the old matron.

The Indian woman stopped before Abbey, her dark eyes bright, piercing. She inspected the English woman thoroughly. Then she nodded, satisfied.

"So you are the one," the matron said to Abbey in English. The Indian was short, thin, and dressed in a long deerskin kilt. A quill-embroidered cape covered the upper half of her body. Her dark hair was tied back at the nape and was streaked with gray. She had the eyes of young woman, but the facial lines of someone who'd seen many hard years of life.

"You speak English!" Abbey exclaimed.

The woman nodded. "I am *O-wee-soo*. Woman of Ice. Head matron of our village."

"Why are we here?" Abbey asked. "What are you going to do with us?"

"The others," the matron said, gesturing to the captives, "they will be sold or kept as slaves to the

24

Onondaga people. As for you . . ." Her dark eyes narrowed. "It is for our sachem to decide."

And it was then that Abbey realized that she'd been singled out from the other captives for a singular and perhaps gruesome fate.

Great Arrow noticed her immediately. How could he not when her hair glowed like the midday sun— and when her fierce spirit made her stand out from the others, a prize among the prisoners?

She was something to behold as she defied his men. She didn't whimper like the others. Even in her weakened condition, she fought back with all her dwindling strength.

She is the one! The thought came unbidden, and Great Arrow rejected it instantly.

She is the woman, the one who will die!

His stomach churned in angry protest. No!

But he knew it was true. Silver Fox didn't have to confirm it. The golden-haired woman was Brecking-ridge's niece.

Great Arrow frowned. It was good that the one to appease Morning Flower's spirit had the courage of a warrior . . . a woman warrior, but . . .

It was a shame, he thought. For the white woman was beautiful. And desirable.

Great Arrow felt something stir in his gut as he observed the woman from the doorway of his hut. Her skin was white . . . flawless. Her limbs were bare; her thin, torn garment afforded the Indian a clear view of her physical charms.

The sachem was startled to feel his staff harden as

he studied her. He was shocked at his reaction. It had been a long time since he felt desire. And it was the first time he'd ever found such pale coloring attractive. Always before, his interest had been in women with black hair and copper-colored skin . . . and dark eyes.

What color were her eyes? he wondered, and then cursed himself for wanting to know.

The woman was the enemy. Breck-ing-ridge's niece. And it was written: *the enemy must be destroyed.*

From his position, Great Arrow watched his grandmother and the English woman. He had witnessed O-wee-soo's approach, and smiled at the way the people revered the old woman. His grandmother was a great woman with power in the village.

O-wee-soo and the white woman spoke briefly. Then, Great Arrow saw O-wee-soo raise a hand, and an Indian maiden came forward. He recognized Morning Flower's cousin, *O-gai-sah Ka-ai-wi-a*. Evening Sky.

O-wee-soo ordered the white woman taken away.

The sachem watched with mixed emotions as the English woman disappeared with Evening Sky into a longhouse. He flushed when he saw that O-wee-soo was looking his way; she'd caught him staring at the beautiful white captive.

Great Arrow fought the urge to retreat into the hut and held his grandmother's gaze steadily. The old woman approached him.

"You saw her," O-wee-soo said.

Great Arrow nodded, his face solemn.

"What will you do with her?"

The sachem narrowed his gaze. "You know what is to be done. It is the will of the people. It is written."

O-wee-soo inclined her head. "That one—she has spirit."

Something flickered across her grandson's face. "I saw."

"It is a shame," the matron said. "Such beauty and fire are rare in a woman . . . in an Englishwoman." Her knowing look made Great Arrow swallow hard. "You are the sachem, my son."

He knew what she was saying, that the decision ultimately rested with him—their leader. He nodded.

Watching O-wee-soo leave him, Great Arrow had to agree with his grandmother. Such traits were rare indeed in a woman. Not just in a Englishwoman, but in any female.

And the sachem frowned.

"Take off." The Indian maiden pulled on Abbey's tattered night gown. *"Take off!"*

Abbey gasped and shrank back with alarm. Her body still stung from the Indian squaws' blows, and the woman's expression was fierce. What cruelty was she going to inflict? In her instant mistrust, Abbey didn't realize that the Indian had spoken English. "Why? What for?"

"No good," the maiden said. She pointed toward a large tear in the flimsy material. "Tear. Bad."

Abbey had trouble keeping her gaze from the woman's naked breasts as the Indian retrieved a garment from the wooden platform built into the side of the longhouse, and held it up.

"Wear this. No tear. Good!"

It was a full length garment made from deerskin that would adequately cover Abbey from her neck to her calves. Beads had been carefully stitched in a gay pattern of color on the bodice and several inches above the tassled bottom edge.

"You want me to wear that?" Abbey asked. The maiden nodded, and relief made Abbey dizzy. "I'll take it off," she said, managing a slight smile. But when she reached for the hem, she found that she was too weak to remove her night rail.

The Indian woman, seeing her condition, took over the task of undressing Abbey, who stiffened at first, but then was too grateful to feel embarrassed. Unsmiling, she handed Abbey the deerskin tunic.

"What is your name?" Abbey asked, upon seeing a softening in the Indian's fierce expression. She was no longer feeling alarm. The woman's touch had been gentle and helpful, not at all cruel. She was a pretty woman with sparkling dark eyes and cheeks reddened by some kind of dye. She wore her black hair in two braids.

The maiden looked blank at the question.

"Your name?" the Englishwoman repeated. She pointed to herself. "Abbey. I am Abigail Rawlins. *Ab-bey* . . ." She gestured toward the young woman. "And you? You are . . . ?"

Understanding lit up the maiden's eyes. "O-gai-sah Ka-ai-wi-a."

"O-gai-sah—" Abbey began.

The maiden interrupted her. "It is, how shall I say, Night . . . no . . . Ev-en-ing . . ." She pointed to the sky.

"Sky? Evening Sky?" Abbey smiled when Evening Sky nodded vigorously. "I am pleased to meet you, Evening Sky." She held out her hand, and the Indian's gaze narrowed as she stared at it a long moment, before slowly, cautiously, holding out her own.

Abbey grabbed her hand, shaking it. "Say it. I am pleased to meet you, Abbey Rawlins."

Evening Sky repeated the words, calling her "Abbey." There was no friendliness in her expression, but there was no hostility either. Another Indian entered the longhouse, and Evening Sky gasped and withdrew her hand.

"My aunt," Evening Sky said. "Come." The Indian was suddenly in a hurry to leave the longhouse. "You wash."

"Wash?" Abbey echoed. She followed the maiden willingly as they left the structure and the stockaded village. The idea of a bath was inviting to Abbey. Water to soothe her aching muscles and tired limbs.

"You speak English," Abbey said.

Evening Sky looked at her, but kept walking. "A little," she admitted. "Not good. A man—" Her eyes darkened with pain. "A white man teach me and some of my people before he—" She averted her glance.

"He was killed?" Abbey's tone was gentle.

The Indian nodded, refusing to meet the Englishwoman's gaze.

Abbey shivered. Was he eaten by the Indians?

She forced away the unpleasant thought, concentrating instead on the beauty of the forest. With the slow darkening of the evening sky, sounds became more distinct. The hum and buzz of insects. The crackle of a dry leaf underfoot. The soft brush of the wind through the trees.

They had traveled some distance when Abbey became aware that they were not alone. Two Indians followed them. She would not bathe before the heathens, Abbey thought.

She was pleasantly surprised when they reached the bathing hole. She hadn't expected hot water or a metal tub. But then neither did she expect to have at her disposal a lake that stretched as far as her eyes could see! Abbey thought the scenery was beautiful. Before her, the huge body of water glistened under the setting sun. At her sides and behind her lay the lush greenery of the forest with its bird and animal sounds and its sweet woodsy scents.

"On-tar-io," Evening Sky said.

Abbey went to the water's edge, dipping a bare toe to test the temperature of the lake. It was brisk and cool . . . pleasantly so. She was suddenly anxious to get into the water.

With Evening Sky's help, she started to remove the tunic and stopped, glancing back. "Your friends . . . do they have to watch?"

Evening Sky frowned and then turned to the braves to give them a harsh tongue lashing. Abbey got the impression that the men were not supposed to be there.

The maiden and the braves argued heatedly. In the end it was Evening Sky who won the argument.

"They not bother us," she said.

"They've left?" Abbey asked, looking doubtful, anxious.

The Indian nodded. "I tell them to go or O-wee-soo will curse their spears to fall off."

Abbey frowned. The maiden explained, "Their spears? Their . . ." She gestured between her legs. Abbey's eyes widened with understanding as she saw the position of Evening Sky's fingers.

Abbey laughed, feeling at ease with the woman. "Their penises," she said without embarrassment, for as a physician's daughter, she'd become accustomed to the term.

"Penis," Evening Sky repeated, her eyes twinkling for the first time. And both women giggled.

It seemed as if Abbey had been in the water only a short time when Evening Sky announced that it was time to return to the village. "The sachem waits," the maiden said.

"Sachem?" Abbey said, rising from the waters of the lake.

Evening Sky nodded, her expression sober. "He is . . . our leader. Great man. Peace man." She handed Abbey a blanket to dry with.

"He is your chief." Abbey slipped on the beaded tunic.

"Yes. Chief." Evening Sky frowned. "He must to see you . . . you and the others."

A shutter came down over the Onondaga maiden's features, and it was as if the two women had never spoken on friendly terms. The air between them had become tense. Suddenly, they were captor and captive again, not two young women sharing each other's company.

"Come." Evening Sky's tone had become brisk. "Kwan Kahaiska waits."

31

Chapter 3

The Iroquois village hummed with excitement as Abbey entered its center. Warriors, women, and children formed a circle about the main yard, chattering noisily in conjecture of their captives' fate.

Evening Sky led Abbey through a break in the circle. Why me? Abbey wondered, feeling the object of all gazes. Why had she been singled out by the Indians? First by the Indian matron . . . and now the entire village?

Abbey stared at her captors. Like the man who'd climbed in through her bedroom window, the men of the village had shorn heads, some with tufts of hair at their crowns, others without any hair at all.

The Onondaga women had long dark hair, worn down their backs in a single braid or loosely tied hank of hair. They were clothed in deerskin skirts; a few wore leggings, but all of them, as Abbey had noted earlier, remained bare-breasted.

Abbey crossed her arms over her chest. Thank God she'd been given a decent garment; these Indians would have been asking for another fight if they'd dared to strip her half naked like the rest of the women!

She caught one woman eyeing her strangely. *Why is she staring at me?* Abbey wondered. She touched her hair. Was it the golden color of her hair that set her apart from the other captives? She frowned, recalling the women captives who had light-colored hair. Perhaps she was the focus of attention because she'd dared to stand up to the heathens.

Man-eaters. Abbey's heart thumped hard with fear. She smelled fire and a new scent of roasting meat unlike the venison she'd smelled earlier. Was she to be their next meal?

She swallowed past a painful lump. To her relief, she saw no sign of any pots large enough to cook her in. Then, her gaze fell on the knife tucked into one brave's breechclout. Abbey shuddered and turned away.

Beside Abbey, Evening Sky remained silent, unlike her fellow tribesmen who taunted Abbey in their strange tongue, their enjoyment of their captive's discomfort obvious in their angular faces.

Determined to appear fearless, Abbey held her head high and kept her gaze trained before her. She fought the urge to check the compound for Rachel, Anna, or any of the other captives to see how they'd fared.

Evening Sky stopped and studied the English-woman. "You wait here," she said. "I go."

"No!" Abbey's facade slipped for a second. Catching Evening Sky's arm, she stared at the Indian maiden with horror. The woman had been kind to

33

her; Abbey suddeny saw her as an ally in an alien world.

She was to be left alone in the middle of the compound, surrounded on all sides by hostile Indians!

There was no glimmer of sympathy in the Onondaga girl's eyes as she disengaged herself from Abbey's grasp. "I go," she said and then left Abbey without a backward glance.

Abbey felt terror as never before.

A woman of middle age broke from the circle and approached Abbey. When she was within several feet, the squaw bent, scooped up a fistful of dirt and stones, and threw the handful in Abbey's face.

Abbey gasped at the unexpected attack. Blinded by dirt and dust, she sensed when others came forward to mimic the woman's actions. The barrage of dirt and stones did nothing more than sting Abbey's flesh; she suffered more from the indignity of her predicament . . . and anger that they'd dare treat her this way. Her fury intensified when the children joined their elders, striking her with sticks, spitting on her.

Stunned, Abbey stood passive; then, her fighting spirit surfaced and she shoved the nearest Indian away.

"Touch me again and die!" she hissed, falling into a protective crouch, raising her hands defensively.

Abbey was struck down by a blow to the head. She never saw the fist coming, but heard the warrior's laugh that followed as she lay on the ground, reeling. She recognized her assailant as the young brave who'd been angered by her earlier show of spirit.

Her head throbbed. Glaring at her captors, Abbey struggled to rise, only to fall again when she was tripped by an Onondaga child. The chorus of delighted cackles made her temper soar. She came up swinging and had the satisfaction of hearing a thud and a grunt when her closed fist made solid contact with an Indian jaw.

The bellows of rage made by the Iroquois made Abbey's blood freeze. She shielded herself with her arms. The expected attack came; she was converged upon by a horde of angry women and children, who hit her with sticks and fists and pulled her hair.

Desperate, Abbey fought her tormentors with the strength of an enraged wildcat. Sobbing and snarling, she swung her hands and kicked out with her feet, biting any exposed skin.

Abbey realized with a sinking heart that she couldn't possibly win the battle. Yet, she kept fighting.

She heard a sharp voice from the distance. Suddenly, Abbey was freed of the pummeling as the Iroquois backed off to the command of someone in authority. Relieved, she lay with her eyes closed, breathing hard, wondering what cruelty fate had in store for her next.

As long as she remained alive, there was a chance for freedom . . . a chance to continue her search for her brother Jamie.

Damn, but she would fight to stay alive!

Kwan stood watching from the shelter of his grandmother's longhouse as his people abused the

35

beautiful English captive. The sight gave him horror but he did nothing to stop it. There was a hunger within the Onondaga for justice; such torment of this captive was necessary in order for the hunger to be assuaged.

Kwan Kahaiska—Great Arrow, sachem of this band of Onondagas—remained in the shadows, waiting until it was time to make his appearance, fighting the urge to go to the woman's rescue. His heart bled for the woman's pain. She had courage; he respected such courage.

Kwan had watched when she crossed the compound with her head held high. She was a magnificent creature. There was much to admire in a woman who fought back. Such spirit was rare in a white female.

O-wee-soo is right, he thought. *This one is special.* How could he allow her to die?

Then he remembered who she was—Breck-ing-ridge's niece. She belonged to the man responsible for taking Morning Flower from this earth. The enemy.

His stomach jolted as his people forced the woman to the ground, covered her from his sight. He heard her sobbing and felt his breath quicken with anxiety as the people beat her.

Enough! he thought. *I will deal with the woman!*

Kwan's gaze darted wildly in his search for his father. Silver Fox stood not far from the longhouse on the fringe of the circle, eyeing his son with an intentness that made Kwan's face heat.

The sachem quickly controlled his expression. He gave his father the silent command to put an end to

36

the proceedings. Silver Fox stepped forward to do the sachem's bidding.

"O wah ai yut! O wah ai yut!"

Abbey heard the Indian brave's strange outcry as she lurched to her feet. She felt dizzy, her stomach queasy. Blinking to clear her vision, she was startled to see that the Indians no longer seemed as angry, as hostile as before.

Puzzled, Abbey hugged herself with her arms. She was a mass of bruised, aching flesh, but she considered herself lucky that she had fared the attack this well.

What next? she wondered, glancing about warily. Were they playing with her before they did their worst? She rubbed the gooseflesh along her upper arms . . . and prayed.

A hush settled over the village. The circle of Iroquois parted near the largest longhouse as three Indians entered the clearing. Abbey judged them to be men of authority by the way the people watched them. The silence in the camp was reverent.

Abbey's breath caught as she noted the tallest of the three. He was dressed much like the others in a breechclout that shielded the most intimate male part of him. He wore deerskin moccasins on his feet. Unlike the warriors and young braves in the village, however, this man had a full head of hair, which he wore long, past his shoulders.

Abbey gasped, meeting his silver-gray gaze with her own. *My God!* she thought. *This man is white!* His hair was a beautiful color that stood out among the other Indians, a rich brown streaked with strands of gold. And those eyes—she'd never heard of an Indian with light eyes!

Who was he? An Englishman sent from the fort to rescue the captives? For a brief second, her heart took flight on the wings of hope. Perhaps he was a special emissary who understood their language, who dressed like he did to be better accepted among the Iroquois.

And then Abbey studied his face. Cold, she thought. Savage. The man's expression was lifeless. There was no sympathy in his silver-gray eyes. Something about the intensity of his gaze raised the little hairs on her nape.

God, no! Why? she cried silently. Abbey knew that there would be no rescue attempt by this man. The man was a savage, just like the rest of them.

Who was he then? Was he a half-breed? That certainly would account for his fair coloring and Iroquoian manner. Abbey's gaze was drawn to the hard, honed muscles of his bare chest. His skin was a sleek shade of copper. Although it was darker than that of any Englishman she'd known, it was obvious that he was white for he was lighter than the other Iroquois.

The man stared at her, and she glared back, her stance defiant. *White blood or not, this man is a savage! I mustn't forget that!* Her mind raced, wondering about the circumstances surrounding the man's presence among the Onondaga people.

The man broke his gaze first, spinning away as if to dismiss her. *Savage Injun!* she thought. How could this man be so cold, so cruel? After all, he might be an

Indian, but he also had white blood flowing within his veins.

Abbey transferred her attention to the Indian on the right, an older man with white hair and piercing black eyes. This man also wore his hair long. She glanced at the circle of savages. In fact, he and the white "half-breed" were the only two men in the village to wear a full head of hair. Why?

Intrigued, Abbey became aware of an aura of authority about the old man. Was he the chief— Kwan Kahaiska?

The third savage, the one on the left, made a sound like a grunt, and Abbey looked at him. This Iroquois was younger with jet black hair and dark eyes. His head was shaven in a way she'd thought was solely Mohawk, a dark crest that ran from the top of his forehead back to his neck. He had a tattoo on his chest.

Abbey blanched. The Indian's gaze glittered with hatred for her—why? What did she do? She had a horrible thought—*What if this man was the chief!*

With pounding heart, she studied each of the three men. Who was Kwan Kahaiska—the man she must appeal to for her release? Abbey decided it was the eldest of the three men. The Indian with the long white hair. A man with the wisdom of age and experience. She hoped he was the sachem. The Indian's expression was unreadable, but he didn't seem as fierce as the others.

Bravely, Abbey stepped forward. "Mr. Kahaiska— Chief," she said, and immediately the camp grew wild with cries and gasps of outrage. She stepped back, startled. What had she done to cause this reaction?

The crest-headed warrior began talking in earnest to the other two, his tone and expression evidence of his anger.

Abbey's gaze sought out Evening Sky where she stood on the fringe of the circle. The Indian woman's expression was brooding. Silently, Abbey appealed to her for help. She saw something change in the woman's face, saw her start in her direction but then check her movement. The old, revered matron whispered something in Evening Sky's ear, and the young Indian woman came forward to stand beside Abbey.

Abbey gave Evening Sky a look of gratitude, but the woman didn't smile or look encouraging.

"I am Kwan Kahaiska."

Abbey jolted from surprise. The "half-breed" had come up to her while her attention had been on Evening Sky.

"You?" she asked, gaping. "You are the sachem?"

He nodded, his face solemn. "We are the *Kanonsionni*, and I am sachem." He eyed her thoroughly from head to toe, and Abbey blushed as his study included a momentary focus on her doeskin-covered breasts. When he met her gaze, his eyes glowed bright silver. "You are the one," he said mysteriously.

"What are you going to do with me?" Abbey asked.

The white-haired Indian approached from behind to touch Kwan's shoulder. The two men spoke in their strange tongue. Abbey wished with her whole heart that she could understand them.

Suddenly, Kwan began speaking with excitement, perhaps anger, shaking his head and gesturing with his hands. The crest-headed warrior joined in what appeared to Abbey to be a debate. Abbey waited, her heart pounding, knowing that it was her fate they were discussing.

"I will decide!" Kwan addressed his father and Bear Claw in Onondaga. "The woman will not die; she has shown courage. A female with such courage should live!"

"Pah!" Bear Claw spat. "You are getting soft, Great Arrow. Her courage makes her worthy of death—our vengeance! The woman must die!"

Kwan stiffened, frowning. Bear Claw had insulted him by implying that he—Great Arrow—would not properly avenge the wrong that had been done to the People.

"Bear Claw," Silver Fox said softly, intermediating. "The decision is Great Arrow's. You forget that it was his loss as well as yours." The old man then turned to his son. "I do not understand your reasoning, my sachem, but I trust you. Your decision has not been any easy one, nor one made lightly." He hesitated. "You mean to trade her?"

Kwan nodded, his brow clearing. "To the French. The woman is English. The French and English are bitter enemies." He shot Bear Claw a narrowed glance. "Justice will be served."

Silver Fox was satisfied. "So it shall be."

"My family—the Deer clan—will not like this." Bear Claw wasn't happy. "They have lost a daughter and have waited a long time for vengeance. You take away their moment of revenge, their chance to find

41

peace once again in their hearts. Why do you gift the English general with his niece's life? Why take her only to let her go again?"

Bear Claw snarled with disgust. "You shame us with your decision, Great Arrow."

"Enough!" The sachem had made up his mind; the subject was closed. He did not shame with his decision. The Onondagas would have their revenge. The woman would live as a slave to be used by her enemy—the French!

Kwan waved the two Indians aside before he spoke to his people. "It is decided!" he announced loudly in Onondaga. "The prisoner—Breck-ing-ridge's woman will be sold to the French. Her vile enemy! Justice will be served! May the woman live a long life as slave to those she despises!"

"So be it!" echoed Silver Fox in support of his son's decision.

A ripple of emotion passed around the circle of Iroquois. It was evident that there were mixed feelings about the sachem's decision. The tide of dissent intensified when the old matron, O-wee-soo, didn't immediately come forward to lend her support.

Kwan, however, was indifferent to the dissension among his people; his attention had turned to the woman captive. The sachem frowned. Bruises and cuts marred the Englishwoman's pale skin; her golden hair was mussed and tangled from the abuse she'd suffered at the hands of the Iroquois.

Ab-bey. Evening Sky had told him the woman's name. Ab-bey. Earlier he had tried out the name on his tongue and had found it pleasing to say and hear it.

She wore a full doeskin tunic unlike the Indian women. He stared at her soft curves. Were her breasts as white as the rest of her? Kwan frowned. Like her visible bruises, had her breasts been darkened in spots by the beating?

His concerned gaze returned to her face. Her lips were swollen and red. She'd been cut across one delicate cheekbone. A shutter came down over his expression, for she stared back at him, her gaze direct . . . accusing.

Blue, he thought with wonder. Ab-bey's eyes were like a clear sky on a summer's day. Suddenly, he saw the vulnerability masked by her glitter of defiance, and his heart tripped in forbidden sympathy. He turned away abruptly. She was the enemy; he could not allow himself to be affected by the woman's plight!

Kwan headed back toward the longhouse, but was forced to stop after taking only two steps. O-wee-soo—his grandmother—had called his name.

He spun to see her approach. "My son," the old woman said. "What of Spring Rain? She has lost a daughter. Who will replace her? Why give the English *Ix e sa ha* to the French when she can be useful here?"

Kwan immediately heard murmurs of agreement. "You wish this?" he asked. He knew what she was asking. Why couldn't the English woman be slave to Spring Rain?

O-wee-soo was the head matron of the village. She and the other women had great power, more so than the Onondaga braves. It was the women of the Onondaga who chose and appointed the sachem. It

43

was the women who could decide that the sachem wasn't doing a good job and replace him, who had the ultimate power over the People. But it wasn't fear of being ousted that made Kwan turn to listen carefully to his grandmother's words, nor was it the knowledge that O-wee-soo actually had the final say. It was because Kwan had long ago recognized the old matron's wisdom, and he respected her judgment.

"I think that Spring Rain needs help with her fire. When Col. Breck-ing-ridge took her daughter from her two summers past, Spring Rain was left with an empty heart. Perhaps having the *Ix e sa ha* will fill the ache inside the mother."

Kwan nodded. "Then it is done. The woman will be given as slave to Spring Rain to use as she decides. That is my final word."

And with that, Kwan left the circle for the sanctuary of the longhouse.

"You have heard your sachem!" O-wee-soo cried. "This woman is now slave to Spring Rain. Vengeance has been served!"

Wild cries of joy rose from the relieved villagers as Evening Sky stepped forward to carry out the sachem's wishes.

"What has happened?" Abbey asked. "Where are you taking me?"

"Kwan Kahaiska—he say you will be given to the French."

"The French!"

Evening Sky inclined her head. "But O-wee-soo she say different. You be slave to Spring Rain. You take the place of the one she lost."

Abbey stopped, grabbing the girl's arm. "Slave? I

44

am to be a slave to an Indian!"

The Onondaga's gaze narrowed. "You like French better? You fear one woman crying for her child?"

"I don't understand."

Evening Sky held up her hand to silence her. "It is not for you to know. It is to be. You now belong to Spring Rain. I take you. She is good Onondaga. You not be broken. This is good."

"Wonderful," Abbey muttered beneath her breath as Evening Sky propelled her in the direction of a longhouse. "I'm to be a slave to some savage and I'm supposed to be grateful."

Well, Spring Rain—whoever you are—the first chance I get I'm leaving this filthy village!

Jamie was still out there waiting to be rescued.

Chapter 4

Evening Sky took Abbey back to the longhouse that was smaller than the rest of the huge, rectangular structures. There were two doors to the building, one at each end. These openings and the tiny smoke holes in the roof were the house's only access to outside light.

As they entered through an open porch and moved inside out of the light, Abbey took thorough stock of her surroundings. Whether she liked it or not, she guessed this building would be home to her for a while. But not for long, she vowed silently.

The two women walked past several cooking fires. Abbey thought it strange that the Iroquois built their fires indoors down the center of the longhouse from end to end. She was thankful that only a few of the fires were burning on this hot summer's day. Though she was aching and weary, she began to question Evening Sky about her new home.

"This belong to the Deer clan," Evening Sky told her, pausing before she entered the longhouse. The building appeared to be twenty feet wide and at least fifty feet long. "I am of Deer clan. Spring Rain, too. You live here with many of the clan."

Abbey would be living with not only Spring Rain, her new master, but with Evening Sky. She scowled as she entered the building. "How many live here?" she asked. Did they honestly believe she would submit to their will?

Evening Sky thought for a moment. "Ten fam—" she hesitated.

"Families? Ten families in one house!"

The maiden nodded. "It is so—ten fam-i-lies. Many matrons. Many warriors."

Something moved in the pit of Abbey's stomach. "Warriors?" She shuddered, remembering the fierce Onondaga brave. She would be living with the cold, sadistic men who'd attacked the fort? And what of the sachem? Did he live here too? Abbey thought she wouldn't be able to bear it if he did.

The Onondaga maiden inclined her head. "Brave warriors," she said proudly. "Men to women of the Deer." She gestured about the longhouse.

"The men are not of the Deer clan?"

"Men of Deer cannot wed women of Deer. Brave of Wolf can wed Deer. Wolf brave move into women's house. It is the Onondaga way."

Abbey forgot her fears, forgot Kwan, in this new knowledge of the Iroquois women. Recalling the old matron and her influence over the villagers, Abbey began to ponder the power the Onondaga women possessed, unlike the English women back home. If she had understood Evening Sky correctly, then it was the Indian women who owned the longhouses.

47

Despite herself, she was fascinated by the knowledge. She studied her surroundings with new eyes.

The longhouse itself was divided into ten cubicles—five on each side, one for each family. These "rooms" were partitioned by walls made of a grass that Abbey noticed gave off a sweet, pleasant odor.

The family had privacy within its cubicle. Each room contained a sleeping platform built about a foot and half off the dirt floor. Soft furs blanketed and afforded comfort to the Indian bed. Several feet directly above was a second shelf used for storage, housing cooking vessels, extra animal skins, hunting gear, and other prized possessions.

Abbey glanced upward. The ceiling of the longhouse was high. The rafters were hung with corn, other vegetables, and various kinds of fruit, including dried apples and something that looked to her like pumpkins or maybe squash.

Evening Sky took Abbey to a cubicle, a short distance from the opposite end of the longhouse. She gestured for Abbey to sit down. "I get water," she said.

"Wait!" Abbey grabbed the girl's arm as she turned to leave. "I—"

Glancing about warily, she felt a sudden chill where only moments before she'd been conscious of the humid, summer heat. Her eyes returned to appeal to the only one in the village who had shown her kindness. "The sachem . . ."

The Indian woman stared at her. "Kwan Kahaiska." Her brow cleared as understanding dawned. "He not live here. He is of the Wolf clan."

Abbey released a shaky breath. Why did she feel so relieved that the sachem wouldn't be sharing the same roof? She recalled his intense silver gaze and felt bumps raise the hairs along her arms. She flushed when she saw that Evening Sky was regarding her strangely.

Straightening her spine, Abbey stared back. What of her master—the woman she was to live with? Who is Spring Rain?"

Evening Sky's dark eyes glistened in the dim light. "You will know. She come. Soon." She escaped from Abbey's grasp. "You hurt. You need water. I come back."

Swallowing hard, Abbey watched her go. Thank God she wouldn't be living with Kwan Kahaiska! Questioning her relief, she told herself it was because she couldn't bear to be near the man who was responsible for taking her from the fort . . . who had wanted to sell her to the French.

She lowered herself gingerly onto the platform to anxiously await Evening Sky's return. She was a slave to savages! Savages led by a wild half-breed!

Abbey's gaze went across the large community space running the length of the longhouse to the "room" across from her. What manner of people were these Iroquois? The items stored on the top shelf looked like those belonging to a primitive, but ordinary people.

Recalling their brutality, Abbey knew otherwise. These people were savages. Cannibals, if the stories she'd heard were true.

She knew the Mohawks had been known to eat humans, what of the Onondagas? Was the same true for all Iroquois? Abbey thought of the other captives . . . Rachel and Anna . . . the children and their mothers, about a dozen victims in all. She'd seen what they did to the soldiers at the fort; she knew the Indians were capable of heinous behavior. But eat a woman or child? She prayed that the Onondagas were different from their Mohawk brothers.

Her cheek throbbed. She touched it, and her fingers came away with blood. Someone had kicked her knee in the scuffle, and she rubbed it now to ease the soreness. Her right elbow was scraped; her head ached abominably from the blow inflicted by an angry brave.

She stared straight ahead, her vision blurring. Unbidden came the mental image of the sachem, Kwan Kahaiska.

Sell her to the French! She shuddered, remembering the stories told of the French by fellow passengers on the ship coming over. The English and the French were enemies. Abbey would have been as bad, if not worse, off if the Onondaga had sold her as a slave.

She blinked to clear her vision. Glancing down at her knuckles and hands, she saw the terrible cuts and bruises. Her legs and feet looked as bad. Would the Indians continue to beat her?

Kwan Kahaiska thinks to make me a slave, does he! Abbey scowled. She wouldn't be a meek servant; she'd fight them every step.

And end up dead or worse? an inner voice queried.

Abbey clenched her fists, gasping at the pain in her fingers. "Unfeeling brute!" she spat. "White savage!"

She experienced a rush of heat as she recalled Kwan's insolent gaze, the way his gray eyes had glowed briefly as they studied her. She felt a tingling along her arms, her spine.

The sachem was a well-built man, she admitted. His shoulders were broad, his muscles hard and developed. It was a curious thing, she thought, that he had no hair on his massive chest. As a physician's daughter who often assisted her father, Abbey had seen a lot of men without shirts, but not one of them had chests as smooth and sleek and as sinewy as this savage's.

Who was he really? Had he lived with the Onondagas all his life? He knew English . . . from his mother? Where was she now? Had she been a captive who'd managed to escape? Had she gone back to England or France—wherever she'd come from across the waters, or was she dead, killed by the same people who made her son chief?

Abbey heard movement at the other end of the longhouse, and thinking it was Evening Sky returning with the water, she rose and headed toward her, the smoke from the dwindling fire obscuring her vision. She froze when she was close enough to see the figure clearly. It was a brave who'd entered, not her gentle Indian friend, but a hideous-looking warrior with an Iroquois head crest and a tattooed face.

Alarmed, Abbey stepped back as the warrior stalked toward her. Her gaze fastened on the knife at his belt, on the leather tassels edging his breechclout.

"Oh-nag-o-noos," he said, lifting an object in the air. Abbey thought it looked like a weapon. A club of some kind.

"Go away," she gasped. "Leave me alone!"

His eyes flashing, the Indian raised the weapon high.

Abbey stumbled in her hurry to escape him. She scrambled to her feet and ran toward the door.

51

Blinded by fear, she never saw the figure who blocked her only exit. She felt the jolt as she ran headlong into an Indian. Panicking, she began swinging her fists.

The first inkling she had that her victim was female was when her fist hit a bare breast and the woman grunted with pain.

Abbey went numb with shock. Her eyes went wide and she tripped backward, right into the arms of the warrior.

The brave hit her along the side of her neck, and Abbey's world went dark.

"Why did you do that?" Spring Rain asked Stone-face, her son. "She will be of no use to me if she is broken."

Stone-face frowned. "The woman is a crazy one. You saw how she hit you. She would have killed you if she could."

"She was frightened." Spring Rain's tone was scolding. "Would you not strike a Mohawk who attacked?"

The brave snorted. "The Mohawk are of the People. We are brothers."

"Until the laws of the Great League are broken," Spring Rain said.

"She is the man's niece." Stone-face studied the captive.

Spring Rain's expression turned grave. "I know. She is slave. I have not forgotten."

When Abbey awoke, she was lying on a platform cushioned by soft beaver pelts. A soft glow lit the interior of the longhouse. It was night and the light came from the fires burning within the longhouse. She wasn't alone; there were others inside. She sat up.

"You are awake." Evening Sky rose from the platform beside her, approaching to put a hand on Abbey's brow.

Abbey nodded, relieved to see a familiar face. "How long did I sleep?" She swung her legs to the floor, gasping at the pain near her right shoulder. She felt a flicker of alarm as she remembered the tattooed warrior. Her sleep hadn't been natural; she'd been knocked unconscious. "That man—"

"*O-nia O-gook-sah* . . . Stone-face." Evening Sky glanced toward the door. "He is Spring Rain's son."

"He tried to kill me!"

The Indian girl shook her head. "With this?" Abbey nodded. "He bring water." Evening Sky showed Abbey the long cone-shaped object. It was a vessel or pot used for carrying water . . . the object held by the tattooed warrior.

Abbey felt foolish. "I didn't know." She rubbed her bruised shoulder. "The woman—I hit a woman." She groaned at Evening Sky's condemning look. "Spring Rain?" she guessed.

The girl nodded. "You belong to her. If it were other than Spring Rain, you would have been beat. Dead maybe."

"You're not serious!"

"Serious?" Evening Sky looked puzzled. "What is serious?" Her brow cleared. "Ah . . . you ask if I tell truth." She inclined her head. "*O-gai-sah Ka-ai-wi-a* always speak truth."

"*O-ga—*"

"*O-gai-sah Ka-ai-wi-a,*" the Onondaga enunciated carefully. "I am called that."

Abbey tried pronouncing Evening Sky's Indian name; and despite the graveness of her situation, she ended up chuckling at her sorry attempt. Her laughter ended abruptly as she recalled Evening Sky's words about punishment. The Indian maiden wasn't smiling.

"If it had been another instead of Spring Rain, I truly could have been killed . . . ?"

The girl nodded. "You slave to Spring Rain. It is her right to—" She hesitated as if searching for the right English word.

"Punish me?"

"Yes. Pun-nish you." Evening Sky gave her a gentle smile. "Spring Rain is"—she thought for a moment—"good." She reached up to the upper platform and placed the retrieved bowl on the furs next to Abbey. "She saw to heal you. You are to help her. Dead you would be no use to her."

"Smart woman," Abbey murmured and offered up a silent prayer of thanks.

"How do you feel?"

"Sore, but I'll live." Her wounds had been tended, she noticed with the interest of a physician's aide. She touched a dressing on her leg and was satisfied that it was clean.

"Come." Evening Sky gestured toward the door. "We go out. Spring Rain waits."

Abbey held back. "But—"

"Come." It was a command, not a request. Abbey seethed with anger as the two women walked past those few who remained inside to tend their cook fires and out into the dark summer's night.

"Where are the other captives?" Abbey demanded as she followed Evening Sky from the longhouse to the village square where many Indians had gathered to sit in a large circle. "Are they all right?"

"They slaves like you, belong to some of my people. Others sent away to French."

Slaves. The knowledge galled her. Abbey worried about Rachel and the German woman's baby. Had they been separated? Were they safe? "My friend—a woman and her baby girl—do you know where they are?" The Indian maiden shook her head. "If they're among your people, will they be treated kindly?"

"If they hear and do good." Evening Sky paused to study those in the circle. "Some Onondaga good to slaves. Some not." Her face brightened as she spied the one she searched for. "There is Spring Rain. Come." She moved forward, and Abbey had no choice but to continue after her.

Abbey's attention was drawn to the center of the circle as the two women traversed the outer perimeter. An Indian brave entered the clearing. He wore a mask which Abbey thought looked more comical than frightening with large, uneven eyes, a twisted nose, and lips curved into a silly smile.

She watched, horrified, as the brave began to gyrate the lower half of his body, to swing his arms. He uttered harsh, guttural sounds as he danced to his own inner music. Abbey decided that it was a ceremony or show of some sort. The brave seemed to be acting, waving a club—a long weapon with a solid wooden ball at the tip. She shuddered, imagining the damage the weapon could inflict on one's head.

The Onondagas in the circle laughed as the brave continued his performance. Abbey stopped and gaped while the Indian whooped and yelled and acted ridiculous. She was astonished to note that the brave's audience appeared to be enjoying themselves. Evening Sky, seeing that Abbey was no longer with her, retraced her steps to urge the Englishwoman on. They continued around the outer circle to the far side.

"What are they doing?" Abbey asked. She was shocked by the scene, reminded anew of the savagery of these people.

Evening Sky paused to glance at the masked brave. "It is the—how say—False . . . False Face."

"False Face?"

The Indian woman nodded. "The Onondaga heals."

Curiosity momentarily replaced Abbey's horror. "He dances to heal the sick?"

"This is truth. Face used for other now. People are sad, but happy. Loved ones avenged, but sorrow remains. Onondaga try to take sorrow. Many hurt. Onondaga stop hurt."

The ceremony, Abbey realized, was a ritual to heal the sick and injured—both physically and emotionally. This day they sought to ease someone's grief. She frowned. Grief? Impossible! These savages had no feelings.

Evening Sky stopped. "Spring Rain," she said.

Spring Rain was a heavy-set woman of indeterminable age with small, dark eyes and a hawk-like nose. She sat on an animal skin, an imposing figure as she watched the dance. Her breasts were huge, her arms big but not fat. The Indian met Abbey's gaze,

56

her expression unfriendly, but for some reason which Abbey didn't understand herself, Abbey felt no fear.

Her new master spoke to her in Onondaga and Abbey, at a loss, looked to Evening Sky for the translation.

"She said you will live. This is good." Evening Sky listened as Spring Rain went on. "She want you to sit."

Spring Rain made room for Abbey in the circle. Her lips forming a slight smile, Abbey obeyed. The smile left her face as she recalled how she'd hit this woman. Fear of reprisal made her offer an apology.

"Tell Spring Rain that I am sorry I struck her."

Nodding, Evening Sky did so. Spring Rain inclined her head and spoke again.

"Spring Rain says it will not happen again."

Abbey felt a prickle of alarm when her new "master" glared at her. Wisely, Abbey refrained from voicing her thoughts. Jamie needed her. She would do whatever she had to do to escape and find him.

The ceremony continued. Abbey felt someone staring from the other side of the circle. She glanced over and was shocked to encounter the intense silver gaze of the sachem.

Kwan Kahaiska.

She looked away, her skin flushing with heat, her nerve endings humming with life. She was unsettled by his continued interest, by her body's instant response. His eyes left her, only to return to study her several more times during the remainder of the Onondaga ritual.

And each time Abbey knew the exact moment when he was watching her.

Chapter 5

Colonel William Breckingridge of the English army stood beside his subordinate, eyeing the carnage of Fort Michaels. His face grew red with rage. "Bloody red bastards!" he bellowed. The veins in his temple rose purple.

"My God," Captain Smythe breathed with horror. His complexion, in contrast to the commander's, was white. "Who, Colonel? Who could have done this?"

The colonel's eyes narrowed. A muscle ticked along the right side of his jaw. "Iroquois," he spat.

"How can you tell?"

"I know." Breckingridge turned his chilling gaze on Smythe. "You saw the dead men . . . their split skulls. Only Iroquois war clubs could do this kind of damage." His breathing became harsh as he looked back at the felled, bloody bodies littering the compound yard. "Those puncture wounds were made by the spike at the ball end of the club. I'd swear it on my mother's grave."

"God damn them to hell!" The soldier reddened

when his commander flashed him a disapproving glance. "Sorry, sir," he mumbled. Tears filled his eyes. "The men . . . they were my friends."

The colonel's expression hardened, and the light of murder sparkled in his dark brown gaze. "We'll find and kill the sonavabitches!"

"Colonel Breckingridge!" A young soldier came hurrying up from the barracks. "It's McKenzie, sir. He's alive—barely."

The three men made haste to the spot where the middle-aged soldier lay on the ground, blood oozing from the corner of his mouth, his body riddled with feathered arrows.

"Mac." The colonel's tone was gentle . . . gentler than any of his men had ever heard.

"Col—nel," McKenzie gasped.

"Who, Mac? Iroquois?"

"Mo-hawk." The man's face contorted with pain; his strength was rapidly leaving him. "Gre . . . at Ar—"

"Great Arrow?" Breckingridge's heart slammed within his chest as a certain memory rushed back to haunt him. "The *Onondaga.*"

The colonel recalled a day over two years ago . . . the sound of children crying for their mothers . . . an Indian's woman's screams as his men raped her, her screams becoming a garbling moan as they finished their sport and snuffed out their victim's life. Then there was the Onondaga brave . . . his oath of vengeance in broken English as the breath of life was crushed from his body by blows inflicted by five English soldiers.

Kwan Kahaiska. Great Arrow. Sachem of the

Onondaga. Chief of the people his men had rounded up and slaughtered. The name was on the dying Iroquois brave's lips as he was repeatedly stabbed by one of the colonel's men. The Indian's look, the way he had stared straight into the colonel's eyes, as he suffered the fatal wounds had brought chills to the British officer's spine.

For weeks—months—afterwards the colonel had his men ready to defend the fort in readiness of the Iroquois attack. But there had been no sign of any Indians . . . no sign of the sachem Kwan Kahaiska. Breckingridge had dismissed the threat as a dying man's only chance at getting back at his enemies.

The colonel had then realized his own fears as foolish. The small band of Onondagas had been alone, gathering what wild fruits and berries they could, taking in the harvest of a field that the Indians had planted before they had moved their village farther north. Who had been left to alert the others?

Onondaga. The word no longer made him uneasy. At least it hadn't . . . until this . . .

He glanced toward where McKenzie lay. "Mac?" He hunkered to his knees, shook the man's shoulder.

"He's gone, sir."

Breckingridge shuddered as he rose to his feet. He stared ahead unseeingly. His men looked at him with concern.

"Colonel?" It was Smythe. He had just finished speaking with a young soldier.

The colonel looked at him.

"Sir," Smythe said hesitantly, "they've taken the women . . . and the children."

Breckingridge's teeth snapped. "I know."

"No, sir. You don't understand. I've been talking to Jones. He checked your house. There are women's things in one of the bedrooms, sir. Your niece—she must have arrived while we were gone. She was here for the attack—"

The colonel gave an ear-piercing howl of rage. "Susie!" he gasped. "They've taken Susie!" Stark pain contorted his features and then was gone. His expression was one his men had never seen before; Smythe and the other soldiers cringed and backed away.

"They'll pay." His dark gaze glittered. "Every last red-arsed one of them!" And the chief, he thought, will be the first to die. He would see to it personally.

A week passed and Abbey's injuries healed. The summer's temperatures continued to soar; the humidity was at times unbearable. Still, the Indian women worked in their fields, tending their corn, beans, and vegetable crops. Abbey, slave to Spring Rain, worked beside them, often pushed to the limit of her endurance. These times Abbey thought she hated the Indian woman. Spring Rain had tended Abbey's cuts during the first two days of her captivity, ensured she was well-fed, and now Abbey knew why. So that Abbey could work for the woman like a pack horse.

The sun was hot, beating on Abbey's back, as she tilled the soil around the bean plants. Flies buzzed about her head. She swung and swatted at several, but killed none, and the pests continued to plague her.

She was perspiring profusely, the sweat trickling

from her forehead, making the doeskin tunic stick to her heated back and breasts. Abbey straightened and rubbed the lower curvature of her spine. She ached in places she didn't recall owning.

Her hand shielding her gaze from the bright glare of the sun, she observed the Onondaga women beside her. They seemed oblivious to the heat; they worked the soil efficiently and non-stop for hours, their copper-colored breasts bobbing as they moved. To Abbey, it seemed that the Indian women worked harder than the men. They didn't seem to mind; they appeared proud of their efforts.

She was so thirsty and hot! They'd been tending the crops for three days now. She couldn't take much more. When would the field work end?

Abbey ran a hand beneath the neckline of her tunic. She felt so sticky! What she wouldn't give for a swim in the cool waters of the lake!

For a brief moment, Abbey envied the Onondaga women's half-naked state. They seemed unaffected by the heat in their short deerskin skirts.

Movement at the edge of the field caught her gaze. Abbey glanced over and saw an Iroquois brave—Bear Claw. He was instantly recognizable to Abbey as the Indian with the tattooed chest who had stared at her with loathing on that first day. He must have been hunting; he carried his bow in one hand, a small dead animal in the other. Abbey couldn't tell whether it was a rabbit or a muskrat.

Bear Claw stared at her, his dark gaze hostile; she felt the force of his hate, her own instant fear in response.

Why did she allow him to frighten her? He hadn't

bothered her during the week of her captivity. She belonged to Spring Rain, and Evening Sky had assured her that he wouldn't harm her. Still, Abbey couldn't shake the notion that Bear Claw was only waiting for the right time to get her alone before he pounced.

"Ab-bey!" Spring Rain admonished.

Abbey jumped, startled. The Indian woman scowled at her and Abbey felt the need to confide her fear. "Spring Rain," she said. "Bear Claw—he frightens me. I don't like the way he looks at me."

Spring Rain stared at her, scowling. "Work!" she said, clearly not understanding.

She glanced at Bear Claw, debated whether or not to try again to make Spring Rain understand. Bear Claw was toying with her; she wouldn't allow him to bother her!

As instructed, Abbey went back to work.

Night fell across the land, shrouding the village in its dark cloak. The Onondagas were in their longhouses, all but Kwan who had escaped the presence of his people to stand on the shore of the great lake.

A scattering of stars dotted the sky; a quarter moon hung overhead, casting little light over the water. Kwan stared at the ripples, his scowl as dark as the night around him. He thought of the blonde captive, Ab-bey, and shifted uncomfortably. He didn't like what he was feeling, his growing fascination for the woman. She was a slave! The enemy! Breckingridge's niece.

63

She was a flesh and blood woman, an inner voice murmured, someone who stirred something within his gut. His heart jumped whenever he saw her.

Kwan continued to brood as he stared out over the lake. He didn't understand what was happening! No one had triggered his manhood since *Atahkwa Tut-kwa-ih-ta,* his late wife . . . not even Morning Flower, the lovely maiden he was to have taken to wife second.

He closed his eyes and thought back to a time of joy and love, and the memory of a laughing face. Atahkwa's.

A fish jumped in the lake, startling Kwan. He glanced back toward the sleeping village before turning once again toward the rippling waters of the lake.

He found his gaze drawn to a large rock near the shoreline, watched as the water licked and lapped at the immovable object, and he recalled a sunny day long ago when he had spied Atahkwa frolicking naked in the cool waters of the lake.

Kwan felt his staff harden as he remembered the vision of globular breasts . . . the way drops of water had glistened on her lush, copper-colored mounds. That day under the hot summer's sun, hiding behind a huge oak tree, he had felt his very first stirring of male desire as he secretly watched the Indian woman bathe. He had fancied himself in love with her from that moment on.

When Kwan turned eighteen, the village matrons decided that he needed a wife. He'd been thrilled but fearful when he learned that his chosen mate was Atahkwa. He had secretly loved her for years, but what of her feelings? Would she be pleased or angry at the match?

Atahkwa was a widow, seven years his senior. To the matrons, the relationship was an ideal one, for Atahkwa would bring the understanding and experience that was needed to teach a future sachem all the joys of married love and harmony.

Atahkwa was pleased with the match, and Kwan was never more happy than when he was wrapped in Atahkwa's arms, burying himself in her softness. Kwan's new wife taught him what it took to please a woman sexually. She knew what to do, where to touch to excite Kwan, to bring him to an explosive, shuddering climax. Life for Kwan was wonderful, and Kwan's joy knew no bounds the day he learned that Atahkwa carried their child.

Then Atahkwa died giving birth to their stillborn child, and Kwan went into a deep state of mourning.

The Onondaga tried everything to help Kwan over his grief. Members of the False Face Society appealed to the spirits; each individual had danced and prayed and attempted to make Kwan smile again. Time healed Kwan's wound, and when the time was right, O-wee-soo and the other matrons had chosen Morning Flower, daughter of Spring Rain, to be the young warrior's next wife.

Morning Flower was as unlike Atahkwa as night was to day. Shy, inexperienced, she was a pretty young maiden with huge doe-like eyes and a gentle smile that could charm a bear cub from its mother. It was custom among the Onondaga people to match one who was experienced with one who has known little of life. This time it would be Kwan who brought the experience to the marriage. Kwan would be the teacher; Morning Flower would be the young but eager student.

But the marriage was not to be. The creek that had supplied the Indians with water had run dry. The land they'd used for farming was no longer fertile, and the entire village had picked up and moved farther north to a rich area near the shores of the great lake. A small field had been left flourishing. It was to harvest this field and to gather berries, acorns and other wild foodstuffs for the winter months that a small peaceful band of Onondaga had returned to their abandoned village site. That fateful autumn day, Morning Flower and other members of the Onondaga party were harvesting the field when they were attacked and slaughtered by English soldiers.

The Indians had done nothing wrong, had harmed no one, but to the English they were just savages to be easily disposed of.

When Bear Claw, a member of the search party that was sent out when the band didn't return, came home with news of discovering the mutilated bodies of their loves ones, Kwan had sworn vengeance . . . as was the Iroquois way. A vengeance that today was being satisfied—at least in part.

Kwan's thoughts came back to the present, centering on Abbey, Breckingridge's niece. By rights, he should have let the women of the village have the English woman to torture as they saw fit. But Kwan found he couldn't stomach the idea. It was Breckingridge who was responsible for the slaughter, not Abbey . . . not the beautiful English captive with the flowing golden hair.

He envisioned her swimming in the lake, much as Atahkwa had, but it was night, not day, with the moon casting its full radiance over her bathing form.

Her breasts would be pale ... gleaming ... as water cascaded over the moon-lit globes, trickling down to her white stomach, to the triangle of dark golden hair at the apex of her thighs.

She'd turn and he'd see the soft, rounded curve of her buttocks ... her long legs ... a small ankle as she lifted her leg from the water ... one perfectly formed foot ... She'd move toward shore; he'd come from the shadows. They'd stop, stare at one another, their bodies pulsating with liquid heat.

Kwan would open his arms, and she'd willingly come into his embrace ... then their lips would meet, tentatively at first and then hard and demanding ... passionately ... savagely ...

They'd become lost in the spiral of sensation that would spin a cocoon of feeling about them until each one would be conscious of only the other.

A snap of a twig pierced the silent night, and Kwan spun around, jerked from his fantasy, drawing his bow. A doe came out of the woods to stare at him with innocent, trusting eyes.

Kwan took aim with his bow and then lowered it. He had no desire to destroy the female ... not while his pulse still raced, his body throbbed with heat. His one desire was to touch and taste Ab-bey.

Cursing, Kwan stalked past the frightened deer, returning to the sanctuary of the longhouse to fight off the tremors of lust.

Chapter 6

"Ab-bey!" Spring Rain shoved Abbey while she slept. "Ab-bey! Wake up!"

Cursing silently, Abbey stirred, opening her eyes. A bright-eyed Spring Rain was fumbling among the utensils on the storage shelf; her son, Stone-face, sat by the cook fire, eating.

The young English woman had come to know several Onondaga phrases since she was brought to the village, like "wake up," "get water," and other commands that Abbey was sick to death of hearing.

Abbey rose from the platform, knowing that if she didn't, her reward would be a heavy-handed cuff across her head. She'd been sleeping soundly the first time Spring Rain had hit her. Days of exhausting work had made her sleep the slumber of the dead. Spring Rain had apparently tried waking her for some time, finally resorting to the one thing she knew would bring the slave instantly to her feet.

Abbey's ears had rung from the blow, and she'd had a headache for the better part of that morning.

Never again, Abbey had sworn to herself. Never again would Spring Rain have cause to hit her while she slept. Since that day no matter how tired she was, she woke up quickly, dragging herself out of bed as fast as her weary body would allow her.

Combing her fingers through her tangled blonde tresses, Abbey stretched. She bent to straighten the fur mats on the bed and suddenly grew conscious of Stone-face's stare.

She refused to look at him. He was a nuisance, but despite his intimidating appearance, he was no real threat. Unlike Bear Claw, she thought. She couldn't seem to shake her fear of that one!

Spring Rain handled Stone-face with a firm hand; he wouldn't dare disobey her. Only once on her second day in the longhouse did he pester Abbey with an order. Abbey, of course, hadn't been able to understand his Onondaga; and when she didn't obey, he'd raised a hand to strike her. Spring Rain had stopped him.

Stone-face never came near her again, except when necessary within the confines of their living cubicle. Spring Rain must have warned him away from the slave.

Ignoring the warrior, Abbey grabbed the vessel used for hauling water and left the longhouse for the lake. Perhaps she'd see Rachel there, she thought.

Abbey saw little of the captives from Fort Michaels. She'd glimpsed at Rachel and her baby Anna on occasion, but only from a distance. She guessed the Indians didn't want the slaves talking to each other, perhaps to prevent plans for escape. Abbey had spoken to white women only once since the day they were captured, and then only briefly down at the lake where she'd gone to fetch water. Of the original seven women who actually made it to the village, there were only five adults left. Two, Evening Sky had told her, had been sold to the French. There remained only Abbey, Rachel, Mary and two others—a soldier's wife and her personal maid. And four children.

To get to the lake, she had to leave the fenced-in village and walk past the warrior-guards. An Onondaga brave followed, several steps behind her. She'd become used to his presence since her first trip outside the village.

Abbey was disappointed; there was no sign of any of the captives along the trail. Yesterday, she'd seen a white child about the village. She appeared well. Where were the others?

When she arrived at the lake, she saw Rachel hunkered down at the shoreline. Her heart lightened as she waved, calling her German friend's name.

"Abbey," Rachel breathed as Abbey came to the shore beside her, dipping the clay vessel in the lapping water.

"Rachel, are you well? Anna . . . is she?" Abbey barely glanced up from the cool waters of the lake.

The German woman sighed. "She is fine." She straightened and met Abbey's gaze. "You?"

Rising, Abbey nodded. "I am well, but long for the day we escape." She glanced furtively behind her to see the position of their Indian guards. The two braves were a few yards away, staring at them.

"We, too, are managing. Song of the Heart is a good woman. I am grateful to her. She allows my Anna to be near me."

70

"Rachel, we must plan our escape."

"Escape?" Rachel shot her a look that said Abbey must be crazy. "How? Vhen?" The brave who followed Abbey moved closer, and the German woman lowered her voice. "Is foolish to do so. I vill not risk our lives. Ve—my Anna and me—ve do all right here."

"You can't want to stay forever?" Abbey looked disbelieving.

"I didn't say that!" Rachel hissed, her gaze flashing to the two guards. "But my baby . . ." Her voice trailed off.

Abbey sighed, but understood. "The others," she said, "I have seen some of them from afar. They fare well."

Picking up her pots, Rachel refused to meet Abbey's gaze.

"Rachel?" Abbey saw something disturbing in her friend's expression. "What is it?"

"Mary is dead." Her voice was toneless.

"Dead!"

"She vas an old woman and sick. They beat her. She never recovered."

"Animals." Abbey blinked back tears.

"I must go back."

Abbey nodded. "We will escape them, Rachel. I swear it."

The German woman gave her a sad smile and headed back to the village.

Dead. Mary was dead, Abbey thought. She cradled the full water jug and returned to the trail. It must have happened while Abbey was unconscious after Stone-face had hit her.

The savages killed Mary! The monsters! She was an old woman, for God's sake!

Her thoughts went to her brother. *Oh, dear God! Is Jamie dead?* She swallowed against a suddenly tight throat. If he was alive, was he suffering at the Indians' hands?

She recalled a time when they were young, and some of the neighboring children had been calling the four-year-old Jamie *bastard,* hitting him with stones. Seeing her, he'd run to her.

"Oh, Abbe," he'd sobbed. Abbey had grabbed a stick and threatened to beat each of the four boys unless they ceased their tormenting. She'd been six and her family situation an unusual one. Their parents lived as husband and wife but weren't legally married. As the children grew older, the bond between them strengthened, and they protected one another against the cruelty of "polite society." They didn't care to be accepted by "decent folk"; they were happy as long as they were together.

But now they were separated . . . and poor Jamie was in the hands of savages! She had to find him! She'd hoped, prayed, that she would learn something within the village about Jamie's whereabouts. But she'd heard and saw nothing that would help her. She felt frustrated . . . and concerned.

How many Indian tribes were there? she wondered. Was Jamie far? How was she going to find out? Colonel Breckingridge must have returned to the fort. Was he now on his way to rescue them?

A horrible thought occurred to her. What if no one at the fort had survived to tell the grisly tale of their abduction?

Abbey switched the jug to her other arm. If someone had survived, would they tell the colonel of his captured niece? The news would ensure their rescue. She could tell from the way the servants fawned over her as Susie Portsmouth that the colonel loved his sister's child. She prayed that a male servant had survived to tell, for only the servants knew of her arrival.

Breckingridge wouldn't leave his beloved niece to the mercy of savages. Thank God, Abbey thought, that the English officer didn't know of her deception!

She went cold with horror as she approached the fence. Had she left anything behind, in her room in the colonel's house, to reveal her deception?

The letter! Oh, God, that damn letter she'd found on a table in Breckingridge's front foyer. She had spied it by accident on her way to her bedchamber that night. Noting the feminine hand and scented paper, she'd picked it up and taken it to read in the privacy of her room. She'd had a strange hunch that the letter was from Susie Portsmouth.

Abbey had been right. The missive had been from Susie to her uncle. The young woman was not coming; she'd run off to marry a gentleman she'd met on the ocean voyage to the New World. Susie Portsmouth was now living happily in the Virginia Colony.

What would dear uncle say to that? Abbey had wondered. She'd been relieved to know that Susie wasn't coming, that for a time, at least, her secret was safe.

She stopped just inside the compound to shift the jug once again. She'd never intended the ruse to

73

continue for long. Breckingridge would have known at first glance that she wasn't his niece. He would have understood once she'd explained.

But the letter! What if, in searching the house for his servants, he found the letter in his niece's room? Would he guess—know—that another had taken her place? Would he then lose the urge to come for her?

"You're being ridiculous!" she muttered. She wasn't the only one captured. There had been a few women and children at the fort. The surviving men would be anxious for their safe return.

And why on heavens would Breckingridge take the time to search the bedchamber? He'd be too upset at Susie's disappearance to be suspicious.

Crossing the yard, Abbey dismissed her worries. It'd been a week and a half since her capture. How long could one be expected to wait? It was time to make definite plans for escape. There was a lot to think about . . . which direction to take when she left . . . what to eat on the trail . . . Fortunately, she'd learned something of food from the Indians. She shouldn't have any difficulty identifying things that were edible among the forest plantlife.

But what of water? What if farther into the wilderness she could find nothing to drink? Would the moisture in the wild berries and fruit be enough? If not, could she manage to secret a small vessel, one that wouldn't weigh her down or hamper her speed?

Abbey walked past the common storage shed, past three longhouses until she came to her own. She paused before entering. The sound of children's laughter drew her gaze to the yard near the longhouse directly across from her.

74

She gasped, her face whitening, when she saw what the Indian children were doing. The object of their sport.

There were two lines of naked Indian boys tormenting and torturing a lone Onondaga youth. The lone boy was being forced to run down the center of the two rows, while the rest of the boys beat him with switches. Some taunted and tripped him as he flew past. Abbey was outraged.

Her anger increased as her color returned. Indian or not, he was a child. How could they do this to one of their own?

Spring Rain called her name from within the longhouse. Ignoring the woman, Abbey carefully laid down the full water jug and marched over to where the children had gathered.

She was so incensed, so determined to put a stop to the boys' sport, that she was only vaguely aware that she'd become the object of several disbelieving stares. The bare-breasted matrons of the village gawked as Abbey grabbed the switch from the nearest child. Several cried out when she took the stick to the boy's bare backside. The other boys gaped at her, even the victim who regarded Abbey as if she'd gone mad.

"Jach te!" an angry male voice boomed from behind her, startling her.

Bear Claw! Abbey froze, alarmed at his expression. As she met his furious dark gaze, she felt her old fear of him intensify. Bear Claw grabbed her and backhanded her across the face. Scolding her in a fierce spat of unintelligible Onondaga, the Indian tossed her to the ground.

Stunned, Abbey lay, winded. She barely had time

to catch her breath when Bear Claw hauled her up by the neck of her tunic, dragging her against him. She felt his hot, fetid breath as he continued to growl his displeasure with her. He wanted to strike her again; Abbey could feel it.

With a grunt of disgust, he handed her into the arms of Evening Sky, who had come up to see the cause of the commotion.

"You not to do that, Ab-bey," the Indian maiden said, bustling Abbey away from an angry Bear Claw and the accusing stares of the village matrons.

"But they were hurting the boy!"

When Evening Sky replied, it was with impatience. "You know not of our ways."

"Damn your ways," Abbey exclaimed, "if it means pain to an innocent child!"

They entered the longhouse. Inside it was dark, and it took Abbey a moment to adjust to the change in light.

"Ab-bey, the *Hux sa ha* must learn to be a *Haing wee*. The boy must learn to be a man," Evening Sky explained so that Abbey would understand. "A warrior must know pain to defeat it."

There was a moment of silence as Evening Sky allowed her message to sink in. She shook her head sadly. "You will be beat this time, Ab-bey. I cannot stop it. You must not inter—fer in Onondaga ways."

"Interfere." Abbey had corrected her automatically. Her head reeled with thoughts of punishment, punishment and the strange Indian customs and beliefs.

The Iroquois allowed their children to torture one another to prepare them for manhood! Abbey thought the idea was preposterous but held back from saying so.

Was it a truly accepted way? Reflecting back, she realized that the boy-victim didn't seem too overly concerned with the youths' treatment of him. In fact, he'd appeared more upset, shocked even, when she'd tried to interfere.

Abbey's thoughts focused on her punishment when she and Evening Sky reached Spring Rain, who stood waiting with hands on hips, impatiently, for the slave to bring water.

Spring Rain spoke in rapid Onondaga to Evening Sky. Abbey saw the woman's face change as Evening Sky answered. She knew the exact point when Evening Sky told how Abbey had struck the boy. Spring Rain's red face turned several shades darker. Her breasts rose and fell with the force of her anger; there was an ominous sparkle in her dark gaze.

"She did not know!" Evening Sky looked concerned.

"That is no excuse! She is slave. Such behavior must be punished."

Evening Sky flashed Abbey a worried glance. "How?" she asked. "How will you punish her?"

Spring Rain shrugged her bare shoulders. She thought for a moment, before her expression brightened. "She will learn what it is to be another's slave." She paused. "Woman With No Heart."

The color left Evening Sky's face. "You will give her to *that* woman! She is a cruel one; she will beat Ab-bey when she has committed no wrong."

"Should I give her to Has-ha instead?"

Evening Sky shook her head. Has-ha—Knife

Woman—was Bear Claw's wife. Abbey would be at the mercy of Bear Claw's hatred. Anything could happen to Breckingridge's niece while she lived in the vengeful warrior's house. Especially when it was Bear Claw's son that Abbey had hit. "Must you punish her?"

"If I do not, she will get herself killed." Spring Rain glanced at the English woman before returning her gaze to Evening Sky. "I cannot protect her if she continues to interfere."

"So be it then," Evening Sky said with resignation in her tone. "What shall I tell her?"

Spring Rain scowled. "Tell her nothing. She will learn her fate soon enough."

Kwan heard Bear Claw shouting well before he saw him in the yard. He left the small hut reserved for the sachem's use and froze, his heart pumping with alarm as he witnessed the brave grab Abbey by the neckline and thrust her away from him.

He stared at the tangle of blonde hair, at the sight of bared limbs as Abbey struggled to rise. She looked confused . . . hurt. Her expression gave Kwan pause, stirred an overwhelming urge for him to come to her rescue. Which, of course, was out of the question! Abbey must have committed a grievous wrong to incur Bear Claw's act of violence. Bear Claw might hate the English woman because of her relationship to the colonel, but he would not strike her for no other reason than her birth ties.

Kwan frowned. What then did Abbey do?

He saw the children with grins on their faces. They

seemed amused at the turn of events. One—Bear Claw's son—was rubbing his buttocks and Kwan saw the mark made by the switch.

Frowning, he approached the group, made direct eye contact with one boy, who quickly turned to speak to the youth next to him. All nine of the young Indian boys spun to regard their sachem. Kwan eyed each one in turn. One child, small in stature, was cut and bruised and covered with a layer of dry dirt dust. Kwan held the child's gaze longer than the others', before he averted his gaze. Bear Claw had stamped off in a huff; it was up to the group of children to tell the sachem what had happened.

"Tell me," Kwan inquired of Bear Claw's son.

"The slave struck me!"

Kwan raised an eyebrow in disbelief as his gaze shifted to the boy's reddened behind. "Why?"

The boy blushed. "She is a crazy one!"

"Yes, an evil one!" said another, and the boys agreed, all but the disheveled child.

"Tell me what happened," Kwan asked him. For some reason, he was disturbed by the boy's expression. Perhaps because he reminded him of himself at that age?

"She does not understand our ways," a feminine voice said from behind. O-wee-soo had come up silently.

Kwan looked at his grandmother with a question in his silver eyes. "What did she do?"

"Little Boar was preparing for manhood," she said.

Kwan glanced at the boy and then back at the old matron. "The gauntlet?"

"This is true."

The sachem frowned. "She will be punished."

"Perhaps you should see to her punishment."

Kwan was startled by her suggestion. "Will not Spring Rain object to this?"

O-wee-soo smiled, the same gentle smile that had early on, during Kwan's first days in the village, soothed the fears of a white captive boy. "You forget. It will be easy for her to accept your word. You are sachem."

The young man thought for a long moment. He *was* sachem; Spring Rain would listen. But was it the right thing to do? And why should he care what happens to a slave?

Kwan gazed at his grandmother, noting the warmth, the wisdom in her brown eyes. O-wee-soo thought it proper, then it must be so.

He nodded. "I will speak with Spring Rain."

The old matron's face was solemn as she inclined her head.

The sachem set off for the longhouse of the Deer clan to decide the fate of Breckingridge's niece.

Chapter 7

"Where is she taking me?" Abbey gasped to Evening Sky as she struggled to keep up with Spring Rain's stride. The Indian maiden turned away without answering, and Abbey felt her heart lodge in her throat.

Abbey's imagination ran wild as Spring Rain tugged her down the length of the longhouse. She knew she was to be punished—but *how?* Her pulse raced with nervous anticipation. Her palms moistened, and perspiration settled above her upper lip. Spring Rain wouldn't even look at her. What was going to happen to her?

Spring Rain stopped suddenly and released her. Abbey fell forward, slamming against the heavy-set woman's back. Placing her fingers against Spring Rain's damp flesh, Abbey pushed herself away.

The Indian woman had accidentally stepped on Abbey's left foot, and Abbey bent to rub out the soreness. She heard someone murmur. Raising her bent head to see who had spoken, what had caused

Spring Rain to stop suddenly, she was startled to find herself the object of a silver-gray gaze. Kwan Kahaiska had blocked the doorway.

The sight of him made Abbey flush. Once again, she was impressed by the sheer breadth and power of him. He was dressed in his usual attire, nothing but a strip of cloth covering his loins. His long hair was disarrayed, as if he'd brushed it back in agitation. For the first time, Abbey noticed the pierced earring, a tiny strap of leather through his right ear. She looked, but could not see his left ear; therefore, she couldn't tell if that one was pierced and adorned as well. She was so busy studying the sachem that she was only vaguely conscious of the fact that he and Spring Rain were carrying on a conversation.

"There has been trouble with the slave," Kwan said to Spring Rain in Onondaga.

Spring Rain nodded. "She goes now to Woman With No Heart. Let the slave know what it is to serve that one! A just punishment, I think."

Kwan frowned. Woman With No Heart was a cross old squaw with the bark of bear and the bite of an adder. "This is wise?"

The Indian woman scowled, but nodded. "The slave Ab-bey must be disciplined. What better one to do that than Woman With No Heart?"

The sachem studied the captive, noting the defiant glitter in her blue eyes . . . the way her hair picked up the tiniest bit of light that came in the longhouse from outside. She was a most unusual woman. Lately, he'd found himself thinking of her too often . . . of her beauty . . . of her courage . . . of touching her smooth honey-toned skin.

His eyes shifted to gaze at her lips. They were full, pink . . . and quivering. He jerked with surprise. Was this courageous one truly afraid?

Obviously, she knew she had done a great wrong, he thought with satisfaction.

"How long?" he asked casually. He couldn't display too much interest; it wouldn't be seemly.

Apparently, Spring Rain had given the matter little thought. She did so now. "Three moons," she decided after several seconds.

Kwan nodded. Woman With No Heart resided in O-wee-soo's longhouse. He'd implore his grandmother to keep a protective eye on her. "I think this best, Spring Rain. Three moons is time enough. You will miss the slave's work."

He could tell Spring Rain hadn't given any thought to *that*.

"Two moons," Spring Rain declared, changing her mind. "If she learns well, then one moon only."

Stifling a smile, Kwan nodded. He then offered to escort the English captive to her new home. Spring Rain accepted his offer.

Abbey jumped, startled, when Kwan grabbed her bare arm. The warmth of his fingers burned against her flesh, sending the blood pumping wildly through her veins. She tried to pull away, but he tightened his hold on her. He didn't look at her as he led her from the longhouse and across the yard.

"Where are you taking me?" Abbey gasped. "Damn you! I know you speak English—answer me!"

Kwan stopped and stared down at her. Silver-gray eyes glowed in an otherwise expressionless face. He was silent for several long seconds, and Abbey felt her breath grow uneven under his piercing gaze. Finally, he spoke.

"You did wrong," he said.

"They were beating a child! I couldn't—"

"We do not hit our young ones." His voice was cold, effectively cutting off Abbey's tirade.

She swallowed, turning away from the force of his silver gaze to look out across the yard. The children were playing their violent game again! Appalled, Abbey turned back with renewed spirit.

"Considering the savagery of your people, Kwan Kahaiska, I find it hard to believe you don't hit children."

Kwan arched an eyebrow in sudden amusement. "We do not punish our young by violence—unlike you English. There are more effective ways of discipline . . . like the threat of a visit from *Long Nose* . . ."

"Long Nose?"

He gave her a wicked smile. "He comes in the night, wearing a mask. He is an eater of humans . . . Our children fear him."

"And you don't?"

Kwan no longer smiled. "It is not wise to tempt evil ones."

And she was left to wonder what he meant by his reply.

With a firm, but gentle grip, he urged Abbey forward. "Our children are smaller than we," he said, "but a woman-slave . . ." His voice trailed off.

Abbey stiffened at the implication. "You're going to beat me?"

He halted, meeting her gaze. Slow to answer her, Kwan continued his study of her, and she found herself held captive by her own fascination with his looks . . . the rugged planes of his handsome face . . . the sensual lips that firmed when he frowned, which he did more often than he smiled.

"Ab-bey," he began, and then stopped.

Abbey caught her breath as he released her arm. Something flickered in his silver eyes; but it was gone before Abbey could identify it.

What? she wondered. What was it he wanted to say?

Suddenly, Kwan was staring at her hard, without expression. "You will be slave to another," he stated coldly, grabbing her arm again. "Come. She will be pleased to use you."

Abbey felt relief. Apparently, he had no intention of beating her. Spring Rain must have been fed up with the slave and simply wanted to rid herself of a nuisance.

Use. Kwan had spoken the word as if she were an object and not a person; Abbey didn't like it. "Who is she? This woman?"

He paused before entering the largest longhouse in the village. Turning to her with a stoic expression, he said, "Woman With No Heart."

And Abbey knew the form of her punishment.

The interior of the longhouse was vast in comparison to that of the Deer Clan. Wide-eyed, Abbey gazed at the number and size of the living cubicles. Why, the building must be home to twenty or more families! she thought. Kwan had stopped to allow their eyes to adjust to the darkness. She looked at him, unable to conceal her astonishment.

He nodded at her unspoken question. "Clan of the Wolf," he said. "Clan of the sachem."

And Abbey understood.

She flushed as she wondered what it would be like living in close proximity to the man beside her.

Close? she mused, again studying the size of the building. Maybe not.

Probably not. Abbey told herself that the twinge she felt was not disappointment.

A small-breasted squaw in highly adorned doeskin skirt caught sight of them and approached. "Kwan," she said barely giving Abbey a glance. "You have brought us a new slave?"

Us? Was this woman Kwan's wife? Was she to be slave to Kwan's household? Abbey shifted, disturbed by the thought.

The woman had spoken English, and Abbey was surprised. She was equally surprised to hear Kwan answer the same way. Apparently, the slave was to hear and understand their conversation.

The woman, who'd been smiling at Kwan, turned her gaze onto Abbey. Her smile vanished; her eyes held contempt. "You are the one who struck Beaver Dancing."

Abbey lifted her chin. "If the boy's name is Beaver Dancing, then yes, I hit him."

A twisted smile came to the squaw's lips. "Stupid slave," she said, which brought Abbey's chin up another notch.

"Woman With No Heart—is she here?" Kwan

86

said, interrupting the current of animosity flowing between the two women.

So this woman wasn't Woman With No Heart . . . nor was she Kwan's wife, Abbey decided.

Good.

"She sits by her fire," the Indian woman said.

Unsmiling, Kwan nodded his thanks and steered Abbey toward the center of the great longhouse.

Woman With No Heart was an elderly squaw with a wrinkled face. Unlike the other matrons among the Iroquois, she wore a full-length tunic that covered her sagging breasts. She sat by a pile of smoldering embers, her back erect, her eyes closed. She was obviously in a state of meditation.

Abbey knew the village men meditated; this was the first inkling that the women might too. She stared at the old woman, fascinated.

Kwan hesitated, clearly unwilling to disturb or frighten the matron.

"So you have brought me the English niece," she said in flawless English, without opening her eyes.

Abbey was taken aback. That made four savages within the village who knew English. And this one had known she had visitors without looking.

The old matron's eyelashes fluttered open, and Abbey saw one white and one dark orb. It was the woman who'd hit her. Woman With No Heart was the squaw with the one blind eye.

She shifted uneasily when she became the focus of the woman's good eye.

"So you are the one," the matron said in a gravelly voice.

"One what?" Abbey asked and saw a glint of anger

come to the good eye.

Woman With No Heart dismissed Abbey to turn to Kwan. "You were right to bring her here. The slave has a sharp tongue. I will douse the fire in this one. She will not be trouble to the Onondaga again."

The sachem tensed, but when Abbey looked at him, he seemed at ease. His rugged face displayed no signs of inner tension. Had she been mistaken?

He is a magnificent looking man, she thought as she continued to study him. Pity, he was a heathen.

"Go," Woman With No Heart said, her eyes on Kwan. "Leave her to me."

"Two moons," he told her. "And then the slave will return to Spring Rain."

The matron's brows rose. "Only two moons?" She sighed. "Woman With No Heart can do it."

To Abbey's surprise, Kwan switched to speaking Onondaga. Whatever he was telling the matron must be unpleasant, Abbey thought, because Woman With No Heart looked angrier by the moment.

Feeling chilled, Abbey hugged herself with her arms, rubbing her shoulders. Was he telling the woman of Abbey's misdeed? *Good lord, don't tell me the boy is this woman's grandson!*

Woman With No Heart was arguing fiercely with the sachem. A sharp word from Kwan ended the quarrel. The matron sat, staring at the fire embers with her one good eye. She was pouting, Abbey saw with wonderment, a fact that didn't bode well for the new slave.

"You will do as she says," Kwan told Abbey. "Make no mistake. She is not like Spring Rain. If you cross her, she will beat you until you bleed."

Abbey looked at the woman before meeting Kwan's gaze with raised eyebrows. Her look said, "She can try . . ."

Kwan frowned, and grabbed Abbey's arm roughly to draw her away from the matron's fire. "I warn you, English niece. She is a dangerous foe. You would be wise to do as she tells you." He was conscious of the softness of her arm, her womanly scent.

Abbey jutted her chin. "She is an old woman."

With a click of his tongue, Kwan shook his head. "Why do you think she is called Woman With No Heart. Because she is soft?" He growled his words with frustration. How could he keep her safe if it was her intention to rile her new master?

"I have no idea."

"Ab-bey—" She liked the way he said her name, even in anger as he had now, hissing it between clamped teeth. He'd said Abbey with a pause between two distinct syllables.

His hands slid to close about her upper arms, and his touch made her tremble, her nerve endings springing to life. "Woman With No Heart once killed a child," he said, "with her own two hands." He released her as if burnt. His eyes narrowed. "She was a little one—an English girl of only three years old. Woman With No Heart was a young maiden then, drawn to comfort the child when she was brought to the village after a raid. The child was crying; she'd been taken from her family and she was frightened. Woman With No Heart took the baby against her breast, but the child fought her. The maiden—Woman With No Heart—bent forward to

89

soothe the child's fears and was gouged in the eye by the child's fingernail . . ."

Abbey gasped, stepping back, her hands covering her mouth in horror. "Her blind eye," she murmured shakily.

"No." Kwan shook his head. "She was blinded—that one—by an enemy knife many moons later after her marriage."

Abbey felt confused. "Then—"

"She killed the girl for scratching near her eye, Abbey. She was not hurt, but for a small mark, yet she killed the one who gave it to her."

"No!" Abbey turned pale.

"*Yes!*" Kwan moved suddenly to grab her again and gave her one hard shake—as if trying to knock some common sense into her. "Beware, fiery one. Obey her or pay the price!"

And with that, Kwan thrust her away and left her to the mercy of the old woman with no heart.

Abbey stood, uncertain what to do once Kwan had departed. The force of his anger remained with her and her legs trembled. Her heart raced as her lungs drew breath.

"Come," the old woman said, not unpleasantly. "Sit here. By the fire."

With Kwan's ominous words still ringing in her ears, Abbey did as she was told, approaching the matron with caution. She felt stiff with unease as she looked at her new master. Had Kwan told her the truth? Had this Indian woman killed a baby merely because she'd been scratched by the child?

"Here." Woman With No Heart thrust a clay bowl onto Abbey's lap. "Beans," she explained, but, of course, Abbey knew what they were and was glad she knew what was expected of her.

Without further instructions, Abbey began to shell the beans from their pods and was relieved to see the matron's nod of approval. Perhaps she was concerned over nothing; perhaps she and the old matron would get along fine.

Woman With No Heart threw a pile of empty bean pods onto the fire embers and the air in the vicinity became smoky as the bean pods struggled to ignite.

The two women worked side by side, not speaking, but working hard. Abbey began to relax. Woman With No Heart seemed harmless. Had Kwan lied to her, made up the story of a child's murder to frighten Abbey into a submission?

She decided to question the matron and find out.

Her tone conversational, Abbey asked, "Is it true you killed a three-year-old child, because she scratched you?" Relaxed, she kept her eyes on the bowl, her fingers busy with shelling beans.

"No." Woman With No Heart's voice was as mild and casual as Abbey's, and Abbey looked up, her lips forming a slight smile. "She was only two summers," the old matron said.

The smile fell from Abbey's face. "Two summers?"

"Two years old." The Indian woman's one-eyed gaze held her slave captive.

Abbey's mouth fell open as she realized that Kwan had spoken the truth. When she bent back over her task, her fingers were trembling.

Chapter 8

It was a steamy summer night; the air within the longhouse was stifling. Abbey couldn't sleep. She felt hot and sticky in her deerskin tunic, but she wouldn't—couldn't!—sleep naked among savages. She was thankful that no one had pressed her, which had surprised her until she'd moved in with Woman With No Heart. The old matron wore a garment to bed . . . unlike the other Iroquois women.

Restless, she rolled over from side to side, gazed into the darkness. She was able to make out the muted glow of the banked fire. It was so hot! Was it really necessary to keep the fires burning all night? she wondered. All summer?

With a low growl of frustration, Abbey sat up in bed. The tunic stuck to her like a second skin. For a brief moment, she almost changed her mind about sleeping in the buff. How else was she to bear this heat?

One glance toward a brave sleeping in the cubicle across from her and she promptly dismissed the idea.

She plucked at the garment, trying to pull it away from her damp flesh, recalling the first time Spring Rain had bid her to join the women for their daily bath.

Each evening, when they were finished with their chores, the Indian women went down to the lake as a community, chattering good-naturedly as they removed their skirts, before stepping naked into the cool water.

Never had Abbey seen the likes of such a people. Bathing every day? she'd first thought. Everyone knew that to do so was to risk illness, exposing a body to the various ailments that could lay one low . . . perhaps even kill . . .

Bathing in Evening Sky's presence had been one thing to Abbey, disrobing for a whole community of females was quite another. When Spring Rain had first gone to the lake, expecting her slave to come, Abbey had managed to find an excuse not to go, choosing instead to bath in privacy at a later hour with Evening Sky as escort and look-out against invasion by the warrior-guards.

Getting out of the ritual, Abbey had been afraid, would be more difficult the second time, but Spring Rain had surprisingly put up little fuss. Apparently, she didn't care that Abbey chose not to join the village women as long as the slave bathed and didn't smell like the other "English ones."

After two weeks of village life, Abbey had been forced to revise her beliefs. The Onondaga were clearly a healthy people, from the bright-faced children to their elderly, who, other than being injured or maimed by accident or battle, were as strong as workhorses. Woman With No Life was blind but she was as sturdy as an ox . . . and she worked hard. Abbey had to admire her.

And Woman With No Heart bathed every day.

Privacy was not a problem at the fire of Woman With No Heart. The old matron did not join the others at bath time. Why? Abbey wondered.

Woman With No Heart was different from the other women not only when it came to bathing, but also in her dressing habits.

Abbey swung her legs over the side of the platform. Three days has passed since she came to Woman With No Heart's fire, and so far she'd managed to avoid engaging the old matron's wrath.

Here, her chores were different. Because of her age and condition, Woman With No Heart worked mainly about the longhouse . . . shelling and preparing beans, husking and boiling the dried corn, curing meat, and tanning the hides from the game killed by the Onondaga men during the hunt.

The corn crop was flourishing, the tall green stalks a spectacular sight. There was talk of a coming ceremony to celebrate. The Green Corn Festival, they called it. A time of thanksgiving.

During the day while the women were out harvesting the fields, Abbey, Woman With No Heart, and the young girls of the village handled the chores about the longhouse.

Abbey didn't mind this. Working inside the smoky longhouse wasn't pleasant, but she preferred it to traipsing about picking beans under the hot glare of the July sun. The breeze that normally came off the great lake had become non-existent these past few days, offering no relief from the summer heat.

But Abbey missed the company of her only friend, Evening Sky. In the house of the Deer Clan, she'd had the Indian maiden to talk with, to answer her questions about Iroquois customs and beliefs. Here, among the Wolf Clan, she was a slave, nothing more. Except for Woman With No Heart, the Indians ignored her. Even the woman who'd first greeted Kwan treated Abbey as if Abbey were invisible, a fact which didn't bother the slave in the least, because the woman had been unpleasant.

Of Kwan, Abbey had seen little. She'd been wrong in believing the longhouse was his home. He lived in a small hut within the stockade fence, beyond the circle of longhouses, in private quarters designed to accommodate the sachem—a revered member of the Great Council.

Kwan had come into the Wolf longhouse only twice since Abbey's move. Both times, it had been to speak with O-wee-soo, the head matron—Kwan's grandmother. On each occasion, Abbey had felt his presence keenly. Who could not help but notice the man? The sachem was an extremely attractive man, who carried with him an air of energy and authority. Abbey found her gaze drawn to him time and again whenever he was within seeing distance. She was disturbed by her growing fascination with the savage.

She rose from her bed, conscious of an odd change within her when she thought of Kwan. Had the temperature in the longhouse grown hotter? Her body felt flushed. She noted a rapid quickening of her pulse.

Savage or not, Kwan Kahaiska was a beautiful specimen of malehood. Abbey's heart fluttered whenever she saw him.

The longhouse suddenly seemed too small to Abbey. The walls were closing in on her; she could barely breathe.

The lake was just outside the village compound, a few hundred yards down the forest footpath. She had missed bathing this evening. What she wouldn't give now for a cool swim!

And why not? she thought.

She knew she could escape Woman With No Heart; the old matron was a heavy sleeper. The Indian hadn't stirred when Abbey had a nightmare her first night here, her cries into the silent night rousing several occupants in the next cubicle.

But could she sneak past the warrior-guards posted about the fence? If she was caught, she'd be punished. The consequences of her actions didn't bear thinking about. She would be whipped, stoned, burned with hot pokers . . . or something equally as horrendous.

The waters of lake seemed to beckon her, promising her safety . . . and relief from the heat.

Her jaw firming, Abbey reached up to the upper shelf, carefully rummaging among the things stored there for something to change into when she'd completed her bath. She hated the idea of donning again her sweat-dampened tunic.

She found a garment among Woman With No Heart's things, an article made of soft doeskin. Abbey spared no time to see what it was. Woman With No Heart had rolled over in her sleep; whatever the garment was it would have to do.

The door leading from the longhouse was open; the smoke of the fires kept the mosquitoes at bay. She had no trouble leaving. Everyone within the building slept soundly. Amazed yet again at the Indians' ability to withstand the heat, Abbey left the building.

Outside, the night was alive with the sounds of summer. A cricket chirped for its mate; an owl hooted from the top of a distant tree. The moon, a bright orb in a jet sky, bathed the land with a soft white glow, and Abbey had no trouble seeing every building and shape within the village.

With thumping heart, she chose a path behind the longhouse past the sachem's hut. She paused before the hut, her stomach flip-flopping with thoughts of Kwan. In the stillness of the summer night, Abbey had a sudden mental image of the man . . . his eyes closed . . . his stern face soft . . . relaxed in sleep. He'd be naked like the others . . . all firm muscle and hard sinew . . . She gasped, seeing the picture clearly. The glistening massive chest. The navel in his flat stomach. The hard thighs and . . .

Mortified, she hurried on past the hut toward the stockade gate. There were no signs of any guards, but Abbey knew better than to take chances. They were out there somewhere; night or day there was always an Iroquois guard.

She hung low behind a wooden log post, her gaze piercing the muted light to where the guard normally stood sentinel beside the huge oak outside the gate.

Movement. The brave was there. Abbey saw him creeping sleathily along the open-slatted fence. She wouldn't have spied him if she hadn't known of his presence. The knowledge sobered her, made her more cautious. What if there were other guards she knew nothing about?

The Iroquois turned and moved away. Abbey slipped through the gate and took off on silent feet for the trail.

The footpath widened as it neared the lake's shore, and Abbey picked up her pace, anxious to swim. She caught sight of the moon-dappled lake through a break in the trees, felt her heart sing with anticipation. Within seconds, she was making her way to the shoreline.

At the water's edge, Abbey stopped and stared. The great moonlit lake was a sight to behold, truly breathtaking in its beauty and size. The sound of the lake caressing the shore was soothing. After setting the deerskin on the grass, she removed her moccasins and dipped a toe into the rippling water to test its temperature. It was cool, not cold . . . pleasant and refreshing.

Abbey reached for the bottom of her tunic. She was anxious to cool her hot flesh, to bathe away the light coating of dry dirt. The tunic stuck to her skin and then caught in her hair. She wore her hair like the village women, drawn back at her nape and fastened with a leather thong.

Her head trapped within the tunic's suffocating folds, Abbey struggled with the deerskin. She tugged hard, nearly fell as she was freed from the damp garment. Gasping, she bent over, drawing air into her starved lungs.

Cool water trickled across Abbey's skin from above her. With a gasp of surprise, she looked up, straight into the silver-gray eyes of Kwan Kahaiska, who was lowering his dripping hand. His chest glistened; he had been swimming. He was unsmiling.

"You! How—where—?" she stuttered. He must have been there all the time! How could she have not noticed?

The sachem raised his other arm; he held her tunic in his hand. Abbey grabbed it, holding it before her, a shield against his interested gaze.

He stared at her with some amusement, his silver eyes glowing. "You needed help."

"I didn't ask you for your damned help!" Abbey glared at him. There was thundering in her ears. Her heart, she realized.

His expression turned hard. "You came past the guards."

Abbey felt a flicker of alarm and then a moment's satisfaction. She scowled. "What if I did? I didn't make it past you."

He nodded, an abrupt jerk of his head that called Abbey's attention to his golden-streaked hair. "I was here at the water." He gestured toward a rock and his discarded breechclout.

She flushed. He was naked! Clutching her tunic tighter, she backed away. "You're—"

He chuckled. "So are you."

Abbey could not help staring. She'd never seen him smile let alone laugh before—the effect was startling. "You . . . you . . ."

"*Ka kho a,*" he said.

"What?"

"*Ka kho a,* Ab-bey. The bird of night that calls out to stranger." His sensual mouth split into a wide grin; Abbey's heart raced. "An owl."

She must have looked confused.

"You—you," he mimicked. "Whoo-whoo! You sound like an owl."

Abbey blinked. "Oh." She held the tunic tighter against her breasts, conscious of the night air on her bare buttocks and legs. And Kwan. She shifted into a half crouch, rearranging the deerskin to better cover herself. "I have to get back—" She tried to edge past him.

He blocked her with his arm. "No."

"What?" she gasped. Swallowing, she studied the muscular arm before meeting his gaze.

"You will swim." He was the great sachem once again. His stoicism told her he meant business.

Abbey swallowed, shaking her head. "I don't think so . . ."

She was naked and alone with a savage! A chief of savages! There was a disquieting intimacy about the moon-lit night. "Please . . . I have to get back."

Kwan arched an eyebrow. "After." He reached for her tunic.

"No, Kwan, don't touch me." She evaded his grasp.

The savage was naked! she thought with a sense of unreality. Naked! She pretended not to notice as she backed away while he continued to advance on her. It was damn difficult to avoid the sight of his revealed male parts!

"I mean it, Indian!" she cried, tripping backward toward the water. She scurried to her feet, her face hot, her dignity bruised. "I said I don't want to swim!"

100

He stopped, his face hard. "You will swim, slave. Now!" The sachem had never before had an order questioned, and it was obvious to Abbey that he was angry.

Kwan gestured toward the water. "Go. Or I will take you."

"You wouldn't dare!"

He smiled an even smile, a smile of male determination and intent. Kwan would, damn him! The savage, Abbey decided, would dare anything!

It was either give in to Kwan's demand, or have the matter taken out of her own hands. Abbey scowled. She'd be damned if she'd let him lay a hand on her! "All right, you ignorant savage!" she snarled. "I'll swim. But not with you standing there!"

She straightened to show him that she could be stubborn too. The movement gave Kwan a tempting view, but Abbey didn't realize . . . until something flickered in the Indian's expression.

"I won't move a step with you watching!"

She felt a tingling along her arms as her gaze fell, drawn, to his manhood. The shaft nestled within the patch of dark pubic hair was huge but flaccid. Relieved, Abbey shuddered and looked away.

"You will not escape?" Kwan's silver eyes seemed to cut through the night, pinning her where she stood.

There was a long moment of silence.

"No, no, I won't," she promised.

To Abbey's astonishment, he nodded and stepped back. Apparently, he trusted her word.

"I will look the other way." Kwan turned, giving her his back, and her privacy.

Abbey stood frozen, fearful. Could she trust *his* word?

The sachem sighed loudly, with a hint of impatience. "Ab-bey . . ."

"I'm going!" she exclaimed, dropping her tunic to hurry into the lake. She shrieked; the water was cooler than she'd first thought.

Hearing her scream, Kwan spun with alarm. He shook his head when he saw her neck-deep in water, shivering. "You wake the forest with your cry." He came toward the water, his intent clear.

Abbey froze, staring. "What are you doing?" she said shakily. She felt tingles along the back of her neck, was both nervous and oddly excited at the same time.

"You are covered." He gestured toward the huge expanse of rippling water. "Is *Ki u ad a dee* not big enough for two?"

She shivered, conscious of his approach, of his hard, sinewy nude form. "Don't!" She sounded panic-stricken.

Kwan smiled. "It is the time of *As so he ka*. I cannot see you." He was lying. He could see her—a hint of white flesh just below the lake's surface. The sight invited him in for a closer look. He felt a definite urge to touch her, to feel if the slave's breasts were as soft and smooth . . . and as full . . . as they appeared.

He saw that she believed him, for she had stopped struggling to swim backward. Either that or she'd realized that her movements only brought her luscious form closer to the surface, giving Kwan a good glimpse.

The sachem took his time entering the lake.

Pausing at the edge of the shoreline, he skimmed one foot across the surface, pretending an interest in the pattern of moving water.

"It feels good." He looked at her. "You feel good?" Eyes wide, she nodded. "Good."

Abbey experienced the strangest desire to laugh hysterically, an urge that was effectively dampened when Kwan dove into the dark water.

The water closed over his head. Abbey shrank back, anxiously searching for him. Where did he go?

"Kwan?" she called, feeling wary all of a sudden. Her hands rose to cover her breasts. "Kwan!" Shivering, she danced about on tiptoes, wondering, sensing that he was somewhere near, deep below the surface.

A splash sounded, and Kwan came up several feet away, rising from the lake like some glistening pagan god. Blinking, he blew out water from his nose and grinned at her.

"Fool!" she began and then screamed. "Kwan! There's something by my leg." Something slimy and slippery. "Kwan!"

Kwan dove into the water like a shot, gliding below the surface like a seal. He slid past Abbey's left thigh; circling her right side, he broke water in front.

"What is it?" Abbey's teeth chattered as she spoke.

"I saw nothing," he said. His gaze fell to her arms where they pressed against her soft womanly curves. The upper swells of her breasts rose like two plump white melons.

Abbey blushed, stepped back, suddenly aware of the direction of Kwan's gaze. It had occurred to her just what the sachem *had* seen under water. Her. Every throbbing white inch of her.

There was a look in his eyes when she met his gaze that frightened her . . . and thrilled her. Her skin tingled; the hairs along her arms and neck rose up on end. Dear God, she thought, what is wrong with me?

"Ab-bey." His voice was low, hoarse.

"No, Kwan, *please.*" Desire hit her hard. The man was a savage—a brutal beast! He moved closer, and she raised her hands to fend him off. "Stop!"

Kwan halted, his handsome face hardening into a dark mask. Only the bright glitter in his silver gaze remained to highlight his lust.

"You are so white . . ." He stared openly at her breasts.

With a gasp, Abbey dipped farther below the lake's surface. "No," she whispered. "No, I'm not."

Unperturbed, he continued to stare and stalk her. "Yes, my *O djis tah.*"

As he moved closer, the water glided smoothly around his bare waist, calling Abbey's attention to the rock solid muscles of his flat stomach. Her own stomach tightened in response.

She made a frantic search of the shore. "The guards—"

"They came and saw me. They will not come back."

What? she thought. The guards had been there! Oh, no! What could they have seen?

"I'll not let you rape me!"

Kwan froze. "We do not rape." He appeared insulted; Abbey had to believe that he spoke the truth. His gaze narrowed on her with intent. She was farther out from shore and had to tread water to stay afloat.

"Please—" She stopped at Kwan's look. Something beyond Abbey's back had drawn the sachem's gaze and he was frowning.

"Watch out!" he cried. *"Ji kon sis!"*

Shrieking, Abbey threw herself into the man's arms. "Wh-what is it?" She clutched onto Kwan's neck, shivering.

To her great humiliation, Kwan chuckled, a deep sound in her ear that caused her nerves to hum, her body to react with the speed of a startled deer. "Pike," he murmured, his breath on her neck. "A fish."

"It's dangerous?" she said nervously.

"No."

Abbey blinked. "No?" Understanding replaced confusion. She released his neck as if stung. "Beast!" She struggled futilely to break away. Kwan held her against his broad chest, cradled within his arms. He stumbled toward shallow water.

"You must stop, *O djis tah*, or you will drown us both."

"I don't care, you stinking animal! You lying lout! You—" She continued to call him all sorts of vile names, hitting him on the shoulders and arms, anywhere her fist could make contact.

"Ab-bey," he growled. He managed to gain control of her hands, no easy feat in the water.

Abbey stopped fighting with an abruptness that nearly unbalanced Kwan. They glared at one another, their breaths labored, their naked bodies pressed close. Abbey gasped, suddenly conscious of the sleek moist heat of his powerful body against her breast and hip . . . the tantalizing scent of wood smoke and clean male that clung to his skin and hair.

Drawn by his hypnotic gaze, by a force more powerful than her own will, Abbey felt herself leaning against him, her face raised upward, her lips slightly parted.

Kwan bent his head and kissed her. Vaguely, Abbey wondered why she wasn't fighting him. And then she became conscious of the pressure of his lips, warm and gentle against her mouth, coaxing a response from her. She felt a tingling from her toes to her nape, heard the blood roaring through her veins and the cadence of her thundering heart. The sensations were new and exciting to her. She was at once both thrilled and afraid.

He left her mouth. She looked up, feeling flushed. Her breath came out in soft pants; she felt like she'd been running. Her face grew hot with embarrassment, and she wanted to look away, but Kwan's gaze held her captive. His eyes glowed with desire, an iridescence that surpassed that of the night's full moon.

"Ab-bey," he muttered, dipping his head once again.

The man was a savage; why was she allowing him to hold her close?

Her body went wild as he kissed her, and Abbey wondered no more. Kwan's passion was volatile; she'd never experienced anything quite like it. Every fiber of her seemed to sing and shiver and pulsate with new life.

He wasn't tender. There was nothing soft or questing about the male mouth. He devoured her lips as if he'd been starved of affection, as if he'd been brought past the point of self-control. He wasn't brutal but there was a roughness about his kiss that heightened the sensation. Abbey was shocked that she enjoyed the contact.

Without breaking the kiss, Kwan released her legs, shifting their positions. Abbey's breasts throbbed and tingled as she slipped into the water to stand straight, their naked bodies brushing in sensitized intimate contact. Slipping his hands behind her back, he kept her against him, skin searing skin, breasts and hips touching. She returned his embrace, her hands at his waist.

Kwan released her mouth to nuzzle her neck and ear. He caressed her back, her lower spine, her buttocks. Abbey moaned and clutched his wet back. He felt warm and rock-hard . . . alive.

He lifted his head. His hands were in her hair, cradling her head with unexpected tenderness. They stood waist-deep in the lake, the water lapping gently against their skin, gazing at one another in awe and physical awareness.

Water glistened on Kwan's eyebrows, tiny droplets holding the moon's light. Abbey watched fascinated as he moved and the pattern of light changed.

Likewise, Kwan studied her. She felt his gaze on her mouth . . . her nose . . . her mouth again. Closing her eyes, Abbey smiled, aware of a new softening in his normally taciturn expression.

"Ab-bey." It was an urgent command to open her eyes.

She did so and suddenly noticed the barbaric leather strip through his one ear. A savage, she thought with sudden horror. She'd kissed a damn redskin!

The "redskin" abruptly frowned as if discerning her thoughts and was angered by them. She saw determination light up his eyes as his gaze settled on her lips. She stiffened, reading his intent as his head bent once again. And Abbey promptly forgot that Kwan was trying to prove his power over her as he kissed her a second time and she became lost in the sweet, flowing warmth of his lips and tongue.

Chapter 9

The kiss ended abruptly. Kwan released her, and Abbey fell back into the water with a splash. She came up gasping and sputtering with outrage.

"Why the devil—" she began. And then she saw his face. Closed. Stern. The savage once again.

"Come," he said coldly. "It is time to go back."

"Damn you," she cried, her outstretched fingers curling into a fist. Her anger was directed at herself as much as him, because she'd responded.

"Silence! You will wake the tribe."

Clamping her mouth shut, she glared at him. The last thing she wanted was to wake the village. It was bad enough that this man had witnessed her humiliation. Must the other Indians know, too?

"Come," he commanded. "Woman With No Heart will be waiting."

Abbey shook her head. "She sleeps like the dead."

Kwan grimaced. "The sun begins to rise. She will be awake soon."

It was then that Abbey noticed the subtle brightening of the sky. Dawn already? she thought. How long had she and Kwan been at the lake? "All right," she said meekly.

The sachem's eyes narrowed in suspicion. "Where is your spirit, *O djis hah?* Before you curse me like a white man, yet now you follow me without fight. Is that what it takes to make you follow? A man's touch?"

She tensed. "It does not!" Her face dared him to argue. "And I can speak the way I damn please! In my family, we were encouraged to speak our minds."

To her astonishment, Kwan laughed. "I am glad to see that I call you justly, *O djis hah.* You have not lost your fire. Come." He extended a hand to help her from the lake.

"I don't want or need your help! I'd sooner rot in prison."

Kwan's lips firmed in anger. "As you wish." He stepped from the water without embarrassment. A glorious picture of unclothed male.

Abbey caught her breath, averting her gaze only seconds before he stopped at the shoreline to wait for her.

"Come."

She met his gaze, glad that from this distance Kwan wouldn't be able to see her blush. "Turn around," she said.

"Come out, Ab-bey." He didn't move but stared. "Now." The last was a low growl.

"I said—"

Kwan strode back into the lake with an air of purpose.

"No, wait! I'm coming." Abbey quickly edged

110

toward the shore. The Indian stopped, his features unreadable, as he paused and waited for her to join him.

She kept her head high, her chin up, as she broke water. The savage would never know how humiliated she felt! Her breath caught when Kwan's gaze dropped to her breasts. Her heart thumped hard as she fought the urge to cover herself with her arms.

When those silver-gray eyes rose to meet her gaze, she felt in control again, but just barely. Turning, Kwan left the shallows for the rock and his belongings. Abbey watched him bend to pick up his discarded loin-covering, turning away as he proceeded to slip the garment between his legs. With flushed cheeks and a mental vision of hard male flanks as Kwan bent over, she retrieved her deerskin. The intimate act of Kwan's dressing was upper most in her mind as she began to dress.

The deerskin garment that Abbey had borrowed was only a skirt—barely large enough to cover her from waist to knee.

What about her breasts? She'd be damned if she'd walk half-naked all the way back to the village under the sachem's eagle eye! She tried ineffectively to position the skirt up higher, under her armpits. There, it did little more than cover her from breast to upper thigh.

In her frustration, she forgot Kwan's presence and tore off the skirt. Grimacing, she picked up her dirty tunic.

"Here."

An article was thrust before her nose. Abbey looked at the length of flannel before meeting Kwan's gaze.

His silver eyes seared her, making her skin burn. "Where did you get this?"

Kwan shrugged. "We trade with white men."

"French?"

He nodded. "Some English."

"It's too warm for this." She handed it back to him.

His eyes grew hard like glittering shards of silver ice. "As you say." He grabbed the blanket and then snatched Abbey's full-length tunic. "It is too hot for this, too."

"Give that back! It's mine!"

He raised an eyebrow. "It is time to go back, Abbey. Dress or not. But hurry, before they know you are gone."

"And if I don't?" She dared him. She had the sudden impression that he was uncomfortable with his tribesmen knowing of the two of them alone together at the lake. A notion that was quickly corrected when Kwan spoke.

"You have been spared the stick, *O djis hah*. But it is there. Do not think you are safe."

"But I'm with you . . ."

A muscle ticked along Kwan's jaw. "I found a slave trying to escape."

"Escape!" She hadn't thought to escape now! And why not, you fool, she thought. You could have been long gone from the village!

Or could she?

"I cannot protect you. You belong to Woman With No Heart. She alone must decide."

Abbey shuddered, remembering the story of a murder—a two-year-old child. She had managed to get along with the old matron, but was she willing to test the woman's wrath?

These Indians were inhuman. She recalled the captives who'd been taken with her at the Fort, who'd been tortured during the journey to the village. Death and pain. The Iroquois thought little of inflicting pain . . . of killing.

She wasn't afraid of death, but she wasn't ready to die yet either!

Ignoring the sachem's piercing gaze, Abbey donned the skirt in silence. Then she hurried back to the longhouse, away from Kwan's hungry eyes.

The Green Corn Festival. It was an Iroquois ceremony, an important one, Abbey decided as she worked alongside Woman With No Heart to prepare for the event. Anticipation within the tribe was high. Representatives from each of the six Iroquois nations would be arriving to share in the celebration.

It's possible that I will hear news of Jamie! Abbey thought upon hearing of the visitors. Her time among the Indians might end up being time well spent.

"Tell me about the festival," Abbey said to Woman With No Heart. The two women were in the great ceremonial longhouse, setting up chambers for the expected guests. It had been three days since the night encounter with Kwan. The sachem had yet to look Abbey in the eye, ignoring her as the Indians did most slaves, and Abbey was more than a little piqued.

The old matron grunted as she shook out a beaver pelt, arranging it with care on the sleeping platform. "It is a time of giving thanks," she said. *"Ha wa ne uh* has been good to us. The *O na hah* is much. We have enough to last us through the time of the great ice."

O na huh, Abbey thought. *Corn*. She nodded. The Indians would be thanking the Great Spirit for the gift of the thriving corn crop. Corn, or maize, was a mainstay of the Iroquois diet. Boiled with beans, it served a tasty dish. Ground corn flour was used in making bread. The Onondagas knew various ways to prepare corn; and during her stay, Abbey had learned most of them. She understood why the Indians rejoiced when the corn crop flourished.

The two women finished in the guest house and returned to their home. There, Woman With No Heart sat near the fire, shelling freshly picked beans brought in by the other women of the house, while Abbey sorted through a basket of wild berries.

"No, stupid!" Woman With No Heart scolded her slave. "Do not mash them!"

Abbey's lips tightened. "I'm sorry," she said. Conscious of the old woman's glare, she managed to stifle a sharp retort as she handled the berries more carefully.

Living with Woman With No Heart wasn't so bad. The matron had yet to strike her, but Abbey regularly suffered the lash of the matron's tongue. There were times, though, when Abbey was grateful for the company. She missed having a family, her brother. Seeing the warm, caring family relationships among the Indians, she'd felt the loss of her parents more keenly these days. She missed Jamie, the way he used to tease her unmercifully. How she longed to see his mischievous smile and twinkling blue eyes!

She had to find her brother—she just had to! And soon!

Her head bent over the bowl of raspberries, Abbey heard Kwan's voice before she saw him. He had entered the longhouse to speak with O-wee-soo, and the two stood side by side, talking in earnest.

Her pulse racing, Abbey looked up and stared. Usually Kwan wore a breechclout and fringed leggings, but today he'd donned a linen shirt—a white man's dress. His broad shoulders and massive chest filled out the white fabric, stretching the seams to near bursting point. The sachem's skin looked savage-dark against the fine snowy linen, yet his English-light hair with its golden streaks proclaimed Kwan as Great Britain's son.

He turned, and Abbey saw a flash of white teeth as he smiled at his grandmother, a glint of silver-gray eyes that softened and lit up the normally stern face. Kwan presented a picture of contrasts, of culture and color and personality. The impact on Abbey's senses was startling.

In the three days since it happened, Abbey had been unable to think of little else but his kiss. Those sensual male lips had been warm and firm on her own, both giving and taking pleasure.

Abbey had been greatly affected by the exchange, but Kwan . . . For him, it was as if their time together had never happened. He was clearly the savage once again; Kwan ignored her as most of the other Indians did the slaves. Abbey thought of her abandonment in his arms and felt herself blush. How could she have allowed him to touch her? And—God help her—she had enjoyed it! Enjoyed his kiss!

She frowned as she studied him. What prompted Kwan to kiss her in the first place? The man had obviously seen a lot of naked breasts; the village was one mass of bouncing naked female flesh!

"You are so white . . ." She recalled his husky words and shivered, a delicious sensation that ran from head to toe.

Was that it? Was it because she was fair in comparison to the Onondaga women? Had he become so fascinated by the difference in color between her and the Indians that he wanted to see if she felt and kissed differently, too?

The memory of his kiss sent the blood rushing through Abbey's veins like hot lava. Apparently, the kiss meant little to him. She wished she, too, had remained unaffected, but she had to admit that she'd never before experienced such raw passion. She couldn't stop thinking about him, and that bothered her. That night she'd seen several different sides of Kwan. She'd seen him laugh. She had felt the fire of his mouth and the power of his embrace. He was all male . . . arrogant . . . used to being obeyed, and easy to anger when someone refused to obey him. Not endearing traits those last three, but there was something else about him . . .

Kwan looked, talked, and thought like a savage, but there was a gentleness within him as well. Abbey caught a glimpse of it now as she watched Kwan with O-wee-soo. Although most of the time he hid it well, Kwan had a tender side to him.

Tenderness and passion, Abbey thought. A lethal combination in a man. To a woman's sense of well-being.

Kwan left the longhouse without glancing Abbey's way, and Abbey bent over her task, gritting her teeth at his indifference.

She had lived among the Onondagas for two weeks, and there was still a lot she didn't understand, and Kwan Kahaiska had proved the most difficult subject.

Abbey glanced over at Woman With No Heart. The Indian had finished the beans and was mending a torn deerskin.

"Kwan Kahaiska. Who is he?"

"He is sachem. He is Onondaga."

"No," Abbey said. "What I meant was . . . he's not of your race."

The old matron tensed. "He is Onondaga. Silver Fox's son. Dead squaw's son."

"Yes, yes," Abbey said with mild irritation. "But he looks English."

Woman With No Heart looked at her hard. She nodded without speaking and went back to her mending.

"Is he a half-breed?" Abbey said.

The old matron met her gaze. "Half-breed?"

Abbey pressed her. "Was his mother white and his father Indian?"

The Indian woman shook her head as she set her mending aside, on the sleeping platform. "He is Iroquois." Seeing Abbey's disbelief, she said, "Not since the summer he became Great Arrow, a fine warrior."

"You mean he was adopted."

The matron inclined her head.

"Then, Kwan is a white man," Abbey murmured,

amazed that an Englishman could become chief of an Indian tribe.

The squaw's scowl was fierce. "Great Arrow is Onondaga." She rose to her feet. "He is of the *Kanonsionni.*"

Kanonsionni. Abbey recalled Kwan using that very same word. "What does that mean—*Kanonsionni?*"

Woman With No Heart was rearranging items on the storage shelf. She turned and Abbey shifted under her gaze; the woman's one good eye seemed to question Abbey's curiosity, to search deep into Abbey's soul. "It means 'People of the Longhouse.'"

Abbey nodded. "Please . . . tell me about him."

The Indian appeared to give the matter some thought. After a long moment, she agreed and sat on the sleeping platform to begin her story.

"He came to us a captive from the Cayugas," she said. "He was but a little one of nine summers."

"Nine years old," Abbey murmured, envisioning his fear at such a young age.

Woman With No Heart nodded as she picked up the partially mended garment that she lay next to her on the platform, threaded a needle, and then went on with her tale. "The Cayugas were cruel to him. The Onondagas were cruel to him, but Kwan was a brave one, and my people respected such courage in one so young." She began stitching the torn tunic.

"They beat him?" Abbey asked, her heart lodged somewhere in her throat.

"You have seen our young warriors. For slaves, it is worse. He was forced to run the gauntlet over and over until he was cut and bleeding . . . and tired. But he never once cried out. He was strong. He was brave.

118

uddered, turning away. He told himself over
‘ again that she was a slave, nothing more. He
rget her.

he continued to haunt his thoughts. The
image of sparkling blue eyes and glistening
kin under the moon's glow refused to leave
ne.

Silver Fox cared for the boy. When three summers had gone by, Silver Fox took Kwan to son." She paused to check her stitches.

"This was a great honor," she continued, "but Kwan did not know this. Soon, he knew. He learned that someday he could be sachem. Kwan came to understand the Onondaga ways. Kwan became a true Onondaga."

Abbey's curiosity had grown as she listened to Woman With No Heart's story. There were so many questions she wanted to ask, so much she needed to know if she were to understand this complex man. How could a white become chief? How old was he when he became sachem?

But Woman With No Heart must have thought that Abbey had learned more than enough about the Onondaga leader, for when Abbey started to satisfy her curiosity, the matron became abruptly close-mouthed. The old woman set aside her mending and stood, signaling an end to the story.

The Indian stared at Abbey until that one-eyed gaze made Abbey uncomfortable, and realizing that Woman With No Heart was dismissing her, the Englishwoman took her basket of berries and went to join the women working in the village yard.

A swirl of smoke surrounded Kwan and Silver Fox where they sat on furs, facing each other, within the sachem's private hut.

"Soon they will come," Silver Fox said.

Kwan nodded. "The messenger said Mud-Slinger will join us. The Seneca comes far from near the waters of the Susquehanna." He drew on his tobacco pipe, exhaling, and was disturbed to see the image of a woman in the ascending cloud of white smoke. Abbey. He forced his gaze from the smoke ring. "It is a good sign."

Silver Fox met his son's gaze. "You think it is true then? That the Senecas are anxious? They are ever on the warpath. Do they turn against us—their brothers—next?"

The sachem frowned at his father. "It is foolish talk, nothing more. I myself spoke to Mud-Slinger. The Confederacy is whole. The English want Indian land. The sachem will meet the English at the great river beyond the first lake."

Kwan had no quarrel with the English, other than the colonel, Breckingridge, for the wrongs he'd committed against the people. But the matter of land was one that concerned him greatly. The whites had become greedy, not satisfied with the gift that God and the Council had seen fit to give them. Now the whites were fighting among themselves. Kwan saw war in the future of the English and French. Where there was war there was the killing of innocent people. The Confederacy must be preserved at all costs; the Iroquois would need its strength to keep what belonged to them.

"The English and French are enemies," Kwan continued. "We must stay out of their battles; we must protect our own. Soon there will be a great war. Many people will die. Brother will fight brother. This we must stop. We must stand together or lose our lands . . . our lives."

Silver Fox's eyes reflected sadness. "This bodes ill

for the Iroquois. The Delawar
sa— the enemy. Too, we must v
He accepted the pipe from his
deeply on the mouthpiece. "Yo
You say the white men will wa
this, my son?"

Kwan met his father's gaze. "
Alarm flickered in Silver F
dream," he echoed.

The sachem nodded. "We m
Spirit to help us. We are a good
Onondaga must not be broken.

"By brother or white man," S
echoing Kwan's thoughts. "Wha
"Our scouts keep watch. Ther
"You think he will come?"
Kwan's thoughts filled with
hair and flashing blue eyes. He r
niece. He will come." Waving a
from his mat. He stood at the
outside. As if conjured up by ma
of his thoughts came into his l

Dressed once again in a full l
had left the longhouse of the W
of women working in the yard
down on the hard-packed dirt
bowl of red berries. The Indiar
as if she wasn't there, but Abbey
by it.

Kwan felt his gut turn as h
swim . . . the mantel of wet g
pale shoulders . . . the brush
breasts against his skin.

Chapter 10

The visitors came trickling into Kwan's village in small groups of three and four. The first to arrive was Mud-Slinger, the Seneca sachem from beyond the first lake in Pennsylvania. Mud-Slinger came in full dress, as Iroquois ceremony demanded. His skull cap was adorned with eagle feathers, his kilt and leggings rich in quillwork. Armbands encircled his dark, muscular arms, and on his feet were moccasins of the finest deerskin.

"Greetings, Oscatax," Kwan said. He, too, wore the ceremonial regalia of an Iroquois member of Council. The muscles of his bare arms glistened with oil; his heavy armbands were made of bright copper.

The Seneca nodded. "Greetings, Kwan Kahaiska. It is a good time—this season of the Green Corn. We have brought meat to share and many gifts. I have been waiting to play the game again." He raised an eyebrow. "I trust your skill has improved."

Kwan laughed. "I have not practiced since I won last, but I feel ready for the challenge."

Mud-Slinger smiled, a thin smile that didn't reach his eyes. "Before the fourth day of the festival is done, we will see who is the winner."

"This is true, Oscatax." Kwan's gaze had narrowed. He sensed a new tension in the air, and he didn't like it. "Brother," he said. It was a subtle reminder that the Seneca and Onondaga were brothers, members of the Six Nations.

The Seneca took the hint. "We have much to be grateful for, Great Arrow."

Kwan nodded as the two fell into step together. "Let us not forget this, Mud-Slinger."

The village was a hive of activity. Women and children scurried to and fro, arms laden with furs, clay pots, and fresh foodstuffs. Dogs, yapping with excitement, ran about the compound, often scolded for getting in their masters' way. The air was filled with the smoke from the cook fires and the tempting aroma of roasting meat. The mood about the camp was joyful as everyone pitched in preparing for the Festival of the Green Corn.

Mud-Slinger and his two braves were soon joined by Senecas from other tribes, among them Man-With-Broken-Nose and He-Who-Comes-From-The-Night. Representatives from all sections of the "Longhouse," the area that comprised Iroquois territory, would be attending. The gathering would not be as large as the great Council meeting, for there would be many such feasts on Iroquois land. Kwan's village had been selected this summer to host the festival in the "Longhouse" center. The Mohawks were the Keepers of the Eastern Door of the "Longhouse," while the Senecas were sentinel to the west. Kwan's tribe and other Onondagas were responsible for the ever-burning council fire in the middle.

The first day of the festival began with a day-long assembly of all who had been called by the Faith-keepers, important appointed tribal members, both male and female.

The Iroquois gathered in the great ceremonial longhouse, the largest building in the village, designed for just such occasions. The Indians filtered inside and took their seats, forming two parallel rows down the length of the structure. When all were seated, Kwan rose to his feet and, as host sachem of the event, addressed the gathering.

"Welcome, brothers and sister," he said. "We have come together to give thanks to the spirits for our thriving corn crop." The room filled with an expectant hush as Kwan spoke.

"We have many gods who have helped us . . . the God of Earth, who gave us this fertile ground . . ." Kwan went on to extol the virtues of this great god, offering up a small burning sacrifice of tobacco, so that this god would be good to the Iroquois again next year.

"The God of Thunder and Rain," he continued, "for giving life to our seeds and making them sprout . . ."

As Abbey stood behind Woman With No Heart, she could not help but be enthralled with the ceremony, the pageantry of Indians wearing their finest. But it was Kwan Kahaiska who most fascinated her. This day he appeared every ounce the great chief, and she couldn't keep her eyes off of him.

Her heart beat faster as she listened to the deep masculine pitch of his voice, recalling again their night by the lake. She experienced again the chills she'd felt when he'd kissed her . . . murmured in her ear.

Beside her, Evening Sky translated Kwan's Onondaga so that Abbey could understand. Kwan's deep emotional tone combined with Evening Sky's soft feminine translation lured Abbey into feeling a part of the ritual, and she saw and understood a side to the Indians that she never dreamed existed.

Kwan's expression was serious; his silver eyes glowed with inner fire. As he spoke, Abbey stared at his sensual mouth.

"The God of Wind has been good to us . . . and the gods of the sun and moon . . ." Kwan moved down the center of the two rows, gesturing with his hands as he spoke. "We are the People, and they have not forgotten us. We must not forget them!"

He continued to thank each and every one of the spirits the Indians believed had a hand in the green corn . . . those who were generous with their life-giving forces, those who held back their destructive powers so that the corn would continue to grow.

The Onondaga words on Kwan's lips sounded like music to Abbey's ears. The sachem had a captive audience, and she could understand why. Kwan's performance was magnificent. Even she had to admit it.

When he had finished expressing the gratitude of the Iroquois people to their spirit forces, Kwan sat down and Silver Fox stood. The old Indian announced that it was time for the Feather Dance.

Several braves came to the center to dance. The Iroquois began to sing, and the chorus of chants made chills run down Abbey's spine. There was something moving about this part of the ceremony. The music continued and all who watched or participated were affected. Even Bear Claw, Abbey saw, much to her own surprise, seemed different somehow. He had joined the dancers on the floor, and he was the picture of concentration and peace as he executed the graceful steps of the dance.

Abbey's wonder grew as Kwan stepped onto the floor to join in the dance. Her mouth went dry as he began to move, his lithe body glistening in the light of the burning fires. His actions were fluid, almost sexual; and entranced, Abbey swallowed hard. His face had a look of concentration. She thought of their shared kiss, and it occurred to her that he focused that same intense concentration on everything he did.

Kwan kept the full force of his passion in check. What would it be like to see it unleashed? How would she feel if she was the focus of such energy, such raw physical power?

Fire shot through Abbey's veins, thrilling her with the prospect. She'd had a small taste of Kwan's passion that night by the lake, and—God help her— she was hungry for more.

"He is a good man," someone whispered in Abbey's ear.

Abbey started and turned to face O-wee-soo, Kwan's grandmother. He? she thought and then flushed, embarrassed. Had her expression given away her thoughts, her fascination with Kwan?

Appalled, she pretended to have misunderstood. "I'm sorry."

"The dance—it is good."

"Yes, yes, it is," Abbey mumbled. Her relief that the old woman didn't pursue the subject of Kwan was short-lived. O-wee-soo looked at her knowingly.

Abbey glanced away, but had trouble finding something to focus on. She dared not look at Kwan, for fear that she'd give herself away to O-wee-soo. She spied the Englishwoman Judith across the yard with her master. Earlier, she'd seen the captive Emily with the Indian women who prepared the food for the event.

A silence stretched between Abbey and O-wee-soo, unrelieved by the continual chants of the Indian dance. Abbey shifted uncomfortably. She felt a need to say something, anything to ease the tension. "It is strange," she said.

"Only to one who doesn't understand," the old woman said softly. Abbey nodded. "But you understand," she continued, staring at her oddly, and Abbey tensed.

This is Kwan's grandmother, Abbey thought. "The sachem . . . is he . . ." Her voice trailed off. Woman With No Heart had become angry when she had questioned Kwan's heritage. Did she dare ask the old matron a few questions?

"White?" the matron said. She seemed unoffended.

"Yes." Abbey smiled. She was amazed at O-wee-soo's perception.

"He is my grandson. Before the time he came to us, he belonged to a white man's family. His name was Lang-don. Kwan was called Ro-bert. This is in the past. To us, to himself, now he is Kwan Kahaiska. Great Arrow. He is sachem to the Onondaga." O-wee-soo's expression was unnerving to Abbey. "You do not hate him."

Abbey jerked with surprise. "How can you say that?" she gasped. "He had me kidnapped!"

"He was doing what is right. In your heart, you know this."

"I know no such thing!"

The old woman just smiled. "Someday you will know this. You will know and respect him for it."

"That's ridiculous!"

O-wee-soo remained unperturbed. "You wait. It will happen. This I know."

The old woman's confidence in her own prophecy brought the little hairs at Abbey's nape up on end. With O-wee-soo's words still ringing in her brain, Abbey glanced at the sachem. She'd hoped that by looking at him she could dispel the attraction, dismiss her uneasiness with the matron's words.

Kwan looked at her, and she felt a jolt of emotion that frightened and yet thrilled her. The Indian sachem held her captive in his glowing silver eyes. Abbey's reaction was immediate. Her breath quickened; her nipples hardened against the deerskin tunic. Every sense and nerve ending was attuned to his interest, responding with the speed of a lightning bolt.

Suddenly, it was as if they were alone, back at the lake again. His arms surrounded her; his demanding mouth captured and ravaged her willing lips.

Abbey blinked. Kwan was several yards away, yet the sensation was so strong, so real, that she trembled and closed her eyes.

The dance chanting stopped, the sudden silence breaking the spell. When Abbey opened her eyes, her heart palpitating to a rhythm that kept the music alive, the sachem's attention was elsewhere. He seemed unaffected by the sexual currents between them, in control.

It left Abbey wondering if her imagination was playing cruel tricks on her.

When the dance was over, the Indians rose from their seats and went outside to the food. The feast combined the community offerings of the Onondagas clans and their guests. Abbey was surprised to see the women wait on the men and then everyone disappear into their own longhouses to eat in solitude. It seemed strange to end the day's events this way, parting company when the feeling of fellowship was at a high, but Evening Sky had told her earlier that it was customary for an Onondaga to eat in the longhouse with the other members of his clan.

The day was a fine one. The temperature had cooled and a light breeze off the lake ruffled the treetops, lowering the humidity. Why go inside when the weather was beautiful? Abbey wondered. She accepted a clay bowl from Evening Sky and filled it with an assortment of Indian dishes along with the fresh vegetables and wild fruits picked earlier along the woods and fields.

Abbey waited while Evening Sky filled her own dish. When the maiden turned toward her longhouse, the English woman stopped her.

"Let's sit there," Abbey suggested, gesturing toward a grassy spot in the shade of a huge oak tree.

Much to Abbey's surprise, Woman With No Heart hadn't objected when Evening Sky had joined them earlier. Surely, the matron wouldn't mind if they spent a few moments together, enjoying the glorious day.

With a doubtful look, Evening Sky glanced at the Wolf longhouse. "You should go to her."

Abbey, who had already taken a seat on the soft, sweet-smelling grass, paused in the act of taking a bite of fruit. "Why?"

"It is our way."

"And if I don't?"

Evening Sky shrugged. "Woman With No Heart be angry. Punish Abbey."

Abbey shook her head. "I think not. She knows where I am." She'd begun to think that the extent of the woman's temper had been overstated. Woman With No Heart had yet to act the fearsome, hot-headed child-murderer that Kwan had painted for Abbey's benefit. "If she wants me, she'll come."

The Indian maiden remained uncertain. After a moment's hesitation, she sat down beside Abbey on the grass.

The village center was empty. Everyone had gone to their longhouses, even the guests who had filed away to the ceremonial longhouse where the day's events had taken place and where yesterday Woman With No Heart and Abbey had prepared the sleeping platforms. Only Abbey and Evening Sky had stayed to enjoy the peaceful dusk. When no one came to disturb them, they relaxed and ate in silence, enjoying the time of the approaching night.

"Abbey," Evening Sky said, breaking the quiet

after a time. "Be you unhappy?"

"Unhappy?" Abbey murmured thoughtfully. "Well, no . . . not exactly." She fixed her gaze on her friend. "But I miss my brother. I'm worried about him . . . where he is, if he's all right." She frowned. "I must find him." She said it with such force that Evening Sky raised her eyebrows.

"*Tai ak e ad a non da . . .*" The Indian girl looked surprised. "You have brother?"

Her eyes sad, Abbey nodded. The conversation reminded her of what she had hoped, but had thus far failed to learn during the festival. She scooted closer, across the ground, lowering her voice to a conspiratorial whisper. "Evening Sky, I need your help. Jamie—my brother—was captured by Indians . . ."

"That too bad." Evening Sky clicked her tongue.

Abbey felt alarm. "Why? Have you seen him? Is he dead?"

The maiden shook her head. "I know not of your brother, Abbey. Who did this?"

"I don't know. He was captured in Pennsylvania, in the forest."

"*Kanonsionni,*" Evening Sky said with confidence.

Abbey blinked. *Kanonsionni.* People of the Longhouse. Onondagas? Senecas? Mohawks? She'd learned that there were six nations in the Iroquois confederacy; all considered themselves People of the Longhouse. Who had him? Why did Evening Sky sound so certain? "Who? How do you know this?"

Evening Sky's expression was shuttered. She seemed to be choosing her words carefully. "Mohawk, may-be. Mohawk take captives."

132

"So do the Onondaga," Abbey quipped.

Evening Sky stared at her. "That different. Onondaga seek justice. English did wrong. Killed Onondagas. Must pay." She glanced away. "How old your Jam-ie?"

"Seventeen."

The young woman swung back to face her. "Young enough, may-be. But may-be no."

Abbey felt breathless. "Young enough for what?" All sort of horrible images flashed through her mind as she waited for Evening Sky's response.

"For making him slave."

"And if not?" Abbey's throat became suddenly dry and she swallowed.

The Indian maiden refused to look at her. Her voice when she spoke was soft, almost too soft to be heard. "The Mohawk torture their man captives. Kill . . . sometimes eat."

Abbey gasped and paled. "Oh, dear God in heaven!" she whispered. Tears threatened to blind her. She blinked them away, her lips firming with determination as she refused to believe in Jamie's death, refused to give up hope that he was alive. *Alive and well.*

"He's not dead," she murmured. "I'd know if he were dead." Her voice rose as she fought off a rising hysteria. "I would know if he were dead!"

She felt a sympathetic hand on her shoulder. Evening Sky's face held compassion as she studied her friend.

"No!" Abbey cried, jerking away, feeling suddenly overwhelmed by everything. "Don't touch me. You're one of them! A savage!"

The Indian girl flinched and pulled back. "Ab-bey."

Abbey stared at her, unseeing, until the image of Evening Sky's pain filtered through her own blinding haze. She closed her eyes. "I'm sorry." It was a whisper. "I didn't mean that."

Evening Sky's gaze was shrewd. "Yes, you do, but it is all right." She paused, apparently struggling with indecision. "I help Ab-bey. I ask *Kanonsionni* about white *hux sa ha*."

"You would do that for me?" Abbey's blue eyes had brightened.

Noting the change, Evening Sky nodded and smiled.

Abbey grabbed the girl's arm. "Thank you!"

The Indian's smile faded. "Do not, Ab-bey. You may-be sad to hear truth. Your Jam-ie may-be dead."

"I know." She exhaled a long breath, shuddering, hugging herself with her arms. Her eyes flashed with fire as she held Evening Sky's gaze. "But I have to keep hoping . . . I have to believe that he's alive."

"Ab-bey, I ask, but then you must ask the sachem. He be the one to help."

"Ask Kwan?" Her stomach flip-flopped nervously. She started to protest but then realized the truth behind Evening Sky's words. She would need Kwan's help once she learned of Jamie's whereabouts. She scowled. Would he help her? And if so, why?

"Go!" Evening Sky's exclamation prevented Abbey from voicing her thoughts. Her friend pointed toward a longhouse as she stumbled to her feet. "The old woman has a stick. Go, Abbey, before she comes to beat you!" She reached into her bowl, transferring

134

two corncakes onto Abbey's dish. "Give to Woman With No Heart. She like *O-hak-wuh*. Tell her it for her."

Too stunned to speak, Abbey nodded, accepting the corncakes before she hurried to the entrance of the house.

Woman With No Heart said nothing as she accepted Abbey's offering. She moved aside after taking the corncakes, gesturing for the slave to go in.

Later, the woman's continued silence as they readied for sleep combined with the mental image of the matron's large stick kept Abbey from a good night's rest.

Chapter 11

The second day of the Green Corn Festival began much as the first, but the event took place outside the ceremonial longhouse in the pleasant warmth of the morning sun. The Iroquois formed a circle in the village compound. In the center, a fire snapped and crackled as it burned. Smoke rose up, tossed away by a light breeze. The air was filled with the scent of burning wood, the bear's grease the Indians used to oil their bodies, and various food odors. The excitement among the Indians continued to be high.

Silver Fox began as the opening orator. Kwan sat beside his standing father, his expression solemn as he listened intently to the old man's speech. Silver Fox's address was much as Kwan's had been. Praises and thanks were given to the Spirit Forces for allowing the corn crop to sprout.

Today's ceremony didn't seem as riveting to Abbey as yesterday's when Kwan had dominated the scene.

It's Kwan, an inner voice taunted her. *He fascinates you.* Abbey realized with a jolt that her enjoyment of the event was linked to her attraction to the sachem.

"Ab-bey." She felt a sharp poke in her ribs and turned to see Woman With No Heart scowling.

The old matron held out a clay pot. "Take to sachem."

Abbey hesitated a moment before taking the drinking bowl. Her stomach contracted at the thought of approaching Kwan. She glanced at him, feeling her face heat at her own sexual thoughts.

"Now, girl! Go!" her master hissed, cuffing her on the shoulder.

Heart pounding with a strange excitement, Abbey hurried around the large circle of Indians to where Kwan sat. She stopped several feet behind him, unspeaking. She was loathe to disturb him, for he looked as if he were in a trance with his head bent, his gaze riveted unseeingly on the fire flickering in the circle's center. She felt the force of Woman With No Heart's displeased gaze from the other side of the gathering. Her breath caught in her throat as she moved closer.

"*Hoh se no wahn,*" she murmured, using the Onondaga word for chief. She saw him tense before he glanced back. Her hands shook as she held out the bowl. He held her captive in his glittering gaze. Accepting her offering, he nodded his thanks and then turned back to the circle.

Abbey hadn't realized that she'd stopped breathing, until she'd released a pent-up breath. Her mission accomplished, she turned to go back to Woman With No Heart. A hand caught her by the elbow. O-wee-soo smiled at her.

"Sit, *Ex aa*," Kwan's grandmother urged, gesturing. Sit, child, she'd said.

Abbey's pulse raced as she saw the empty space. It was next to Kwan. Knowing it was unwise to argue with the village's head matron, she did as she was told and sat, positioning herself beside Kwan, but slightly to the rear. His glistening male arm was only inches away; she felt the strongest desire to touch it. Aghast at herself, she looked away and straight into Bear Claw's hostile gaze.

She glared back, ignoring the warmth of her rising blush. Had the warrior guessed her attraction to his chief? She was tinglingly aware of Kwan's rock-hard body as she and Bear Claw engaged in a silent duel with their eyes.

You are the enemy; you cannot fool him, Bear Claw's expression seemed to say.

She sent back a silent message. *You can't intimidate me. I won't let you!*

Kwan shifted next to her, and Abbey broke eye contact with the angry warrior. The sachem rose as many in the circle began to sing, accompanied by their drums, while others danced around the fire. Kwan joined the dancers, his oiled body shimmering beneath the summer sun, looking like some glorious savage god. His hair appeared more gold than brown in the sunshine. His eyes gleamed like polished silver. He moved fluidly to the rhythm of the Iroquois song and the steady beat of the drums.

Mesmerized, Abbey stared. Her breasts tingled. A pleasant warmth invaded her most private parts. She wanted to run her fingertips over Kwan's oiled muscles, touch her lips to his sensual mouth, and feel the thrust of his tongue against her teeth . . . deeper . . . What would it be like to lie beneath him, to be swept away by his savage passion?

Oh, God, he's my enemy, she thought, *but I want to know what it is to be loved by him.* She shivered with sensation. The memory of his kiss was strong.

The primitive beat of the Indian drums echoed about the forest, heating Abbey's blood, burning, sensitizing every fiber and nerve ending in her body.

The dancers were all male warriors in prime physical condition; yet, it was Kwan who held her attention . . . his beautiful male body moving sinuously as he executed the dance.

He was dressed in only a breechclout—a thin strap of deerskin that went between his legs, covering his manhood, tied on with a thin leather strap about his hips. The Indian men had abandoned their full dress for comfort under the hot summer sun. Or perhaps to come before the Great Spirit as simple warriors, Abbey surmised. Whatever the reason, the effect of so many scantily clothed, oiled male bodies of copper dancing to the primal beat was startling to her. Her gaze widened as it glanced off each of the dancing braves before sliding back to Kwan.

Abbey swallowed hard. The circle of performers had widened, bringing Kwan within three feet of where she sat. Her eyes were level with his hard thighs. Her gaze rose to his corded back, to the fall of sun-streaked brown hair that swept his neck and shoulders as he moved. She could smell him; the scent was heady, heightening her already soaring senses. Her feelings scared her, but she gloried in the sensations as well. She felt so alive.

The music stopped abruptly. The dancers froze, and for a heart-stopping minute, Abbey felt the silence. It hung like a cloud; it vibrated across her skin, raising the level of emotion within her to a fever pitch.

The dancers moved back to their places in the circle. Abbey's throat went dry as Kwan came back to his seat. She didn't look at him; she felt too raw, too exposed for the intensity of that silver gaze.

His man smell was stronger from his exertions. The scent of sweat, bear's grease, combined with his own male musk should have been offensive to Abbey, but it wasn't. The earthy, primeval odor reached out to tease and tantalize her, striking a chord of womanly desire. It agitated her insides, arousing her. It inspired mental images that made Abbey flush and squirm, and look anywhere but at Kwan.

She could feel the heat of his body. It radiated from his skin in thick pulsating waves. He looked at her then, drawing her glance, and she gasped. He felt the attraction, too. It was there glittering in his eyes, in his brooding expression.

He stared at her a long moment, silently. In that moment, his gaze stripped her naked and intimately caressed every living, breathing inch of her. She grew hot and tingly all over.

She had to leave him. This village. Abbey was afraid. Afraid of a desire so strong it swept away reason. A feeling so intense that she'd forget that Kwan was her captor. Her enemy.

And—God help her—she'd forget that her brother was out there waiting to be rescued.

The thought of Jamie sobered her, reminding her

of her intent to question the Indians. Where was Evening Sky? The Indian maiden had said she'd help her. Glancing about the circle, Abbey could find no traces of her friend.

O-wee-soo touched her shoulder. "Ab-bey, come."

Abbey went, glad to be free of Kwan's disturbing presence so she could concentrate once again on her brother's rescue.

Her relief lasted only until they came to the area where the food waited.

"You will feed Kwan," O-wee-soo said.

"Feed him?" Abbey's heart tripped.

The old matron nodded. "Bring him food. Has no wife. Kwan needs to eat."

"Yes, but—" Her voice trailed off. *No wife.* The two words reverberated within Abbey's mind. Kwan was unmarried.

"Here." O-wee-soo handed Abbey a bowl. "He is waiting. He is hungry. Must hurry."

Where is Woman With No Heart? Abbey wondered, silently praying for the matron to appear and demand the return of her slave. Her attraction for the man combined with the reminder that Kwan was unmarried made her feel more vulnerable, more endangered from his charms.

Abbey listened silently while O-wee-soo advised her on what to feed Kwan, and then headed back to where she'd left him. But Kwan was no longer in the circle. All of the Iroquois had risen from their seats and gone to their longhouses.

Had Kwan gone back to his hut? Heart thumping, Abbey glanced down at his bowl. Surely, O-wee-soo didn't expect her to follow him?

She saw O-wee-soo and Woman With No Heart talking in earnest. Were the two women arguing? It appeared so seconds later when Woman With No Heart stalked angrily away from the head matron.

O-wee-soo caught sight of Abbey standing idle with Kwan's bowl. The matron frowned as she approached. "He waits for you in his house. Go, child. Hurry!" she scolded.

Abbey nodded and headed toward Kwan's hut, located behind the Wolf longhouse.

Once outside Kwan's open doorway, she hesitated, feeling the strongest desire to flee. She could hear her beating heart, feel the blood rushing to her brain as she fought for the courage to confront the one man who took her off balance. Kwan had kissed and caressed her, making her feel things that no decent, God-fearing woman had a right to feel, especially with a savage. How could she face him?

Kwan Kahaiska. The man's image taunted her every waking hour . . . and invaded her dreams each night. The bowl in her hands shook as she moved before the door.

"Uk no hah." Kwan's deep voice startled Abbey, making her gasp.

Abbey recognized the Onondaga word for mother. "No," she murmured, stepping inside. He looked up. Their eyes met, and she felt the impact of his startled gaze. "O-wee-soo sent me," she said. "I've brought food . . ."

Kwan's gaze narrowed. He was seated on a beaver pelt, smoking a pipe, his features softened by the swirling haze from the burning tobacco. "Come." He waved her inside.

She entered and held out the bowl. "Here."

"Sit." He ignored her outstretched hand, laying his pipe down.

Frowning, Abbey glanced toward the door. "I have to get back . . . Woman With No Heart . . ."

His head snapped in her direction. "Sit!" he commanded.

Taken aback by his harsh tone, she sat down across from him. She was quiet, watching him from beneath lowered lids, wondering what to do next when Kwan grew suddenly impatient.

"A slave serves," he said.

Flustered, Abbey tried to hand him the bowl.

Kwan shook his head. "No," he said. "A slave feeds."

"What!" She was appalled. "I will not!"

"Ab-bey." He was angry. His silver eyes glinted; a pulse beat at his temple. His very maleness reached out to her, making her feel alive, all woman. Yet, at the same time, she felt the strongest urge to clobber his arrogant head.

"I don't have to feed you. I don't have to do anything for you!"

"No?" It was a direct challenge. "You are slave. You do what Woman With No Heart says. You do what I say!"

Aroused by her show of spirit, he grabbed Abbey's arm, dragged her across the ground to lay against him on the beaver pelt. He'd moved so quickly that she was taken off guard and had little chance to evade him. He rolled her over so that he was lying above her, his weight pinning her to the animal skin.

She felt enveloped by his nearness, strangled by the

143

force of his virility. Abbey's breath rasped from her throat as she fought to breathe, to think rationally and sort out her confused feelings. His hand cupped her jaw. His eyes glowed, his head bent, and she panicked.

"Let go! You're hurting me!" She struggled to get out from beneath him.

He released her jaw to thread his fingers in her hair, effectively blocking her chance for escape. The air crackled with energy. They gazed at one another in silence, their expressions fierce with anger . . . with longing. The only sound was that of their rasping breaths.

Kwan cradled her head, raising her so that they were close . . . nose to nose . . . mouth to quivering mouth . . . He pressed her to the beaver pelt. His head loomed closer, and his breath and then his lips grazed her cheek.

"No," she whispered. She had difficulty breathing.

His mouth hovered near her lips. He murmured in Onondaga—a word she'd never heard before—and pulled her onto his lap.

Abbey pushed to be free, but his body wouldn't budge. "Kwan! W . . . what are you doing?" she gasped when he moved to the side, and his hand moved, caressing her neck, her left shoulder before sliding down toward her aching breast. "Kwan?"

He stilled his fingers. "I will not hurt you." Then, he spoke to her in Onondaga. The words were foreign yet soothing to Abbey; and she closed her eyes, anticipating his touch. He cupped her throat, sliding his hand up and down the fragile, throbbing column.

Abbey's breath quickened as she began to explore his male form. The smell and feel of him were heady to her senses. His skin was moist and slick under her palms. His thighs beneath her were like molten steel . . . hard, hot, and smooth.

Kwan's flesh burned against her hand. She opened her eyes and was mortified to find her fingers on his nipple. With a gasp, she repositioned her right hand, only to encounter the steady drum of his beating heart, which disturbed her even more than touching his nipple did. She had the power to arouse him!

Abbey caressed his chest, felt his instant response. He felt so good! She moved her hand down to his stomach, and he gasped as the muscles contracted.

What am I doing? she wondered. Kwan was a savage! Her enemy! She mustn't allow this!

But he can help you find Jamie.

At what expense? Fornication?

She had a mental image of the two of them lying together, naked, on a pile of thick furs.

"Ab-bey," he said huskily. Kwan's breath smelled sweet. *"E-ghe-a . . ."* Yes.

She felt his mouth sear her neck. Closing her eyes, she arched back, enjoying the sweet sensation of burning lips and tongue.

His head lifted. He studied her, his silver eyes gleaming hotly.

And then Kwan bent and took her mouth.

His kisses were hot, furious, demanding, as his lips slanted across her own. He shifted her, bending her, twisting her, until her hair swept the beaver pelt.

It was an uncomfortable position for Abbey and she whimpered. Kwan immediately changed tactics,

145

his lovemaking turning tender, but no less intense. Such gentleness from a fierce man undid Abbey. Moaning, she gave into his kisses, sighing when his teeth nipped her earlobe. She alternately gasped and groaned while he kissed and caressed her through the deerskin tunic. He seemed to know all the right places to touch, just how to touch her to bring her the most pleasure.

"Yes," she whispered. "Yes, Kwan . . . Oh!"

Suddenly, he released her, setting her back on his crossed legs. "You will undress."

You will undress. The command was cold, lifeless. Abbey stared at him. His eyes were glittering—yes, but it was clear that he wasn't nearly as affected by their lovemaking as she.

Savage. He's a savage. What did you expect? Reason returned like a shock of cold water.

Abbey scrambled off his lap. "I won't do this, Kwan."

He stared at her broodingly, making no attempt to bring her back. "Come here."

"No."

He raised his eyebrows. "I am sachem. You are slave. Come here."

"Savage!" she spat, rubbing her hand across her mouth as if to wipe away the kiss. He looked so sure of himself she wanted to smack him.

"I would not," he advised, apparently reading her mind.

She narrowed her gaze. "Would not what?" she said, pretending innocence. Her breath was still uneven from the passionate encounter.

He sighed with impatience. "Ab-bey, come, or—"

"Or what?" she dared, raising her chin. "Will you tie me to the stake and roast me alive? Or . . ." She affected a shudder. "Will you kiss me again?"

He looked amused. "You want Kwan to kiss you." He said it with a sureness that could only be male.

"You must be joking!"

He grinned. "Come."

"Never!"

He tensed. Or so Abbey thought. She wasn't sure, for next he'd shrugged as if tired of the game.

Kwan gestured to the bowl of food. "Feed me," he said, his eyes daring her to refuse.

Abbey bit the inside of her mouth as she picked up the bowl. She studied its contents for a few moments.

"I will have cakes of *O-na-hah*."

So he wants corncakes, does he? she thought. Her jaw clenched. She picked up a corncake, studying it. Crumbling it in her hand, she threw it at him. "Eat then!" The crumbs hit his face.

Kwan bellowed with rage.

Abbey jumped up and fled the hut. And was disappointed when he didn't follow her.

Darkness cloaked the land, and the Indians gathered around a huge fire in the compound. It was late but everyone within the village was in attendance. Guests had arrived—two white men from the French settlement up north.

With a frown, Kwan watched his people. The white men had brought fire water, and the sachem worried that the Onondagas and their guests would drink themselves into oblivion, leaving them vul-

147

nerable to attack.

He-Who-Comes-From-The-Night. He scowled as he eyed the Seneca brave. He-Who-Comes-From-The-Night was responsible for the presence of the French men. It was the Seneca who had been pressing the League to join forces with French against the *Yen'gees*—the English. While Kwan didn't mind trading with the white man, he saw danger in taking sides. The Iroquois must stay out of the white man's wars. Both French and English would only use the Indian people; they'd care little for the loss of Indian life or the damage that might be done to the League.

Kwan remembered little from his life with his English family. All he knew of the white man he'd learned from the British soldiers and the French.

Ages ago, the Iroquois had fought amongst themselves, just like the white man. But the League had changed all that, making brothers out of enemies. It had brought loyalty between the Iroquois tribes. Members of the League looked out for each other, protecting their own. As long as the confederacy remained intact, then the rights of the Iroquois would be safe. The joint tribes made a formidable enemy for anyone who dared to cross them.

Kwan watched the Seneca guzzle from a whiskey jug before passing it on to the brave next to him.

It wasn't the French who were a danger to the people, so much as it was a few of the People themselves . . . discontents like He-Who-Comes-From-The-Night, who listened to the white men's lies and sought to make trouble within the League.

The sachem had been surprised to see the Seneca in his village. His distrust of the brave came from a disagreement he and the Seneca had had at the last great council meeting. About the French.

He frowned when He-Who-Comes-From-The-Night rose and reeled drunkenly. The Green Corn Festival was a sacred gathering; it pained him to see his People acting this way. Whiskey did terrible things to the Iroquois. It didn't affect him the way it did the others. He supposed it was because of his English blood. He'd never seen a white man get drunk as fast as an Iroquois brave. And a drunk brave could be a dangerous one.

The speeches of the day were over. Kwan sent up a silent prayer to the Great Spirit to protect the People from betrayal and harm.

"Ees!" A Mohawk warrior stood swaying before, holding out a jug. *"Nay'-tah! Oh yah-heh!"*

Shaking his head, Kwan pushed away the Indian's offering. *"Hee-gah. Ot'gon.* The drink is evil. Warrior's enemy!"

The Mohawk laughed. "Kwan Kahaiska is weak. He fears big. The Iroquois are powerful. Have no enemy. We fight all and win!"

"How can you fight when you cannot stand?" Kwan said. "It is wrong to take the white man's drink."

"Hau!" The Mohawk gulped from the whiskey jug. "Firewater is *Yan lee!"* Good.

The smell of whiskey was thick in the air and made Kwan wrinkle his nose with disgust. It had spilled down the brave's chin, dripped down his tattooed chest.

"Sah'dend'-yah," Kwan said. "I do not want your firewater." He sighed as he watched the Mohawk

stumble away. There'd be little sleep for him this night.

As the night wore on, the Indians drank more and became obnoxious. Kwan sought out his father.

"They will not stop. Bear Claw . . . Stone-face. They will not listen. They drink until they cannot see."

Silver Fox nodded gravely. Like his son, he had refrained from partaking of the French firewater. Too often he had seen what the drink did to good warriors. Made them act like children. Made them draw weapons and fight.

The imbibers were getting impatient of the Onondaga children. Some threatened the youngsters with tales of Big Nose; one brave kicked a young girl, a terrible thing to do, for the Iroquois didn't believe in hitting their children. They used embarrassment and humiliation to keep the young in line. Never violence.

The Iroquois mothers took their offspring off to bed, and both Indian and English slave women kept back from the gathering for fear of molestation—or worse.

Ab-bey. Kwan searched the compound for her. Her golden hair would make her stand out from the other women. Earlier, he'd been furious to note one of the Frenchmen studying her with lust. The idea of another's hands on Abbey filled Kwan with jealousy.

A woman screamed, and Kwan jumped up, searching for the sound's source.

He knew who it was when she began shouting English obscenities. *Ab-bey!* Kwan's heart thumped.

He found himself running.

150

Chapter 12

"Relax, chèrie . . ."

"Let me go, you French dogsbody!" Abbey struggled against the trapper's hold. They were outside the stockade, far from the celebration. Abbey had left the compound with O-wee-soo's permission, fetching water from the lake and stopping once in the woods to relieve herself. Returning to the village, she was accosted by the Frenchmen. "Let me go, or I'll—"

"Leave her alone," a deep voice interrupted.

Kwan stood on the trail, his gaze burning with anger, his fists clenched by his sides.

"Kwan!" Abbey whispered. She felt giddy with relief.

The Frenchman seemed unconcerned with the arrival of the host. "If you will wait just a moment, monsieur . . . over there. Jacques will be finished soon." He bent his head and ground his mouth against the woman's lips.

Abbey whimpered, repulsed by his fleshy kiss. She

shoved him away. His breath smelled of liquor; his body reeked of unwashed human flesh. "Let go!"

She fought to be free, kicking him in the shin, but the trapper only laughed and pulled her closer.

"*Oh-neh!*" Kwan growled. "Now!" With a savage snarl, the sachem grabbed hold of the trapper's shirt and threw him aside like a sack of grain. The Frenchman landed in the woods with a thump.

"Kwan!" As the trapper lay in a daze, Abbey ran into Kwan's arms. "Thank God." His muscled arms pulled her against him, holding her close. Sighing, she buried her face against his bare chest. She felt safe and warm . . . and tingly.

"Monsieur." The French trapper had stumbled to his feet. Murder glinted in the brown eyes. Murder and lust. He pulled a knife from his belt and threatened Kwan. "Come, Indian! Come see Jacques!"

"No!" Abbey screamed in warning.

Kwan tossed her aside as the trapper lunged.

Abbey fought back a rising panic. Kwan needed a weapon! But he was the peace leader; he never carried a knife.

She watched the two men circle like hungry wolves preparing to attack prey, the Frenchman wielding a deadly knife, Kwan weaponless. She searched frantically for a stick, a club . . . anything to aid Kwan.

Where was the guard? Abbey wondered. She rummaged in the brush and found a tree branch. Throwing it down, she searched for something bigger.

"I take no orders from a savage, Monsieur Kwan," the Frenchman snarled while making a strike. The blade grazed Kwan's arm, but he didn't flinch. "I will kill you, monsieur."

"And the Indians will kill you," Abbey gasped. Kwan was cut! "Drop your knife!"

Damn, why couldn't she find a branch big enough! She retrieved the first stick. "Kwan! Here!" It wasn't much of a weapon, but it was better than nothing.

The Frenchman laughed as Kwan caught the branch. "You think to conquer Jacques with that?" He made a swipe with the knife, cutting away the tip of Kwan's weapon. "I don't think so, Monsieur Savage."

Apparently, the man was too drunk to care about what could happen should he kill the Indian. A fearless fool made a dangerous adversary, Abbey thought.

Kwan's silver gaze flashed menacingly as he crouched, his muscles tensed, ready to fight.

"Jacques!" The other French guest had arrived on the scene.

Abbey watched him warily as he approached the small group. She picked up a rock, preparing to throw it should the trapper attempt to join forces with his friend.

Pierre looked at Abbey, and then Jacques. His eyes widened. "Are you crazy?" he said. "This Indian is chief. Do you want to get us killed?"

Jacques barely glanced at his friend. "I am not afraid of the redskin."

"Well, you damn well should be!" Abbey exclaimed, lowering her arm. The rock was heavy.

She grabbed Pierre's arm. "Tell him," she urged. "Tell him to drop his knife."

The Frenchman stared at her as if mesmerized. "You are a beauty, ma chère."

"Oh, God!" Abbey said. "You're crazy. You're both crazy!"

Shaking his head, the man sobered and turned to his comrade. "Jacques—my friend," he pleaded, "you'd best drop the knife."

"I've seen what they do to their enemies," Abbey said. "Do you want to be tied up and tortured?" It was a lie. She'd seen the prisoners treated cruelly by a few Mohawks, but not since coming to the village. She'd witnessed none of the atrocities the Iroquois were known to commit against their men prisoners. Although she'd been spared, Abbey knew the Indians did, in fact, torture and kill their adult male victims, often reviving the poor unconscious men so they'd continue to suffer pain.

"Kwan," Abbey gasped. "Tell him you'll let him go if he puts down the knife."

Kwan tensed.

"Kwan . . ." she begged.

He glanced at her and then back at Jacques. "You ask much, Ab-bey."

Please, Kwan. She feared not for the trapper, but for the savage who had worked his way into her affections.

"Put down your blade, white man," the sachem ordered.

"Jacques . . ."

"Kwan . . ." A burst of Onondaga announced the arrival of the warrior guard.

Both Frenchmen stiffened. "We are dead men, Jacques," Pierre said.

154

Jacques looked at the sachem. "You will let us go if I put down my weapon?"

Kwan hesitated. After a glance in Abbey's direction, he nodded.

"Give him your word, Kwan," Abbey said when the Frenchman hesitated to give up his knife.

Kwan turned to the guard, Big-Turtle. *"Hah-nya-denh-goh'-nah, sah-dend'-yah."*

"What-what's he saying?" Pierre asked Abbey.

"I am sending Big-Turtle away." The sachem narrowed his gaze. "You will leave the village and Onondaga land. You will not return."

Jacques lowered the knife. "So . . . monsieur." His eyes glittering dangerously, he fingered the knife blade.

"Dus'-hah-wah." Kwan asked for the knife.

"I think not—"

"Give him the knife, Jacques," Pierre said.

"Skeh-nong'-hah," Kwan said. "Slowly."

Jacques handed Kwan the knife. The sachem took the weapon and then knocked the Frenchman out cold with his closed fist.

Kwan stared at Pierre, looking every inch a savage warrior. "You will take your friend far from this village."

Pierre nodded nervously and bent to pick up his senseless friend. The guard reappeared, and the Frenchman started nervously.

"He will help you to leave," Kwan said.

Pierre nodded, and accepting the Indian's help, he left, taking the unconscious Jacques.

"Are you all right?" Kwan asked.

Abbey looked at him, tears filling her eyes. Damn,

why did she feel like crying?

"Ab-bey," he breathed, and opened his arms to her.

With a cry, she ran to him. He embraced her and soothed her with soft words as she sobbed like a child. She felt foolish; she'd been through a lot worse than suffering the Frenchman's attention. Why couldn't she stop crying?

Kwan's hands rubbed her back. The heat of his muscled chest warmed her cheek. His clean man smell invaded her senses; she felt safe, secure in his arms.

He continued to hold her after she stopped crying. He stroked her hair, playing with the golden strands. Abbey closed her eyes, relishing his touch.

"Ab-bey."

She raised her head and gazed into his handsome face. "Thank you. If you hadn't come . . ." She shuddered.

He cupped her face, staring down at her lips. "Did he hurt you?"

She shook her head.

Something flickered in his expression and was gone. "Good." He released her, turning back toward the trail. "Come. It is time we return. Woman With No Heart will worry."

"Spring Rain," she murmured. "I am again serving Spring Rain." Kwan started down the forest footpath. "Wait!" Abbey said, feeling keen disappointment in his sudden detached behavior. "What about your arm? Jacques cut you!"

He glanced down at the nicked skin. "It is nothing."

"Let me look." She'd been the daughter of a

156

physician; she would be the one to judge whether Kwan's injury was indeed nothing.

"No!"

Abbey flinched at his tone. "What's wrong?" she asked. "What have I done?"

Kwan fixed her with his silver gaze. "You have done nothing," he said. His expression forbade further questioning. "Let us go."

Her chest constricting with pain, Abbey had no choice but to obey him. Tender one moment, savage the next. Would she ever understand this white Indian?

Kwan was thoughtful as he walked beside Abbey back to the village. The depth of his feeling for the slave frightened him. He'd believed his obsession with the Englishwoman rooted in sexual need, but now he realized that he felt more for her than lust. He'd never felt fear as when he'd found her fighting the Frenchman's attentions.

"Kwan?" Her voice was weak, uncertain.

"Spring Rain will be waiting." Kwan knew he was treating her badly. He felt her pain and wanted to offer comfort, but he didn't. *He couldn't.* His feelings for her were wrong. He was a sachem, she slave. And she was Breckingridge's niece. The enemy. But the reminder did little to quell his desire for her.

Silver Fox was at the gate when Kwan and Abbey returned to the village. "What has happened, my son?" the old man said in Onondaga.

"The Frenchmen have left."

Silver Fox looked at the woman beside his son.

157

Abbey's face was pale, her lips swollen and bruised. There was a noticeable tear in her deerskin tunic. "Is she all right?" the old man asked, accurately guessing what had occurred.

Kwan nodded. "What of our braves? What of Bear Claw?" he asked.

"Gone to his longhouse. So too the others. Spring Rain is looking for the slave. Stone-face is ill and needs water."

The sachem turned to Abbey. "You go to Deer longhouse."

Abbey looked as if she wanted to say something to him. His gut wrenched at the sight of her soulful blue eyes. "Go!" he ordered brusquely.

With a cry of distress, she left.

"You were harsh with her, my son. She did no wrong. O-wee-soo tells me. She went to get water, nothing more."

Kwan's expression turned hard. "I know this. But she could have been hurt. The Frenchman . . ."

Silver Fox nodded. "The braves have gone to their platforms. Big Turtle and Night Eagle will keep watch. They have not taken the firewater."

Kwan nodded. "When the sun rises, Oscatax and the others will be angry. The French are gone; they will not be back."

"They will be too sick to care."

The sachem scowled. "I pray to the Great Spirit that you are right, Silver Fox."

Seconds later, Silver Fox left for his longhouse, while the sachem turned toward his hut.

The new knowledge of his feelings for Abbey confused and angered Kwan. Morning Flower had

158

never stirred him this way, and Atahkwa . . . Atahkwa had made his manhood rise, had taught him the ways of love, but he had never felt protective toward her. Atahkwa had been older, more experienced than him. Abbey was spirited, courageous, but there was something vulnerable about her. She was innocent in the ways of love; Kwan fantasized about making love to her. In his dreams, he brought her toward the peak of ecstasy until she'd cry out, shuddering with pleasure. He wanted to teach her the joys of joining, of all the ways to pleasure a man . . . him.

Only him, he realized. The idea of another man touching her was repugnant to Kwan, filling him with anger and jealousy.

What was becoming of him that he could feel this way for a slave?

The center of the village was empty. Everyone had retired to their longhouses. It would be up to the few who did not drink the white men's firewater to protect the village this night. Those few and the Onondaga women.

Later that night, Kwan wandered about the sleeping encampment, plagued by the day's events. The Seneca must be getting restless, he thought. What of the Mohawks?

If the council didn't convince certain factions of the danger of the French, there was sure to be war between the Iroquois nations. Kwan had noticed the discontent during the last council fire. Apparently, it was spreading, and he worried that by the time of the next League meeting, it would be too late to do anything about it.

Perhaps he should send word to the other thirteen Onondaga sachems. If they felt the same way as he, he could call a special council meeting. After all, they tended the council fire. It was time to use that power for the well being of the confederacy.

Movement in the darkness caught Kwan's attention, making him tense. He glanced toward the longhouse of the Deer and was startled to see Abbey emerge from inside. He recognized her instantly by the way she moved . . . by her golden hair.

He saw her hurry toward the stockade gate. Kwan frowned. Was she trying to escape? If so, she'd picked the wrong night to do this, the two Frenchmen were out there. She'd be in terrible danger should she stumble across their path.

The thought of the French angered Kwan. Ab-bey had asked more of him than she realized when she'd begged him to let the men go. Jacques had done Kwan a wrong; it was the Iroquois way to seek revenge for that. Even now, hours later, Kwan wanted to see the man suffer a slow death.

A second figure left the Deer longhouse, and Kwan recognized Evening Sky. Abbey stopped in the yard, waiting for the Indian maiden to catch up with her. The two women engaged in conversation, and Kwan wondered what it was they talked about.

Was Evening Sky helping Ab-bey to escape?

He saw the Indian woman hand something to Abbey. A bundle of some kind. Supplies for her journey?

Kwan relaxed when he saw that it was just a water bowl that Abbey held. Did Spring Rain send the slave

160

for more water?

The women stopped near the gate. Evening Sky called out to the warrior-guard—mimicking the *hoot-hoot* of a wood owl.

Kwan's breath caught as the warrior appeared and opened the gate. Abbey went out of the compound; Evening Sky made her way back to the longhouse.

The sachem stepped into the Indian's path. "Where does she go?" He looked menacing in the dim light.

Evening Sky gasped. "Kwan?"

"Where does Ab-bey go?" he repeated.

"Stone-face is still ill. She gets water and medicine roots for the brave's *o-yon-wah*."

"Stone-face has taken too much firewater. He needs sleep not medicine."

Evening Sky agreed, but told Kwan that Spring Rain felt differently. The Indian maiden saw the sachem glance toward the gate. She smiled. "Ab-bey will be safe. Night Eagle will care for her."

Kwan tensed. "Night Eagle is to stand guard!" he snapped. "Who will alert us should the enemy come to attack?" He turned.

"I will take Ab-bey to the lake," he said, stalking away from Evening Sky, to follow Abbey and the brave. *You're jealous of Night Eagle*, an inner voice told him. *It's not concern for the village that makes you seek to take Night Eagle's place.* But Kwan refused to listen.

He reached Abbey and Night Eagle on the trail. "Night Eagle!" he said coldly. "You have left the gate. You will return now!"

"Don't be angry with him, Kwan. It's my—"

161

"Silence!" The two had been walking closely together; jealousy clawed at Kwan's insides, making him see red.

"I will return," Night Eagle said. He didn't argue, but left willingly.

The haze of Kwan's jealousy lifted. "You are a good warrior, Night Eagle," he said as the warrior swept past him on his return to the village.

"You were unfair to him!" Abbey exclaimed when Night Eagle had left.

Kwan stared at her. She looked breathtaking in the dim light from the night sky. He'd been plagued by desire for her since he'd first seen her come into his village. He felt it again as she gazed up at him. His loins tightened as he studied her lips. He fought the urge to take her into his arms and kiss her wildly . . . to throw her onto the ground and bury himself deeply into her soft warmth.

He gestured toward the trail. "You need water. Go! Spring Rain is waiting." Desire coiled about his shaft, hardening the member until it strained his breechcloth.

"You're impossible!" she burst out as she hurried down the trail to the lake. "The most arrogant . . . unfeeling," she sputtered, "savage . . . beast!"

He snorted with amusement. "Watch your step or you trip," he said.

Abbey froze in her tracks. "Damn you! I don't know whether I like you or hate you! You've got me so confused!"

His only answer was to point to the lake.

With a sound of irritation, Abbey stomped down to the water's edge and bent to fill Spring Rain's bowl.

162

Heat seared Kwan as he recalled how he'd cupped her naked behind, squeezing the soft lush mounds with his hands.

The breeze off the lake ruffled her hair as she straightened from the shoreline. She repositioned the water jug and walked back toward the trail.

"Ab-bey."

She kept going, ignoring him.

"*Ab-bey*."

Abbey stopped, slowly faced him. "What do you want?"

For a long moment, he gazed at her. The wind tossed his hair, fluttering it about his face, and Abbey fought to control her own golden strands . . . and the emotion swelling within her breast.

"What do you want?" she repeated.

He appeared to be fighting an inner battle . . . fighting and losing. Finally, his lips moved. "*Ees,*" he said hoarsely. You. "Come here."

She blinked. "No."

"*Gah'-jee.*" His face had softened. His smile, she thought, was almost tender. He came toward her, opening his arms.

A strange force seemed to propel her forward. His gaze mesmerized her, calling her to him. "I have to get back. The others . . ." she whispered. She flowed into his arms.

"Can wait," he murmured against her hair. He set her away, raising her chin to gaze into her eyes. He caressed her jaw with his fingers.

The flame of desire burned in his eyes. "Kwan want . . . need Ab-bey. *Now.*"

Chapter 13

They found a forest clearing, away from the village and prying eyes. Kwan laid Abbey on a blanket of matted grass and then stepped back, his hands moving to loosen the ties holding his breechclout.

The air was perfumed with the scent of sweet grass. The sounds of the forest were all around them—the *chirp-chirp* of a cricket . . . the night owl's *hoot-hoot* . . . the breeze rustling the treetops. Trees, brush, and grass surrounded the area, creating a secluded hideaway.

Her senses reeling, Abbey watched Kwan undo the leather ties of his garment. Her heart pounded with a strange excitement. Anticipation hummed through her veins, making her feel alternately hot and cold. He held her gaze steadily as he released the cloth.

Abbey swallowed. Unlike that night at the lake, Kwan's shaft was turgid with desire. Her own feminine core throbbed in response as he came to her, kneeing beside her, worshipping her with his silver gaze.

"A-nik-ha Ix-e-sa-ha," he murmured. Kwan touched her cheek, and she shivered with pleasure.

"What does that mean?" she asked breathlessly. Her gaze fastened on his sensual male mouth.

He smiled. "Maiden of the Sun."

Maiden of the Sun, Abbey thought and was pleased. It felt like the moon had burst through the clouds, lighting the earth with its soft radiance. Kwan stroked back the golden strands that clung to her face and forehead.

His fingers continued to move, feather-light against her skin. He seemed entranced with her as he caressed her jaw . . . ran a finger to her ear and then down her throat where he paused to feel her rapidly beating pulse.

"Kwan . . ." She felt her nipples strain against her tunic. What if someone saw them? What if that beast Jacques returned, taking him by surprise? "Kwan—"

He tensed at her tone.

Her lips quivered. "The Frenchmen . . ."

Kwan seemed unconcerned. "They will not bother us. They are far from our camp."

"But the others . . ."

He smiled away her fears. "Do not worry, *O-ka-o*. It will be all right."

And she believed him, was surprised to find she trusted him.

Abbey sighed, closing her eyes. His touch was magic against her neck, slipping beneath the deerskin to crest her pink softness. He withdrew suddenly, and her eyelashes fluttered open.

Kwan was staring at her, his brow furrowed. Clearly, he was displeased with something.

She was startled when she met his gaze. "I . . . I'm sorry," she whispered. "I don't . . . know . . . what to do."

She blushed.

His face softened. "Rise," he ordered in that familiar commanding tone of his, but she took no offense.

Kwan helped her to sit upright, his hand lingering caressingly on her leg. "You are pret-ty, Ab-bey."

Her breath caught. "Thank you." She searched her mind for the Onondaga word for handsome. *"A-gon-le."*

He chuckled. "You come to know our language. What else have you learned?"

She smiled, remembering his kiss. "Many things," she said impishly. "But I won't tell you, for you think too much of yourself already."

Kwan scowled and Abbey laughed, a tinkling sound of pure delight. "You have become used to being king of these Indians, haven't you?"

"King?" He shook his head. "I am not king. I am sachem. Not the same thing."

"But you're used to getting your own way."

He was thoughtful. "No. This is not true." He paused, his gaze caressing. "You wear your tunic still." He reached for the hem.

Blushing, Abbey caught his hand, stopping him. "That's not what I mean—"

In a sudden move, Kwan silenced her with his lips. Pressing her to the ground, he executed the kiss like he did the dance . . . skillfully and with intense emotion. He nibbled each corner of her lips. She gasped, and he took advantage of her open mouth to delve deep inside with his tongue.

"Kwan!" she cried out. He had dipped his hand under the hem of her tunic, and now he stroked her thigh.

Kwan watched the play of emotion on the woman's face. He felt a burst of satisfaction as he squeezed her firm flesh gently, ran his fingers up higher until he found the moist secret part of her.

With a cry of astonishment, Abbey arched off the ground. Spurred on by her response, he probed gently between her legs with his finger, invading her center. He found the sensitive feminine nub and rubbed it, enjoying her look of astonishment . . . the glaze of passion dulling her blue eyes.

His finger probed deep inside of her, playing her, readying her for his entry. Kwan caught his breath. She was magnificent . . . moist and warm and sweet. He wanted to observe her face while she climaxed, to hear her cry out as she convulsed.

His touch gentle, he grabbed hold of her woman nub and squeezed. At the same time, he placed a hand on her breast, tenderly pinching the pebble-hard nipple.

Abbey's response was instantaneous. She bucked off the ground, her beautiful blue eyes widening with astonishment. "Softly," he murmured in Onondaga. He felt an overwhelming tenderness for this fair-skinned beauty.

He slid his fingers down her belly and was aware of the sharp contrast between their bodies. She was white where he was dark. She was satin where he was steel.

He bent to kiss her flat stomach, and felt it quiver

against his lips. The urge to take her was strong. His manhood was near bursting with his desire. But Kwan fought to control himself; he wanted Abbey to experience the joy of their joining.

Abbey inhaled sharply and tried to close her legs when Kwan's head moved down to her belly, to the curling triangular nest of hair that shielded her womanhood. She stiffened when he bit the inside of her thigh. She'd never experienced such pleasure-pain before, and she was frightened . . . and ashamed by her response.

His head lifted and moved downward again. With a murmur of protest, Abbey tried to roll away, but Kwan held her captive, murmuring to her soothingly. She relaxed when he changed his intent and caressed her with his hands instead of his lips. And she allowed the wonderful new feeling he created to wash over her . . . to build and build.

"Good, Ab-bey. *Yan-lee!*"

He pressed her in that one special spot, sending her over the pinnacle of ecstasy, making her cry out as her muscles contracted, and she felt a gushing warmth.

Kwan reached for her, drawing her into his arms, but now that the pleasure had passed, she was embarrassed and fought to be free of him.

"Oh, God, no!" She had let an Indian make love to her! She turned her head, hiding her face. The area between her legs still tingled and throbbed. She lifted her hands to cradle her hot cheeks.

"Ab-bey?" Kwan sounded puzzled. "Ab-bey, *saht-gaht'-to*. Look at me."

She refused.

"*Hoht-nen'-geh*." He touched her shoulder, trying

to turn her. "Did I hurt you?"

"No, no!" Without thinking, she spun to face him, then gasped and quickly averted her gaze again.

"*Hau!* What is it then?"

"I . . . you . . . I should never have . . ."

Suddenly, Kwan understood. She had experienced her first taste of ecstasy while he had sat back and watched. Apparently, she didn't understand that he, too, had been affected. That he was still waiting to feel it too . . . that there was time yet for them to reach the top together.

"*O-ka-o.*" The endearment came out as a breathless, throaty whisper. He had called her "his sweet."

Surprised at Kwan's tone, Abbey glanced at him. Gone was the stern savage; in the sachem's place was an ordinary male . . . a flesh and blood man.

"Touch Kwan, *O-ka-o.*" He grabbed her hand, moving it to his staff. Her first impulse was to retreat, run from the savage as far and as fast as she could. But she didn't . . . couldn't. Kwan looked like a male tortured, in pain.

And then Abbey understood . . . and she was no longer afraid or embarrassed, because Kwan shared the same feelings . . . desire . . . confusion . . . love . . . *Love?* No. Not that.

Kwan shifted, and his shaft moved. He felt hot and hard in her hand. She gasped, fascinated by the pulsating male flesh.

Emboldened by her obvious power over him, Abbey began to fondle him, and found herself aroused by his unrestrained response. He groaned, his face convulsing with pleasure.

She sat up, shifting closer. Abbey enjoyed touching him intimately, understood what Kwan must have felt only seconds before when his kisses and caresses had brought her to earth-shattering heights.

"O-on-ha," he rasped. "It is alive for you, Ab-bey." The Indian sat back on his haunches. She could see the tension in his coiled muscles as Kwan closed his eyes and threw back his head.

The sounds coming from deep in his throat made her skin tingle, her body heat with desire. On impulse, Abbey leaned forward, placing her lips on the arched column, kissing and tasting his dark skin. He jerked with surprise and peered at her through heavy-lidded eyes.

"Where, Kwan?" she asked softly. "Where shall I touch you?" Holding his gaze, she ran a hand over his sleek, muscled chest. "Here?" She moved her fingers downward to his flat belly. "Or here . . ."

Kwan gasped. *"E-ghe-a . . . Abbey. E-ghe-a, O-ka-o . . ."*

She enjoyed observing him as she touched him . . . hearing him groan. Gasping, he reached for her, but she held him back.

"No, Kwan . . . Not yet." The area between her legs was throbbing. One touch from his skillful hands, and she'd be up and over the edge again . . . lost. This time she wanted to know how it felt to have Kwan deep inside her . . . thrusting against her. The image made her gasp. Her breasts tingled.

The only thing separating them was the deerskin tunic. Abbey released Kwan to undress. She wanted to be naked, to feel him against her, their bodies touching . . . searing . . .

His breath labored, Kwan watched her, his silver

eyes burning brighter as he realized her intent.

Haste made Abbey clumsy; Kwan helped her, tossing away the garment. The discarded tunic landed beside them on the ground.

Holding her gaze, Kwan cupped her breast. She felt her flesh throb and fill his hand. Murmuring softly, he then bent his head, taking her nipple into his mouth, licking and nipping the bud gently. Abbey moaned, her fingers entangling in his long sable hair to clutch him close.

The savage worshiped both of Abbey's breasts, paying them equal attention with palms and fingers, lips and tongue. When he rose, she felt the air tickle her wet skin, her nipples. The sensation heightened her desire, and she reached out to him, grabbing his head to kiss him.

Kwan pressed her to the grass. Groaning against his lips, Abbey fell back, sighing with pleasure as he stretched out beside her. He shifted, and she felt enveloped by his sinewy length as he eased his weight onto her soft form.

And then he was probing between her open legs . . .

He was gentle, but Abbey felt the pressure of his manhood and she cried out as he eased into her fully. The pain lasted only a moment until her flesh adjusted around him.

Then Kwan began to move, grinding against her. And Abbey felt that pleasure-pain again as her womb tightened and tingled and she learned the joys of mating.

Kwan kissed and caressed her, bringing her with him as he strained toward the climax. Whimpering with the wonder of her feelings, Abbey clung to him as they both climbed high.

The sachem gasped and shuddered, his response sending Abbey over the crest and she sobbed her release, clutching his broad shoulders. Her head spinning with the wonder of their shared ecstasy, Abbey felt a lethargic warmth invade her mind and body, and she smiled.

Sated, Kwan and Abbey lay quietly, muscles and nerve endings throbbing in wake of their joining. Minutes passed, and they fell asleep, locked in each other's arms.

Somewhere in the forest of the New York Colony . . .

"Colonel—sir, we have prisoners. We found them wandering outside our camp, sir."

Breckingridge frowned. "Savages?"

The young soldier shook his head. "French, sir."

"Bloody same if you ask me," Captain Smythe said.

"What the hell are they doing here?" the English colonel wondered aloud.

"They say the've been run off by redskins."

"Oh?" Breckingridge's eyes gleamed as he eyed the young soldier. "Bring them here then." He turned to Smythe when the boy had hurried to do his bidding. "Well, John, it looks like we may be close after all. These Frenchies may be able to help us find Great Arrow."

The captain looked unconvinced. "They're French.

172

The enemy . . ."

"So? After we're done with the bastards, we'll kill them."

Moments later, led by the young soldier, the two French trappers stumbled into camp, red-eyed and reeking of whiskey.

"Sit down, gentlemen." The colonel smiled grimly as he gestured toward a fallen tree.

The men looked at each other nervously before taking a seat on the hollow log. The English army had set up for the night in a clearing surrounded by forest thicket. The young soldier who'd made the capture was just one of several guards posted about the crude camp.

"What are you going to do to us?"

Breckingridge raised his eyebrows. "Well, now that depends on the answers to a few questions. First, who are you and what are you doing in this neck of the woods?"

The oldest of the two men spoke. He was a scruffy-looking character with a full, matted beard. He blinked up through bleary eyes. "We're trappers." He slurred his words. "We were trading with some Injuns when we were run off by the swivin' chief."

The colonel stared at him hard. "You are French."

"What makes you say that?" The youngest man's expression turned wary.

The bearded man seemed unafraid. "We are, monsieur. Is that a problem?"

The colonel smiled grimly. "As I said, that depends on whether or not you are willing to cooperate with us."

"To do what?"

"Jacques!" the younger man exclaimed, obviously upset with his friend's boldness.

Breckingridge stared at the young trapper. "And you are?"

"Pierre, monsieur," he mumbled. "Pierre Charcot."

"Have you ever heard of a savage called Great Arrow, Pierre?"

Pierre's face brightened. "Jacques, isn't that the—"

"Sh-sh!" Jacques's expression turned shrewed. "You are looking for a redskin, monsieur?"

The English officer nodded. "Great Arrow. Sachem of the Onondagas." His gaze narrowed. "You've met the man."

The Frenchman shrugged. "Could be, monsieur."

Breckingridge managed to control his excitement. "You've been to his village?" He stared at the two men hard.

"This chief . . . is his skin not fairer . . . unlike the others?"

The colonel nodded, and Pierre said, "I think he is the one who ran us off!"

"It seems, monsieur," Jacques said, "that your Great Arrow is Kwan Kahaiska. We've been to his village. You *are* looking for Kwan Kahaiska, are you not?" He paused long enough for the officer to nod. "Well, colonel, if we help you, what's in it for us?"

Breckingridge laughed, but inside he was seething. The nerve of the French scum! "If you take us to the man's village, gentlemen, I'll see you're not only let free, but rewarded handsomely." He named a figure that made both prisoners gasp.

"Your generosity overwhelms me, monsieur."

"Then you will take us to him?"

"With pleasure." Jacques noticed the sudden change in the Englishman's expression. "Why do you want him?"

The colonel's smile was tight-lipped. "Let's just say he has something that belongs to me. I want it back and to see the bastard pay for the crime."

"Oh? And what is that, monsieur?" The Frenchman seemed only mildly curious, but he was actually very interested. The information could be prove invaluable for future use in dealing with the English officers.

Breckingridge's features hardened. "My niece."

"Ab-bey." Kwan's urgent voice brought her awake. "It is time to return."

Abbey blinked. Was Kwan angry? They must have fallen asleep, she decided. She remembered Spring Rain and immediately understood his concern.

"Oh, my God!" She scrambled to her feet, and finding her tunic, proceeded to dress. Kwan, she saw, had already dressed.

"Kwan, the water!" She fumbled on the ground, crying out in frustration when she came up empty. "Where's the jug?"

He moved in the darkness and then handed her the filled jug. "Not to worry, Ab-bey. I fill again while you sleep."

Abbey gazed at the Indian with worried eyes. She didn't want the whole village to know that she and Kwan had . . . had what? Made love? Fornicated like two animals in heat?

175

She was mortified at her behavior. How could she have responded so wildly? All of this was so new to her, so disturbing. And it wasn't because she'd lain with a man without marriage. Her parents had loved each other. Unable to wed, they'd lived and enjoyed a life together, raising two children out of wedlock. Abbey and her brother Jamie had been raised to be proud of their parents' relationship, for wasn't it love that counted above all things?

But was what she and Kwan shared love? She wasn't sure how she felt about him. She was physically drawn to him, yes. But love?

And as for Kwan . . . She studied him. There was no tenderness in his expression, and his indifference hurt her. Was it because Kwan was also uncertain of his feelings? Was he, too, struggling to decide whether or not he loved her?

"What will we tell Spring Rain and the others?" she asked.

"They will not ask. I am their sachem."

Abbey stiffened, annoyed with his male arrogance. "And you believe this?"

He presented his back to her as he retrieved an object from the bed of grass. "I know this. It is so."

"But Evening Sky—"

Kwan turned to her, scowling. "Evening Sky will say nothing." He grasped her arm. "Let us go." As they started back, he released her.

They walked along the forest footpath without speaking. The sun had yet to make an appearance, Abbey was thankful to note. Perhaps they hadn't been gone as long as she'd first thought.

When the man beside her continued to be silent,

Abbey's irritation grew.

Didn't what happened between them mean anything to Kwan?

"Kwan." She touched his shoulder, instantly aware when his warm flesh tensed. "What we did?" she mumbled. "Back there . . . D-did it mean anything to you?"

He stopped to glare at her. "I am sachem. What we did was wrong."

How could she reply to that? *Wrong?* she thought. *How could anything so beautiful be wrong?*

There was a long moment of strained silence.

"This should never be," he said.

"Us?" she whispered. Her chest constricted with pain. *He's just a savage.* The reminder was little comfort, because he wasn't just a savage. He was a man.

Kwan nodded with an abrupt jerk of his handsome head. "Come," he ordered. "We must go back."

Abbey must have looked crestfallen because suddenly his face softened. "It will be all right," he said. "We did wrong, but no one will know."

"Damn you, Kwan Kahaiska!" She was furious. He had made it sound as if they'd committed a criminal offense.

His gaze narrowed. She reached out to strike him, and he caught her hand, squeezing hard. "Do not try it, *O-ka-o.*"

She slumped in defeat. Sadness replaced her anger as he released her and they continued their trek back.

I've been a fool, Jamie. I've given myself to a savage—a damn, unfeeling Indian! She felt the sting of tears.

It was time to leave. Her brother was still waiting for her to rescue him. There was nothing for her here; she had lingered long enough. She knew enough of these Indians to know their ways, to escape.

With that decision made, Abbey felt her heart lighten. Tomorrow she would talk with Evening Sky. Depending on what the Indian woman had learned, Abbey would go on to the next village or return to the English fort. Breckingridge would surely have returned. After what the Indians had done, he was certain to help her.

Come nightfall tomorrow she would leave these Indians . . . and forget Kwan . . . and his magic touch.

Chapter 14

Abbey began preparing for her escape during the fourth and final day of the Festival of Green Corn. None of the Mohawks attending festival had seen or heard of a young English male captive with hair the color of ripened wheat. Nor did any of the Iroquois tribesmen whom Evening Sky had questioned.

With the Indians busy celebrating, she found it simple enough to move about the village, gathering foodstuffs and secreting supplies without suspicion. The community storage room at one end of the Deer longhouse proved to a good place for Abbey to hide her provisions. The Indians would not notice her small satchel among the extra stock of the Deer clan.

She would make her escape at night, Abbey decided. Which night she wasn't sure yet. *I mustn't allow my haste to jeopardize my chances!* The safe thing to do would be to wait until she was sure that she could get past the warrior guards.

That night as she lay on her platform, waiting for the Indians to sleep, she reviewed the day's events.

The festival was over. With the Frenchmen gone and their whiskey disposed of, the Indians continued their feasting without incident.

The Iroquois from other tribes remained as guests. Should she escape this night while she knew their whereabouts? Or would it be wiser for her to wait a day or two before leaving even though there was the risk of meeting them on their journey home?

Rachel Votteger. Abbey thought of her friend with sadness. She wanted to take Rachel along with her, but she doubted the German woman would agree to come. The danger of discovery with the baby Anna would be too great. Rachel had told Abbey on more than one occasion that she was content within the village, but Abbey suspected and understood that fear for her baby's safety would be the woman's greatest concern. And what about the others?

I'd never be able to forgive myself if anything happened to them. Abbey decided that it would be best if she went alone and sent back a rescue party. Then, she would be the only one to suffer if the escape attempt failed.

She was frightened. The thought of venturing out in the wilds on her own made her more than a little nervous. The Onondagas might be heathens, but she had come to know them, to see their gentler side. They no longer posed a threat. Savages or not, she had learned how to deal with them, while beyond the stockade fence lurked danger. Terrible, terrible danger in the form of fierce wild animals . . . man . . . and nature's habit of being unpredictable.

But I will face it. For you, Jamie. She needed to see her brother more than ever now. She was anxious for their reunion. Tears burned her eyelids as she thought of their father on his deathbed. He had given her a message—for Jamie.

"Tell him—tell him," he'd gasped, "that I did my best . . . fer your mother." Abbey had nodded, crying silent tears. Rawlins had then looked at his daughter with love. "I love you, Princess. James, too." He'd stopped, coughing, and spit up blood. When he spoke again, it was a hoarse whisper, barely discernible to Abbey's ears. "Jamie . . . find him, girl. Good boy . . . Needs you. Look . . . out . . . fer him." And with that, Dr. Rawlins died, leaving Abbey to mourn him alone.

Abbey closed her eyes, envisioning Jamie's young face. He had to be alive. She had promised to find him. As her father had said, her brother needed her. Surely, she'd know—sense—if he were dead!

There was activity within the longhouse. Abbey listened to the night sounds. Beside her, Spring Rain stirred restlessly in her sleep, while on the far side of the matron, her son Stone-Face slept, snoring loudly.

She could hear the soft murmurs from other members of the clan. Would they never go to sleep? she wondered.

Her mind wandered as she lay there. The night seemed to drag on relentlessly. As during the long hours of each day, Kwan infringed on her thoughts, tormenting her with sweet memories, plaguing her with desire.

Seeing Kwan these past two days, knowing what had transpired between them, had been torture for Abbey . . . especially when it seemed that he'd re-

181

mained unaffected by their encounter. It was as if nothing had happened, as if they'd never kissed and caressed and made love.

The knowledge gave her pain. She had given herself to a man, and he had accepted her gift without feeling. She was so ashamed.

She should have left weeks ago. Her fascination with the sachem had literally kept her a willing prisoner, and she felt guilty at letting her brother down. Jamie was out there waiting for her while she'd allowed herself to be seduced by a damned savage!

The sooner she made her escape the better. Once free of his presence she'd get on with her life, forget all about Kwan Kahaiska.

Liar! an inner voice taunted. *The man will continue to haunt you for the rest of your life.*

"No," she insisted silently. "I'll never again be vulnerable to a man's touch . . . his kisses. Not Kwan. Not any man!"

She felt a constricting pain whenever she thought of Kwan. He had taught her the joys of making love, taught her what it was to be a woman. Even now, her breasts seemed to tingle with the burning imprint of his fingertips. It was hours later, yet her belly quivered still in memory of his caressing lips.

Would she ever be truly free of him? She wanted to believe it, but she admitted that he was unlike any man she'd ever met or would ever be likely to meet. He was a puzzle . . . arrogant and savage, but he had a tender, passionate side to him. How could she resist him? How could any woman?

She wondered long into the night, waiting for the

others to quiet. Finally, she gave up hoping to escape this night and fell asleep.

"Jacques!" Pierre whispered. "Are you sure this is it?"

The bearded trapper scowled at his friend. "Of course, I am sure. See that trail?" Jacques grinned. "We have been here before. The savages are near. They are there over that rise, my friend."

Pierre sighed with relief and allowed his tense shoulders to relax slightly. They'd been traveling for the past two days, having become lost after the first hour after leaving the British camp. This past hour the colonel had been fast losing patience.

The young Frenchman smiled. If Jacques was right, he thought, then the Indian encampment was close by, over that rise. Soon he and Jacques would be free to go. *With the reward money.*

Jacques stopped suddenly, held up a hand. Pierre halted, his gaze on his friend and the English commander.

"Colonel, the village of Kwan Kahaiska is directly ahead of us," Jacques said. "I suggest you quiet your men—" He raised his eyebrows. "Unless you wish to extend the redskins an invitation to attack?"

The British officer stared. "You'd better be right this time, Frenchie. If you're lying, I'll slit your throat."

Jacques laughed. "I do not lie, monsieur. I merely change the truth a bit. However, in this case, I do not do either. Kwan Kahaiska lives up that trail. You, Colonel, owe us a great deal of money."

Colonel William Breckingridge and his men reached the outskirts of the Onondaga village an hour later . . . exactly one half hour after they'd disposed of the dead Frenchmen's bodies.

The Indian women were out in the fields. Abbey worked beside Spring Rain and Evening Sky, weeding the second planting of the bean crop, her thoughts not on her task, but on the one man who had turned her world topsy-turvy. Kwan Kahaiska.

These past two hours had been especially trying for her. Since she'd come to experience the joys of Kwan's lovemaking, she'd been unable to think of little else . . . especially now that her decision to escape was made. When the wind stirred the treetops, she imagined it was the soft murmur of Kwan's voice. Each time a plant leaf brushed up against her, she had a memory of his gentle touch upon her skin. Abbey saw his glowing eyes in the flickering flames of Spring Rain's fire, and the warmth the fire generated was like the heat of their passion, burning, alive.

Tonight. Tonight she would leave here, escape the village and her obsession with the Onondaga sachem. She'd stay up all night if she had to, do anything that would speed her on her way to a safe journey.

Abbey glanced at Evening Sky. She would miss her Indian friend. Straightening to rub her aching back, she studied the young woman who was bent over a row of plants, carefully working the soil around the tender roots. Evening Sky's skin was a rich, reddish,

184

copper color, smooth and lovely; her bare breasts hung forward, small but firm, jiggling as she moved. She wore a beaded skirt and fringed leggings to protect her legs against brush and insects. Abbey, too, wore leggings beneath her tunic; fortunately, the day was cool, making the garments quite comfortable.

Fingering her own blonde tresses, Abbey stared at her friend. Evening Sky's black hair had been greased with sunflower oil, parted and braided into two plaits; she had painted her center part with a mixture of red and orange pigments.

Abbey bent once again to her row of plants, noting the new light honey color of her hands. The Indian women wore powder and face paint, both articles of cosmetics made from the plants found near the village, both designed to redden their skin. As a slave, Abbey wasn't expected to make herself pretty; she was to be useful, nothing more. She looked pale in comparison to her Indian counterpart.

Evening Sky was a beautiful maiden, Abbey realized. Her beauty was more than skin deep; she was a warm and giving person. Abbey would never forget her.

You and Evening Sky are different as night and day, yet Kwan was attracted to you, an inner voice said.

Was he? she wondered. She plucked a weed from the ground, tossing it into a pile. Recalling the look of passion on Kwan's face as he rose above her, remembering his deep groans as he thrust into her warm, willing body, Abbey had to admit that it was true. Kwan had thought her attractive.

Had. He ignored her these days. His desire for her

had waned. Having once tasted the fruit, Kwan must have decided that he didn't care for it.

The opposite was true for Abbey. Having enjoyed a sample of Kwan's lovemaking, she was eager for a second helping. *I have to get out of here, before I lose the desire to leave!*

Abbey was jerked from her reveries when she heard the ear-piercing call come from the warrior-guard. A imitation of a crow, a warning of danger.

The women had little time to flee the field, before the men broke from the forest. White men. British soldiers bellowing war cries, carrying guns and knives.

"Ab-bey, run!" Evening Sky waved her away.

Abbey hesitated. These men were British soldiers! Here was her chance for escape.

"Ab-bey!" Evening Sky screamed. *"Kih un i ag wa sa!"* The enemy!

The young English woman heard a ear-splitting shriek, was shocked to see a soldier bayonet a young girl. *My God*, Abbey thought, *she's only a child!* There had been two small Iroquois children playing at the edge of the field. Heart pounding, Abbey searched for them. They stood together, crying for their mother. Summer Thunder was nowhere in sight. Abbey took off to gather the sobbing children.

"Ab-bey!"

She heard her name called as she scooped up the little girls. Frightened, the toddlers clung to her.

"Ab-bey!" Evening Sky was on the other side of the field. The English soldiers trampled the bean field, crushing the tender plants as they attacked.

"Susie!" a man shouted, and Abbey looked at him.

186

"Where's Susie?" She knew immediately that he was the leader. Susie, she thought. Portsmouth?

Within moments, the braves from the village were fighting the English soldiers. Knives flew through the air, hitting their targets. Shots rang out as British guns were fired, and Abbey felt chilled at the inhuman cries of pain.

Her gaze encountered that of the English commander. A cold shiver ran down her spine, and she felt the strongest urge to flee. The man, she thought, looked crazed . . . capable of anything. She realized by his look that he saw her not as a white woman, but an Iroquois squaw. He seemed oblivious to her blonde hair and pale skin. His dark eyes gleamed with hatred.

"Get her!" the officer's harsh voice commanded. "Get all of them!"

Abbey ran, clutching the children. As she fled the increasing swarm of men, her heart pounded with horror and fear. She offered a silent prayer that she wouldn't trip or lose grip of her precious burden. The two beautiful little girls needed her. She had to see them safe.

Surely, this can't be Breckingridge! she thought. This man was a monster, not a rescuer. And his soldiers were animals, not civilized men!

Suddenly, Abbey saw the Indians as the victims they often were, the whites as attacking savages. Being on the other side of the fence, so to speak, was enlightening. Her desire to escape had passed at the first Indian scream. *Oh, God, will it never end!*

A bullet whizzed by, striking a brave in the shoulder. Bear Claw went down, clutching his wound. The brave had been nothing but hostile to Abbey, but she felt for him, wanted to doctor his injury and offer comfort. The children in her arms came first, and Abbey stumbled into the shelter of the woods. She raced through the thicket, ignoring the pain as her skin caught the thorns that blocked her path.

The babies continued to cry, but didn't struggle to be free, and Abbey was thankful. She tried to reassure them with soft words, but she knew that they could sense her fear . . . and they were frightened by the continual hail of gunfire in the field they'd left behind.

Abbey ran until she could run no more. Her muscles called for her to stop. Her lungs felt sore from ragged breathing. Her every body part screamed with pain, but she kept on until she knew it was safe to slow down.

She found a secluded clearing, concealed by dense foliage and briar thicket. Here, she stopped, but only because she was sure that no one had followed her. Releasing the sobbing toddlers, she sat them on the soft earth and crooned to them. As the girls quieted, Abbey gently dried their tears.

Her own thoughts filled with the dread of death and pain for her Indian friends, she seized the babies to her breast and found comfort in their warm, cuddly softness. Tears stung her eyes. Evening Sky. Spring Rain. Were they all right?

She had the terrible mental image of the two women lying in a pool of blood while the British commander stood, laughing, over their dead bodies.

What of Bear Claw and the other braves? What

of . . . *Kwan?* Had the sachem come to fight? Since her tussle with the Frenchman, Kwan had begun carrying a weapon. Abbey knew he wouldn't stand by idly while the English attacked and murdered his people.

Oh, dear Lord! Is he all right? She couldn't bear the thought of anything happening to him. *Not Kwan!*

Abbey had to fight the urge to return to the village. She couldn't leave the children here, and she surely couldn't endanger them by going back so soon.

All she could do was pray . . . which she did. *Dear God in Heaven, help them.*

The hours that followed proved hellish for Abbey as she battled with fearful images and emotions, and the desire to go back. To Kwan. To see if he was all right.

Finally, she could wait no more. She woke the girls, who had fallen asleep with their heads in her lap, and then started back to the village, praying, hugging the sleepy children.

Chapter 15

The Indian sliced open the man's flesh and placed a hot, glowing ember into the fresh wound. She watched stoically as, howling with pain, the soldier writhed against his rope bindings. The coal fell from the cut to the ground as the squaw stirred the fire.

"Bastards!" the white man gasped when the pain subsided enough for him to speak. "Savages . . . *No!*" His face went death-white as the woman dipped into the flames for another ember. He struggled against the ties, his features contorting. "Let me go! Oh, God, let me go, you red bastards!" Fear shone in his blue eyes, mirrors of stark terror.

A young Indian boy took hold of the woman's knife, brought it against the soldier's belly. "Watch, *Yen'-gees!*" he hissed in Onondaga. "Watch as I cut open your *o-yon-wah*. See the coward you are when I rip out your organs and shove them down your throat!"

The knife blade quivered against the man's skin. "*Please . . .*" the soldier pleaded.

190

"Wait," Kwan commanded, and the boy turned to him. The sachem approached, his gaze hard as he studied the bound soldier.

"I will speak first," he told the Indian family who was torturing the British officer. "There is much we must know."

Nodding, the squaw waved away her son. It was the woman's right to torture and kill this white man. During the attack, the soldier had taken the life of her husband—the boy's father. Red Squirrel had been a good provider and brave.

Kwan eyed the captain's face, noted the way the man begged for mercy with his blue gaze. He hardened himself against the Englishman's suffering. Too many of his People had been wounded and killed. Abbey was missing. Abbey and two children—Summer Thunder's little girls.

The British soldier deserved to die.

"Who are you?" Kwan demanded. The image of Abbey's lovely face came to mind as he anticipated the white man's answer. Had she too been injured or killed? Or had the soldiers taken her away?

The man stared at him through a haze of pain. "Bastard! Animal! I'll tell you nothing!"

With a wave of his hand, Kwan called back the squaw.

"Wait!" the soldier cried fearfully as the woman returned with a spiked Iroquois war club. "I'll—I'll tell you!"

The squaw stopped at her sachem's bidding.

Kwan grabbed hold of the man's hair, jerked back his head, so that the soldier had no choice but to stare into Kwan's gleaming silver gaze. "Who sent you?"

Captain Smythe swallowed. "Breckingridge," he whispered. He closed his eyes; and tears seeped from under his lashes, tricking a trail down his dirty cheeks. "C-Colonel William B-Breckingridge."

Breckingridge. Kwan nodded. He had suspected the colonel, but had needed to hear the man say it . . . needed to know whether or not Abbey had left of her own accord. His mind rebelled at the painful truth. Maybe he was wrong. Maybe she hadn't wanted to leave. "Why have you come?"

"The colonel's niece . . ." the captain gasped.

Kwan's heart tripped. Pain wrenched his gut as his suspicion was confirmed. Abbey had escaped. His fingers gripped the man's hair hard, and the captain cried out. She had left willingly with the English army.

Forcing the hurt away, Kwan gazed at the young captain. "How did you find us?"

Had it been easy for Breckingridge? he wondered. He had always known that the colonel would come. That the commander had gotten what he'd come for so easily disturbed Kwan.

Would the colonel return? Would others follow? Would his people be safe against further attack?

Kwan felt an increasing rage. "Tell me!" Gripping the man's hair, he shook the soldier until he heard the snapping of teeth. "Who led you?"

"French." Smythe's head jerked so hard he had difficulty answering.

The sachem froze. "French." Holding the captain's head up high, he glared down into the man's face. "Two men?"

Smythe nodded, swallowing.

192

Kwan released his grip. He should have killed the men instead of listening to Abbey; he should never have let them free. He turned away, waving to the Indian woman as he went. "Continue," he told her.

With thoughts rolling about in his brain, the sachem sought the peaceful sanctuary of his hut. He was oblivious to the Englishman's last cries of pain.

The field was empty when Abbey stumbled from the woods. There were no sign of any dead bodies; the victors—either Indian or British—had removed them. The bean plants were trampled, and a dark stain marred one area of ground, but the scene was otherwise peaceful. Who had won? Abbey wondered. Had Kwan—and her friends—survived?

One of the little girls woke up and began to whimper, no doubt frightened by the field and the memory of what had taken place.

"Sh-sh," Abbey soothed her. "You'll wake your sister. Don't you worry. I'll find your mother. She's all right." Her throat tightened. "They're all all right." She bit her lip. "They have to be." *Please let him be alive! I love him. Let Kwan be alive!*

The knowledge of her love for the sachem had come to her on the return journey. She had given herself to the man willingly. She would never have done so if she hadn't loved him, she'd realized. Nor would her fear for his safety these last couple of hours have been so great.

Abbey smelled smoke as she neared the village. A good sign, she thought. She froze in her tracks. Unless the English had taken over the Indian longhouses. If so, what should she do? She wasn't sure she could reason with them. They had attacked with a viciousness she'd never thought civilized men capable of. She remembered hearing a woman's scream. The English soldiers she'd known would never have harmed women or children.

She hugged the little girls, nuzzling their hair. She couldn't blame the youngsters if they carried with them forever a hatred of white men. They were innocent children. How could they understand why the English had attacked? How could they when she, an Englishwoman herself, didn't—couldn't—understand?

The stockade fence loomed ahead. Abbey relaxed when she saw Big-Turtle. Her relief at seeing the Indian warrior at his guard post made her feel guilty. The Indians must have won.

She tensed. But how many had been slaughtered defending their village? Bear Claw? Night Eagle? *Kwan* . . . ?

In her haste to know, Abbey hurried toward the gate, yelling at Big-Turtle, waving her arms. The brave stared at her, and then cupping his mouth, made a sound to alert the others.

Within moments, Abbey was surrounded by chattering Onondagas. Some eyed her with suspicion, but most seemed surprised and grateful for the return of the little girls.

"Kwan Kahaiska?" she asked anxiously. "Kwan—" She felt a light touch on her shoulder.

"He is well."

"Evening Sky!" Abbey gasped, and the two women hugged.

The Indian maiden smiled when they broke apart. "You come back. It is good to see you."

Abbey nodded. "I'm so glad you're all right." She held her friend's gaze steadily, knowing her heart was there for Evening Sky to see. "I couldn't stay away."

Evening Sky looked pleased. "Come," she said, drawing Abbey's hand through her arm. "The sachem awaits."

Abbey mentally prepared herself. Kwan was waiting beyond the fence. Would he be surprised—*pleased*—to see her? Would he greet her with joy? Or would she know the pain of a spurned love?

Abbey. She was gone. Run off with that cruel uncle of hers . . . Breckingridge. Kwan knew he shouldn't be surprised—hurt—by her actions, but he was. Deeply. *Because you love her* came the traitorous thought.

No, it wasn't possible, he decided. A sachem couldn't—mustn't—love a slave. The enemy.

But he did love her, he admitted. It was the truth. May the Great Spirit help him, he had come to care for the white woman. She had changed him since he'd first laid eyes on her and he'd felt desire again. It had been years since he'd experienced a stiffening of his manhood, yet one look upon the white woman and it had risen like an ironwood war club. He'd been touched by her spirit, her courage . . . her caring for those she believed needed help—like the boy who'd gone through the gauntlet. It hadn't mattered to her that the youth had been one of the "savages"; believing him in danger, she had jumped

195

in to save him.

Kwan knew he'd become obsessed with Abbey, compelled not only by a physical force, but an emotion pull as well.

And now he knew . . . the emotion was love.

I should have sold her to the French, he thought, recalling his first decision. *Then I would not hurt so.* But he hadn't sold her to the French. He had listened to O-wee-soo instead. And he would listen to his grandmother again, he realized. Such was his respect for the old woman.

"My son." O-wee-soo stepped into Kwan's hut as if conjured up by the dream spirits.

"She is gone," Kwan murmured. "Ab-bey went with the man—Breck-ing-ridge."

The old woman's eyes narrowed as she noted her grandson's pain. "She will be back."

He seemed startled. "Back?" he echoed. "She is *Yen'-gees*—one of them. She will not return to our village. Here she is slave."

"She will come," O-wee-soo insisted with confidence. She had seen the look in the white woman's eyes. Abbey had love for her grandson. Of this, O-wee-soo was certain.

A spasm of emotion crossed Kwan's face. "You sound sure, my mother. How so?"

The matron smiled with gentle fondness for her dead daughter's son. "This old woman has been around many summers, Great Arrow. She knows the truth of many things."

"Great Arrow!" An Indian youth appeared at the sachem's door. "The white woman—she has returned. She brings daughters of Summer Thunder!"

O-wee-soo chuckled as Kwan shot to his feet. Her grandson's face told her many things. One . . . he loved the white woman, Abbey. "You see?" she said. "O-wee-soo knows. She has come back to you, Great Arrow."

Kwan seemed to sway on his feet. His face paled, but his silver gaze glistened . . . with hope . . . and relief.

The grandmother caressed Kwan's bare shoulder. "Go to her, my son. Go to Ab-bey. She left a slave, but in safely returning Summer Thunder's daughters, she has come back a true daughter of the Onondaga."

Abbey entered the village, surrounded by the excited Onondagas and their dogs who barked and ran about their feet. Children frolicked laughingly among their elders, shaking their fathers' ceremonial gourd rattles, mimicking great warriors in battle. Summer Thunder's daughters—two of their own—had come home safely. Despite the sadness of the lost or wounded in the attack, it was a time to rejoice for the little girls.

Watching the youngsters at play, Abbey thought of Bear Claw, remembering the moment he'd been shot. Was the brave alive? Bear Claw had never had any liking for her, but still the thought of his death bothered her.

She turned to Evening Sky, "Bear Claw . . ."

She never heard her friend's reply. Kwan was coming. She knew the exact moment he stepped from his hut, for her skin prickled with warning and her pulse picked up speed.

197

The Indians quieted at Kwan's approach, the gathering parting to allow him easy access to the returning white woman.

Their eyes met as he crossed the compound, and Abbey experienced a jolt. How could she have forgotten how magnificent he was? His handsome features . . . his body all firm muscle and sinew . . .

His movements suggested power. Studying him through the eyes of love, Abbey saw not the savage, but the leader of men. Kwan, she realized by studying his pale, strained features, had been deeply affected by the attack on his people. She wanted to draw him to her breast for comfort, soothe away his lines of suffering and pain.

Her gaze swept him from head to toe, checking for signs of physical injury. *Kwan looks well,* she thought. Relief made her slightly dizzy. Gladness bubbled up inside of her, a feeling she didn't try to conceal. She saw something flicker across his attractive face, saw Kwan hesitate in his long strides.

Abbey inhaled sharply. Joy? Had she actually glimpsed his joy at her return? She couldn't be certain; the look lasted for only a brief second.

He stopped before her, his silver gaze studying her with an intentness that was disconcerting to her.

"Hoh se no wahn," she murmured, her blue eyes sparkling. "Chief."

Kwan stared. He wanted to spirit her away to a private place, take her into his arms, and love her as she'd never been loved before.

She came back! The knowledge brought a happiness so strong that he wanted to hold a celebration . . . to dance . . . to sing and offer thanks to

198

the Great Spirit.

For now, he had to content himself with looking upon her beauty.

"You came back," he said. There was a question in his tone.

She nodded. "Summer Thunder needs her daughters."

Kwan felt a surge of disappointment. "I see," he mumbled. His voice was barely discernible.

The Indians began chattering again. The children were too excited to sit still, and their parents scolded the noisy rascals. The dogs jumped up on their masters, howling and whining for joy.

In the midst of all the commotion, Abbey and Kwan stared at each other.

"I had to return," Abbey admitted.

Kwan felt his heart trip. "Why?"

She seemed unwilling to answer, quickly changing the subject instead. "How is Bear Claw? I saw him fall."

The sachem frowned. "He lives—barely."

"I want to see him." She explained softly, "I'm a physician's daughter. I know about healing. Let me see what I can do."

She was the niece of his enemy, but Kwan trusted her. She came back. She protected Summer Thunder's daughters. Why didn't she leave with her uncle?

"I won't hurt him!" Abbey was angry. "I only want to help!"

Kwan suddenly realized that he was scowling. His face softened. "Come," he said. He turned, expecting her to follow.

Staring at the rippling muscles of his bare back,

Abbey felt the strongest desire to throttle him. He was still the most arrogant . . . frustrating . . .

She glared at him, refusing to move. He stopped, apparently sensing her hesitation, and faced her.

"What is wrong?" he said.

"You."

He raised his eyebrows. "You want to see Bear Claw. I take you. I do what you say. I do no wrong."

Abbey's blue eyes flashed fire. "Do you have to act so superior all the time?"

"Sup-er-ior?" Kwan stiffened.

She growled with frustration. "Like you're the big chief or something."

Amusement lit up his silver eyes. "I am chief."

"You know what I mean!"

"Come," he said. His lips twitched. "Please."

Nodding, she went.

The longhouse where Bear Claw lay unconscious was dark when Abbey entered. The warrior's family was with him. Members of the False Face Society chanted their rites over the injured victim, beseeching the Spirits for the brave to be cured. A single fire burned near the cubicle, casting an orange glow over the prone body and the others who stood sentinel over the wounded man.

Abbey broke from Kwan's side, hurrying to Bear Claw's platform. Knife-Woman, Bear Claw's wife, blocked her way. The woman gave the English-woman a hostile look.

"I want to help," Abbey said. "I know about medicine."

Kwan joined her, translating her words into Onondaga, so that Knife-Woman would understand.

200

The matron looked unconvinced. The sachem spoke a few soft words to her, and the woman consented to have Abbey examine her spouse. Kwan ordered the False Face members to step aside, to give Abbey room. The longhouse seemed to echo eerily with their continued chants as Abbey moved closer.

The warrior looked pale and lifeless against the beaver pelts lining his platform. Unconscious, Abbey thought, Bear Claw appeared less savage, less threatening, despite the Iroquois war crest along his bald head and the row of colorful tattoos across his bare chest.

He'd been wounded in the right shoulder. Abbey bent to check the nature of Bear Claw's injury. The flesh looked raw and angry. Despite the swelling of the surrounding tissue, she was able to spot the bullet, where it remained lodged in muscle and bone. Abbey knew that Bear Claw would have a better chance of recovery if she removed the shot. Her concerned gaze found Kwan's. Could she do it? How could she prevent the wound from festering?

"The whiskey," she said. "Is there any left?" Kwan frowned. "The ball is still in there, Kwan. It has to come out." She glanced at Knife-Woman. "The whiskey . . . something to clean the wound . . ."

Kwan nodded in understanding. He called out to Beaver Dancing, Bear Claw's son, and explained what was needed. The youth inclined his head, flashed Abbey a look of suspicion, and then left, supposedly to get the liquor.

"There is one jug," Kwan said. "I found it hidden by the lake." He was angry. After the incident with the Frenchmen, he had forbidden the use of the white man's firewater. One of his braves, however, had stashed the whiskey away for future use. The sachem had left it there in the hopes of discovering who had done so.

Abbey stared at her patient. What could she use to extract the lead from Bear Claw's shoulder? What she wouldn't give for her father's bag, his instruments. She turned to the man's wife. "Has he been doctored at all?"

Kwan translated, and Abbey was glad. Her grasp of the Onondaga language wasn't good enough that it would come easy to her in such a serious situation. The woman replied in rapid Onondaga.

"Yes. He has seen the shaman," Kwan said.

Abbey frowned. "What did this shaman do?"

Knife-Woman looked to Kwan for understanding. He explained what Abbey wanted to know, and she answered that she had no idea what had been done for Bear Claw.

"Who is the shaman?"

"My father. Silver Fox," Kwan said.

"Would you get him? I need to find out what medicine he used on the wound." Abbey felt a little better knowing that the shaman was Silver Fox. She had great respect for the gentle man.

Kwan, unwilling to leave Abbey's side, sent one of the braves of the Deer clan to find Silver Fox. "You can help him?"

"I don't know," Abbey whispered. "I can only try."

Knife-Woman, perhaps sensing Abbey's uncertainty, began to argue against the help of the white woman captive. Her rapid-fire Iroquoian tongue sounded angry and loud.

Abbey saw Kwan's face darken as the woman continued to rant and rave. Her chest tightened. What if she did something wrong? What if because of her Bear Claw died? "Kwan? What is she saying?"

The sachem scowled. "She is afraid to let a *Yen'-gees* touch her husband. Her man is sick, maybe dying, because of the *Yen'-gees*. Because of the *Yen'-gees*, one of her clan's daughters has gone from this earth."

"A woman was killed? They killed a woman?" Abbey felt the blood drain from her face.

"It was many moons ago." Kwan refused to look at her. "The English colonel, Breck-ing-ridge, came and killed many of us—many women and children." His jaw clenched, and Abbey could see his pulse throbbing near his left temple. He faced her, his expression a mirror of anger and pain. "Our people had done nothing! Nothing! Yet the *Yen'-gees* had hurt them, taken their lives. Bear Claw and Knife-Woman lost someone they cared for much. Two summers have come and gone, but the hurt remains. That is why she fears to have you—a *Yen'-gees*—touch her husband."

When Kwan was done, Abbey was trembling. She wasn't God! For all she knew, only a miracle might save the Onondaga brave. How could she help him, knowing that his life—and perhaps her life—hung in the balance? "Kwan—maybe I shouldn't . . ."

"You are afraid?" Kwan said softly.

Abbey nodded. "I'm not a physician . . . only a physician's daughter . . . and we've no proper tools." She grabbed hold of his arm. "What if I do something to make him worse? What if he dies?"

Kwan glanced at Knife-Woman. "You think you can help him?"

"I thought so . . . but I don't know anymore."

He ordered Knife-Woman away to wait, to the opposite side of the longhouse where she won't distract Abbey or make her nervous.

He then addressed the women he loved. "You will do what you can," Kwan said. "Kwan will help you. No one will harm you if Bear Claw dies."

He held Abbey's gaze, infusing her with a new confidence and warmth. Clearly, he believed in her. The knowledge gave Abbey courage and strength.

She gave him a wobbly smile. "I'll need a knife—a small one . . . not that monstrosity of Bear Claw's."

Lips twitching at her choice of words, Kwan inclined his head and sought out the proper tool. When he handed her the instrument, she said, "Kwan . . . I'll have you by my side. Bear Claw is unconscious, but when I begin to dig for the lead, he is going to hurt like hell and may awaken. I'll need you to hold him down." She swallowed hard. "So he doesn't cause further injury . . ."

Beaver Dancing returned with the jug of whiskey, handing it to Kwan while casting a look of hatred in Abbey's direction. Kwan scolded the hostile youth severely. The boy looked stunned and then crestfallen as he went to sit on the other side of the longhouse where he'd been ordered to keep his mother company.

Abbey stared at the knife, saw it shake within her trembling fingers.

"What else you need?" Kwan said tersely.

Gathering her wits about her, Abbey got back to the matter at hand. "Tweezers! God, how can I do this without something to grab hold of the shot with!"

"Tweezers," Kwan echoed.

Abbey demonstrated the working action of the instrument with her fingers. "To pluck out the bullet."

Kwan had a sudden mental image of a tiny metal instrument . . . a memory from his English youth. What did they have that would work like these tweezers he remembered? "Wait!" he said. "I find you tweezers."

Before Abbey could voice her astonishment, he was gone from the longhouse and within minutes was back again. "Here."

Abbey took the rough tool. It was a thin piece of copper—perhaps an awl hammered flat and bent in half or maybe the first stage of an Onondaga arm or wrist band. She squeezed it, testing its strength. It was a far cry from her father's precision instruments, but it was better than just her fingers or the knife, which were the only other choices Abbey had.

"This might work," she said, smiling briefly. "Thank you."

She set the copper "tweezers" on the storage platform, within easy reach.

"What do I do?" Kwan asked.

"Whatever I tell you when I tell you," Abbey said. Then, white-faced, she raised the knife and bent over her patient.

Chapter 16

"I can't do this," she gasped. Abbey trembled from head to toe as she held the knife above Bear Claw's shoulder. "I can't see! It's too dark!"

Kwan caught her hand, his fingers caressing. He held her gaze. "I get you light." She felt his tender touch as he gave someone a command.

Tears stung her eyes; she wanted to sob out aloud. *How can I do this? Please don't make me do this.*

"You can help." Kwan's quiet voice pierced her wall of growing panic. He smiled a warm, gentle smile that made Abbey feel all warm and fuzzy inside.

Silver Fox arrived then, his brow furrowed, as he approached. "You call me, my son?"

Kwan nodded. "Ab-bey . . . she needs to know what magic you worked on Bear Claw."

The old man's eyes grew sad. "Silver Fox worked no great magic, Great Arrow. He did what a shaman does. He blew the burning ashes over Bear Claw's body, calling him back to life. He burned the tobacco, calling on the spirits to heal. He called on

206

the False Faces to help."

"What—what did he say?" Abbey asked anxiously.

"He knows not of your medicine. He called on our spirit gods . . . that is all."

The Iroquois brave returned with a burning torch. Abbey saw it and was satisfied. Held near Bear Claw's head, it would afford ample light for the delicate operation. "I'll need something to stitch closed the wound," she said. Kwan nodded and then murmured something to the brave.

The brave returned with quill needle and rough thread. Abbey shook her head. "That won't do." When Kwan raised his eyebrows in question, she said, "Infection." She brushed back a lock of hair. "I'll have to cauterize the wound."

Kwan climbed onto the platform to position himself for the task of holding the patient down. Earlier, Silver Fox had taken the torch from the brave, and now he held it aloft Bear Claw's head. Behind them on the far side of the longhouse, members of the False Face Society sang and prayed and shook their rattles.

The first touch of the knife brought little reaction from Bear Claw. Abbey probed more deeply, and he struggled against Kwan's hold, moaning in pain. Sweat broke out on Abbey's brow as she carefully drew aside torn tissue with the knife. Blood oozed out, riveting down the patient's chest, staining Abbey's fingers. She bit the inside of her mouth, trying to ignore Bear Claw's thrashings, his groans of suffering. Finally, the piece of lead was exposed enough for extraction.

Using the copper tweezers along with her two

fingers, Abbey sought for a grip on the lead ball. The shape of the bullet gave her little to grab a hold of. Fortunately, the ball wasn't lodged in the bone as she'd first thought; it was cradled in between. The shot moved at each touch; Abbey's concern was how to lift it without creating more damage to the shoulder area. Bear Claw would need the use of his arm if he lived. Abbey tried not to think of that now; her main concern was with improving the man's chances for survival.

Kwan murmured to her through the entire procedure, encouraging her, soothing her with his low husky voice. If she hadn't fallen in love with him already, she would have right then. She was awed and touched by his faith, his confidence, in her. His deep tones were like a lifeline to someone floundering in a dark, angry sea.

Abbey was able to maneuver the bullet free, using the knife, tweezers, and her fingers. Relief brought tears to her eyes as she held up the piece of shot.

We did it! Abbey looked at Kwan with love, knowing that without him, she would never have found the courage to continue . . . to save a life.

Kwan smiled at her, his gaze full of pride for her accomplishment. *You* did it, his eyes seemed to say. It was a special moment, shared by two people who worked together to do something wonderful.

But the danger wasn't over. The bullet was free, but Abbey needed to close the hole.

Bear Claw's blood had slowed; miraculously, he'd lost little of the precious lifeflow. Abbey asked for the whiskey jug. Unstopping the vessel, she asked for a small bowl and proceeded to pour out a portion of the dark liquid.

"Kwan," she murmured, her gaze drifting to the tattoo on Bear Claw's breast, "this is going to hurt him. Hold tight—please. We've come too far for us to lose him."

He nodded and fortified his grip. Abbey tipped the bowl, spilling a little of the whiskey into the wound; and as expected, Bear Claw stiffened and cried out and then struggled. She continued to cleanse the cut, but it wasn't easy to ignore Bear Claw's pain. She stopped when she was satisfied that she had done everything possible to lessen the chances of infection. Finally, the warrior went slack.

"I should stitch the wound," she murmured, "but I haven't the proper tools." She bit her lip. "I need a hot ember."

"Get it for her," Kwan said to the Iroquois brave.

The Indian handed her the coal in a thick piece of tanned animal skin. "The cut needs to be closed," she said, meeting Kwan's glance. "I'll have to burn the tissue."

She proceeded to do so only after explaining the procedure and obtaining consent from Knife-Woman. Abbey felt calm and steady as she carefully cauterized the bullet hole. The warrior's face contorted with the sizzle of his raw flesh.

Finally, Abbey finished, carefully removing the coal and setting it aside where no one could get burned.

Reaction set in as she moved away from the bed. Abbey started to shake violently; she couldn't control it.

"*O-ka-o,*" Strong male arms surrounded her

shoulders, and she felt the instant comfort of Kwan's presence. "Come." He tried to lead her from the longhouse.

Abbey protested. "Bear Claw . . ."

"He will be all right. You have done much for him." He had clasped her to his breast, and his breath stirred her hair, his deep voice rumbled above her ear. "Come, *O-ka-o*. It is over." He paused, and his next words sounded thick, emotional to Abbey's hearing. "*Nee-yah-weh'-ha.* Thank you."

She looked up to meet his gaze, studying his attractive face through a haze of tears. "*Nee-yah-weh'-ha,*" she echoed. "I couldn't have done it without you, Kwan." A lump rose to clog her throat. She blinked up at him and smiled. "You are a great man, Kwan Kahaiska." *And I love you.*

He nodded his thanks, and it seemed to Abbey that he appeared strangely vulnerable at that moment. He was suddenly all brisk and superior male as he led her away from the longhouse.

Abbey lay awake, staring at the shelf above her platform in Spring Rain's cubicle. The village was sleeping. It had been a trying, sorrowful day, but there had been joys, too. The joy of Summer Thunder's daughters' return. The joy of knowing Bear Claw was on his way to recovery. The joy of seeing Kwan again . . .

She'd missed a chance to escape. But she realized now that when the opportunity presented itself she'd felt no great desire to escape. The British soldiers' brutal attack had shocked her, horrified her. Still, if she had really wanted to go . . .

Kwan feels something for me. The thought played itself over and over again in her mind, and she knew why she'd elected to stay behind. To help the children—yes. And because she didn't want to leave Kwan.

She felt that Kwan cared for her, despite the fact that he'd done little to show he cared since they'd left the house of Bear Claw. Abbey couldn't forget the tenderness in his touch as he held her hand . . . the warmth of his gaze as he gave her the courage to go on . . . the heat of Kwan's surrounding arm as he led her away from her patient.

She yearned for his nearness . . . his touch . . . with a passion she'd never experienced before meeting him.

Kwan had taken her from Bear Claw's bedside and outside where he seated her by the fire burning in the village center. He'd brought her food, insisting she eat, watching to make sure she finished what he'd brought; then he'd returned her to Spring Rain. By that time, the sun had set, and the light had turned to darkness. The children had been tucked up in their bed furs, and the Indians had gathered in clans in their longhouses.

Spring Rain had greeted her with a warmth that had surprised Abbey. She'd been so disappointed with Kwan's departure that Abbey hadn't noticed the change in the matron's attitude at first. Soon, it had become obvious to her that all of the Onondagas treated her differently. She was no longer ignored as slave. Tonight, all of the clan members had gone out of their way to speak to her, even if just to wish

211

her a pleasant sleep.

Abbey was somewhat confused by the change, but pleased. Kwan was the one person she'd hoped would regard her in a different light. And he had . . . for a while. The bond between them while they worked together on Bear Claw had been real. She'd never before felt so close to another human being. That she had forged such a feeling with an Indian—a savage— might have shocked her at one time, but not now. Not since she had come to know these Iroquois Onondagas. They were people . . . just like her. They had hopes and dreams . . . and wanted to live happily and in peace.

Could she dare hope to have a future here? To share a life with Kwan? And what of Jamie? She still longed to find him, to ensure his happiness and deliver her father's message. If God had been good to them both, then perhaps Jamie's fate was better than what she'd first imagined. She had found the Indians to be less cruel and vicious than she'd believed . . . perhaps Jamie had too.

She tried not to think of what Evening Sky had told her . . . that Jamie might have been taken by Mo- hawks . . . tortured and killed.

Evening Sky had said that Kwan would be the one to help her, that through him she might be able to obtain Jamie's rescue. Should she go to Kwan and ask him? Would he deny his help or willingly agree?

Thoughts of her brother's rescue triggered mixed emotions within Abbey. She wanted to be reunited with Jamie again, but at the same time she wondered how their reunion would affect her life. Would Jamie wish to return to Philadelphia where he could continue his silversmith apprenticeship?

She wanted to be with Kwan. If Jamie wanted her to go back with him, how would she feel about leaving Kwan? And would Kwan even care if she left?

The longhouse interior was in darkness. The only firelight this night was on the far end of the building, far from Spring Rain's cubicle where Abbey lay. She felt nothing but curiosity when she detected movement at the door near her end. It was only when the figure came closer that her heart picked up speed. The way he moved made her breath still, her body come alive, for when her senses became alert she knew who it was immediately.

"Kwan." It was barely a whisper on her lips.

He was suddenly there, standing above her, gazing down at her with his hot silver gaze. *"O-ka-o,"* he mouthed silently. He gestured for her to follow him.

She didn't hesitate. She rose carefully and like a sleepwalker drifted behind him . . . from the longhouse and into the summer night.

They kept speechless as they glided past the row of longhouses, moved past the gate and the warrior-guard. Kwan nodded to Night Eagle, making him aware of their presence. Then, he led Abbey down the forest trail, toward the shimmering waters of the great lake. With each step, Abbey's pulse raced faster.

Kwan reached the shoreline first. There, he stopped and faced her with flaming silver eyes. His hands rose to the fastening of his breechclout. With thundering heart, Abbey watched him undo the ties. Her breasts tingled with anticipation; the nipples grew erect, tiny buds of sensation that strained against her tunic.

His loincloth fell away, revealing his taut, rock-hard thighs . . . his manhood which was erect with desire. He beckoned her closer. "Ab-bey. *O-ka-o, gah-jee.*"

Swallowing hard, Abbey glided toward him, her blood roaring through her veins. She loved him. There was no shame in what they were about to do. Her body hummed with increased feeling as she moved closer. Her whole being cried out with her longing to love, to join with, this magnificent man.

Kwan opened his arms, and she flowed into his embrace. "Woman," he muttered in Onondaga, "I couldn't stay away." He set her back to study her.

Abbey caught her breath at his smoldering look, closed her eyes and swayed toward him, mouth raised and lips parted. She sighed softly at the first touch of his male lips, her sigh quickly becoming a deep groan as he deepened the kiss . . . and the ecstasy with gentle, yet urgent caresses . . . with quietly spoken love words.

"Kwan. Kwan." In her joy, she murmured his name over and over. She clung to his hard form, her fingers exploring, fondling his warm flesh. Their caresses became frantic with their desire.

Kwan grabbed her tunic, pulling it off, staring at her hotly as he threw it onto the shore. "You are beau-ti-ful, Ab-bey. So soft and white . . . I want you." He touched her secret moistness.

"Yes," she gasped. "Touch me. Love me!"

But Kwan was in no hurry now. He enjoyed the vision of her naked beauty, discovering it with his hands . . . his lips . . . his tongue. He lifted her easily. Carrying her in his strong arms, he waded into the water. He lowered her ever so slowly into the gentle waves which lapped and licked at their sensitized skin. Abbey inhaled Kwan's scent, enjoying the wonderful, familiar, earthy male odor.

She stared at him, noting the tiny little things about him that pleased her . . . the way the water glistened on Kwan's copper skin . . . the glow of his eyes as he gazed at her . . . the way his breath grew labored after kissing her and his heart thundered against his chest muscles at her touch.

"Kiss me," she begged.

Kwan obeyed, capturing her lips tenderly, before bruising her with his mouth. She clutched his shoulders, gripping him with surprising strength. He groaned and shuddered and held her tighter.

Then, he was nibbling on her neck, and she was arching backward, thrusting her breasts up and out of the water. Kwan stared at the wet, shimmering globes . . . the contrast of dark areola against smooth white flesh. With a deep-throated moan, he bent his head to suckle the pert nipples. Gasping, Abbey held him to her breasts, tinglingly aware of the way his long, sable hair brushed against her bare skin.

The water was warm . . . pleasant. Abbey allowed herself to drift, buoyed by the waves . . . Kwan's strength.

Kwan shifted, grabbed her ankles, pulling her against him, wrapping her legs about his waist. She felt his tumescent staff bump up against her thigh. Muttering in Onondaga, he readjusted their positions for joining.

His tip probed her pulsating warmth. Abbey reached down between them for his shaft, rubbing the head until his whole body quivered, and then she guided it home.

Once they were joined, Kwan began to move. The water heightened the intimacy, dipping, stroking every curve and cranny. With his heels planted firmly in the lake bed, his hands beneath her buttocks, he orchestrated the rhythm of their lovemaking.

Abbey felt him deep inside her, felt his fingers squeezing her supple flesh, and she whimpered and moaned before she grabbed his head, forcing her mouth to his lips. She thrust her tongue past his teeth and mimicked the cadence of their lower torsos.

Kwan groaned against her mouth, his muscles stiffening as he ground against her. With a harsh cry, he climaxed, pumping his seed into Abbey at the exact moment she sobbed out her own release.

They floated for a time, parting only long enough to come together breast to breast . . . belly to belly. The effort of making love in the lake had cost them.

"You are like a wild woman, *O-ka-o*," he growled. His silver eyes twinkled with warmth and amusement before he lay back in the water and closed his eyes. "Kwan is tired. You have taken his strength."

"Oh?" Abbey regarded him with sudden mischief. "I am stronger than you . . . the great sachem . . . the mighty hunter of the Onondaga?"

At that his head shot upward. Her lips curving in a sly smile, Abbey caught hold of his penis, worrying the male tip until it grew hard and moist.

Kwan sucked his breath, astonished at how easily she had made him ready again. "Ab-bey," he rasped.

"Yes, Kwan. Oh, yes . . ."

They slipped from the rippling waters and onto a

secluded grassy spot along the shore.

A while later their joint moans of ecstasy rent the stillness of the summer night.

Gesturing with her hands, Spring Rain spoke to Abbey in rapid Onondaga while Evening Sky stood beside her, smiling.

"What does she want?" Abbey asked. "She's talking too fast. I can't understand her."

"She does so, because she is excit-ted. Happy," Evening Sky said.

Abbey grew curious. "About what?"

"She has decided to make you daughter instead of slave."

"Daughter?" the Englishwoman echoed. "You mean she wants to adopt me?" The Indian maiden nodded. "But I am a grown woman!"

"It matters not. Two summers past, the *Yen'-gees* took away Spring Rain's daughter. It is her right to replace her. Because of your goodness and courage, she has chosen you."

Spring Rain murmured to Evening Sky. When Abbey looked at them questioningly, Evening Sky said, "Spring Rain wishes to know if her decision displeases you."

The Englishwoman smiled, and tears filled her eyes as she thought of her own dead parents. "How can I be displeased? Spring Rain pays me a great honor with her decision."

Her friend quickly translated Abbey's words. Spring Rain grinned and pulled Abbey into her arms for a hug.

"Tomorrow, Spring Rain will tell the head matron about her wish."

Abbey nodded. "And then I'll be a daughter . . . just like that?"

Evening Sky smiled. "No. There will be a special ceremony. You will be asked to join us." She paused. "The women will bathe you."

Bathe her? One look at her friend's face, and Abbey realized why Evening Sky had hesitated before telling all that would transpire. She would have to submit to bathing with the community of women. She would have to undress fully before the village matrons. "Will I have to give up my tunic . . . afterward?"

The girl's lips twitched. "This I know not. I believe they let you keep it if it pleases you."

Abbey breathed a sigh of relief. "All right then. If I don't have to go about the village half-naked afterward, I'll consent to the public bathing."

"Good."

Spring Rain nodded, smiling. "Good," she mimicked.

And Abbey laughed, feeling happy.

Chapter 17

Kwan sat at the shore of the lake, staring out across the sun-dappled water. He had seen Abbey back to the longhouse hours ago, insisting on returning her before they fell asleep and the others within the village awakened. Troubled by the day's events and his feelings for Abbey, he'd been unable to sleep. He'd come back here instead . . . where he had been sitting alone with his thoughts since.

Abbey. What was he to do? She was slave, the enemy. He was sachem, chief. There was much about her to admire, but every way he looked at it, their relationship was wrong.

Why did she come back? To bring back Summer Thunder's daughters, she'd said. Why did she take them in the first place? Because of her uncle? Because of Breckingridge? Had it been his idea to kidnap the children? Had Abbey been unable to go through with her uncle's plan?

The whole thing didn't make sense to him. Breckingridge was still alive. Abbey was within the village. If she could have left the children without being caught, would she have done so?

Having failed to get his niece, Breckingridge would be back for her; Kwan knew this as surely as he knew O-wee-soo was head matron of his tribe.

"What troubles you, my son?"

Startled, Kwan spun around. Silver Fox stood a few yards from the shoreline, his gaze full of concern as he observed his son. "Have I said I am troubled?" Kwan said, glancing back toward the lake.

The ground crunched beneath moccasined feet as the old man approached. "You do not have to say it; this I can see with my own two eyes."

"The *Yen'-gees*—they will be back."

Silver Fox sighed. "I know. They have lost what they came for. The white woman."

Kwan flashed him a glance. "I do not understand. Why did she return?"

"Perhaps her heart lies here within our village."

Kwan's heart thumped. "She is the enemy. She is slave."

"Is she? Her actions say this is not true."

The sachem frowned. "She is Breck-ing-ridge's niece!"

His father shrugged. "You have forgotten many things. You were once one of them. You were a *Yen'-gees*."

"I was but a child."

"She is a woman . . . with tenderness in her heart. The white woman saved three of our people. Summer Thunder's two girls and Bear Claw."

Kwan nodded. "How is Bear Claw?" He worried for Abbey's safety. Should Bear Claw die, he would

220

try to protect her against his people's anger, but would the Onondaga listen to their sachem? They had lost much at the hands of the English. It was their right to see justice done.

"He is resting, my son," Silver Fox said. "He appears well."

Inclining his head, Kwan closed his eyes. *I must thank the spirits*, he thought.

Silver Fox sat down beside his son, observing Kwan intently. "There is to be a special ceremony today."

"Oh?" Kwan was curious. "I have heard nothing of this."

"It was decided when the sun first rose in the sky . . . by O-wee-soo and the other women of our camp."

"To welcome back our young daughters?" He smiled, remembering Summer Thunder's joy at seeing her little girls again.

"To welcome into the tribe a new daughter."

Kwan felt a jolt. "The white woman."

Silver Fox nodded. "Ab-bey. This pleases you not, Great Arrow?"

His gaze on the rippling water, the sachem shrugged. "It matters to me not."

"I think it does."

Kwan shot him a look of surprise. "How so?"

"She is Breck-ing-ridge's niece. The man did you a wrong. He took away your woman. He hardened your heart against all whites."

"That is not true!"

"Then you should be happy for the white woman. Spring Rain has taken her to replace her lost

221

daughter." Silver Fox rose from the ground. "Will you accept Abbey as one of us? Forget that she was once *Yen'-gees?*" He started down the trail back to the village, calling over his shoulder as he left, "Think long and hard on this, Great Arrow. It is time to go forward, forget the woman you once thought to make wife."

Kwan frowned. It was true that Breckingridge had taken Morning Flower from this earth, but it was also true that he had finished mourning for the Indian maiden. His hatred of the English colonel stemmed not from her death alone, but for all the deaths of the Onondaga, all the Indians that the officer had killed.

He should never have gone to Abbey's longhouse last night. But he couldn't stay away. His desire for her was like a fire in his soul; he ached every moment with it. He'd hoped that by having her one last time he'd be able to conquer the weakness and put the white woman from his mind . . . his heart.

His time with her had only strengthened his hunger for her.

Kwan heard a woman's giggle and then the chatting of several females. The women were on the trail, coming to the lake. To bathe, he realized. Not wanting to be seen, he rose quickly and fled into the woods, taking refuge in a dense copse.

It was a private moment; he shouldn't be watching, but something kept him there. *Abbey*. He had no idea if she was with them, yet hopeful, he stayed. Kwan felt again like the naughty young boy who'd spied on the naked Atahkwa while she swam.

They came from the trail, laughing and singing, women of all ages and shapes. Abbey was there, her golden coloring, her full length tunic, making her stand out from the others. She was quiet . . . appearing almost nervous.

And then Kwan understood. *The adoption ceremony*, he thought. The women were here at the lake to make Abbey an Onondaga daughter.

Abbey felt nervous, but strangely excited by the Iroquois rite of adoption. She had some understanding of the procedure, having questioned Evening Sky. She knew the ceremony began at the lake, where Abbey would be stripped from her garment and submerged in the cool crystal-clear water.

It was the first time Abbey had consented to the communal bath, and she was self-conscious about being naked. The women, she knew, were curious about the white woman.

Earlier, she'd been pleased to see Rachel and the two captives among the group. As they neared the shore, Abbey caught Rachel's glance, saw the German woman looking at her oddly. She smiled, and expressionless, Rachel turned away. Her friend's behavior hurt. Was she wrong in agreeing to the adoption? Abbey wondered. Rachel's look had made her feel like a traitor.

Muttering earnestly in their Onondaga tongue, the women formed a circle around their daughter-to-be. Spring Rain came forward. As new mother, it was her right to uncloth Abbey, to take her into the lake.

Abbey felt the cool air brush her bare skin, hugged herself with her arms, as Spring Rain led her into the water and shoved her under, head and all. Surprised,

Abbey came up sputtering. Her shocked cry turned into a gasp of pain as Spring Rain and the other women scrubbed her down with sand and scouring rushes. The matrons cackled and chortled as they rubbed and dunked Abbey, leaving no place of her body unattended. Even her hair had special attention. When they were done, Abbey was pink and tingling from head to toe. Embarrassed, she wanted to disappear into the forest, but the women, she noted, seemed matter-of-fact about the whole process.

Satisfied that Abbey had been cleansed properly, Spring Rain led her from the lake where the matrons patted her dry with soft animal skins and then gave her a new tunic—one of fine white doeskin. The garment was beautiful, embroidered with dyed deer hair, the multi-colored pattern resembling little curls. The bottom hem of the tunic was fringed and long, nearly to Abbey's ankles. The skin felt soft and comfortable against her pinkened flesh.

The women worked on Abbey's hair and face next. After carefully untangling her blonde tresses, Spring Rain parted the hair into two sections. One matron came up, carrying a bowl of sunflower-seed oil. Spring Rain, Abbey was grateful to note, spoke rapidly and shook her head. Apparently, Spring Rain did not want her new daughter's golden hair oiled, which was just fine with Abbey. However, the new mother did consent to having Abbey's part painted a bright red, after she and Evening Sky had braided each hair hank.

Then, Evening Sky used a fluffy cattail to powder Abbey's face with a reddish powder made from dry-rotted pine wood, while Woman With No Heart rubbed Abbey's cheeks with red berry juice.

Dressed and painted and with the funny feeling that the forest had eyes that were watching her, Abbey went with the women back to the great ceremonial longhouse in the village. At Spring Rain's instructions, she sat on a rush mat on the floor along with the other women. The longhouse began to fill with the rest of the tribe.

Kwan was the last to enter the longhouse. Abbey's heart seemed to stop as he took the empty place directly across from her. She couldn't keep from looking at him. The memory of his lovemaking made her face heat; she was glad for the red-berry coloring on her cheeks.

His features appeared unreadable. Abbey wondered what he was thinking. Did he approve of the adoption? Did it matter to him one way or the other?

She stared at him, trying to get him to look at her, but he refused to meet her gaze, and she grew frustrated . . . and angry.

Why won't he look at me? Abbey hugged herself with her arms, feeling a sudden chill. *Why won't he acknowledge the passion we shared . . . the love?*

Spring Rain rose from her mat, gesturing for Abbey to rise with her. The laughter and conversation within the longhouse ceased abruptly. Kwan stood and addressed the gathering.

Abbey understood little of what Kwan said. She heard Spring Rain's name and then the Onondaga word for daughter. Watching Kwan speak, his strangely dispassionate tone and his face clear of emotion, Abbey felt a pain in her mid-section. The sachem looked anything but happy to welcome her into the Onondaga family. In fact, she thought her lover looked more than little displeased.

Having finished his speech, Kwan sat down. Spring Rain caught Abbey by the shoulder and began to lead her around the large room, past all members of the tribe.

"Anikha Sagoha. Anikha Sagoha." Spring Rain chanted the words over and over again as she steered Abbey about the crowded longhouse. When the two women had circled the longhouse, returning to the point where they'd started, Silver Fox stood and in a loud, booming voice, shouted, *"Wa-a-ah!"*

The people shrieked back, *"Wuh! Wuh! Waaah!"*

Silver Fox came from his place and took Abbey by the arm. He escorted her up and down the longhouse floor, singing as he walked. And the Indians chanted, *"Heh! Heh! Heh!"* in time with Silver Fox and Abbey's steps until finally the old man stopped.

"Un-hay-yay-way wuh!" an Indian called, and Abbey turned, knowing it was Kwan.

The Iroquois tribal members responded with another strange cry. Then several others spoke or sang, while the others answered. Abbey listened, in a daze.

Kwan came to her when the speeches and singing were done, placed a hand on her shoulder. *"Anikha Sagoha!"* he said, and Abbey tingled at his touch.

"Anikha Sagoha!" the Indians shouted, and the ceremony was over.

The sachem withdrew, and Abbey felt a loss. She was overwhelmed by both the ceremony and Kwan's strange behavior.

Anikha Sagoha. She must have been given a new name. An Onondaga name. Her suspicion was confirmed by Evening Sky as she accompanied her new mother and friend from the longhouse.

"It means Sun Daughter," Evening Sky explained. Pleased, Abbey knew it was because of her light hair. She felt proud to be an Onondaga. *From slave to daughter.* She thought how much things had changed in the month and a half's time since her capture, how differently she regarded these people.

"Welcome, daughter," Spring Rain said.

And Abbey grinned.

Chapter 18

"But, Colonel," the young man exclaimed, "the savages will kill us!" He flinched at the look on his commanding officer's face. "Ah . . . what I mean, sir, is—"

"I know what you mean, lieutenant!" Breckingridge bellowed. "You're a bloody coward, that's what you are!"

Terrington blanched. "No! That's not true." He wished he could bite back the words the moment he saw the colonel's look.

"I'm happy to hear you say that, lieutenant. You'll be in charge of the attack. We'll leave at first light." The commander prowled about the campsite like a caged bear. "My niece is somewhere within that village." He stopped, fixed the younger officer with a glance. "I want her rescued, and I expect you to be the one who brings her back safely."

The young officer had no other choice but to nod. "Right, sir."

Having barely escaped with their lives, the English

army had set up camp deep in the forest. There were ten men left of the original twenty-three. Several of the survivors were wounded; it was for those men's care that Breckingridge had reluctantly postponed a second attack. Some of the others suffered mental injuries, wounds too deep to see. Terrington prayed that the rest of them would leave the village alive. He wondered if he'd ever escape the nightmare of what he'd recently seen.

"And, lieutenant, I want you to find Captain Smythe." Breckingridge cursed. "Damn, but I miss his company and quick wit!"

Terrington thought of Smythe's capture, knew there wasn't a hope in hell that the soldier was still living. The last thing he wanted to do was to fight Iroquois . . . the fearsome "man-eaters." They'd need reinforcements, he mused.

"What of the chief? Shouldn't we return to the fort for more men?"

The colonel frowned. "Kwan Kahaiska? Save the sorry bastard for me. *I* want the pleasure of skinning the red savage alive. And as for returning to fort . . . I suppose a few days won't matter. Yes, I believe we'll return to Fort Michaels for more troops."

The sachem saw the runner arrive at the gate and went to meet him. Kwan had sent Crooked Ear with a white wampum belt for each of the other sachems of the Onondaga tribe. He was calling together a meeting of chiefs to discuss unrest within the Seneca members of the League. The time of the Great Council Fire was still to come, but Kwan thought to

229

meet with his tribesmen first. The presence of the French at the Green Corn Festival had distressed him.

"Crooked Ear." Kwan waved the brave into his hut. He took a seat and gestured for the young brave to sit across from him.

"Our People ask about the meeting of Onondagas," Crooked Ear said. "Why do you not call together all of the League?"

"What did you tell them?" The sachem handed the warrior his filled tobacco pipe.

"I told them of our Festival of Green Corn . . . of the two Frenchmen and He-Who-Comes-In-The-Night." The brave accepted the pipe with a nod of thanks and proceeded to light it.

"They will come?"

Crooked Ear inclined his head. "When the moon rises full in the night sky, our leaders will leave their villages. They come, because Great Arrow has willed it." He paused to remove something from his belt pouch. "Wolf of the Forest sends you *Ot-ko-a*." He handed Kwan a string of shell beads. "He says it was given to him by He-Who-Comes-In-The-Night."

Kwan was startled. "This is true?" He stared at the wampum within his fingers.

Crooked Ear nodded while he drew deeply from the tobacco pipe. "Perhaps the message of the *Ot-ko-a* will give the Onondaga answers. The brave has sent these beads to many of our chiefs."

"But not to me," Kwan murmured thoughtfully. The knowledge didn't sit well with him. Why would the brave send beads of wampum to only some of the Onondaga sachems? Was the Seneca planning to go to war? Had the warrior sent beads to those he thought might side with him? If so, how many belts of wampum had he sent? How many chiefs were listening to He-Who-Comes-In-The-Night's call to war?

Kwan was glad he had called for the meeting. The need for discussion was stronger than ever now. "You have done well, Crooked Ear."

The brave inclined his head in solemn acknowledgment.

"You will come to the council meeting. I will have you tell all that you've seen and heard among our People."

"*Nyoh,*" the young warrior replied. *So be it.*

"Sun Daughter," Spring Rain said, "you seem sad. Are you not happy within our family?"

Abbey glanced up from the giant mortar, her hands continuing the steady up and down movements that ground the dried corn beneath the wooden pestle. She gave a slight smile. Her new Indian mother had spoken half in broken English, half in slowly enunciated Onondaga so that Abbey would understand. "I am not unhappy here, *Uk no hah.*" She stilled the pestle and scooped up the corn meal, allowing it to sift through her fingers. "You've been good to me. The People have been good to me . . ."

"Then what is it, *Ex aa?*" Spring Rain put down her quillwork. Rising from the ground, she approached where Abbey worked. "Is it Stone-Face? Is he unkind to you?"

Abbey shook her head. "It's not Stone-Face." To her surprise, the fierce-looking tattooed warrior had seemed to accept her as a member of his clan. In fact, all the Indians had accepted her happily . . . except Kwan . . . She was unaware that she'd voiced her thoughts.

"Our chief has not welcomed you?" Spring Rain had tensed. "I will speak to his grandmother," she said angrily. "O-wee-soo will see that Great Arrow changes his ways!"

"No!" Abbey exclaimed, feeling a prickle of alarm. The last thing she needed was for someone to interfere with her relationship with Kwan. After all, the man had a right to his feelings, didn't he? If he saw her as *Yen'-gees*, who was she to argue with him? She *was* English born and raised; there was nothing she could do to change that.

"It is time for Great Arrow to forget. My first daughter is gone; we cannot bring her back to life."

"Daughter?" It was the first time that Abbey had a inkling of an involvement between Kwan and Spring Rain's deceased daughter.

Pain darkened Spring Rain's features. "We do not talk of our dead, but since you were once *Yen'-gees*, I will explain." She grabbed the pestle from Abbey's hand, set it down into the mortar gently. "Come."

She took Abbey into the longhouse where she rummaged through the things stored on the top shelf. With a triumphant cry, she found what appeared to Abbey to be a copper wrist bracelet.

"Here." Spring Rain pressed the piece into Abbey's hand. "This belonged to Morning Flower." She paused, her eyes glistening with tears.

232

"My daughter."

With mixed emotions, Abbey studied the shining wristlet. "It's beautiful," she mumbled.

The matron nodded. "Morning Flower was beauti-ful. Very young. Sixteen summers." She paused, and Abbey looked at her, aware of a feeling of anticipation. "Take," Spring Rain said. "You are Onondaga daughter now. Band belongs to you."

"No," Abbey said. "I couldn't." But Spring Rain insisted, and so the new daughter was forced to accept the dead girl's bracelet.

Why do I have this sudden image of Kwan and a young girl? Abbey wondered. She recalled Kwan's pain-filled expression when he'd spoken of a relative of Knife-Woman . . . a young woman who'd been killed by Colonel Breckingridge and his men.

"Knife-Woman," she said, "is she of your clan?" She knew that all members of the same clan were considered family. Could Knife-Woman's relative and Spring Rain's daughter be one and the same girl?

"This is not so," the matron said.

For some reason, Abbey felt relieved at the woman's answer.

Spring Rain looked curious. "Why do you ask this?"

"Kwan . . . the sachem . . ." Abbey flushed. "When I doctored Bear Claw . . . he spoke of a young woman. A dead woman . . . murdered by the *Yen'-gees*."

Spring Rain nodded. "Yes, this is Morning Flower. Bear Claw, Knife-Woman's husband, is of the Deer Clan. When the *Yen'-gees* killed my daughter, there was much sorrow in Great Arrow's heart." She met Abbey's gaze. "Great Arrow was to take Morning Flower to wife."

Wife. It was the only word Abbey heard. "Kwan and your daughter were married?"

The old woman shook her head. "Morning Flower was taken away before the wedding ceremony. Still, Great Arrow grieved for her . . . just as he did Atahkwa, his first wife."

Abbey was in shock. Kwan had not only been betrothed before, but married . . . "What happened to Atahkwa?" she breathed.

"She died giving birth . . . to Kwan's son."

She was angry with herself because she was jealous of the two women who had come before her. The poor souls were dead—why should she feel envious of them?

Abbey had a mental image of Kwan making love to another woman—a woman with no face. The knowledge of his intimacy with another hurt her. She knew that while he might not have made love to the young Morning Flower he most definitely had, of course, with his first wife. What was her name? Atahkwa.

Abbey felt a squeezing pain in her stomach. *What was this Atahkwa like? My God, Spring Rain spoke of a son! What of the child? Was he one of the children running naked about camp?* She forced away the painful thought. Still, she was curious to know this child of her lover's.

"You look as if you've seen Big Nose, Sun Daughter," Spring Rain said. "Are you unwell? Should I call the shaman?"

Abbey shook her head. "No. No, I'm fine." *Kwan*

234

was married! "Kwan's son . . ."

Spring Rain clucked her tongue. "Kwan's wife died giving birth to a dead son."

"Oh, no! Poor Kwan . . ." Abbey felt an overpowering surge of sympathy for the mighty sachem. No wonder he looked stern . . . unfeeling. The man had suffered greatly during his young life.

She thought of Kwan's wife . . . of his second love, the young girl Morning Flower. Abbey felt threatened by Kwan's memory of his former loves.

They are gone! an inner voice scolded her. *They are no threat to you!*

No? Abbey thought. *What if he loves one of them still? What if he still mourns for Morning Flower? What if there is an emptiness in his heart that cannot be filled . . . especially by a white woman—a Yen'-gees?*

You will never know if you don't confront him, the voice taunted. *Find him. Talk with him. See if he is as angry with your adoption as you seem to think.*

Abbey nodded. She would have to do that. If she were ever to obtain any happiness in this life, then she would have to take chances . . . even if the end result meant heartbreak.

She smiled in reassurance when she found Spring Rain looking at her with concern. "There is no need to speak with O-wee-soo. I will speak to the chief myself."

The old woman blinked and then smiled in sudden understanding. "You are learning our women's ways—that is good."

Abbey agreed, although she was unsure what the matron's words had meant.

Two days later, the matron elders gathered together for a meeting. Abbey and the other young women of the village weren't invited. Curious, Abbey questioned Evening Sky, who admitted to not knowing what was on the elders' minds.

"May-be they discuss war," Evening Sky suggested. "There's talk among the People. The Seneca are unhappy . . . may-be looking to fight."

Abbey was surprised. It was the first knowledge she'd had of problems within the League of Iroquois Nations. It occurred to her why Kwan had seemed preoccupied of late. Perhaps he wasn't angry with her adoption, perhaps he had his mind filled with the trouble among the Seneca.

"I am surprised that your women discuss war," she said.

Evening Sky raised her eyebrows. "Our women say much on all things. We have much power within the tribe. When the sachem dies, we women choose our next leader. If the living sachem does bad, it is the women who call on him, tell him he's done wrong. The sachem always listens to the matrons. If not, the matrons can replace him."

"I like that!" Abbey laughed, delighted with the women's position within the tribe. "Do you meet on all matters?"

"This is so. If our braves want war, but their mothers think it unwise, then the women band together and work to change the minds of our men."

"Oh? How?"

"If our warriors don't listen, we keep food from

them. If they do not listen still, we keep other things from our braves . . ." Evening Sky blushed. "These things, of course, I have yet to learn about."

Abbey's eyes widened as she understood. The women held back their favors! A small smile played upon her lips. What ingenious creatures these Iroquois women were! She decided she could easily enjoy being an Onondaga wife.

But she couldn't enjoy anything until she could improve her relationship with Kwan. She had yet to talk with him. There just hadn't been the opportunity . . . until now. With the matrons of the village occupied at their meeting, she could seek out the sachem. If she was fortunate, she'd find him somewhere alone . . . somewhere where she could speak freely.

And if I lose the courage to talk with him about us . . . I'll speak to him about finding Jamie. Evening Sky said he would help. Surely, it can only help . . . the fact that I'm now considered an Onondaga.

Abbey frowned. *Unless he hates me for taking Morning Flower's place!*

She spied Kwan leaving the village—apparently unaccompanied. Excusing herself from Evening Sky's presence, Abbey hurried to follow him.

Chapter 19

She caught up with Kwan at the edge of what had once been the Indians' bean field. He was staring at the ruined green plants, his face grim.

Abbey hung back, unsure whether to approach him. She glanced about and saw no one. There would be warrior-guards nearby, but Kwan was otherwise alone. She stepped forward.

"Kwan," she said softly.

He spun at her call, his eyes wild. His expression, a mirror of pain, quickly became unreadable. "Abbey."

Her breath quickened as she studied him. His male beauty set her heart to fluttering each time she set eyes on him. Her gaze went from his unusual silver eyes to his angular nose . . . his sensual lips . . . He wore an odd string of white beans about his neck, a necklace she'd never seen before. The sight of it against his tanned bare chest made him appear more primitive, more savage. He shifted; and she saw the way his arm and chest muscles rippled at the slight movement.

She had a sudden vision of him raised above her, his face passionate, while they made love. Heat warmed her insides. He frowned, and she felt awkward.

"I'm sorry," she said. "I didn't mean to startle you, but we need to talk."

He looked instantly wary.

"Kwan, please . . ."

"Speak."

Is this the same man who made tender love to me at the lake? she thought. Abbey swallowed. "What's wrong?"

He scowled. "I know not what you mean."

It was her turn to frown. "I think you do. You've been acting strangely. Have I done something to offend you?"

He blinked. "Offend?"

"Hurt," she explained. She bit her lip and decided to be frank. "My adoption. I think it bothers you."

"Spring Rain is happy. It is her right to make you daughter."

"Because of Morning Flower."

Kwan tensed. "We do not speak of our dead ones. Who told you this?"

His harsh tone made her flinch. "Spring Rain. She thought I should know." Abbey longed to touch him, to run her fingers across the creases in his brow.

He seemed surprised, thoughtful.

Boldly, she stepped closer. "Why didn't you tell me about Morning Flower?"

He stared at her hard. "It is past, and you were slave."

"I'm not a slave anymore," she said softly. Abbey

gave in to the urge to touch him. She caressed his arm, rubbing her fingers against the hardened muscle. He stiffened and pulled away. Hurt, she gazed at him.

"You were married," she said in a choked voice.

His eyes widened. "Spring Rain?"

Abbey shrugged, unwilling to have him angry with her new Indian mother. She saw his pulse throbbing along his jaw, felt the tension emanating from his taut frame. "Does it matter?"

It was his turn to pretend indifference. "It matters not. It is past."

"Is it?" She grabbed his shoulder, spun him to face her. "Is it!"

Kwan gazed at her with a blank silver gaze, and Abbey was furious. She longed to shake him . . . anger him. She thought any emotion was better than that damned look of indifference!

"What do you want me to tell you?" he asked.

I want you to say you love me . . . more than Atahkwa . . . more than Morning Flower. "The other night . . . why did you come for me? You said you couldn't stay away . . ." She stared at him. Her voice went soft. "Why not?"

He turned away from her. "It matters not."

"Damn you! Why the change? Is it because you think it's wrong that you and a slave made love? That you made love to a *Yen'-gees*?"

Kwan faced her. Something worked in his expression. Finally, he said, "Why did you not go with Breck-ing-ridge?"

So it was the colonel, Abbey thought. "The children," she stammered, unwilling to admit she'd actually thought about escaping. "I couldn't leave the children . . ."

He arched his right eyebrow. "You should have gone. He will be back. Bring many *Yen'-gees*. Danger to our people."

"Maybe he won't come back . . ." But Abbey knew he would. At least, if he believed the Iroquois still had his niece. What if there was some way to get word to the man that his niece, Susie Portsmouth, was with her new husband in the Virginia Colony?

"Can we get him a message?" she asked. "The man wants his niece. If we tell that she's not here . . ."

The sachem scowled. "How can you say this when it is not true?"

"It's true! Susie is in Virginia. I know. I read her letter myself!"

"Susie?" Kwan echoed. He looked puzzled.

"The colonel's niece."

"But you are the colonel's niece."

Abbey blinked. "Me?" She shook her head.

"Sen-dah-no'-gehs! You lie! You came from the *Yen'-gees* house. Many there said you are niece!" His warriors had told him she was taken from the niece's room, and his warriors would not lie to him. Abbey must be the one who lies, he thought.

"I'm not, Kwan . . . really." She had spoken softly, and she touched his arm.

Her blue eyes glistened. Her face seemed sincere, yet he was afraid to believe her. Why couldn't he believe her? He had trusted her with Bear Claw's life. Why not now?

"If you are not Breck-ing-ridge's niece, then who are you?"

"I told you I'm Abbey. Abigail Rawlins from Kent, England."

"What were you doing in Breck-ing-ridge's house?"

She looked guilt-ridden as she looked away.

"Ab-bey?" he prompted.

"I was waiting to see the colonel." She glanced at him then. "I was told he could help me find James—Jamie."

"Jamie? Who is this Jamie?" A man? Not her husband . . . nor her lover, he thought. She was pure when he'd first lain with her. Still, he hated the thought of her being friends with another man.

"My brother," she said, and the tension eased from Kwan's frame. "He was captured by Indians while delivering silver to a family in Pennsylvania. Several people in Philadelphia told me that Colonel Breck-ingridge of Fort Michaels could help me find Jamie. To rescue him. When I got to the fort, though, the colonel wasn't there, but he was due back in few days. I had no money, no place to go, and I was desperate. Then I learned that the colonel was expecting his niece, so I pretended to be her . . . Susie Portsmouth. It was easy, because the servants already thought I was her."

She brushed back several stray golden hairs that had escaped her braids. "I knew my secret would be safe until the colonel's return. I had found a letter on the hall table. Susie Portsmouth wasn't coming. She met someone coming across from England. A planter. She had written her uncle to tell him that she was marrying the man, going to his home."

Abbey grabbed his arm, and this time Kwan didn't

242

pull away. Silence reigned for a long moment as they locked gazes. "I know it was wrong . . . deceitful, but I had no other choice. Don't you see? I had nowhere to go! No money! And I was sure the colonel would understand once he learned the truth."

She swallowed. Now that she knew the nature of the English commander, Abbey wasn't so sure that Breckingridge would have understood. She'd assumed the officer would be courteous, heroic . . . a true English gentleman. Not a murderer of innocent people!

"Why do you tell this?" Kwan said.

"Because . . . you've acted so strangely to me lately, and I thought . . . Damn it, Kwan! You've lain with me twice. Doesn't what we shared mean anything to you?"

He seemed amused, and she felt her blood boil. "You brute! What's so funny!" she said.

"You tricked Breck-ing-ridge." He paused. "Like Onondaga." He grinned, and Abbey's heart tripped.

"Spring Rain tells me I am considered Onondaga now. *Anikha Sagoha,*" she said.

His expression turned solemn. "Sun Daughter."

"Kwan—"

"*Gah'-jee.*"

Come here, he'd said. She experienced a jolt in her stomach. Kwan's gaze seemed different somehow. The silver in his eyes glowed with inner fire. His mouth had softened into a slight smile.

"I'm still English," she stammered, feeling the need to make things clear between them. "You can't change that." She gazed at his mouth, fascinated with its shape, feeling the strongest urge to press her lips there.

He gave her a tender smile. *"Gah'-jee, Anikha Sagoha."* He opened his arms to her. They were standing at the edge of the field, but near the forest woodsline. *"Nay'-toh."*

"Kwan, the guards . . ."

And then the messenger's call came, the interruption seeming an omen from the gods. *"Go'-weh!"*

Kwan stiffened and stepped back from her. "Night Eagle," he acknowledged the brave's approach and then waited patiently for the guard to speak.

The warrior nodded to Abbey, before answering. He turned to Kwan. "O-wee-soo . . . she looks for her grandson. Sends me to find him. She says she must talk now."

Kwan frowned. "Is she all right?"

His gaze sliding toward Abbey, Night Eagle nodded. Abbey thought he was eyeing her strangely.

"Kwan, what is it? Is everything all right?" She had an odd feeling that something momentous was about to happen . . . if it hadn't already.

Kwan turned to her unsmilingly. "O-wee-soo calls me. She says she must speak with me."

"The women were in council," Abbey said. "What were they talking about?"

Kwan shrugged. "With O-wee-soo, one never knows."

"Evening Sky thought they were talking of war."

His eyes flickered. "Evening Sky did not go?" The sachem was thoughtful. He frowned when Abbey shook her head. "This is strange . . ." He took her arm. "Come," he said.

They headed back to the village.

The matrons had gathered in the village proper, seated themselves in a small circle. Outside the ring, the children played with the dogs while the men within camp went about their duties, readying themselves for the hunt.

"It is right," O-wee-soo said. "They are well-suited. I approve of the match."

Several of the women agreed with the head matron.

"It is true that he needs a wife," someone said. "Our sachem is past the mourning state. He needs someone to care for him. He needs daughters and strong sons."

"But what of Singing Bird? What of my daughter? She is true Onondaga. She would make better wife. Any of our daughters would make better wife."

O-wee-soo shook her head. "Singing Bird is too delicate for my grandson. Kwan needs someone strong, someone like Sun Daughter."

"But she is a *Yen'-gees!*" Singing Bird's mother insisted. "She will betray us. She will take sides against the Iroquois people."

"She saved Bear Claw," Spring Rain said in defense of her new daughter. "She brought back Summer Thunder's little ones."

And so all but one of the matrons agreed. The decision was made. Kwan Kahaiska would marry *Anikha Sagoha.*

The first person Abbey noticed when she entered the village was Bear Claw. The recovering brave was at the door of his longhouse, his arms laden with a few hunting weapons. His dark gaze met hers briefly before sliding away.

O-wee-soo rose and smiled at their approach. She broke away from the group to greet Kwan and then Abbey with a hug.

Abbey was taken aback at the head matron's display of affection. Kwan, she noted, wore an odd expression. Apparently, he, too, seemed surprised by O-wee-soo's behavior.

"Kwan. *Anikha Sagoha*. Welcome. We have been looking for you." O-wee-soo gestured toward the Indian women who nodded and smiled their slight smiles.

"For what do you need me, grandmother?" Kwan asked.

The old woman pointed to the circle. "Sit, my son." Turning to Abbey, she said, "Sit, *Ex-aa*."

Puzzled, curious, Abbey sat. Kwan took a seat to her right. She could feel the tension in his muscular frame, and she wondered what had brought it on.

O-wee-soo's voice drew everyone's attention. "The women of our village have been talking," she said. "We feel it is time that our leader—our sachem— marries again." She paused, and a ripple of excitement passed through the village . . . among the unmarried Onondaga women.

The old matron waited a moment until the murmurs died down before she went on. "As it is our way for the women to decide such matters, we have come together to discuss the marriage." She hesitated, eyeing her grandson. "Kwan, what think you on this matter?"

Kwan rose to his feet. Abbey stared at him in a daze. Marriage? She understood Onondaga well enough to know that the women had decided that Kwan must marry. She was terrified of losing the one man who'd come to mean everything to her. How could she live knowing Kwan was another woman's husband? His handsome features wavered in her gaze. Who? she wondered. Who had they picked for the man she loved?

Abbey glanced toward her friend, who stood in the doorway of the Deer clan longhouse. *Evening Sky?* She thought of those she knew among the Indian maidens. Recalling her first visit to the longhouse of the Wolf Clan, she was more than a little discomfited by the memory of the young woman who had greeted Kwan there . . . the one she'd first suspected might be his wife. What was her name? She-Who-Runs-Fast. Abbey remembered the way the woman had looked at Kwan. It had been obvious; She-Who-Runs-Fast desired the sachem.

Kwan had not yet spoken; O-wee-soo waited patiently to hear his thoughts. "You have not spoken, my son. Does having a wife again bother you?"

Kwan didn't answer. A wife, he thought, startled by the question. He resisted the urge to look at the one woman he desired. Abbey.

He shook his head.

"Yan-lee." O-wee-soo seemed pleased. "A sachem needs a woman to feed him. To give him children." She studied him for a long moment, a small smile playing about her lips.

"You have decided?" Kwan said. His expression

247

was solemn. Would he be able to accept the matrons' choice? he wondered. Who had they chosen? Singing Bird? She-Who-Runs-Fast?

His grandmother nodded. "We have decided."

Kwan's face didn't alter as he waited for O-wee-soo to continue.

"In three days' time, you will marry *Anikha Sagoha.*"

And he felt his heart slam in his chest at the same time that he heard the woman beside him gasp. Abbey, he thought. They had chosen Abbey.

Chapter 20

Marry Kwan! Abbey felt a numbing panic as several Indian women worked to prepare and dress her for the wedding ceremony. It had been three days since O-wee-soo's startling announcement. Three days later and Abbey was caught in a whirlwind of events that would change her life forever. And she was powerless to stop them. Because she didn't want to. Because she loved Kwan.

That the head matron of the village was pleased was evident to everyone. Spring Rain, the bride's new adoptive mother, was happy, too. Her late daughter, Morning Flower, had died before becoming the sachem's wife, but now her new daughter would have the honor.

There were a few within the tribe, who did not share the others' excitement. These people were bitter, hostile to Abbey, although not in a blatant way. O-wee-soo and the other women were too overjoyed with the event to notice them.

At first, Abbey had been confused by their

behavior. Later she came to realize that the discontents had young, unmarried daughters with an eye and a desire for the handsome chief. Recalling her own jealousy when it came to Kwan, Abbey was unoffended. Eventually, these people would come to accept the marriage, to accept Abbey as the sachem's wife.

But would Kwan? she wondered. She'd seen little of him since the matrons' decision was announced. He certainly didn't act like a man who was glad to be getting married. He barely glanced at his future wife, and at a time when Abbey needed his reassurance. If he didn't want to marry her, why didn't he say something? she wondered. Why was he going through with it?

Abbey stared down at Evening Sky's bent head as the maiden straightened the fringed hem of Abbey's bridal skirt. Made of soft doeskin, the garment was part of a two-piece set. The fringed cape-like top was the same lovely white color and adorned with fancy embroidery much like many of the warriors' clothing. Looking down at herself, Abbey thought how like an Indian she'd become. Her skin had darkened to the color of rich honey; she could see how pale her flesh was in the private places where the sun had been unable to work its golden magic.

Why is Kwan going through with the wedding? The question returned to haunt Abbey again and again, until she wanted to scream. She spoke her thought aloud to Evening Sky, who straightened and regarded Abbey with two bright, dark eyes.

"The matrons have decided," the Indian said. "Kwan will follow their wishes."

"Whether he wants to marry or not?" Abbey was appalled.

Evening Sky shrugged.

It was apparently common practice for two people to be joined forever without love, Abbey thought. "A marriage should be based on love," she said. "Kwan doesn't love me!" She experienced a growing panic.

"You are woman. You have power to change his mind."

"I can't do this."

"You must or shame Kwan. Shame you. You are afraid? Kwan is a good man. He will not hurt you."

I will not hurt you. Kwan had said that very same thing to her once before, and he had kept his promise. At least physically. The way she felt right now was something else altogether. She was afraid of getting her heart broken. She had never counted on falling in love with a savage.

Jamie needs me to rescue him, she thought as Evening Sky began to comb the tangles from her shining blonde hair. She should be gone from the village. How many times had she reminded herself? Why was she still here?

Now that she knew the kind of man William Breckingridge was, she couldn't very well go to him for help. She could never trust such an unfeeling monster. His tactics for rescue would probably endanger Jamie more!

Then Abbey remembered Evening Sky's words that Kwan would be the one to help her find Jamie. Wouldn't he be more inclined to help her if she was his wife?

Perhaps.

Then she would stay and marry him. For Jamie's sake.

You are lying to yourself, an inner voice scolded her. *Admit it. You are marrying him for yourself.*

When it came time to begin the wedding ceremony, Spring Rain and Evening Sky escorted Abbey out of the longhouse of the Deer and into the circle of waiting tribesmen.

Abbey was in a turmoil. The voice inside her wouldn't let her alone; it seemed to be taunting her for some kind of admission.

Why are you marrying him?

"For Jamie," she murmured silently.

Because you love him.

"All right, because I love him."

Did he care for her? she wondered. Even a little?

Abbey's breath caught when she saw him. He was standing outside the circle, waiting, his silver gaze glowing with an emotion she couldn't define.

Spring Rain led Abbey to the circle's center where a woven rush mat lay on the dirt ground. Hugging her daughter briefly, the matron then stepped back to join the other Indians.

All eyes went to Kwan as he came forward, dressed as fitting his station. His only garment was a kilt, beautifully made, highly adorned. He looked the savage with his bare muscled chest, the wide gleaming armbands that encircled his thick corded arms. And through his earlobe—both ears, he wore those barbaric-looking thin strips of leather. Abbey thought she'd never before seen a male so beautiful.

Kwan knelt on the mat, facing the center. Abbey watched as O-wee-soo came to stand behind him and

252

place a work-roughened hand on her grandson's shoulder. The silence in the village was deafening. Abbey could hear the blood roaring in her ears, the steady heavy pounding of her heart.

With a nod, O-wee-soo gestured Abbey to join Kwan on the mat, facing him. Spring Rain returned then, carrying a bowl made out of wood, which she carefully handed to her daughter. Accepting the offering, Abbey saw that it was filled with hominy, which the Onondagas called *oh-no'-kwa*, and two carved wooden spoons.

She set the bowl on the mat between Kwan and herself, somehow sensing that she should do so, realizing that the Onondaga marriage ceremony involved her sharing a meal with her bridegroom. Abbey glanced briefly at O-wee-soo as she picked up one spoon. The matron nodded and looked down at her grandson, and Abbey knew then what was expected.

"You will say as my grandson," O-wee-soo said. "Then you will feed him food."

Abbey nodded solemnly.

Kwan spoke. *"Oh-neh' wa-ong-nee-nyah'-kay!"*

"What does that mean?" she asked softly, words meant only for Kwan's ears.

"Now we two marry," he said, and he repeated the Onondaga phrase again so that Abbey could say and understand it.

"Oh-neh' wa-ong-nee-nyah'-kay!" she echoed, and she knew by Kwan's startled gaze that she had spoken with great feeling.

"It is time to feed him," O-wee-soo said.

Abbey dipped the spoon into the hominy, aware of

Kwan watching her steadily with his silver-gray gaze. She nearly dropped the utensil on the way to his mouth, for he was eyeing her with amusement, and it was then that she recalled another time when he had ordered her to feed him and she'd refused.

The spoon wavered in her hand. She smiled mischievously, sending him a silent message that as she had before she might throw the food at him. He blinked, taken aback, and then his lips curved ever so slightly in a tender smile designed to make her melt. And she did.

It was an intimate, sensual experience for Abbey to place the spoon in Kwan's mouth. His lips opened to encompass the wooden utensil, and she felt his breath as they closed over a point high on the handle near her fingers. The warmth of his mouth seared her knuckles, her fingertips. She watched, fascinated, aroused by the sight of him taking the hominy onto his tongue.

Abbey flushed, shot O-wee-soo a glance, and was relieved to see the old woman had not noticed. The matron simply inclined her head and smiled at her approvingly.

Now it was Kwan's turn to feed Abbey. With his piercing gaze never leaving her face, he took the other spoon, filled it with hominy, and held it before her open mouth. She ate the food, saw the way Kwan was staring at her lips, and realized with surprise that he was as moved by her eating as she was by his.

They continued to share the *oh-no'-kwa*, until the bowl was empty. Then Evening Sky brought them more food in a basket—sweets of tiny corncakes made with tree sugar. Kwan and Abbey fed each other one cake, before passing on the basket of cakes to share with other members of the tribe.

O-wee-soo announced that Kwan Kahaiska and Anikha Sagoha were now married, and Spring Rain and several others echoed the announcement in loud voices.

The ceremony was over. The sachem had a new wife. Abbey had a new husband.

The newlyweds were escorted by the people to the sachem's hut. Normally, the husband went to live with his wife's family; it was simply the Iroquois way. In this case, things were different; because Kwan was sachem and had special privileges, among them a private hut, where bride and groom would take up residence.

Abbey was grateful to learn that she and Kwan would have the privacy afforded newly-married English couples. It would be difficult enough to adjust to the marriage without the added tension of being watched by Spring Rain and the other members of Abbey's new clan.

Still, it was with mixed feelings that Abbey waved to her Deer clan family and proceeded Kwan into her new home.

She stood nervously inside, waiting for Kwan to adjust the fur across the open doorway of the hut. She was conscious of the sound of his movements, of the power of his presence in the small room.

Abbey studied her surroundings, seeing the hut through the eyes of its new mistress. It wasn't what she'd envisioned as her dream house, but she liked what she saw, knew she could be happy here.

The sleeping platform was against the far wall.

She saw the pile of thick furs and knew that someone had been here, preparing the house for her arrival. O-wee-soo? Kwan himself?

She flashed him a look and was taken aback to see him standing by the closed door, staring at her with that unnerving, unreadable expression of his. She forced her gaze back to the platform and the storage shelf above. Abbey recognized a few of her own personal belongings as well as several gifts that had been given to her these past days. Bridal gifts, she'd surmised.

She was startled anew by the reminder that she had married an Indian. She turned to face him. He was her husband; she had to confront him sometime. The night would be awkward for them both. It would be their first time together as man and wife.

Man and wife. Abbey stared at her husband and felt a lump rise to her throat. He looked so stern, so angry, she thought. Because he'd married a *Yen'-gees?* Would he never soften, accept her as his wife?

Then, something in his look changed . . . a subtle relaxing of his rugged features. Whoever had readied Kwan's hut had stoked the fire and it burned off-center on the dirt floor, a small flame that cast an orange glow over the hut's interior . . . over her-self . . . and Kwan.

He shifted, moved from the door, and her pulse roared loudly through her veins. If he rejected her this night, it would set a tone for the rest of their marriage . . . however long destiny decided that would be, she thought.

"*O-ka-o,*" he murmured.

Abbey swallowed hard.

256

"You dress different this night."

She nodded. Although she wore the garb of an Onondaga woman, she'd refused their other adornments: their face paint and powder, the vermillion red paint they applied to their hair.

Her lips moved ever so slightly. "I come as myself," she said in a shaky voice. "I am Onondaga in the eyes of your people, but I am English and nothing can change that." She hesitated, trying to gauge his reaction. "You married a *Yen'-gees*, Kwan. Can you accept that? Me?" she added in a weaker tone.

He nodded abruptly. "As English blood flows through your veins, it does mine." He saw her start, her eyes widen with the truth. Abbey was not the niece of his enemy. He could accept her, desire her . . . love her. *"Gah'-jee."*

"No, Kwan."

He raised an eyebrow. Not married but a short time and already she was defying him. "Have we not wed?"

"I don't know," she whispered. "Have we?"

Kwan frowned.

The sound of giggling outside the hut drew Abbey's attention. "Who's that?"

He shrugged as he glanced toward the doorway. The sound came again.

"Kwan," she exclaimed. "Is someone outside?" She started to move past him toward the door.

He blocked her way. "It is nothing."

"Nothing?" she squealed when the giggling came again. "You call that nothing. Kwan, someone is eavesdropping on us!"

"Ab-bey . . . *O-ka-o*, they but wait for us to be man and wife."

"They wait," she echoed. Her eyes widened with understanding, and Kwan thought he'd never seen a woman so beautiful. He ached with the desire to hold her . . . to claim her once and for all as his own. The nights since he'd had her last had been long and lonely ones.

One look at Abbey's expression, and Kwan knew he'd have nothing as long as the others stood outside, waiting. With a sigh, he went to the door. Would his People understand?

Kwan opened the fur flap. *"Sah-dend'-yah*. Go away," he commanded. "I can do this alone."

There was a stir among the crowd. Abbey, peering out from behind her new husband's back, was astonished and appalled to see how many people had been out there waiting for them to consummate their marriage.

The crowd began to disperse, but not without sounds of grumbling.

The moment was awkward for Abbey; she had the feeling that in sending them away she had done something wrong. Would the marriage be valid without witnesses? she wondered.

"Kwan." She reached out to his shoulder, stopping short of touching his light copper skin.

He spun from the door, and she jerked backward, stumbling.

Her face grew hot with embarrassment as she righted herself. "Must there be witnesses?" she asked.

"It is the way of our village."

Abbey bit her lip. The whole idea was repugnant

258

to her. Someone listening in on their private moments, for God's sake! What kind of custom was that!

"How many?" she said. When he raised an eyebrow in question, she added, "How many witnesses? Will one be enough?"

Kwan gave the matter some thought. He nodded. "Yes."

"Silver Fox."

The sachem smiled. Then he summoned his father to stand outside, a discreet distance away, to be the official "witness" to the marriage.

The situation seemed awkward, almost ludicrous, to Abbey but she would bear it for Kwan's sake. She loved him. It was as simple as that. She wouldn't have lain with him if she hadn't; she most certainly wouldn't have married him—no amount of pressure from Spring Rain or O-wee-soo would have made a bit of difference.

Kwan saw his new wife's lips quiver and felt an overwhelming sympathy for her. How hard it must be for her to understand our ways, he thought. Her blue eyes glistened in the firelight. She looked more than a little scared, and his heart ached for her.

"Gah'-jee, O-ka-o," he murmured, holding open his arms to her.

She started forward, then hesitated. She glanced toward the closed door, and Kwan knew then what he must do. He left the hut and approached his father. In the spirits' eyes, Abbey was already his wife, he thought. There was no need to follow his people's customs.

Abbey was stunned when Kwan left the hut

abruptly. She went to the door flap, peered outside, and was surprised to see Kwan talking in earnest to Silver Fox. The old man had his head tilted to one side as he listened. A myriad of emotions passed across the shaman's face, but then he nodded, seemingly satisfied with what Kwan was telling him . . . and then Silver Fox left.

When Kwan turned to reenter the hut, Abbey was waiting at the doorway, her face puzzled.

"Where did he go?" Abbey asked.

"He has returned to his longhouse. I told him that in the Great One's eyes we were man and wife."

She blinked. "And he accepted that."

Holding her gaze, Kwan nodded. "It is so. We have lain together twice. The marriage is sacred. There was no reason for my father to stay."

Abbey felt a mixture of embarrassment and relief . . . embarrassment that the old man knew that she and Kwan had been intimate before the actual wedding . . . and relief that she and Kwan's first night as man and wife would be private and not take on the form of a circus show at a county fair.

Once the flap of the hut closed, Abbey knew that they were alone—truly alone. She was suddenly nervous of her new husband.

"You like your home?" Kwan asked. He began to putter about the place, and Abbey smiled as she realized that he was trying to put her at ease.

"Yes," she said shakily. "It's very nice." *I'm scared, Kwan,* she thought. *What happens tonight can make all the difference in our future together.*

"*Sahd-yenh'.* Sit." He gestured toward the platform with his muscular arm.

Abbey's gaze was drawn to his thick copper armband. She sat on the edge of the platform, conscious of the soft animal pelts beneath her . . . the intimate orange glow of the room . . . the scent of wood smoke and sweet grass . . . and Kwan.

He came down beside her, pulling her into his arms. She stiffened as he caught her shoulders; she relaxed when he maneuvered her gently, tenderly, onto his lap. He seemed in no hurry to take her; his soft finger-light caresses down her arms as he cradled her against his chest said that he had all the time in the world.

Abbey sighed and nuzzled against his neck. It felt good to be held, good to be treated with loving reverence. When Kwan turned up her chin, bent down to claim a soft kiss, Abbey responded willingly. She made no protest when he carefully, skillfully deepened the kiss. He shifted until she was stretched out on the fur, her blonde head pillowed on a beaver pelt.

Kwan studied his wife, enjoying the contrast of her golden hair against the dark fur . . . the luminous quality of her lovely blue eyes . . . the pink lips swollen from his kiss.

She reached up, grasped his neck to guide him down to her. Kwan inhaled sharply, feeling an instant surge of desire. When her soft warm mouth touched his jaw, his cheek, his chin before pressing firmly against his lips, he felt his heart jerk in his breast and a hot hardening of his manroot. He was no longer able to control himself, but took of her freely. His caresses became frantic, almost savage as he found the two twin mounds of heavenly flesh

261

beneath her cape-like top. He palmed the lush curves, feeling the nipples pebble beneath his hands, feeling his own body's instant response to her wild cry of pleasure.

"Ab-bey," he inhaled sharply when he'd pushed up her top so that he could see what he was touching. *"O-ka-o."*

Her dark areolas stood out against the pale skin. He bent down to lick first one breast and then the other, enjoying the feminine taste, the texture.

Abbey whimpered, arched upward. She clung to Kwan's shoulders, moved a hand into his dark hair as he sucked and nibbled at her breasts. Her body was flaming with desire. The heat flowed over her in thick waves, tingling along her skin, burning her lower half.

"Kwan," she gasped when he touched the secret moist part of her. "Kwan!" she cried out as he rubbed the nub gently, but with enough friction to make her mindless of all but his moving hand.

Her responses spurred on Kwan's desire, and he quickly undressed her and hurriedly rose to remove his kilt.

He watched her as he struggled to undress, was pleased with her passion-drugged expression, with the harsh sound of her breathing.

She grabbed him as he leaned above her, pulled him down, until their bodies met, bare flesh to hot bare flesh. He rose and shifted, fitting his shaft into her opening. She moaned and lifted her legs, wrapping them about his back, and he went wild as he thrust into her, long deep thrusts that drew little cries from deep in the back of Abbey's throat.

They ground against each other, gasping out love words, stroking and caressing . . . kissing with open mouths.

The frenzy of sensation reached a fever-pitch, topped the pinnacle of pure ecstasy. Abbey's cry of release was quickly followed by her husband's deep-throated groan.

Kwan rolled to the side of her, and then they held each other. Their bodies still pulsated in the pleasurable aftermath, that moment when energies drained, but the passion still tingled deliciously through tired limbs.

Within moments of their joining, Abbey drifted off.

She was a joy to love, quick to cry out when she was pleased, and uninhibited with her responses. Kwan marveled that her capacity for loving equalled her spirit and courage. And she was his wife. Only his.

But she was English, and niece or not, Brecking-ridge was sure to return for all the captives . . . for her.

He gripped her with a fierceness that woke her. And to his wife's delight, Kwan began to love her once again.

And again. All through the night.

Chapter 21

Married life within the Onondaga village gave Abbey privileges that neither a slave nor an Indian maiden had. With the matron status came not only certain benefits such as being consulted on all important matters, but responsibilities as well.

A wife was in charge of the food supply and satisfying her husband's appetite. Abbey had been startled to learn that an Iroquois male never asked for food; it was his mate's duty to set it before him whenever he returned from the hunt or his duties about the village. If a woman forgot or deliberately chose not to feed her man, the man would go hungry. Nothing would impel him to ask for food; it simply wasn't done. Abbey understood then how the women were able to "persuade" their men to their way of thinking. A man with a belly crying out for food was more apt to listen to reason.

Abbey and Kwan had been married two days when Abbey thought of asking her new husband to help her find Jamie. They were in their hut, sharing the evening meal, when she decided that she would broach the subject.

"Kwan." She handed him a second helping of hominy. Since the sensual exchange during their wedding ceremony, it had become her favorite meal.

He looked up and smiled. Abbey, studying his rugged face, felt an overwhelming surge of love for him. Thus far, he'd proven a good husband. He was ever the chief to his people by day, but at night . . . He was all hers then—a passionate, attentive lover.

Kwan accepted the bowl, thanking her in Onondaga. His expression was soft with affection. "You have learned to prepare our dishes well."

Abbey flushed. "Thank you." Why was it that she could be intimate with this man and yet at odd moments, such as this, feel shy of him?

"You are happy?" he asked. The question sounded casual, but something in Kwan's look told her that he was anxious to hear she was.

She nodded. Then it occurred to her that here was the perfect opening for her to ask for his help. "Mostly," she said. "But I worry about Jamie."

His eyes glowed. "Your brother."

"Yes. It pains me to think he may not be as well as I among the Indians."

Before he could respond, she continued, "Kwan, can you help me? Can you help find Jamie?"

He frowned. "This is not possible."

His refusal stung her. "Why not?"

Kwan looked sincerely apologetic. "These times are bad for the Iroquois. Many problems to deal with. Many lives at stake."

"But what of Jamie?" she exclaimed. "What of his

life? Couldn't you at least inquire about him?" She rose up on her knees to touch him. His shoulder burned beneath her hand.

His face softened, and he smiled. "You care for your brother, *O-ka-o*. This is a good thing. If times were different, I would be happy to help you. But not now. Tonight is the night of the moon. Tomorrow when the sun rises, our sachems will come. I cannot think of your Jamie, *O-ka-o*. May-be later when those within the League quiet."

How could she not help but understand? Abbey was disappointed but she couldn't argue with him. Her blue eyes tearing, she attempted to smile but failed.

"*Gah'-jee,*" he murmured, offering her comfort. She moved into his arms. "I am sorry, *Anikha*. You must understand."

"I do, Kwan, but—"

He placed a silencing finger across her lips. "When this time is over, I will help you. But for now, it must rest. Tomorrow I must meet with my friends. It worries me greatly." He caressed her cheek. "There is this night, *O-ka-o*, and we need comfort." He kissed her, a hot volatile meeting of mouths.

And Abbey forgot all but her new husband.

The sachems came into the village one by one, each arriving from different sections of the Iroquois "Longhouse." Abbey stood to one side and watched her husband greet each chief solemnly.

The Indians were then led into the great cere-monial longhouse. The women had prepared for the

266

event the day before, spreading rush mats over the dirt floor for seats, cooking an enormous amount of food.

Abbey studied each guest with open curiosity, comparing the sachems' ages and looks to that of her husband. From her judgment, Kwan was not only the youngest chief but the most handsome, and she was proud of the way he handled himself, of the respect afforded to him by the other League sachems.

As matron and Kwan's wife, Abbey was allowed to attend the meeting. She did so when it was time, taking a seat with the other women who had gathered at one end of the building.

Kwan was the host, having called the meeting, and the officiator of proceedings. His voice rang out loud and clear as he addressed his fellow chiefs. His words were filled with feeling as he expressed his concerns about the Senecas' dealings with the French and their hunger for war.

Abbey had to listen intently to understand, but found her attention wandering to gauge the various reactions in the sachems' faces to Kwan's words. Surprise. Anger. Determination.

All the Onondaga chiefs apparently agreed that they must watch the Senecas, alert the other League tribes: the Cayugas, the Mohawks, the Oneidas, and the Tuscaroras. Something must be done to prevent the Senecas from joining forces with the white French, with any white man. Such action could only weaken the Iroquois' strength, the force that had thus far protected the People from their enemies.

When Kwan had finished his speech, one gray-haired sachem rose from his mat. "You speak of trouble. I have felt it in the wind. I have felt it in the night. But what can we do to stop it? Our Seneca brothers are most powerful. How can we stop He-Who-Comes-In-The-Night without making the Seneca our enemies?"

"I do not know," Kwan admitted. "This is why I have called you to my village. Many of you have received wampum from the brave. I have not. We must read the wampum beads to understand the Seneca's mind. We must find a way to put out the fire of hatred that will come with the white man's wars."

Each sachem had his chance to speak. When they had spoken their peace, those who had received Seneca wampum belts brought them forward, one by one, to be read and interpreted.

Abbey watched and listened, but had trouble understanding all that went on. She was glad, therefore, when Spring Rain tapped her shoulder.

"The men will want food," her adoptive mother said.

Nodding, Abbey followed her from the longhouse to an area where the food had been set out in readiness to be served. Several other of the women joined them, while others remained behind at the meeting.

"Here." Spring Rain handed Abbey two large baskets of fruit. "Give to Knife-Woman. She will serve them."

Abbey nodded, turned toward the longhouse, and then hesitated. "What are they saying?"

Her Indian mother looked surprised. "You do not understand?"

She shook her head. "They all speak differently . . . and too fast."

The matron agreed. "They talk of war. They talk of the white man. The Seneca want the Iroquois people to join forces with the French against the *Yen'-gees*. Kwan says no. The white man—any white man—will only destroy the confederacy, weaken our power against our enemies."

"And you?" Abbey had come to love her adoptive mother and respect the woman's opinion.

Spring Rain smiled at her with affection. "I think the Onondaga should listen to him. The sachem is a wise man . . ."

Abbey flushed. She had gotten the impression that her adoptive mother had been referring to Kwan's wisdom in not only his abilities as sachem, but in his choice of wife.

"You think he is wise?"

"He is a good man," Abbey said. *And a stubborn one,* she thought, recalling his refusal to help her find Jamie. Still, he *had* promised to help her later. "He is wise."

Spring Rain nodded. "He is your husband. This is good." She picked up a bowl of cakes, handed it to a young woman with a smile. Then, she addressed Abbey, "Great Arrow will do right . . . but not when his *O-yon-wah* is empty and pains him." Her dark eyes twinkled.

"Oh! Yes," Abbey said, and she hurried to deliver the fruit baskets.

Sometime later, after her duties of food delivering were done, Abbey chose not to return to the meeting. She couldn't understand what the men were saying, and although she enjoyed watching her husband, she was afraid that anyone looking at her would read her thoughts . . . which were full of the memory of their lovemaking.

Kwan's skill as a lover far exceeded her own. But she was learning under his tutelage, and remembering her lessons well—or so he'd said. But she didn't need to reflect on the lessons during such an important meeting. She knew she should leave the first time Kwan caught her staring at him, and his expression had changed as if he'd read her mind. The last thing Kwan needed at this time was to be distracted.

Abbey left and wandered about the village. Not all of the women had chosen to attend, although they were all allowed. She smiled at several, who had become more friendly toward her since she'd become Kwan's wife, and walked past the longhouse of the Snipe clan, where she decided to enter and visit Rachel.

The change in her friend's behavior bothered her, and she wanted to see Rachel and smooth away the woman's recent hostility toward her.

No one questioned her right to enter the longhouse. She found Rachel in her master's cubicle, husking corn. The woman looked up, saw Abbey, and looked away without uttering a sound.

Hurt, Abbey stepped forward. "Rachel." The German woman ignored her. "Rachel, talk to me!"

She glanced up. "You are von of them now."

"You seemed content enough to stay with them when I wanted to escape!" Abbey exclaimed.

Rachel's lips tightened. "Because of Anna . . ."

Abbey sighed. "I know." There was a lengthy

silence. "I'm still me. The adoption ceremony didn't change that."

"Vhat of your marriage?"

She blushed. "I love him." It was the first time she'd admitted it to anyone.

Rachel looked surprised. "You do?"

Nodding, Abbey said, "He is a good man, despite the fact that he had us kidnapped. He's an honorable chief who tried to seek justice for an Englishman's crime."

"Breckingridge?" Rachel asked.

Abbey inclined her head. She joined Rachel on her mat and started helping her friend husk corn. "Trust me," she told her friend. "Perhaps I can convince him to free you . . . you and Anna."

"You vould do this?"

"If I can."

"He loves you?" Rachel asked.

"I don't know. He . . ." Abbey felt her face heat. ". . . wants me."

"Ah . . ." The word was rich with sound and understanding. "It is possible then, yes." Rachel eyed the sachem's wife speculatively.

Abbey looked away. "You didn't want to leave," she said. "I assume you've changed your mind."

"If ve can leave safely, then I vant to go. I must know if my John is still alive."

John Votteger was Rachel's husband. Abbey had learned a little about him during those first hours of their shared captivity.

"I understand," Abbey said. "If I thought something had happened to Kwan . . ."

Rachel nodded, and for the first time in several

days, Abbey detected an easing of strain in their relationship. She was quick, though, to point out that things would take time.

"I can't bother him now with the request. He has worries . . ." And because she could see Rachel was curious, Abbey explained what she knew about the problems within the League.

"I think your husband is right," Rachel surprised her by saying. "I know my John. I know the men. They care little for the savages."

Abbey agreed with the theory, although she no longer thought of the Indians as savages. They were people just like the English.

"How is Anna?"

Rachel smiled. "She is fine. She has captured the hearts of these Onondaga."

"Good." The corn was all husked, and Abbey rose to leave. "If you need anything . . ."

The German woman smiled with warmth. Abbey left the longhouse, knowing she had a friend again.

The meeting of Onondaga sachems ended after hours of discussion. The chiefs left the following afternoon to return to their own tribes. They had interpreted their wampum belts; they had talked of their dreams and their meanings. Abbey learned that all the sachems agreed to send messengers to their Iroquois brothers. They would meet with their fellow chiefs on a individual basis to express their concerns about the Seneca and the French.

During her two months with Kwan's tribe, Abbey had come to understand the Indian people. She had come to the village a beaten captive and had been made into an unwilling slave. She had served under two women, both different in nature—Spring Rain and Woman With No Heart. She felt a connection with these people, an active familial love that had been missing in her life since the death of her mother, since her brother Jamie had left home. Her world as she'd known it had been torn asunder with her mother and brother gone. Her father, a broken shell of a man, had lived the rest of his days grieving for his lost ones, virtually ignoring the daughter who'd chosen to remain by his side.

Standing on the banks of Lake Ontario, Abbey studied the glistening water. The sky was clear, a breathtaking shade of azure, and the sun's warmth felt heavenly against her flesh.

Closing her eyes, she tilted her face upward, enjoying the light breeze that blew in from the lake. She wore her hair loose today, unlike the other wives in the village. Kwan seemed to like it better that way, long and flowing about her neck, and back. The wind played gently with the golden tresses, stirring the strands against her cheeks. She enjoyed the tickling sensation of hair against skin and opened her eyes to admire the magnificent scenery.

Abbey was happy. She thought of her life before coming to this place and longed for her English family to share her joy, her peace, here. But, of course, her parents were dead, her brother missing. Her eyes watered.

"We'd be accepted here, Mother, Father," she said aloud. "No one would treat us as outcasts, because we didn't fit the role others thought we should."

She recalled her beautiful mother and smiled. "Mother, you would love him." She had a vision of Kwan meeting her parents for the first time. "Your parents would no doubt gasp and fall down at my marrying an Indian, but I know you would understand."

It wouldn't matter that Kwan was in actuality an Englishman. He was more savage than white man, and Abbey knew that nothing would change that in him. And she was glad, for she loved him just the way he was.

"I know you'd understand, Mother, because you stayed with Father against your family's wishes."

Her father would be a different story. James Rawlins would not have been as accepting of Kwan, but once her mother had spoken with him he would have come around to her way of thinking. *Father, you always did what Mother wanted, because you loved her so.* She felt a moment's sadness. *When she died, you willed yourself to die . . . to be with her . . .*

Reflecting on her father's feelings about his spouse, Abbey couldn't help but feel a warmth for him. "Your mother is all a man needs, Princess," he'd once told her. "A bright sun in this old physician's dark and drab life."

Anikha Sagoha. Sun Daughter—her Indian name. An apt name for the daughter of woman who was referred by her husband as the sun.

Abbey hoped, prayed, that someday she'd have a love as strong as her parents. She didn't know if it was possible. Could Kwan ever love so completely? She knew he had desire for her. Would he ever come to love her?

She thought of the people she knew back in England. What would they say if they could see her now? She glanced down at herself and grinned. In her doeskin tunic and moccasins, she looked like a savage herself. Her pale skin had surprisingly darkened further, the shade now matching her husband's.

The English people she knew would not believe in the validity of her Indian wedding, but Abbey did. Her parents had never legally married. James Rawlins had already been wed when he'd met Elizabeth Tumbrell. His legal wife had been mentally ill and living in a convent under the care of the good Catholic sisters, a humane alternative to those horrible institutions for the insane.

James had been a young man and lonely when he fell in love with Abbey's mother. Summoned on a sick call to the great mansion of the wealthy Tumbrell family, the doctor had taken an immediate fancy to the beautiful blonde Elizabeth. And she, watching him work on her ill younger sister, had become fascinated with the handsome man.

Pleased by the doctor's success in treating their son, Elizabeth's parents had called on the young physician again and again to treat not only themselves but their relatives and servants, too. The feeling between James and Elizabeth grew as they spent more time with each other. One day Elizabeth had professed her love for the doctor, telling her parents that she had decided to move in with him.

The Tumbrells were appalled. They had no idea that James Rawlins was married. It was bad enough that he was a poor country doctor with nothing to offer their eldest daughter. They had locked Elizabeth in her room to prevent her from leaving, kept food from her in an attempt to sway her to their way of thinking. But Elizabeth was a determined young lady. She was loved by the household servants and with their help she managed to escape.

When she'd showed up on his humble doorstep, how could James turn her away? To his credit, when he had learned of Elizabeth's love for him, he had pleaded with her to forget him. What did he have to offer her? She was used to the finest living quarters, clothes, and food. He couldn't give her his name; he was a married man. But Elizabeth didn't care. She'd been adamant and persuasive, and he'd loved her so.

James spent the remainder of his life pleasing her. They had little money, for a doctor's life was a poor one; and the scandal following her move into his house severely damaged Elizabeth's reputation, making it difficult for her to hold her head up in public.

But the lovers were never more happy then when they were together. They had lived together ten months when the missive came from the French convent informing James of the death of his wife. Still they never married. They didn't need to wed; in their own eyes, they were already man and wife, and Elizabeth was with child then—Abbey.

Abbey was born to the lovers seven months later; their son Jamie came two years later. The Rawlins household was filled with love and laughter. It wasn't until Abbey was five that she first heard the word "bastard" in connection with herself. By the way the boy had said, it, Abbey knew it must be something terrible. She had run home crying to her mother. Elizabeth had taken her daughter onto her lap and hugged her.

"You are your father's little princess and your mother's pride and joy, and you have nothing to be ashamed of. We love you, never forget that."

When Abbey grew older, she learned more about how her parents met, about the circumstances surrounding their relationship. Elizabeth, disowned by her family, with only the clothes on her back and a ruby brooch given to her by her maternal grandmother, had loved Abbey's father so much that she'd sacrificed all to be with him. How could Abbey question a love so pure, so good? And so she had grown up learning about prejudice, and how to ignore it.

Kwan saw his wife at the shoreline and took a long moment to admire her beauty. He approached her on light feet and placed his hand on her shoulder.

As if knowing who it was, she turned slowly with a smile, grabbed a tender hold of his hand. *"Haiw-nah,"* she said softly.

A warmth filled him to overflowing. My husband, she'd said.

Kwan knew how to please a woman, believed that Abbey's pleasure was due to his skill in the art of making love. How could his wife love the man who'd had her kidnapped, beaten, taken from her former life?

He pulled her into his arms and kissed her hard with the desperation of knowing that he wanted something that was beyond reach. Love.

He would make her forget Jamie. She would be much happier without her brother, better off living with him as wife.

Deep down, Kwan knew why he wanted Abbey to forget her brother. He was afraid that once Jamie was found, she would abandon him, return to the life of the white man.

And he couldn't—wouldn't—allow her to leave him.

Chapter 22

Days passed, and Abbey became frustrated with Kwan's refusal to search for Jamie. The more she thought about it the more she was certain that Kwan could send word to the other tribes asking after her brother, without any reprisal or danger to the Iroquois League.

One morning she spoke to him again, pleading with him to send a runner to the nearest village to begin the search, but her husband remained adamant in his refusal.

"I cannot do this, *O-ka-o*," he told her impatiently. "I tell you this once before."

"But, Kwan, it couldn't hurt to simply ask them! *Please!*"

"No, Ab-bey." Anger emanated from his taut frame; his silver eyes glowed with his ire. "I cannot."

"Can't or won't?" she challenged him.

"It matters not," he said and left their hut.

Abbey's mind began working as she thought of ways to change his mind. She blinked. Food, she thought. It worked for Onondaga women, why not for her?

The first time Kwan returned to their hut at mealtime, he said nothing when Abbey neglected to put food before him. She felt him watching her closely, but she managed to move casually about the hut. It wouldn't do, she thought, to be too obvious at first. Let him sweat and wonder if she'd simply forgotten to feed him or whether it was a deliberate action to keep food from him.

Finally, Kwan left. He was angry, but said nothing as he stalked from the hut. Abbey secretly had to laugh at his expression when she'd finally met his gaze. He'd looked astonished that she would try such a thing, clearly frustrated by his feeling of helplessness . . . and hunger.

He didn't look at her when he returned later that evening. Abbey had managed to avoid speaking with him, a calculated maneuver designed to let him know that she meant business . . . that if he didn't see her way of things, he would starve.

She heard his stomach growl and had to stifle the giggle that threatened to burst free and that would ruin her chances of successful "gentle persuasion." Kwan was angry, it was true, but he knew it was perfectly within her right as Onondaga wife to use food as a tool for changing her husband's mind. If he thought that she was deriving a great deal of amusement from the situation, he'd be too furious to ever see the light; Abbey wasn't about to destroy her best hope for finding Jamie.

And so the game went on . . . for two days. And each day Kwan grew hungrier and hungrier . . . until his pallor looked ghastly and Abbey felt her resolve weaken.

On the third day when Kwan woke from the night's sleep, Abbey placed a bowl of hominy before him and was further moved to pity when he looked at her with overwhelming gratitude. She tried talking with him again—about Jamie, but Kwan, ever the sachem, stood firm in his decision. He would not begin the search—not yet . . . perhaps not ever.

Each night when Kwan drew her into his arms, she allowed him to hold her, but she fought her responses . . . the instant desire at his touch. She was mad at him. She didn't want to love him. Her husband, however, seemed determined to bring her to the peak of pleasure. Kwan skillfully overcame her resistance, and the two continued to enjoy the wonderful ecstasy of being in each other's arms.

Then Abbey got smart. She had thought long and hard before she remembered Evening Sky's words. The new method of persuasion might prove as painful for her as for her amorous husband, but Jamie needed her and she was determined to find him.

And so she withheld her sexual favors.

And she suffered . . . but managed to keep Kwan from knowing it.

Abbey loved her husband and enjoyed being his wife, but she'd had enough of the man's stubborn nature. *It's what comes from being the big chief,* she thought irritably. She missed making love . . . Kwan's kisses . . . caresses. It was difficult living in such close proximity with the virile man and pretending an indifference that wasn't there.

She couldn't give in on this, though. How could

281

she find any happiness with Kwan when Jamie was still missing and in danger? She tried to persuade herself that her brother could be happy as a male captive among the Indians, but it didn't help her. Because she didn't believe it—couldn't believe it—until she could see and judge with her own two eyes.

Finally, with her failure in changing Kwan's mind and her desire and need to find Jamie at a breaking point, Abbey decided to take matters into her own hands. There was nothing else to do but strike out on her own to find her brother. She didn't relish the prospect, but neither did she think she'd be in any great danger.

That night she allowed Kwan to make love to her again. The next day she began to make preparations for her journey.

Abbey decided to leave by daylight. As Kwan's wife, she had the right to come and go from the village as she pleased. The warrior-guards were no longer there as a threat against escaping, only to keep her safe from the Onondaga's enemies.

Of Breckingridge, there had been no sign. Now that she knew what kind of monstrous man he was, she was glad she'd never had a chance to appeal for his help.

She tried not to think of Kwan's reaction when he found her gone, wondered if he'd be upset at her leaving . . . or relieved. They had come to an amicable living arrangement. Kwan seemed to enjoy having her for his wife, but love . . .

She had no clue whether or not he cared for her in that way, and she felt the pain of wondering like a deep ache in her breast.

The day before Abbey had planned to leave, she told Evening Sky of her plans. She couldn't tell Kwan; he would stop her from going. She trusted the Indian maiden enough to know that Evening Sky would abide by her wishes, informing Kwan of his wife's decision only after the discovery of her absence.

"I'm leaving tomorrow at first light," she'd told her Indian friend. "I can no longer wait to find Jamie. I've waited too long already."

Evening Sky looked worried. "You will travel on your own? Tell Kwan; he will help you."

Abbey shook her head, feeling sad. "He refuses to help now. I tried to change his mind, but . . ." She placed a hand on the girl's shoulder. "Please don't tell him . . . Wait until after I'm gone." She drew a deep breath. "If I don't return, tell him . . . tell him . . ." She swallowed against a lump in her throat. Tears stung her eyes, making it difficult for her to see.

"I think you are wrong to do this, but I understand it. I will tell Kwan you go to your brother, but that you will return. He will be angry . . ." Evening Sky stared at her hard. "You will come back?" she asked, seeking reassurance.

Abbey nodded. "I'm Kwan's wife. I'll come back."

Evening Sky smiled. "Then I will bear his anger." Her expression sobered. "Where will you go? You know little of our people? They are not all good— Wait!" She left, entering the house of her clan, returning within moments with a string of beads made of white whelk shells. "Take this *Ot-ko-a*. It is one of the wampum belts of our village. Tell them you are *Anikha Saghoa*—Great Arrow's wife. Show them this and they will help you."

"Thank you." Abbey accepted the belt, held it reverently as she studied the strange pattern of the shells.

"Do not lose it, *Anikha Sagoha*. It is the only thing that will save you from being slave again."

It occurred to Abbey that Evening Sky might have done something wrong in giving the precious belt to her. "Where did you get it?" The belt was beautifully crafted of the white shells patterned with slightly darker ones.

Evening Sky had averted her glance. "I take it from the house of my clan. We hold and guard the Onondaga wampum—the belts of our village."

Abbey guessed from Evening Sky's behavior that the Indian maiden would be confronting not only the anger of her sachem but of the entire village as well. "I can't keep this," she said, trying to give the belt back.

But her friend refused to take it. "Go. You are Kwan's wife. He would see you safe. I do it for him as for you. I do only what is right."

Abbey wore the belt attached to a loop in her tunic as she left the village. The day was but a soft white promise of bright sunshine as she entered the woods and began her way.

She had hidden a stash of food the previous afternoon in a copse in the forest. She headed for the thicket first. After retrieving her small animal-skin bundle, she found the trail frequently used by the Indians to travel the length of the Iroquois Longhouse. The path was clear in both directions. Abbey chose to go north-northeast toward the Oneida tribes . . . and the feared Mohawks. It would be better to brave the worst first, she thought, the most obvious place for English captives.

And so Abbey began her search for Jamie with only a satchel of food and a white wampum belt to aid her in her quest.

The English colonel and his men broke their camp at first light. They had come far to return to these Indian lands. It had taken them longer at the fort than planned. Shortly after their arrival at the post, new troops had arrived as replacements for those killed during the Indians' attack. Breckingridge had to deal with the paperwork and then the choosing of recruits for the journey back into Iroquois territory.

Everything had taken too much time, the colonel thought. The new men were clearly an inexperienced bunch, so the selection process had taken patience—something the British officer had in short supply.

"Colonel, Rush has spotted a woman on the trail."

Breckingridge frowned. "An Injun?"

"He's not sure, sir. She's wearing savage clothes, but she's blonde, sir."

The colonel was instantly interested. "Get her and bring her to me." It had been sometime since he'd had a woman. He'd question the wench and then if she were comely enough he'd enjoy her fruits.

He felt his eyes bulge when they brought her before him. She was dressed in an Indian garment, as Rush had said, but without a doubt, she was a white woman. A beautiful, blue-eyed wench. He could ignore her tanned skin in favor of the lush, full curves beneath her deerskin tunic.

Playing the gentleman, he introduced himself, and then he moved away to speak privately with his lieutenant. They were no longer in any hurry to leave the encampment. The men would stay another night here. Someone had been found who might help them. Someone who had been captured and brutalized by the savages, who would surely be seeking her own revenge.

"What is your name?" he asked the woman after issuing his commands to his man.

The young woman hesitated. "Abigail—Abigail Rawlins." She looked oddly frightened, a fact that irritated the colonel until he realized what the woman must have gone through. He smiled inwardly; he would use that fear to his advantage. Once having gained her trust, he would easily have his way with her.

"It must have been terrible for you, my dear," he said. "Thank God, you escaped." He gestured for her to sit beside him on a large flat rock.

When she hung back, he purred, "Don't be frightened. You're with me now. I won't hurt you."

Abbey wanted to kill the man, but she managed to keep her thoughts hidden. It wouldn't do for him to know her true feelings. The only way to escape her new predicament was to catch him off-guard. In order to do that, she would have to pretend to believe in him . . . to be grateful for his "rescue."

She approached him cautiously and took a seat. When he placed his arm about her shoulders, it took all her mind-power not to strike him, to act like she'd fallen willingly into his hands. *Murderer! Monster!*

she thought. And then she nodded and smiled at something he said.

Kwan woke up to find Abbey gone from their platform, but it didn't concern him. She often rose before him to join the other women at the lake. He stretched, and a small smile played about his face as he recalled last night and his wife's passionate cries as they'd made love.

When she'd turned to him in the night, he'd been astonished. These past few days she'd done everything possible to try to change his mind about finding her brother. He'd been furious when she'd refused to feed him, and when she'd turned away when he tried to love her, his temper had been tested to the limit. He'd wanted both to throttle and physically excite her at the same time.

Kwan didn't know what to do. How was he going to handle the situation of Jamie? If he sent word and the brother was found, he would lose his wife to the white man's world again. Abbey seemed to have adjusted to life within the village, but he was afraid that once reunited with her English brother the call of that world would be stronger than the peace found here by the great lake.

Kwan climbed off the platform and fastened on his breechclout. He closed his eyes, recalling the magic touch of Abbey's trembling fingers as she explored his chest, his stomach . . . his shaft. Desire hit him like a bolt of lightning. If she were beside him now, he would bury himself in her softness, stroke and caress her until she was whimpering his name.

He loved to watch the way her blue eyes widened with wonder whenever he brought her to new heights of pleasure. He enjoyed seeing her lips pink and swollen from his kisses . . . her blushing cheeks.

The sachem was no stranger to physical excitement; Atahkwa had been a good teacher, but there was something different about Abbey . . . He'd never felt so drawn to a woman before; it frightened him.

He was the leader of his people. He'd faced danger in all forms, but never had he felt more vulnerable. Abbey had become necessary to his sense of well-being. With her by his side, he could conquer anything. He would die for her and feel as if he'd come out the winner.

The urge to see her drew him from the hut. Outside in the cooling air, he searched for her among the village matrons. Abbey was nowhere to be found. With an inner smile, Kwan headed toward the lake where he was sure he would find her doing one chore or another. Bathing alone, he hoped.

There was no one at the lake, but Evening Sky. The young woman was filling a water bowl. She looked up at his approach, and Kwan met her gaze, felt a sense of foreboding at the sudden fear in her face.

"Great Arrow." Evening Sky hurriedly straightened. She seemed unusually tense, and he stared at her with a sudden wrenching in his gut.

"Teh-ne-taiw—my wife—"

"I'm sorry," the girl breathed.

Kwan grabbed her arm. "Tell me. Something is wrong. Where is Ab-bey?"

Evening Sky swallowed hard as she gazed up at him with glistening dark eyes. "She is gone."

"Gone?" Shocked, he released her.

The girl nodded. "To find her brother."

The sachem closed his eyes. "When?"

"She left at first light." She touched his arm. "Kwan, I know you are angry—"

His lashes opened and he fixed her with an anguished gaze. "She is gone." He felt his heart start to pound as he realized the dangers Abbey would face—a woman alone in these woods. He caught Evening Sky's shoulder. "You will tell me where she goes. I will find her."

"This I do not know, Kwan . . ."

"You will help me! There are many who would harm her . . . the French . . . the *Yen'-gees!* Our Iroquois brothers! They will not know who she is. They will make her captive!"

"She had the *Ot-ko-a.*"

Kwan gazed at her in shock. "You did this?"

Averting her glance, Evening Sky nodded. "I told her to stay. She would not listen. I had to protect her. It was the only thing to do."

The sachem frowned. "You did wrong. Many will be angry. Spring Rain. O-wee-soo. Your heart was true, so may-be they will understand."

"But not you," Evening Sky said.

"You did what was right, you say. I do not believe this. The right thing to do would have been to come to your sachem. You have not done this, and now Abbey is in danger." He paused. "If she dies, then I will never see Evening Sky . . . never speak to her again."

With tears in her eyes, Evening Sky nodded. She understood it would be this way. Many in her village would feel so.

The sachem left, and the Indian maiden prayed to the Great Spirit for her friend's safe return.

Chapter 23

"Now, my dear," Breckingridge purred, "you must tell me . . . from whose village did you escape?"

Abbey shuddered. The colonel was too near to her, and his scent, his presence, made her feel physically ill. "I don't know," she said in a weak voice.

"There, there," he soothed, "I know it was terrible for you, but try to think . . ." He stared at her, and she was afraid that he could see beneath her act. "How long were you with them?"

She knew she couldn't actually lie about this. "Weeks . . . I guess. Maybe months." She blinked up at him, her eyes filling with tears. Her breath caught on a sob. "They . . . it was all so terrible!"

Abbey saw the look change on the English officer's face and felt a sharp prickle of alarm.

"Can you describe them for me?" He began to stroke her hair, and Abbey had to fight the urge to jerk away. Breckingridge was a handsome man by some women's standards, she presumed, but there was something about him that was not only evil but unsavory. A woman would never feel safe around him. But, it wouldn't do for the man to realize that Abbey could see through his sweet-talking, smooth manner. He had two things on his mind—attacking the Indians and his lust for the woman who'd stumbled into his camp.

"They . . . the men . . . were bald, most of them," she said, knowing that the same was true for many of the Indian tribes, ". . . with little clumps of hair on the top of their head."

"Iroquois," the colonel said, nodding with satisfaction.

"How do you know?" She acted impressed.

He puffed out his chest. "Experience, my dear. Experience." When Abbey continued to gaze up at him with limpid blue eyes, he urged. "What else?"

His hand moved to the curve of her neck. A shiver of revulsion ran through her, raising the hairs at her nape, burning in the pit of her stomach. The colonel smiled at her, his eyes glowing with desire, and Abbey knew he thought she was pleasurably affected by his bold touch. *Not in your vile life, Breckingridge!*

"The women," she managed to choke out against her outrage, "they were . . ." She averted her glance as if too embarrassed to describe the state of nakedness.

"Yes, yes, I know." he murmured. His eyes gleamed with lust. "They wear nothing up top."

She looked at him, nodding shyly.

"Shameful, simply shameful." But his gaze fell to her breasts, and Abbey wanted to strike him.

"Did any of them—" He hesitated. "—hurt . . . you?"

Do you mean rape, you lowlife? Abbey thought. "The women beat me," she said, pretending to be overly horrified. "Why? How could people be such animals?"

"There, there." He patted her shoulder. "They're not people. They *are* animals." Breckingridge ran his beefy hand down the length of her arm to her hand. He wove his fingers through hers and stroked the back of her hand with his thumb. "It must have been terrible."

"Yes, yes, it was!" Her vehemence was fueled by her disgust for the British officer.

"Well, you're safe now." The way he looked at her said she was anything but safe.

"Am I?" she couldn't help retorting. Then, she quickly covered her lapse with a sob and a "What if the Indians come after me?"

"We'll protect you. I have men trained in firearms. You have nothing to fear from them." His gaze fell to the wampum belt attached to her tunic. "Is there any reason to think that they would follow you?"

Abbey had seen the direction of his glance. "Yes, well, I . . ." She looked away guiltily. "I stole this." She fingered the white shell beads.

"I see." He grabbed the end, studied it carefully, before looking up at her with a smile. "Too pretty to resist, eh?"

She gave him a slight smile.

"Relax. We'll see you safe."

Abbey pretended to be grateful. "I've come a long way," she lied. "May I lie down? I'm so tired."

"You are?" Anger flashed in the man's gaze, and she saw a glimmer of his unbalanced state of mind.

She knew it was dangerous dealing with the colonel. She'd have to be extremely cautious. "I'm sorry. You've been so wonderful . . . feeding me and all, but . . ."

The colonel's expression softened. Obviously, he believed her. She could almost hear his thoughts, "No matter. Rest. There's time for what I have in mind for us later."

"How thoughtless of me, my dear—"

"Not at all, Colonel," she interrupted, placating his ego. "You've been a most gracious host."

He nodded. "You can rest easy in my tent. There will be a guard posted outside to . . . protect you."

"Thank you." Abbey swallowed. The guard was more likely to keep her from escaping than protect her from the Indians.

Her thoughts went wild as she followed him to his tent. Would she be safe there for now? How was she going to escape? How was she going to continue to evade the man's obvious lust for her until she could get free or be rescued?

Kwan would know now of her plans. He'd be furious with her. Would he try to find her or simply dismiss her as a loss?

I'm his wife. Surely, he'll try to find me.

"He's your husband," an inner voice taunted, "because the matrons decreed it and for no other reason."

But he desires me, and he's treated me kindly.

The voice spoke again. "He's under the watchful eye of the head matron. He's been good to you because he's felt duty-bound."

No, she couldn't believe that. She had to hope that he cared enough to come after her, if for no other reason than because she was his wife.

His wife. If Breckingridge knew that she was the wife of Kwan Kahaiska, the man he was seeking revenge against, she'd become a tool in Kwan's destruction. She'd lie and die first before she'd see Kwan hurt.

"Here you are, my dear." Breckingridge had stopped before the largest of two tents. "Use my bunk . . . I'll check on you later." His tone and the gleam in his eyes made Abbey more than a little nervous as she ducked under the tent flap and went inside.

"We must find her. The English are not done with us. Neither are the French. She is in great danger."

Silver Fox gazed with compassion at his son. "Why did she leave you, Great Arrow?"

Kwan's jaw tightened. He knew what his fellow braves were thinking. It was common practice that when a wife was unhappy with her husband, she could divorce simply by putting his belongings outside their home. Did the white woman not know this? Was that why she ran away?

The sachem was angry that he had to explain his wife's actions. "Her English brother has been taken by one of our Iroquois brothers—or so she believes. She had gone to find him."

"Alone?" Bear Claw seemed amazed by the extent of the woman's courage.

Kwan stared at him hard. "She would not wait for me to help her. I would have her wait until after the Great Council Fire. This she would not do." But he knew it was because she had sensed that he'd had no intention of looking for Jamie. Did she realize why?

Bear Claw spoke up. *"Anikha Sagoha* is strong, that one. She has courage to face our mightiest braves. We will find her before the Mohawks do. She will fight off her enemies when they come."

Surprised by the brave's words, Kwan nodded. "I have sent runners in both directions of the Longhouse. She may have gone far, but we will soon know where." He rose from a kneeling position to pace back and forth. He stopped, addressed the three men who had gathered to meet with him. "I will go when one of them finds her trail. *Anikha Sagoha* is my wife. I will see her safe."

"I will go with you," Bear Claw said. "She has magic healing powers, that one. She has done much for me, for our people. Anikha Sagoha belongs here in our village."

Stone-Face, too, wanted to come. *"Tai-o-he-ad-a-non-da,"* said. She is my sister.

"What of her brother?" Silver Fox said.

"Jam-ie," Kwan said.

The old man inclined his head. "She will leave again. She will find him. This white brother means much to her." Silver Fox gave his son a meaningful glance.

"I know this is so," the sachem admitted. "I will ask after her Jam-ie." *I will chance losing her to the white man's world. Anything to see her safe.* Since discovering her gone, Kwan had imagined all sorts of dangers she might encounter. He was frightened. What if his enemies found her first? What if she was made a slave?

If Silver Fox hadn't stopped him, cautioning him against running unarmed into the forest, he would have gone to find her without weapon, plan, or thought. The realization made him aware of how much she meant to him.

"The runners will be back soon," Kwan said. "One of them may have Sun Daughter, or she may have traveled too far from our camp."

"But we will know her path," Bear Claw added.

Kwan nodded. "And we will leave to follow her."

The first runner returned shortly afterward. There was no sign of the sachem's wife to the south, toward the houses of their Seneca brothers.

The chief was both worried and relieved. He was worried that she'd fallen into the hands of the Mohawks, but he was relieved that she'd stayed clear of the Senecas, whom Kwan was afraid to trust, who were sure not to reason with him for her release.

The Mohawks were a fierce, blood-thirsty lot, but Kwan was certain they would give him back his wife.

"Let us go. Night Eagle has not returned, but we know she has gone north."

They all agreed. Kwan, Bear Claw, and Stone-Face readied their weapons and gathered their supplies. The shaman, Silver Fox, would stay to guide their people.

"Father, we will return when we find her," Kwan said.

The old man was solemn. "Her family is concerned for her."

Kwan nodded. So was he.

The last runner met them several feet outside the stockade fence surrounding the village.

"Night Eagle," Kwan greeted the brave.

The warrior looked anxious. "I have found *Anikha's* path. She has gone north to the Mohawks."

"This Running Wolf has told us."

"I have found something else—" Night Eagle flashed each one of them a glance. "I have seen the *Yen'-gees*."

Kwan tensed. "Breckingridge?"

"I think this is so."

"Ab-bey?" the sachem breathed. In his fear, he'd used her English name.

"Your wife—she is with them."

Kwan felt a blinding pain. "By her own choice?"

This Night Eagle didn't know. "I went to the camp and saw her talking with the leader. She looked . . . unhappy."

The sachem didn't know what to think. Had his wife met Breckingridge by design? It mattered not, he decided, because she was his wife and he would not allow her to leave him.

"Let us go. The Englishman is a dangerous one. We will need more warriors."

A short time later, Kwan went into the forest, leading a band of painted Onondaga warriors.

Even in her sleep, she sensed immediately that it wasn't Kwan kissing her. Abbey's eyes flew and she screamed. Breckingridge loomed over her, his gaze gleaming, as he lowered his head again.

297

"No!" she cried. "Leave me alone."

"Sh-sh." The colonel tried to soothe her. "It is all right, my dear. It is me. William."

Abbey scrambled up and away from him on the cot. She hadn't meant to fall asleep! She'd simply pretended to so that she could escape the man's company for a while. But she must have dozed. How could she have slept knowing she was in such a man's clutches?

She should have known he'd try taking advantage. His lust for her had been evident from their first meeting.

"Get away from me." Abbey attempted to gain control of the situation. She glared at him, unwilling to cower, and he seemed taken aback by her show of spirit.

His face darkened. "You are not as vulnerable as you seemed."

"You would attack a sleeping woman!" she gasped.

"I was only kissing you."

"I don't want your kisses! I don't want you near me! You call yourself an English officer; I call you a filthy swine!"

The man's expression lit up with a look of murder. "Bitch!" He sprang for her without warning, but she evaded his grasp and pulled out the knife she'd hidden beneath her skirt.

"Come again, and I'll slit your throat," she warned him.

The colonel laughed. "You!"

"I've spent over two months with the Iroquois—do you doubt my ability?"

Breckingridge's confidence wavered. "You wouldn't kill me."

"Because I'm a woman?" Abbey's chuckle rang harshly about the tent. She brandished the knife, cutting the air like she might a man's flesh.

Breckingridge's gaze followed the blade's movements. He turned slightly, and Abbey gauged his intent. "Call your man," she said, "and I'll cut out your gizzard." She rushed forward to press the knife point to his jugular. "My father was a physician. I learned not only how to heal, but the places most sensitive on a man's body. Shall I test my skill?"

She drew the knife down his neck toward the area near his heart. Breckingridge had discarded his uniform coat and wore only a thin white-linen shirt. "Bone and muscle here, colonel, protect your heart. But I know a way around them, just where and how to drive in this blade . . ."

Abbey pressed down on the point until he winced and she knew she had nicked his skin.

"You don't understand—" The colonel was flustered. "I only wanted to—"

"Rape me?"

"No, no! Pleasure is all!"

"While I slept?" She raised her eyebrows. Her blue eyes flashed fire. "Don't lie! You came while I was sleeping so I wouldn't have a chance to fight you. It didn't matter if I said yes or no. You never asked me!"

The officer's face was a deathly white. He'd never seen a woman so completely in control before . . . not with that cold look of purpose.

"Give me the knife," he begged. "I won't hurt you. I would have stopped when you said."

"Like you stopped killing that child at the village?" Abbey shuddered, recalling the attack at the bean field. The screams of a young girl as Breckingridge's men took her life.

His features contorted. "You were there—weren't you? With the Indians." His lips quivered in his anger; his face turned a bright shade of beet red. "You're one of them!"

"They, Colonel, are people like you and me. No! Let me correct myself—like me. You, colonel, are an animal!"

"Colonel! Sir! There are savages—" The rest of what the soldier was saying was lost in the sudden commotion outside the tent. Abbey heard the wild war whoops of attacking Indians.

"Kwan," she breathed, praying it was him. Without conscious thought, she lowered the knife.

"Bitch!" the colonel growled. He grabbed her arm and wrestled away her weapon.

"Kwan!" she screamed.

The officer backhanded her across the face. Tossing the knife away, he pinned Abbey to the cot and ground his lips against her soft mouth.

Abbey fought him. Kicking and struggling, she managed to hit him in his private parts, and he yelped but he lowered his head again. She bit his lip, and blood spurted from the cut flesh.

Breckingridge called her all sorts of uncomplimentary names as he held a hand to his bleeding mouth. Seeing her advantage, Abbey sprang from the cot and retrieved the knife from the dirt floor. Then she backed toward the tent flap.

The canvas opened, and Abbey gasped and spun.

She nearly fainted with relief to see Bear Claw. The look in the warrior's eyes gave her pause as they stared at one another. Bear Claw glanced at the colonel and then at Abbey's knife. Suddenly, his gaze brightened. *"Anikha Sagoha,* come."

She nodded and rushed through the opening. All hell had broken loose in the English camp; Onondagas were fighting hand to hand with British soldiers, but not without the discharge of gunfire as a soldier or two managed to use their guns.

Abbey stood, wondering what to do. She saw Kwan locked in combat with a tall, hefty soldier. She watched with sick horror as the two fell and grappled together on the ground.

Where is Bear Claw? Somehow she'd lost him in the fray. She gazed back at the tent, saw the brave ducking beneath the flap with raised Iroquois war club. He had gone back to deal with Breckingridge. Moments later, he came out of the tent.

Abbey had spied Kwan in the midst of the fighting. "Bear Claw!" she shouted, calling for him to aid Kwan. The brave nodded and ordered, "Go!" He gestured toward the forest.

"Kwan!" she cried. Bear Claw wanted her to flee into the woods. But how could she leave her husband to the enemy?

The warrior scowled at her. "Go! I will help!"

Nodding, Abbey did as she was told, hurrying toward Night Eagle, who waved her to join him, away from the campsite.

She didn't know what happened after that. Night Eagle spirited her away from the scene of the fighting, and there they waited near a small trickling stream. It seemed like hours before Kwan and the others joined them. Abbey took one look at her handsome husband, and the tears came; she couldn't stop them.

Kwan came to her, drew her into the security of his strong arms. Abbey sobbed with relief at his safety. "It is all right, little one. You are safe now. The soldiers will bother us no longer."

When she was done crying, Kwan released her and walked away. Abbey felt the instant wall he erected between them, a wall of silent tension. The barrier traveled with them to their Indian home.

Chapter 24

"My son, how long will you hold your tongue?" Silver Fox eyed Kwan with a concerned gaze. "Your woman hurts; it is easy to see that."

Kwan turned from the waters of the great lake to face his father. When he was troubled, he frequently came to the shoreline. His study of the rippling water soothed him. But these past two days, his dispirit remained. There was anguish in his eyes as he met Silver Fox's gaze. "She left me," he said. "The pain is mine."

"You are a fool if you believe this," the old man said. "Look with your two eyes open. Hear with listening ears. You are a man with pride. May-be it is your pride that hurts you—nothing more."

The sachem frowned. It was true Abbey had hurt his pride. Everyone in the village knew that she had left; his people looked at him speculatively, searching for answers. But it was more than hurt pride that plagued Kwan. The fear—the ache—of knowing she'd left had been too real, too difficult to forget.

She should have trusted in him.

He felt instantly guilty. He'd had no intention of looking for her brother, but she hadn't known that . . . or had she somehow sensed it? If she had guessed the truth, how could he condemn her for his wrong?

"You must speak with her," Silver Fox said, startling him. Kwan had forgotten his father's presence. "The sun has come up twice since your return. This silence between you is a bad thing."

Kwan nodded.

"She cares for you," his father continued. "I've seen it in her eyes. I've seen it in her heart. A wife would not hurt so if she did not love her husband." He paused. "She cries when she thinks she is alone."

"You've seen her crying?" Kwan experienced a sharp twinge in his chest region.

The white-haired Indian inclined his head. "She stares across these waters and weeps. She weeps in the forest while gathering food."

Kwan scowled. "She cries for her brother."

"May-be," Silver Fox said. "But she looks at you and her eyes fill with tears. O-wee-soo tells me Anikha Sagoha is unhappy and it is you. Your grandmother is a wise woman. If she sees the truth in this, then I believe her."

Was it true? Did Abbey love him? Kwan wondered. Hope filled his heart like the rain shower fills a dry stream bed.

He met his father's gaze. "She is *Yen'-gees*."

"If she is, then you are, too. In your heart, you are Iroquois. Give her a chance . . . she will be Iroquois, too. For me, she has already proven so."

Kwan thought on this. It was true that Abbey had adapted well to village life. She'd seemed to enjoy being his wife—he had to smile—and the powers that came with being a village matron. And he knew she enjoyed his kisses . . . his touch. But was that all it was that drew her to him? How could he know whether it was love that bound her to him or his skills with physical pleasure? When the desire waned after a time, would she still care for him?

The idea didn't sit well. He wanted Abbey's love—freely and without condition. He was sachem—chief of his tribe, but with her, he was only a man . . . who wanted—*needed*—his wife's love.

Kwan came to a decision. "I will talk with her."

Silver Fox looked relieved. "Good. She is a good woman. You must care for her. If she remains unhappy, then . . ."

Kwan knew what the old man was saying. As an Onondaga matron, Abbey alone had the right to divorce him. By simply placing his belongings outside the hut, she would be free to love another.

He had the desperate need to put things right between them. He didn't want to lose her . . . yet he must give her a choice. It was only fair; he had taken her from her people.

But if he gave her that choice and she still wanted to stay with him, he would love and care for her until the end of their lives.

"Do you know where she is?" Kwan asked.

Silver Fox gestured toward the forest. "O-wee-soo sent her to gather nuts. Evening Sky went with her."

There was a look in the old man's eyes that said it was time, too, to forgive the young Indian maiden who had proven to be his wife's true friend.

Kwan silently agreed. He moved toward the woods. "I will find them."

The two women worked beside one another without speaking. A tension had entered their relationship, a strain fueled by guilt and pain, and the displeasure of their fellow tribesmen.

Abbey felt the ever-present lump in her throat that had come since returning to her Indian home, and she swallowed once again to relieve it. But the lump—and the pain—remained.

If only she hadn't left, she thought. Her life here as she'd known it had changed and all because she'd chosen to honor her promise to her father . . . and herself.

Oh, Jamie! I miss you. I need you more than ever. I've angered my husband. I've alienated my friends . . .

She plucked a berry off a bush, studying its plumb fullness. She saw Evening Sky bend beside her to pick a leaf, which her friend put in a basket.

Abbey wanted to apologize to the Indian maiden. It wasn't until her arrival back at the village that she'd realized the extent of Evening Sky's act of friendship for her. The Onondagas, angered that the girl had stolen the wampum belt and aided Abbey in her escape, had treated Evening Sky as an outcast. Abbey had been horrified when they'd spoken to her but not to her friend. She thought it grossly unfair. Evening Sky was actually paying for her friend's sins and not her own!

The tension grew in the continued silence between them. Unable to bear it any longer, Abbey laid a hand on Evening Sky's arm. *"O-gai-sah Ka-ai-wi-a,"* she murmured. "Forgive me."

Evening Sky looked at her, her eyes glimmering with tears. "I would do it again. It was the right thing."

With a sob, Abbey reached for her friend, and they hugged. The Englishwoman felt a warmth and caring she'd never before experienced from a friend.

A sound interrupted them—someone clearing his throat. The women broke apart.

"Kwan!" Abbey stepped back.

The sachem nodded to Evening Sky. "I would speak with my wife." His voice sounded brusque.

The Indian girl solemnly agreed to leave the two alone. Kwan halted her as she passed by him on her way back to the village and held her gaze. "You are a good friend to *Anikha Sagoha*," he said softly, gently. "And to me. I thank you."

Evening Sky's lips curved into a wide smile, before she left.

Abbey was discomfited. She couldn't hear the exchange of words between Kwan and Evening Sky, and she wondered what it was Kwan was saying. When she saw her friend smile, she felt relieved though still confused. The last thing she'd expected was for him to seek her out. He'd said very little to her since their return. He'd kept his end of their conversations to one-word replies to her questions.

"Would you like more meat?" she'd asked.

His answer had been *"No."*

307

"Did you have enough to eat?"

"Yes."

Kwan barely looked at her when speaking these days, and Abbey hurt constantly from the pain of his rejection of her.

Why had he come? she wondered. Tears filled her eyes as she gazed at him. She loved him, but how long could she endure the endless hurt? Why did he rescue her from Breckingridge when it was clear that he no longer wanted her for wife?

"You left me," he said, and by his tone, Abbey knew how much she'd hurt him. She saw the look in his eyes and wanted to take him into her arms . . . but she was afraid.

"I'm sorry," she whispered. "I'm sorry . . ." She turned away. She should have told him of her plans, she realized. As a matron, he wouldn't have been able to stop her from leaving. Would he have insisted on helping her once he'd known the extent of her determination?

Kwan stepped closer. "You are unhappy here?"

Abbey hesitated. Only lately, she thought, since she and Kwan had become estranged. "I love the village."

"Your home? Our house?" he asked, watching her closely.

"I like that, too."

"Then I make you sad."

"No!" she exclaimed. "Well . . . only with your silence these last two days."

He nodded. "This silence is bad between man and wife." He paused. "You are my wife."

She stared at him, waiting for him to continue, too

308

surprised by the direction of their talk to say anything.

"The ways of our people say that when the wife is unhappy she can divorce her husband."

Abbey's heart began to beat fast. Was Kwan asking to be free of their marriage? The English would never condone such practices, but Kwan wasn't English anymore . . . and life within the village was different. Besides, she thought, her own parents had taught her that marriage was a commitment between two people whether legal or not. If Kwan no longer wished to be married, then how could she stop the divorce?

She swallowed against that painful lump. "Am I a bad wife?" she asked, trembling.

Kwan looked surprised. "You are good wife."

She blinked against tears. "Do you want to get rid of me? Is that why you talk of divorce?"

Her husband's face became a study in emotions. "I tell you, because it is your right to know. You are Onondaga and not *Yen'-gees* here. You can undo our ties if they make you sad."

"But marriage is a commitment! Do you take your commitments so lightly?"

"You will explain—"

"Promises!" she explained, angered by the talk of divorce. Why didn't he just tell her how he felt? Why play games with her?

"It is your right." Kwan firmed his lips.

"Well, I don't care to exercise that right now, thank you!" Furious, Abbey stalked away from him, farther into the woods.

Damn savage! she thought. Would she ever be able

to understand his mind? Did he or did he not want to stay married to her? And if he did, why tell her of divorce?

God, how she loved him! *Although right now, I have the strongest urge to hit him—not kiss him!*

She was frustrated. How does one deal with the man?

Kwan had known she'd needed to find Jamie. Why had he been surprised when she'd decided to seek her brother on her own? After all, he'd all but refused to assist her . . . and she'd been tired of waiting for his help.

His behavior was puzzling to her. Abbey wandered through the forest, trying to decide what to do.

At first, she didn't realize how far she'd walked. The woods had grown thicker, but Abbey was off the path and thought nothing of it.

The growl was low at first; she wasn't sure she'd heard it. She stopped, listened. The wind tousled the treetops, but the forest was otherwise silent. And then the growl came again . . . and Abbey knew it was an animal.

She wasn't afraid of the dog. She'd seen a lot of the animals about the village, for the Indians kept many of them. It wasn't until she saw the flash of his sharp yellow teeth that she became uneasy.

The dog stiffened its back, raising its fur. It bared its teeth, and a menacing rumble came from the back of its throat.

Abbey froze. The beast, she saw at second glance, looked unkempt, wild. The dogs in the village were well cared for by the Onondagas. This animal was not one of the tame Indian pets.

She stepped back, and the animal snarled. Heart pounding, Abbey checked all avenues for her escape, but she was surrounded on two sides by brush and briars. Behind her lay the route she'd taken, but it was too overgrown to flee across hastily. One stumble, she thought, and she'd be on the ground with the snapping, snarling animal on top.

She stayed still, hoping the dog would tire of its prey and move on. But he showed no signs of leaving.

A twig snapped nearly, and Abbey felt a prickle of alarm. *Dear Lord, is he just one of a pack of wild beasts?*

She didn't move; she was afraid to.

"O-ka-o." Kwan's voice pierced her fear, calming her like sweet music. "Do not move. I will lure him from you."

"Kwan!" she gasped. "Be careful!" She sensed when he moved closer. Her husband came on silent feet until he stepped on something that crackled. The dog immediately focused his attention on Kwan. His snarl made the hairs rise at the back of Abbey's neck. Inside her chest, Abbey's heart pounded like thunder.

Oh, no! Not Kwan, she thought. Did he have a weapon? She recalled the horror of his weaponless battle with the Frenchman Jacques. She turned, maneuvering slowly. Kwan had a hand at his belt, and Abbey saw the knife. Relieved, she slowly released a pent-up breath.

Abbey heard Kwan telling the dog to go away.

"Tsh-ech-ha! Tsh-ech-ha! Sah-dend'-yah!" he cried. Dog! Dog! Go away! Kwan sprang forward. There was a flurry of movement as Kwan and dog

311

collided with force. They fell to the dirt in a tangle of bare human muscle and dark fur.

"Kwan!" Abbey screamed.

"Stay back!" he ordered.

She obeyed him, gaping in horror. Then, she grabbed the nearest stick, circled the area where man and beast struggled. Abbey searched for an opportunity to strike the dog, but the two combatants rolled so quickly over the ground that Abbey was afraid she'd hit Kwan.

The sounds of Kwan's male grunts mingled with the horrible growling of the wild dog. Abbey's breath slammed in her throat as she caught sight of her husband's knife blade as it arched through the air seeking its target.

The knife hit dirt, and dust flew at the impact. The dog went for a tooth hold on Kwan's arm, but Kwan evaded the beast's mouth and managed to get a grip on the dog's body. He tossed the animal aside, and it landed in the brush with a yelp. Abbey watched her husband scurry toward the stunned animal with his knife raised. She closed her eyes, unwilling to witness the slitting of fur and flesh.

The dog's inhuman cries of pain brought chills to Abbey's spine, and she brought her hands up to her ears to stifle the pitiful sound.

The cries stopped abruptly. Abbey opened her eyelids and saw that the dog's death had been merciful. Kwan had taken the advantage to bring a swift end to the beast.

There was blood all over Kwan's chest and arms. His hands were a bright crimson. Abbey gulped against bile.

Was Kwan hurt? Surely, all that blood couldn't be the dog's!

Kwan swayed on his feet.

"Kwan!" she cried and ran to him. "Oh, Kwan! Are you hurt?"

He looked at her blankly, and then his gaze cleared. "You are well?" he asked, and she nodded. "I am fine," he said.

"Thank God!" she exclaimed with great feeling, and Kwan's lips curved upward in a sudden smile.

"You sound as if you are glad, *O-ka-o*."

Abbey's eyes flashed blue fire. "Of course, I am. You're my husband. I care what happens to you. I—" Her voice trailed off. *Love you*, she thought.

He stilled. "You . . ."

She shook her head, unable to admit her love for him, afraid that his feelings were not the same. "I . . . don't want to see you hurt."

Kwan seemed disappointed, but his look lasted only a second. "Trouble likes you, *Anikha Sagoha*. It follows you wherever you go."

She was surprised to see his silver gaze twinkle. He couldn't be too hurt, she thought. Abbey drank in the sight of his handsome face like a woman with a terrible thirst for love. His hair appeared darker in the forest where the thick treetop foliage allowed little sunlight to brighten the woods' floor.

There was a smear of blood on Kwan's cheek. Abbey touched her fingertips to his face to wipe it away. She felt no revulsion for the blood; her only thoughts were of Kwan and how long it had been since he'd held her.

She dared to caress his jaw. His skin burned

beneath her hand. So long, she thought, since she'd touched him freely. Too much anger . . . too much pain.

"Kwan . . ." Her eyes filled with tears.

"It is all right, *O-ka-o*," he said.

She blinked. "Is it?"

He drew her against his breast, embraced her with his powerful arms. Sighing, Abbey laid her head against his chest. It felt good to be home again, she mused, startled by the intensity of her feelings.

Should she tell him how she felt? She glanced up. Kwan had his eyes closed, a peaceful expression on his face.

No, she decided. For all his gentleness, he was still a savage, and while he was no longer quite a mystery to her, she had no idea how he felt about her, was afraid to learn that her love for him wasn't returned to full measure.

He stumbled and opened his eyes to smile at her weakly.

"You *are* hurt!" she said.

"Only a scratch, *O-ka-o*," he said. Kwan shifted and winced, arching his back.

Abbey hurried around him and inhaled sharply at what she saw. A dog bite . . . on Kwan's back.

The flesh wound was already swelling and turning purple.

314

Chapter 25

The Indian village maidens gasped, horrified to see the blood spattered over their sachem. All wanted to tend his wounds, but Abbey sent them away with firm words, words designed to remind them that Kwan belonged to her. She was annoyed that since her return some of the young women had tried to gain his attention, as if he were no longer married . . . as if she—Abbey—didn't exist.

Clearly, for her to leave had been a terrible thing. But the matrons understood, she realized, and the thought gave her a measure of comfort. Now if only things could be better between herself and her husband.

Kwan sat on their sleeping platform, while Abbey cleansed the injury to his back. She bathed his chest and arms first, glad to see that the blood there had been the dog's and not Kwan's.

She dipped a piece of soft cloth into a bowl of water and sponged away a layer of dried blood. "It's not as bad as it first seemed," she said, conscious of the glistening trail across his copper skin that was left by the wet fabric.

He grunted. "You were not the meat of the dog's mouth."

Abbey stood back and gazed at him with amusement. "So it hurts that much," she murmured.

He nodded.

"But you will live." Suspecting that he was playing up the pain to gain her sympathy, she wiped the outer area of the bite a little less gently than she had before.

"Yes," he grated between clenched teeth.

Contrite, she immediately gentled her touch. "I was worried the bite would fester. If the dog were ill . . ." She held his gaze, her blue eyes full of concern.

"Bear Claw checked the animal. It was angry because it was hurt." He appeared to have forgiven her roughness.

"A gunshot, you said." Abbey lifted the cloth from her husband's back. Cleared of blood, Kwan seemed to have suffered only a few minor scratches; even the dog bite was superficial.

"This is so," Kwan said. "A white man's work."

Abbey experienced a tightening in her stomach. "Are you reminding me of my place? That I'm white and, therefore, below contempt?"

Kwan frowned. "I know not what you mean. You are wife. Onondaga." He reached out to touch her face. "What is this con-tempt?" he asked softly.

"Hate."

He withdrew his hand, his features shocked. "You believe this of me?"

"The *Yen'-gees* killed Morning Flower."

"You did not."

"Yes, I know, but—"

He tugged her into his arms, kissed her hungrily.

"I do not kiss a *Yen'-gees* murderer. You are not. You are *Anikha Sagoha*. Sun Daughter."

"Abbey Rawlins," she said.

He nodded. "That, too." His lips formed a sly smile. "And it is Abbey Rawlins I like kissing best."

Kwan captured her mouth a second time, making her moan as desire spiraled within her and her senses reeled. He released her lips.

"Are you done with my back?" he asked. He had averted his gaze, but Abbey saw how his chest labored as he breathed—the effect of their kiss, she realized with happiness.

Bemused, Abbey nodded. How could he talk of his back when it was obvious that they were both thinking of other things . . . like lying down on their platform and making love?

"Ab-bey?" he asked, and she met his gaze.

"Yes, yes. I'm finished."

"*Oh-yah'-neh!* Good." He shifted his position so that he was facing her. "It is time for healing other things."

"Other things?" she echoed, suddenly mesmerized by the strange light in her husband's eyes.

"The hole that is between us. We are man and wife—one. It is not good to be apart." As he spoke, Kwan reached for Abbey's tunic hem, easing it up over her stomach and full, throbbing breasts, and finally over her head.

Abbey closed her eyes in anticipation of his touch.

317

The air in the hut was cool—the first sign of the coming cold months. She waited with lids closed, heart thumping, and blood pulsing through her veins. But he didn't touch her. She heard no movement, and she opened her eyes.

The solid impact of his silver gaze made her gasp. She saw her longing mirrored in Kwan's rugged features. She felt as if his look stroked and caressed every tingling inch of her.

"Kwan." She trembled.

"You are a brave woman, *O-ka-o*.'

She frowned. "Brave?"

"To go after your Jamie."

Abbey tensed. The subject of her brother remained painful to her. He was still out there waiting to be rescued from captivity; she felt like she'd failed him.

"Softly, *O-ka-o*," Kwan urged. He must have sensed her mood. "I will help your Jamie."

The change in her was instantaneous. "You will?"

He bent his head to lick her nipple. Straightening, he smiled. *"Do-gehs'*. Truly. If it will please you."

"Oh, Kwan!" she cried. Capturing his head between her two hands, she brought his mouth close for a thorough kiss.

The warm, willing responsive mouth beneath his own made Kwan groan. He should have agreed to help her sooner, he thought, enjoyed the wild mating ritual of lips and tongues. *I will find her Jamie, and she will be happy and will not—must not—leave me.*

"Kwan?" Abbey must have sensed the tension in him, for she gazed up at him with concern. "What's wrong?"

He shook his head and touched his fingertips to

318

her upper lip. "You are beau-ti-ful, *O-ka-o*. I am glad to have you to wife." It was the closest he'd ever come to admitting his love for her.

Abbey looked radiantly happy. "And I am glad to have you to husband," she whispered, leaning against him, straining her naked curves against his flesh.

He inhaled sharply at her actions, and hope swelled within his breast. "This is good." He stroked her between her legs, enjoyed the way passion deepened the color of her blue eyes, the way her mouth softened in response.

"And this is good," she said. She placed a hand on his hardening male member, and Kwan moaned his agreement. "And this," Abbey said, her voice soft. Her hand moved to his thigh . . . his belly . . . back to tantalize his swollen shaft. "And this . . . and this . . . and this."

Kwan groaned and gasped as her hands continued to fondle him. He explored her as she did him. They caressed and kissed and whispered love words, urging each other on toward that place where their bodies soared and their hearts leapt in joyful unison.

When Abbey was ready, Kwan stretched out above her, impaling her with his staff. Abbey cried out with joy as he thrust into her. The rhythm was ancient, the music was love. And it was good for the both of them. It had been a long time, and each was hungry to touch the other's soul.

The next morning Abbey woke up feeling content.

Kwan was beside her, sleeping. The warmth of his frame reached out to envelop her, making her feel cherished, loved.

Could it be true? Had Kwan admitted love for her? *Perhaps not in so many words,* she thought, *but surely he was telling me he loves me when he said he enjoyed having me to wife.*

Hope blossomed in her heart like a wild rose, bringing joy and color to her world.

Only Jamie remained between them. Kwan had promised to help her find him, but he had implied so before . . . Would he go back on his promise? If so, how could she ever again trust his word?

They had been so busy making love that she'd never thought to ask him when. When he'd search for Jamie.

Abbey studied him. Kwan lay close to her on his back. His chest rose and fell with each breath. Fascinated, she placed her hand against him, watching, feeling the up and down movement.

Should she ask him? she wondered. What harm could it do to mention it now that he'd agreed to help her?

His lashes fluttered open. *"Gah'-jee."*

She obliged him by pressing her lips to his sensual mouth. Abbey straightened with a smile. "Good morning, Kwan."

Should she ask him? she wondered again. She regarded him thoughtfully. The last thing she wanted was to anger Kwan . . . not with this new peace between them.

"What is it, Ab-bey?"

She met his glance. "I was thinking . . ." Kwan

320

frowned, and she hurried on, "About my brother . . ."

"Yes?" He ran his fingers over her shoulder, and she closed her eyes. It was difficult for her to think; his feather-light touch made her skin rise in little bumps like goose flesh.

She opened her eyes and stared. He didn't seem angry; Abbey was encouraged. "When will we begin the search?"

"Soon. When the moon rises full in the night sky."

"But that's nearly a month away!" she protested.

He grasped both of her shoulders. "*O-ka-o*—Sun Daughter, this day we begin to make ready for the Great Council Meeting. Tomorrow, we leave when the sun brightens the day sky." He pierced her with his silver gaze. "There will be many of the People at the Council fire. Many Iroquois. There I can ask after your sun-haired brother, but you must wait, *O-ka-o*. I am the sachem. You must leave this matter to me. This I promise you—we will find your Jamie." He paused. "Does this please you?"

With tears in her eyes, Abbey nodded. "I'm sorry," she whispered, feeling like a fool. "I didn't know."

"That is why I tell you. But, Ab-bey, you must hear me and you must listen. There will be many brothers at Onondaga, but there will be enemies, too. I will ask questions. I will decide when and how we find Jamie. Do you understand?"

"Yes, but—oh, Kwan, what if none of them know him? What will I do then? I promised Father!"

Kwan regarded her solemnly. "I will find him, *O-ka-o*." *Dead or alive*, he thought, *I will find him for you.*

The camp of the English soldiers was quiet. It was dawn, that time between total darkness and bright sun, and many of the men still slept.

The army had moved after the attack by the Indians. A number of the soldiers had been killed, but a good size gathering had remained to continue on, to follow their colonel's orders.

William Breckingridge sat by the remains of yesterday's campfire. He stared off into space, contemplating his next move. His head was bandaged at his brow. He had suffered a slight blow to the head when the Iroquois had hit him, but otherwise he was fine. Why the Indian didn't make sure he was dead was a mystery to him. He'd been puzzling over this since the attack.

He thought of the woman Abbey and his teeth snapped. Bitch! he thought. It was her fault he'd been taken off guard. She was the one responsible for the death of his men!

Breckingridge cursed her and himself for playing the fool over a curvaceous body. *Oh, but she smelled so sweet!* He could still detect her fragrance, feel her lush, full softness crushed against his chest. And her mouth . . . He felt his body harden; he closed his eyes.

She'd struggled, but oh how he loved a woman who fought! It made the game for him that much more exciting. He enjoyed the feeling of power over women. It made him feel strong, masculine . . . in control.

But damn if the bloody bitch hasn't escaped me! He wasn't finished with her yet—not by a long shot.

He experienced a burning heat in his loins as he envisioned what he'd do to her when he had his hands on her. There were so many ways to use her . . . so many ways to amuse himself . . .

"Colonel." Terrington, his lieutenant, stood before him, eyeing him with wary eyes.

Annoyed at the interruption, the colonel looked up. "What is it, Lieutenant?" he growled. His staff was straining against his breeches; he could feel its throbbing heat.

The young officer flinched. "It's Rogers, sir. He's taken the fever."

Breckingridge frowned and then snapped, "What do you want me to do, Terrington? Work a bloody miracle?" He waved his arm. "Make him as comfortable as you can and then leave him. We've no time for ill men! They only hinder us against the Indians!"

Terrington was appalled at the colonel's lack of regard for human life. "But, sir, Rogers . . . he has a wife . . . children."

The colonel looked away. "We all have those we care about, Terrington. It's most unfortunate, I grant you, but what else are we to do? Wait here until the savages attack again?"

The young man thought to remind the colonel of family love. "Sir, your niece . . ."

"Yes. My niece . . ." Breckingridge's gaze took on a look of pain. "The savages have her. I must get her back. I must pay back the Iroquois for their wrongs!"

"But Rogers's wife. Think how she'd feel if she were here . . ."

"Are you trying to tell me how to run this army, soldier!" the colonel exclaimed.

323

Terrington shook his head. "No, sir—"

"Oh, very well, soldier! I'll have a look at Rogers—for his wife's sake." He glanced about. "Where is he?"

"By the stream, sir."

The colonel rose and took a moment to dust off the seat of his breeches. "Damn nuisance if you ask me!" he grumbled as he moved in the right direction.

His subordinate followed him, fury raging within his breast, for the young man was sure of it now . . . nothing would stand in the way of the colonel's lust for Indian blood. William Breckingridge, Terrington realized, was a cold, heartless madman hellbent on revenge.

"Rogers." The colonel bent down to the sick man. "How are you, son?"

"C-cold, sir." The man was shivering, but not delirious. A good sign, Breckingridge thought. Rogers was the tracker for his troops. To lose the man would be not only inconvenient but dangerous as well. If Rogers died, they would go on; it was too late to turn. But the way would be easier with Rogers's help.

"Terrington, get this man another blanket!" the British commander bellowed.

"But sir . . ." the lieutenant objected. "Won't that bring up his temperature?"

The colonel reddened with rage. "And how do you know this?"

The young man blushed. "My mother, sir."

"Oh." Breckingridge immediately backed down. A person's mother was a wealth of good advice. If the boy's mother had said it, then it must be so. He eyed the streambed. "Have you tried bathing him with cold water?"

"Yes," said the man nearest Rogers's head. "And it's lowered the heat some, sir, but—"

"Well, take off his clothes," the colonel interrupted, "and dump him in."

Two of the three soldiers there looked horrified, all but Terrington who glanced at Breckingridge with surprise.

"Do it!" the lieutenant said. "Sir, it makes good sense to me."

Amid grumbling against the ills of bathing a naked, sick man in the forest, Rogers was stripped of his uniform and set down gently into a shallow area of the stream. He sat looking like a small boy, shivering and pale.

"Sir," he said between chattering teeth. "I saw him, sir."

The colonel frowned. Perhaps the boy was becoming delirious. "What are you saying, boy? Who, soldier?"

"Great Arrow."

Breckingridge leaned forward, alert. "When?"

"During the raid. The one yesterday."

"And you didn't tell me before this!" the officer boomed. Kwan Kahaiska fighting beside his braves? It didn't make sense; the man was a sachem. Sachems didn't fight.

"The Indian looked familiar," Rogers was saying. "It t-took me a while to r-remember who he was." He hugged himself with his arms. His lips were beginning to purple. Breckingridge waved the men to lift the boy from the water.

"I saw him that d-day at the village . . . when Smythe was c-captured," Rogers said as two soldiers hefted him up by his arms.

"Why would a sachem fight?" Breckingridge wondered aloud.

"The woman," Terrington said.

The colonel looked at him. "The blonde—Abbey?" He suddenly smiled, a slow smile full of evil intent. "Yes, yes, it does make sense." He addressed Rogers. "Do you remember the woman at the village?"

Rogers smiled gratefully as one of the soldiers wrapped a blanket around his naked form.

"Rogers!" Breckingridge snarled impatiently.

The young man jumped. "The woman?" He swayed dizzily as he tried to think. "I may have . . . there were others there. White women." His expression brightened. "Yes, I saw her. I remember seeing her with two little girls."

Breckingridge was all smiles. "Good work, soldier!" He was pleased with Rogers, who had just proven himself once again. He turned to Terrington, "See that he's dried and dressed. Then, get him something to eat. Keep him comfortable." He saw the lieutenant's look and said, "We're not going to leave him."

The lieutenant looked relieved. "Yes, sir."

"If his fever rises, bathe him again with the cold water." The colonel barely saw his man's nod before he turned back toward the unlit campfire.

Abbey Rawlins is Great Arrow's woman. Breckingridge grinned. "Good," he muttered beneath his breath. "Before he dies, the savage can watch while I use his woman!"

That day and the night that followed, the Indians made preparations for the journey to Onondaga, a place only an hour north where the eternal fire of the League burned. The heart of the confederacy.

Abbey worked beside the other matrons, readying the food supplies, packing cooking utensils and other necessities including furs and extra weapons. She picked up a knife, fingering the blade. If this was a peace mission, then why did they need to bring weapons?

"You wish to use that on me?" Kwan asked as he approached.

She smiled as she tucked the knife into a satchel. "Only thinking about it . . . so for now, you're safe."

Eyes twinkling, her husband inclined his head. He placed his hand on her head, running his fingers through her blonde hair. "You work hard, *O-ka-o* . . . as well as any of them." With a nod of his head, he gestured toward a group of women husking corn.

She experienced pleasure. "So you are pleased with me?"

His lips curved into a sensual smile, and a warmth invaded her stomach, radiating through her whole being. "I am pleased." He leaned close to whisper in her ear. *"Ah-gwas',"* he murmured.

"Ah-gwas'?" she asked. She was unfamiliar with the word.

His eyes flamed. "Very," he said, and she blushed

at his frank look of male desire. "You are almost done?" he said.

"All I have to do is pack these weapons." She bit the inside of her cheek. "Kwan? I thought the League was a peaceful one. You spoke of enemies. Is that why we need weapons?"

He seemed reluctant to answer her. "I have learned a great lesson. One must always carry arrows . . . to forget is calling out to those who would attack."

"Kwan." O-wee-soo approached, eyeing her grandson and his wife with satisfaction. "Sun Daughter," she greeted Abbey. Then to Kwan, she said, "We will be ready soon."

He smiled. The old woman was more than sixty summers and yet there was an energy and youthfulness about her that made her age seem a lie.

The matron turned to Abbey. "Knife-Woman's son has nicked himself while cutting fish. She asks that you tend to him."

Abbey nodded. She was pleased to be of service to the Indian people. Her knowledge of healing had brought her a measure of respect within the tribe.

"In the longhouse?" she asked.

O-wee-soo inclined her head. "You have made a loyal friend there, Sun Daughter."

It was true, Abbey thought, that Knife-Woman had become more friendly to her since she'd saved the life of the woman's husband. "Knife-woman," she murmured.

O-wee-soo raised her eyebrows. "Bear Claw."

"Bear Claw?" Abbey blinked. The brave had not been as hostile as when she'd first come to the Onondagas, but a loyal friend. "Bear Claw?" she

328

echoed, sounding amazed.

Kwan grinned while the old woman chuckled. "Bear Claw is a man of little words, *O-ka-o*," Kwan said. "You have captured his heart with your kind ways."

Like I have captured yours? Abbey thought, wishing it were true.

"*Anikha Sagoha!*" Evening Sky came from the longhouse belonging to Knife-Woman's clan. "Knife-Woman looks for you!"

"Go, *O-ka-o*. I will see you later."

Bear Claw? Abbey thought with wonder. Her lips twitched. Bear Claw—her friend. She had a mental image of the fierce-looking warrior with Iroquois war crest and painted face smiling and waving at her.

No . . . Bear Claw never smiled. She couldn't expect to see him smile.

She doubted the warrior ever lost that stern face. Abbey chuckled as she entered the longhouse. She had pictured the brave making love to his wife with a scowl on his face.

Chapter 26

Abbey eyed the canoe with misgiving. "Is it safe?" The vessel was made of the bark from an elm tree. The bark was sewn together and spread with a pitch made from the pine trees, which was mixed with some kind of fibrous pieces. The vessel had thin wooden poles inside for shape and strength.

"Would I ask you in if it were not so?" Kwan asked, his eyes sparkling with amusement. He reached out his hand to her. *"Gah'-jee, O-ka-o."* I will not let you drop."

He stood calf-deep in the water, while she was on the shore.

"Come," he said. "We must go by water. It is faster this way. I am sachem and must get to the Council Fire before the others join us by foot."

"I don't know . . ."

"Give me the pack," Kwan said.

She handed her husband the small satchel. The bulk of their belongings would travel with the tribe following the Iroquois Trail.

"What if the canoe tips over?" she said as he waded to the vessel and stowed their supplies. "We'll lose our things."

"And you will fall in?" he suggested as he returned to her. His lips twitched. "I will not let you drown." He suddenly chuckled.

Abbey was annoyed. "What's so funny?"

"You, *O-ka-o*. You stand up to your enemy, ready to fight. You stand up to the *Yen'-gees* colonel, yet you are afraid of a good canoe."

She looked startled, and then she allowed herself a small smile. "I guess you're right. I'll go." She reached out to him, and Kwan swung her up onto his powerful arms.

He grinned down at her as he splashed back to the canoe. "I will keep you safe, *Teh-ne-taiw*," he said, calling her wife.

His smile sent Abbey's pulse racing. She found it difficult to breathe. "I will hold you to that promise, *Haiw-nah*," she replied, referring to him as husband.

Kwan raised his eyebrows as he set her into the canoe. The vessel rocked back and forth. Abbey shrieked, sat down with a plunk, and clutched the sides with white-knuckled hands.

"Not that way," he told her. He instructed her how to sit in the vessel—on her knees. He helped her up. The shifting movement caused the canoe to tip and rock precariously. Abbey gasped and caught her husband's shoulders.

Laughing, Kwan tried to steady both her and the canoe.

"You—you!" she sputtered, noting his mischievous twinkle. "You did that on purpose!" She kept grasp of his shoulders; his flesh was firm and warm beneath her hands.

His mouth widened with delight, a flash of white teeth. She was momentarily taken aback by the sight of his boyish look. Here was a side of him she'd never seen before, and it only strengthened the feelings she harbored for him in her heart.

The vessel stilled abruptly. Abbey glanced to the other side and saw Bear Claw. He had steadied the canoe, and he inclined his head, telling her that he would continue to hold it while she maneuvered herself into the right position.

Once situated, Abbey met the warrior's gaze. "Thank you," she said softly.

Bear Claw nodded without a word and left. His help had stirred up Abbey's memory of O-wee-soo's words, "You have made a loyal friend there, Sun Daughter." And then her husband's statement, "Bear Claw is a man of little words . . ."

Perhaps it was true, Abbey thought. She smiled.

Kwan climbed into the canoe with barely a stir of the water, which only confirmed in Abbey's mind that moments ago he'd been playing with her. At first, she was angry, but her displeasure didn't last long, for she got caught up in the canoe ride, in the wild beauty surrounding her.

There were four elm-bark canoes making the trip. O-wee-soo and Silver Fox rode together. Spring Rain, her son Stone-Face, and Evening Sky were also of those allowed to travel by boat.

Abbey had been embarrassed to see how easily O-wee-soo and Silver Fox boarded the watercraft. It made her fear seem foolish.

"How far is Onondaga?" she asked Kwan when she'd unbent sufficiently in her anger to speak to him. Onondaga was the name given to the place of the ever-burning Council Fire as well as those who tended the flame.

There was a slight pause. "A short journey by water," he said.

A short journey? she thought, worrying about the length of her canoe ride. How long was that? Abbey held tight to the canoe's sides as the vessel left sight of the village shore.

"You are stiff, *O-ka-o*. Do not be. Relax. Allow yourself to move. I will steer the *Ka-o-wa*."

Staring straight ahead, she gave an affirmative jerk of her head. *Ka-o-wa*, she supposed, meant canoe, but not in Onondaga, for she was familiar enough with the language to have heard their word for boat, which was *Kun-e-a-e-tah*.

"*Ka-o-wa* is what language?" she said. The languages of the six Iroquois nations were similar in many ways. Although some words were different, the tribes had no trouble understanding each other.

"Cayuga," her husband said.

"That's right. You spent time with the Cayugas, didn't you?"

"Yes." His tone said that he didn't care to talk about it.

Abbey remembered O-wee-soo telling her that Kwan had come to the Onondaga people from the Cayugas, who had been the ones to capture him as a young boy. She understood that the memory wasn't a pleasant one.

From the corner of her eye, she could see the paddle

dip into the water, feel the movement of the canoe as it went forward. She heard Kwan's chuckle.

"You will hurt by the time we reach Onondaga if you don't do as I say," he said.

Abbey forced herself to relax. The canoe eased through the water with the ease of a swan gliding across the lake. She began to enjoy the smooth ride.

The area looked different from this vantage point, Abbey thought. Why was it that the colors in the New World looked more natural, more vivid?

The sky overhead was a glorious azure blue. She could see several shades of green in the foliage along shore, from the dark rich color of the tall pines to the lighter hues that were reminiscent of the leaves at springtime.

The lake was huge, like an ocean. It seemed to stretch on forever, a rich vibrant, clear blue.

Kwan was silent behind her as he propelled the craft toward their destination. The only sounds Abbey could hear came from the birds overhead, the dip and swish of the canoe paddle in the water, and the low murmur of conversation from the other three canoes.

Abbey closed her eyes and felt in tune, as one, with her surroundings. The motion of the canoe was soothing, and she was smiling when she opened her eyes again. For the first time since they'd left the shoreline, she chanced a glance back at her husband.

"You enjoy the ride?" he asked, returning her smile.

She nodded her head. "It's beautiful. I'm no longer afraid."

"Good," he said, and she faced the front.

The journey to Onondaga, the seat of the League of Six Nations, was a short one—as Kwan said. About twenty minutes, Abbey gauged. They had turned onto a river; Onondaga, the meeting place, was a slight distance inland from the great lake.

As they moved toward shore, she caught sight of other canoes coming across the great lake toward the river from different directions. They were not the only ones traveling by water, she realized. The other tribes had farther to go. The waterway was probably the most direct route for many of them.

"Kwan." She gestured toward those vessels moving up behind them. They were still some distance away, but she didn't have to squint to tell that the occupants were Indians.

Kwan had climbed out of the canoe. He held it steady as he eyed the approaching craft. "Seneca," he said.

Abbey perked up with interest. "Senecas? Aren't they the ones . . ."

He nodded. "There are those among them that are unhappy with the League." He swung his gaze from the crafts to meet his wife's look. "Do not think they are all enemy. They are not. The Seneca are our brothers. There are many among them who are friends."

Her attention was so taken with the Seneca canoes that Abbey climbed from their own canoe, unaided.

Someone approached—an elderly Indian with long hair. He was the head sachem of this village, the keeper of the Council Fire.

The sound of drums and primitive song filled the air as Kwan and Abbey followed the Onondaga chief up the path from the river to the meeting site. Abbey glanced briefly over her shoulder for one last look at the picturesque view of the lake. Canoes were gathering at the river mouth.

She happened to catch sight of Silver Fox's white hair. He had stopped to speak with an Onondaga warrior, one unfamiliar to Abbey. O-wee-soo and the others were with him.

"Wait, Kwan," Abbey said.

Kwan caught the objects of her gaze and nodded. As they stood patiently while the others climbed the embankment to join them, Abbey thought she detected a blond head in one of the approaching Indian canoes. She became excited. Another captive?

"Kwan!" she gasped, grabbing his arm. "Look!"

Her husband narrowed his gaze toward the canoes. "Seneca."

"No! The young man in the far canoe. He has light hair like mine. See!" Her eyes lit up as she swung to regard Kwan. "He's an English man."

Kwan gazed down at his wife and frowned. "You do not know this."

"We can wait for them. Or ask them. Perhaps he's seen Jamie. *Please, Kwan.*" But when she looked back at the lake, the canoe she thought she'd seen was gone. "What!" It was as it had disappeared into thin air. She moved toward the river.

Kwan stopped her. "You must have been wrong," he said.

"No! No, I wasn't!" She squeezed his arm. "Someone else must have seen him."

"What is wrong?" Silver Fox said as he came up to

them. O-wee-soo, Evening Sky, and the others joined them.

Abbey turned to Kwan's father. "I saw someone who can help find my brother!"

"You look for me?" Stone-Face said as he approached, hearing only "brother."

She shook her head. "Silver Fox—did you see him?" Her eyes widened. "What if it's Jamie? What if that man is my brother!"

The old man shook his head. "I am sorry. I did not see."

"Ab-bey," Kwan said, sounding impatient. "You do not know this. It may have been the Spirit of the Sun on a warrior's head."

"He had fair hair, Kwan!" Abbey was angry. "Golden hair, damn it!" Her eyes stung with tears. "Why won't you believe me?"

"Softly," Kwan said, trying to soothe her.

O-wee-soo's brow furrowed. "What is this, my son? Did she see her brother?"

"She saw a canoe and thought one of the Indians must be an Englishman."

"He's not Indian!" Abbey insisted.

"Can we not ask Oscatax?" the old matron suggested.

Kwan shook his head. "The time is not good. But I will do so . . ." His face hardened as he studied his wife. ". . . after the great opening of Council."

O-wee-soo nodded and turned to her grandson's wife. "He will ask after the one with hair of sun."

"Why can't he ask now?"

The Indian shook her head. "You do not understand yet the ways of the Council. There is much to

337

talk about. The time is not right to discuss a *Yen'-gees* slave."

"But what if he's my brother!"

"Ab-bey!" Kwan snapped, all patience gone. "You will draw eyes with your anger. Please stop now. I am your sachem and I have spoken. I will see after your Jamie later."

Abbey had to be satisfied with her angry husband's promise. She felt frustrated, but to protest further would make her seem childish and unreasonable. *Please understand! It looked like Jamie in that canoe!*

She was trembling as she followed the others into the great council house. *Soon, Jamie. Soon!* she thought.

The longhouse was larger than any she'd ever seen before, at least ten times the size of the biggest longhouse in Kwan's village. Other than its size, Abbey had very little impression of the building. She was too restless, too upset.

She tensed when her husband glanced at her. Kwan was angry with her and perhaps he had a right to be. But she couldn't help herself. She was so close to her beloved brother—the only link to her former life.

"We will sit with the others," O-wee-soo stated, speaking of the Indian women already seated.

Abbey searched for her Indian mother, but was unable to find her. "Where is Spring Rain?" The woman had been with them only moments ago.

"She had gone to the trail to wait for those of our tribe."

Abbey was surprised. "But that could take a while. We've only arrived ourselves."

Silver Fox spoke up. "The Iroquois are fast. They will be here soon." He left to join the men, and the women sat down.

Abbey stared across the expanse of the great longhouse, hoping for a glimpse of a blond head—Jamie's. He was close—she could feel it!

She strained her eyes over the crowded gathering, her heart pumping when she encountered the sight of a blonde head. Her spirits plummeted when she realized that the fair-haired figure was a woman. A captive, no doubt, she thought. Perhaps one made wife to a sachem as she had been to Kwan. Could she be the one she'd seen in the canoe? Abbey hoped not.

She closed her eyes, wanting to scream with frustration. If only she could leave the meeting to search for Jamie among those outside. Not everyone was allowed to attend Council.

Her thoughts took her back to her childhood, back to the days when her mother was alive and her father was happy. There'd been so much love in their little household. Jamie and she had been raised to be close, affectionate, friends and allies against a world that had labeled them outcasts of society.

Her parents had been solid examples of the power of true love, inspiring their children, teaching them. And Abbey had been awed further by her physician father who had extended that love to include his patients.

Life changed with the death of Abbey's mother. Abbey felt the pain of remembering the loss, the grief, and the horrible confrontation that had followed between her brother and father.

"Why didn't you save her!" Jamie had shouted,

tears streaming down his young face. "I thought you were a physician! You're nothing but a helpless old man . . ."

"Jamie!" she'd gasped.

But the damage had been done, and in a way, she had understood that grief and pain had made Jamie say things he didn't mean . . . or didn't want to.

Abbey could still clearly recall her father's expression. His face had resembled death, for when his wife had died, something within him had died, too. The will to live.

In the days following his outburst, Jamie had been hurt, angered to see their father's decline in both spirit and health. He hadn't understood that each person grieved in his own way, that their father couldn't help being only a shadow of his former self. Jamie had grown impatient with James Rawlin's melancholia. "Snap out of it, Father! There's still life, for God's sake. You have a daughter and son!"

Finally, Jamie reached a point where he'd been unable to live in the sad little cottage in Kent, England. Offered a fine opportunity to travel to the New World to learn a trade, he'd turned his thoughts and energies toward a new life. It was the first time since the death of their mother that Abbey had seen her brother's enthusiasm, his smile.

"I'm going to the colonies," he'd told his family.

James had stared, but had said nothing. Abbey had been too stunned at first by the announcement to form a response. Jamie was leaving? How would she manage without his company?

"I'm not leaving without a look back, Abbe," he'd assured her. "As soon as I can, I'll send the funds for you and Father to come across. I'm going to be a

340

silversmith. Walt and I are going to work for his uncle.''

Abbey had patted his cheek and forced a smile. How could she damper the boy's happiness? He deserved his chance in the world. Who was she to stay in his way?

And so Jamie had left. Abbey had bundled up her ailing father and taken him to the port to see Jamie off on ship. Their parting had been tearful and difficult. "I love you, Abbe," he'd whispered. He'd looked more of a man than a boy, and she couldn't help but feel proud.

Jamie had left England on a cold, gray morning, bound for Philadelphia. He'd written her once. He'd begun his apprenticeship within a day of his arrival in the New World. His news had been so happy, so full of life.

Tears flooded Abbey's eyes, and she blinked to clear them. He was happy, she thought, until he was captured by Indians. Only God knew what his life was like now.

Her lips moved silently. "I have to find you, Jamie. No matter what I have to do, no matter what it takes . . .''

She could hear the Iroquois speaking, but their words didn't register. The desire, the need, to find Jamie had grown so strong that it overrode all else in her life.

The meeting broke up for the day, and Abbey was glad to leave. Outside the building, she could search among those who had come with their sachems. The air outside the longhouse was cooler than before with a crisp edge to it that announced the time of autumn.

Without conscious thought, Abbey stopped in the path of exiting Indians and studied the sea of Iroquois humanity. There was no sign of Jamie's familiar face.

"Ab-bey." Kwan came from behind her, grabbed her arm. He led her out of the Indians' way and stopped in a clearing by the woods' edge. "You look for someone . . . me?"

She flushed guiltily and looked away.

"*O-ka-o*, I will look for Jamie. You must not do so. The peace between brothers is easily broken."

"But, Kwan—"

He grasped her shoulders, lowered his face close to hers. She could smell his luring scent, felt his breath tickle her skin. "I mean what I say, wife. Do not wander where only fools go." He narrowed his gaze. "You will listen?"

Head bowed, Abbey nodded. Then, she glanced up. "But I don't have to like it, do I?" she said, challenging him.

Kwan's face softened and he chuckled. "No, *O-ka-o*, I am not such a fool as that." He placed his hand in the curve of her neck, caressed her skin. "Come. Let us join O-wee-soo and the others. It is getting late."

Which meant he was hungry, Abbey supposed. She met his gaze, saw his glistening silver eyes, and melted with love for him. "All right," she said. She wasn't going to give in easily, but . . .

Kwan's lips twitched as if he were amused. Then, he bent his head and kissed her briefly. A reward, she thought bitterly, for agreeing to obey his commands.

Chapter 27

"I am proud of you, *O-ka-o*," Kwan murmured against her shoulder. "You listen well." His lips moved down her arm, kissing and worshiping her smooth skin.

Abbey didn't answer. She felt more than a little guilt, for she hadn't obeyed him. Before they'd left Onondaga, she'd given in to the urge to speak with the Senecas. How could she not?

She'd been good at first. Her eyes had looked, but she had refrained from questioning the Indians. She'd had every intention of listening to Kwan. But then she'd seen those Senecas, learned who they were . . .

She gasped. Kwan's mouth was doing exciting things to her belly, nuzzling and licking her white skin. Her stomach muscles quivered. He moved down to her right thigh, and she moaned and clutched his head, threading her fingers through his hair.

"Kwan . . ." She stroked his silky head, arching

her body off their platform. Kwan rose up onto his knees, smiling at her with his eyes. He was pleased with her; she didn't have the heart to change that, to confess her sin.

"You like?" His voice was husky with desire.

She nodded and pulled him down to her. "I like," she whispered.

Kissing him fiercely, she squirmed beneath him, the contact inflaming her need.

Kwan groaned, enjoying the writhing movements of his wife's form. Abbey had pleased him. She'd known when to obey him, her husband—her sachem. He was starting to believe that she actually cared for him . . . that it was more for her than just physical desire.

He caressed her in all her sensitive places, making her moan and gasp and sob out loud. She touched him back, her fingers searing his skin, making his heart pound and the blood rush, roaring, through his body.

"Kwan . . . please," she gasped.

"Yes, *O-ka-o*. Yes. I come to you."

In her desire, she opened her legs for him. He positioned himself above her, staring down at her, enjoying the passionate look on Abbey's face.

His staff was hot and hard when he slid into the moist haven between her silken thighs. He was slow to set a rhythm, taking his time to move in and out of her. Kwan loved the little sounds she made when he made love to her, and he wanted the whimpers to continue. They drove him wild.

But soon Abbey became impatient as if she were frustrated with the slow pace of their lovemaking.

She clung to his back, bucked against him. She kissed and nipped him . . . his neck . . . his shoulder . . . his jaw.

They made love savagely. Abbey's response seemed almost desperate to Kwan, but he had no time to question it. Soon, he was caught up in her momentum, in the scent, the texture, the sweet essence of her body.

Abbey cried out, her muscles tensing, as ecstasy washed over her in thick, pulsating waves.

Kwan groaned as he spilled his seed into his wife's womb. He buried his face in the curve of her neck, as his limbs relaxed and he gasped for air.

It had been a passionate, almost violent joining. Abbey was stunned by the force of her desire, by the wanton, wild way she'd reacted.

Neither spoke as Kwan rolled to the side, but he kept his wife close to him, tucking her against his right breast.

Abbey lay within Kwan's arms, her eyes closed. The sense of peace and contentment that usually came to her after she and Kwan had made love was illusive. Her feelings of guilt and betrayal were too strong. She had defied her husband by going against his wishes and questioning the Senecas, and she'd been haunted by her guilt ever since.

Which must account for the sick feeling in her stomach, she thought. The illness seemed to come and go with her attacks of conscience.

She loved Kwan. What if her actions caused reprisals for the Onondagas? For the League? What if she'd said or done something to offend the Senecas? That brave she'd spoken with . . . what was his name? He-Who-Comes-In-The-Night. He'd seemed so fierce, so unfeeling. It had been a mistake to mention Kwan's name. The brave's scowl had deepened, and she'd immediately sensed his hostility.

Abbey rose while Kwan slept and slipped on her tunic. She then crept from the hut to wander about the village yard. She needed to think . . . Kwan was sure to find out she'd disobeyed him. It would be better to tell him first before he found out on his own. *Or would it?*

There was only a sliver of moon to light up the night sky. The encampment was dark and quiet as Abbey went to the stockade gate.

Kwan seemed at ease since leaving the council meeting, she thought. Perhaps all the tribes had come to an agreement. Maybe the bond of brother to Indian brother was stronger than the Senecas' desire to join the French.

There was a renewed measure of peace established within the confederacy at Onondaga. Abbey was told that the Senecas posed no immediate threat to the League of Six Nations.

Am I worrying for nothing then? she wondered.

She knew the trail to the lake by heart, so the absence of light didn't bother her. There was a soft breeze; it teased the tendrils of her blonde hair, caressed her skin, reminding her of Kwan's touch.

Abbey stopped and closed her eyes. What would she do if Jamie wanted her to return to Philadephia with him? How could she leave Kwan?

She couldn't leave her husband! She loved him. Jamie would have to understand. He, too, could be happy among the Indians if he wanted.

She sent up a silent prayer that the future for all of them would come easy, that no one would get hurt in the end.

But she had her doubts. And she was frightened.

"Colonel?" the soldier whispered. "There she is!"

Breckingridge strained to see the woman through the darkness. He captured a glimpse of her golden hair. "That's her all right. They've got the guard?"

"Yes, sir. He's dead."

"Good. Wait until she gets to the water. There'll be less chance for her to flee." The colonel grinned. He couldn't believe his luck! The woman had come to him; he hadn't had to attack the village.

"Colonel."

"Ready, soldier?" Breckingridge said, and the man nodded. "Let's move!" the colonel growled. "Don't hurt her. She's mine! She's the bait to lure in the savage—Kwan Kahaiska."

And the British army moved forward.

Abbey stood by the lake and contemplated taking a swim. The night was cool, however, and she hesitated. The breeze at the water's edge was stronger than in the village. It chilled her to the bone, making her skin prickle.

She had forgotten her moccasins, and she dipped her toe in to test the temperature of the lake. The water felt warm, which surprised her. The thought of a swim became more pleasing to her, and she reached to remove her deerskin tunic.

Abbey was in the act of undressing when she heard a sound. She dropped her tunic hem, and it fell into place, covering her decently . . . but not before the men who surrounded her got a good look at her naked curves. She heard the soft catcalls and crude, whispered comments of the English soldiers.

"Well, my dear," a familiar voice said. "We meet again. Such a pleasure to *see you.*"

"Breckingridge!" Shocked, Abbey gaped at him, too stunned to be embarrassed at being caught half naked by a group of men. "I thought you were killed!"

"Apparently so did your Indian friend."

"Bear Claw?"

"So that is the beast's name, is it?" He turned to one of his men. "Remember that name, Rogers. The savage will need to be singled out for extra punishment."

Abbey was horrified.

"Let's go!" Breckingridge ordered his men. Immediately, a man appeared at each side of Abbey. They grabbed her arms.

"Where are we going?" she asked. "Where are you taking me?"

The colonel smiled, an evil flash of white teeth in the black night. "To finish what we started, my dear. I want to try out a few ways to make you scream and beg for mercy. You and I will put on a good show for the redskin. The last thing he'll see before he dies a slow death!"

When Kwan woke up, Abbey was gone, and he was

lonely for her company. The first thing he did when he left their hut was call for a messenger. It was time to keep his promise to begin the search for his wife's brother.

He requested the same runner who'd gone to the Onondaga sachems—Crooked Ear. The brave was fast on his feet; Kwan knew he could trust him to make record time. Crooked Ear had a special talent; he had the ability to get others to talk with him without their taking offense at his curiosity.

"*Anikha Sagoha*—my wife . . . she has a *Yen'-gees* brother," Kwan told Crooked Ear when the brave appeared. "You must ask questions. We must find him. Begin with the Keepers of the West Door—our Seneca brothers. It is her brother we may have seen at Onondaga . . . in a Seneca canoe."

"This brother," the brave said, "what is he called?"

"His *Yen'-gees* name is Jamie. You will know him by the color of his hair. It is gold like the sun . . . like my wife's."

Crooked Ear inclined his head. "I will look as well as listen," he promised. "I will run like the wind and return by the time the sun rises twice to light the sky."

Kwan's expression was solemn, but approving. "My wife is sad. She will be happy to know that her Jamie lives . . . that he is being treated well by our Seneca brothers. But even if he is not . . . if he is slave or dead, we must know this. It is important to her."

"*Nyoh,*" the brave said. *So be it.*

The runner left him, and Kwan who was hungry went to search for the keeper of his appetite—his wife.

"O-wee-soo, have you seen Sun Daughter?" he asked his grandmother. The old woman was crossing the yard.

"Did you try the lake? She loves the water, that one, but only when she is alone. She is not yet used to our ways of bathing together as women of the tribe."

"I will go to the lake." Kwan smiled his thanks and went on.

But Abbey was not there and no one along the path had seen her. Kwan walked about the forest, checking the area where she usually went berry-gathering. She was not there either. What he found, though, brought fear to his heart, chills to his spine. There were signs of the white man. *Yen'-gees*—English? French? His need to find Abbey grew urgent. The thought of her in the hands of white men terrified him.

He hurried back to the village and became further alarmed at a recent discovery made by Night Eagle, one of the warrior-guards. A brave was missing; he'd been on guard last night, and there were signs of a struggle near the Onondaga's post.

What happened to Abbey and the brave? Was Breckingridge dead? What if Bear Claw hadn't killed him? Kwan had a gut feeling that the British officer was alive and responsible.

"She is gone," Kwan told his father, "and I fear the *Yen'-gees* colonel is the one who has her."

Silver Fox looked grave. "He is not dead?"

Kwan went in search of Bear Claw. "Is this possible? Could the man have escaped death?"

The warrior frowned. "I hit him with my *Ka-jee-kwa*. He should be dead. If not, then it must be Big

350

Nose, the bad spirit, who is with him. Bad, powerful medicine."

"He may have Sun Daughter," Kwan said.

Bear Claw tensed. *"Anikha Sagoha?* We must find the white man. We must kill him and all who talk with him."

The warrior left to organize the band of Indians who would search for and rescue their sachem's bride.

Was it possible that Abbey had left on her own? Kwan wondered. None of the others had mentioned it. It hadn't even crossed their mind.

He recalled the desperation in his wife's love-making last night. Had it been Abbey's way of saying goodbye?

Chapter 28

Kwan's messenger reached the first Seneca village that afternoon. Crooked Ear asked the sachem if he knew of a golden-haired *Yen'-gees*, who'd been taken captive several moons ago.

The sachem did not have such a slave. He never kept male captives, he said, only the little ones. He had heard of a golden-haired warrior, though, one of their Seneca brothers. Crooked Ear nodded his thanks and left for the next village.

The brave was greeted by He-Who-Comes-In-The-Night next. The Seneca warrior was the one who had been at odds with Kwan over the French.

"I am Onondaga," Crooked Ear said. "I come from my sachem's hut."

"Who is your sachem?" He-Who-Comes-In-The-Night said.

"Great Arrow of the Wolf clan."

The Seneca scowled. "What news does the sachem send? Does he seek to make war?"

Crooked Ear was startled. "Great Arrow wants

only peace. He seeks to make He-Who-Comes-In-The-Night his friend. He asks a great favor of you. He knows you are a just warrior and will not hold your past differences against him in his time of need.''

The Indian looked pleased. ''What is it that Kwan wants?''

''We are looking for a *Yen'-gees* captive. A man with hair the color of the bright sun.''

He-Who-Comes-In-The-Night stared at him. ''Why do you search for him?''

''He is the brother of Great Arrow's wife, *Anikha Sagoha*.''

''I know not of the brother. This—''

''Jam-ie.''

The brave nodded. A man approached He-Who-Comes-In-The-Night from behind. ''I would speak with you,'' the man said.

''I will return,'' He-Who-Comes-In-The-Night said to Crooked Ear. ''Sit. My woman—Slow Dancer—has brought you food.'' He moved away several yards to speak with the man in private.

Crooked Ear sat down and smiled at Slow Dancer as she handed him a plate of fruit and meat. He was grateful for the rest and food; he was tired and hungry. While he ate, he kept a close watch on the two Senecas as they talked. The second one was gesturing with his hands. Crooked Ear heard the Indian scolding He-Who-Comes-In-The-Night for being less loyal to his Indian brothers than to the French. Finally, the conversation was over, and He-Who-Comes-In-The-Night came back to Crooked Ear.

"We may know of the *Yen'-gees*," he said grudgingly.

Crooked Ear perked up. "He is here?"

The Seneca shook his head. "He is gone on the hunt. He will be back soon."

"He is not slave then." The *Yen'-gees* was allowed to hunt? This news greatly interested the Onondaga.

"White Bear is one of us now. He is wed to our sachem's daughter." The Seneca brave seemed angry, and Crooked Ear wondered why.

"Your friend—" Crooked Ear gestured toward the other Seneca.

"Our sachem," He-Who-Comes-In-The-Night said. "White Bear's new father. Man with Eyes of Hawk."

Eyes sparkling, Crooked Ear nodded his thanks. The older Seneca was the chief. Kwan would be interested in the Senecas' words. It seemed that Man with Eyes of Hawk thought differently than He-Who-Comes-In-Night. If Kwan talked with the Seneca sachem, perhaps their troubles with the French would be over.

As the Seneca brave left, he smiled. He had learned something of value for the League. Now he would wait and meet with this White Bear.

"I feel sick!" Abbey said. "Please . . . take me to the woods."

"Leave her!" Breckingridge commanded his lieutenant who had been bending over the woman with concern. "She's lying."

Abbey clutched her stomach, moaning. She really

was ill, and she didn't know why. She'd refused all offers of food; they couldn't have poisoned her.

"Please, Lieutenant!" she groaned. She blinked up at the young officer with tear-filled eyes.

"Colonel!"

Breckingridge looked over with annoyance. He saw his subordinate's expression and switched his attention to the woman. Abbey did look pale . . . and a bit green. "Oh, all right," he said. "Take her. We don't need her vomiting here. But, Lieutenant—and I'm holding you personally responsible for this—don't let her escape!" He narrowed his gaze. "She's a tricky one. She's liable to try anything—even fake illness—to get away."

Abbey flashed him a vile look. She could understand why the man might believe she was lying, but it didn't lessen her hatred for him.

"If you'd care to wait, Colonel," she gasped, reeling under an attack of dizziness, "I'll be happy to prove just how sick I am."

She gulped and covered her mouth.

"Lieutenant!" Breckingridge boomed. "Get her out of here. *Now!*"

Abbey was led by the young man to the woods where she promptly rid herself of her stomach's contents.

"Are you all right, Miss?" the man asked her.

She stood a moment with her eyes closed, her hands on her stomach, waiting for her nausea to pass.

"Miss?"

She swallowed and looked at the man called Terrington. "I'm sorry, Lieutenant. I'm . . . better. Thank you." The earth spun, and she grabbed the young officer's shoulder to gain her balance.

"Miss," he said worriedly, "shall I get the colonel?"

"No!" Abbey took a deep breath. "That won't be necessary. I'm feeling fine now . . ."

Why am I sick? Nerves? She'd begun to feel ill since the Council Fire when she'd disobeyed Kwan. Of course, being held captive by a madman hadn't improved her sense of peace.

Still . . . She tensed. How long had it been since she had her monthly courses? Three weeks? Four? Five?

Abbey closed her eyes and cradled her belly with her hands. A baby? Was it possible she carried Kwan's child?

Not only possible, she thought with a growing feeling of awe, *but probable.* A baby! Kwan's baby!

"Miss, if you're done . . ."

She looked up, saw the lieutenant blush, and realized how important it was that she escaped. There was more at stake here than just her life. There was Kwan's. Breckingridge planned to use her as bait. There was Bear Claw, whom the colonel intended to punish for his attack. And now . . . there was the tiny life growing inside of her. Their baby. Hers and Kwan's.

Abbey felt a new resolve to get away as she walked back to the campsite and sat down, as instructed, under a large tree.

"Well?" Breckingridge asked.

Terrington approached him. "She was ill, sir."

The colonel glared at Abbey. "You'd better get well quickly, wench, or I'm liable to take advantage of the situation." He laughed as he moved away.

Abbey sat under the tree and stared ahead. So far she'd been safe from the colonel's attentions, but her time was running out. Now that she was with child, it was even more imperative that the man not lay his hands on her. No man must touch her, but Kwan.

Kwan. Would he be happy about the babe? She frowned. Atahkwa had died giving birth, would Kwan be concerned with her own time of lying in?

She heard movement in the clearing. Breckingridge was on his feet, pacing back and forth before their campfire.

The man was fast regaining his health and strength. They'd traveled far the first day, far enough from the Iroquois to fear reprisal in immediate attack.

Breckingridge had been too tired to fulfill the promise of his threat. But soon . . . tonight . . . She'd be at the animal's mercy!

Abbey thought hard. How could she keep him at bay? She couldn't bear it if he touched her. With Kwan it was making love; with Breckingridge, it would be the violent, unspeakable act of rape.

Breckingridge loved power over those weaker than himself. How could she pierce that male confidence, that cocksure attitude, that made the man a dangerous adversary?

Hit him low, she thought.

An idea came to her then, and she smiled secretively.

Crooked Ear, Kwan's messenger, couldn't believe his success. He was in a Seneca canoe and on his way

357

back to the Onondagas with not only the knowledge of Jamie's whereabouts—but the man himself.

The brave glanced at the figure beside him. This was a *Yen'-gees!* Crooked Ear thought. When he'd first met Sun Daughter's brother, he'd been astonished by the man's appearance. Jamie was no pale-faced *Yen'-gees* with light eyes and curly hair. The brother had become White Bear, Seneca warrior with hair worn in an Iroquois war lock.

Kwan's woman was in for a shock, the Onondaga thought. The man beside him must be a far cry from the brother Sun Daughter knew back in England. Her Jamie.

But White Bear was Jamie. The light of recognition in the young man's eyes when Crooked Ear had spoken Abbey's name had been convincing enough . . . and then there was the youth's willingness to come and see his sister.

"Your wife is Wind Singer," Crooked Ear said.

White Bear nodded. "She's a good woman."

"You were once slave?"

"Yes, for a time. Man with Eyes of Hawk admired me and gave me to his sister's people. Soon, I became son."

Crooked Ear smiled. "Your sister—her story is near to that."

The warrior's blue eyes blinked. "Abbey is well?"

Crooked Ear said she was. "She is married, like you. To Kwan Kahaiska, our chief." He could see that the Seneca had trouble envisioning his sister in Indian life.

"How far is your village," White Bear asked.

"We are almost there. Just below Onondaga and

the Council Fire."

"I was near the fire—briefly. I didn't stay. Man with Eyes of Hawk had other commands for me."

"It was you that she saw then," Crooked Ear murmured.

"Abbey?"

"*Anikha Sagoha,*" the Onondaga messenger said. "Sun Daughter."

"Sun Daughter." White Bear smiled as if caught up in a past memory. "Yes, it suits her."

"Sun Daughter is a strong, spirited woman," Crooked Ear said.

The Seneca grinned. "I know."

The soldiers were sleeping when Abbey managed to escape them. It wasn't a miracle that she'd done so; she'd had help. Terrington, the lieutenant, had felt sorry for her and had left her rope bindings loose enough for her to wiggle free. And the guards selected by Terrington each had the brains of a small peahen. It had been easy to slip past them.

It was pitch black in the woods, and the territory was unfamiliar to her. She concentrated not on the dangers she might encounter, but on her main goal, which was to get as far away as possible this night from Colonel Breckingridge and his men.

This evening she had angered the colonel until he'd turned beet red in the face; but he hadn't raped her, he'd been unable to.

Abbey grinned as she pushed back brush in her search for a footpath. Breckingridge had come to his tent where she'd been held captive for a time, his manner taunting, assured. But she'd been ready for him. Pretending fear at first, Abbey had cowered as he'd told her of the terrible things he would do to her, do to Kwan.

The animal! she thought, recalling part of their conversation.

"I'll torture the bloody savage until he begs for mercy!" the colonel had growled.

"What do you have against him?"

"He attacked the fort!"

"You murdered his people—his future wife!"

Breckingridge's face had darkened. "No matter. They're heathens all of them. What do we need with the savages? We don't need them! They kidnapped my Susie."

"Susie Portsmouth?" Abbey said, enjoying the astonishment on his face.

"You know my niece." He grabbed her arms, his expression anxious. "Where is she? Is she alive? Did the bastards hurt her? If they did—"

"Virginia, colonel." Abbey pulled away. "Your niece is safe and sound in the Virginia colony with her planter husband."

"You're lying!"

"Am I?" She had stared at him. "I was the one in your house, colonel. The servants thought I was Susie. I let them believe it!" She raised her eyebrows at his look. "You don't believe me? Shall I describe your home for you?" She went on to describe in detail the layout of his house, the color of the rugs, the walls, the pieces of furniture in the different rooms.

"Virginia?" he said, looking stunned. She nodded. "No matter. The savages raided my fort, kidnapped my soldiers' wives. They took my man Smythe. Where is he?''

"I've never seen or heard of your Smythe, colonel.''

Breckingridge had gazed at her. "They have to pay—every last one of them. You're his woman. You have to pay.''

He had stepped back from her then, his features changing, mirroring his lust for her. His hands went to his breeches, releasing the strings. "I'm going to enjoy this, my dear, but I'm afraid you might find it a bit rough . . .''

Breckingridge eyed her wickedly as he removed his clothes. "You may scream if you wish. I like a woman's scream . . .''

Abbey kept silent, feeling horror. She reminded herself if she was to outsmart the man, she must stay calm.

As she traipsed through the forest, Abbey looked back on the moments that followed with a silent prayer of thanks. She remembered how she'd laughed at the colonel's naked body. She'd ridiculed his manhood . . . its size, its color, and its shape. Then, she'd gone on in detail and to great length on how amusing he looked . . . his chest . . . his arms . . . his hairy buttocks.

The British commander had been so stunned by her accolade that he'd been speechless at first. Then came his rage, but Abbey had kept laughing, and when he'd attempted to rape her, his staff had been useless, lifeless . . . limp and small, just as she'd said.

Abbey touched her bottom lip, which was slightly swollen. Breckingridge had struck her across the mouth, so hard that he'd made her lips bleed; but she was grateful, for he scrambled into his clothes and left, ordering his men to remove her from the tent.

Her mouth stung now, but she considered herself lucky. Breckingridge hadn't raped her. He'd been so startled he hadn't even thought to humiliate her by offensive touching.

Abbey was amused. Oh, what a fragile thing was a man's pride!

As she stumbled through the thicket, her only desire was to return to Kwan. What must he be thinking with her gone? Did he believe that, like the last time, she'd left him on purpose? How could he know that she'd been kidnapped by the one man they all thought dead?

She was a long way from the village. She was tired and sore, but she couldn't stop. When the colonel learned of her escape, he'd be insane with anger—like the madman he was. Abbey said a prayer that the colonel didn't suspect that it was the young lieutenant who'd helped her. It would mean the English soldier's death if he did.

She continued her trek through the dark, at times scared but unwilling to submit to fear. She needed to see Kwan, to explain that she hadn't left him willingly.

Abbey wanted to tell Kwan that she loved him.

She walked and walked until she could move no more. Exhausted, she found a secluded spot in the woods, and she curled up on the ground, covering herself with dead leaves and dried brush. Thinking she was safe, Abbey dozed for a time, until something woke her. Voices. Indians.

She froze, afraid to move, but the Iroquois had already spied her. Her brush covering was tossed aside, and Abbey scrambled to her feet, moving away. Mohawks? she wondered, examining them closely. She swallowed. She'd had little contact with the Mohawks of the League, but they were known to be fierce. Man-eaters.

Without thought, she moved her hand, searching for her knife, which wasn't there.

The Indians looked much as the other Iroquois. There were five of them. Two of them wore the cock's crest; two others had the small dark tufts at the crown of their heads. One, the youngest, had a full head of hair; Abbey was eyeing this brave with interest, when the Indian spoke, addressing his friends.

The warrior was little more than a boy, she noted, listening carefully to their pattern of speech. There was something powerful about the youth; the others seemed to view him with respect.

Abbey knew Onondaga well enough now that she was able to make out some of his Iroquoian tongue. The brave was speculating who she was. He discussed with his friends what to do with her.

She spoke up. "I am *Anikha Sagoha,* wife to Kwan Kahaiska, sachem of the Onondagas." The youth studied her from beneath lowered eyelids. "I am lost," she continued. "I was kidnapped by the *Yen'-gees,* but I escaped. I mean to return to my village. Can you help me?"

When she was done speaking, there was instant reaction among the Indians. The young brave stepped closer.

"I am *Swe-an-da-e-a Kagh-ka*—Black Crow," he

363

said. "Sachem of the Cayugas. I know of Great Arrow. He is your husband?" The Indian looked skeptical; his expression demanded some sort of proof from her.

Swallowing hard, Abbey nodded. "I was slave once. Then, I was adopted by the Onondagas. O-wee-soo, my husband's grandmother, is a wise woman. She decided the match for us. It is a good one . . ." Her voice dropped off, and her eyes filled with tears. She missed Kwan, longed to be with him. She needed to feel his strong arms around her again . . . the sweet savagery of his lips.

"You will come to my village where you will eat and sleep." Black Crow's words brought her attention back to the brave.

Would they help her? Or was she to be a slave again? She wished for the presence of the wampum belt.

"You will sleep and then we will take you to your village. We will take you to Great Arrow."

She smiled, and her tears became tears of gratitude and joy. "Thank you."

Black Crow grinned. "It will be good to see the sachem again. There have been many changes in our tribe since he was with us."

Cayugas, Abbey thought later as she reached their village. Could these be the same Indians who'd captured Kwan when he was a boy? She found the notion was discomfiting.

The sight that met her gaze when she entered past the stockade fence was a familiar one to her. Children played naked about the yard, while dogs barked and ran about their masters, often stopping to nibble the food scraps tossed to them by bare-breasted Indian women.

Abbey became homesick, overwhelmingly so. She wanted nothing more than to be home with the Onondagas again . . . with Kwan.

"You are hungry?" Black Crow asked. They came into the center of the compound and were surrounded by the families and friends of the young sachem and his men.

She was too emotional to answer him. All she could do was look at him and nod.

The young chief's face softened. "Eat and do not fear," he said, his voice gentle. "Black Crow always keeps his word."

"Nee-yah-weh'-ha," she managed to choke out. *Thank you.*

Chapter 29

Crooked Ear arrived home at his village as Kwan and the others were preparing to leave. He spied the sachem across the yard, talking with Bear Claw.

"*Hoh-se-no-wahn!*" he called out to Kwan, excited with his success. "I have brought good news. I have—" He stopped when the sachem turned around. Kwan's face looked haggard. There were lines of worry about the silver eyes. "Kwan, what is it? What has happened?"

"*Anikha Sagoha*—she is gone."

Crooked Ear felt the woman's brother tense beside him. He held out a hand to keep him silent. "Gone? She has left?" His gaze met White Bear's briefly before sliding back to Kwan.

"*Yen'-gees.*" Kwan slipped his flint knife into the ties of his breechclout. "Running Deer is missing. There are signs of a fight."

"So she did not go to her brother?" Crooked Ear asked.

Kwan frowned. "No." His eyes flickered as they

noted the Seneca beside the brave. "You have word of Jam-ie?" He looked at Crooked Ear.

The brave nodded. "I have more than news. I—"

"I am White Bear," the Seneca said, introducing himself.

Kwan stared at him, his brow furrowing. There was something about the Indian. His stomach rocked. Those eyes. They were Abbey's eyes. He glanced up at his war lock. Sure enough, his hair— what little there was of it—was gold like the sun. "You?"

The man nodded and switched to speaking flawless English. "I'm Jamie Rawlins." His blue eyes blinked. "You're my sister's husband?"

The sachem inclined his head. "I am Kwan Kahaiska. Sun Daughter—Ab-bey Raw-lins—is my wife." He could see the mixed emotions on the Seneca's face as White Bear—Jamie—realized he, too, was once English. He wondered if his own thoughts showed as clearly. This was a *Yen'-gees?* He smiled slightly as he envisioned Abbey's reaction to her brother's savage appearance.

"My sister is gone? Where?"

Kwan's expression grew tortured. "We leave to find her. There are tracks left by those who took her."

"I will go with you," White Bear said. "You said the English have her. Why?"

"Breckingridge—the colonel—has her. Sun Daughter is a beau-ti-ful woman."

The brother's face darkened. "Sonuvabitch," he said. "Let's go then."

They left with six Indians in their party. The Iroquois followed the tracks for hours. During that time, Kwan watched Abbey's brother, wondering if the man would return to Philadelphia and the English way of life once he was reunited with his sister. He felt a measure of hope. Jamie Rawlins was a Seneca now—White Bear. The brave looked anything but ready for the white man's way of life.

The Indians stopped briefly to drink from a forest stream. Both husband and brother had grown increasing concerned for Abbey's safety. They should have reached the *Yen'-gees*. Had they misread the signs? Kwan's gaze met White Bear's in silent acknowledgment of shared fear.

The Iroquois reached the British encampment after dark. Crouched in the brush, Kwan eyed the soldiers, trying to gauge their number. He saw eleven about the campfire. There was no sign of Breckingridge. If the man was still alive, there'd be twelve Englishmen to six Indians. Good odds, Kwan thought. They could easily handle twelve *Yen'-gees*.

A tent was set up to the right in his view. The opening flap faced the fire, which crackled and popped as it burned. *Stupid Yen'-gees*, Kwan thought. It had been the flames and smoke of the fire that had drawn them to the site.

The tent flap moved, and Colonel Breckingridge exited the structure. "Terrington," he bellowed, "you bloody bastard! Where the devil are you?"

A young man rose from his position by the fire. "Yes, Colonel?"

"It's your bloody fault—all this! You'll be written up for this. Sent home in disgrace. If not for you, we'd still have our hands on the savage's bitch!"

Kwan stiffened and met the gaze of the man

hunkered down next to him. White Bear. Abbey's brother.

"She is not there?" White Bear mouthed silently.

The sachem nodded, his face strained.

The Seneca raised his eyebrows as if to say, "Shall I alert the others to attack?"

Kwan gave the go-ahead signal. He grabbed his knife from his waist, gripping the handle tightly. Hatred roiled in his gut for the English colonel, bringing up bile.

"Where is she, you scum!" he heard, the whispered words mimicking Kwan's thoughts. White Bear had returned.

The sachem exchanged looks with Abbey's brother. "I want him," Jamie said. Kwan hesitated. The Seneca's eyes so like his sister's had a glint to them that warned of danger. The sachem felt his lips curve upward. He recognized that familiar spark as one he'd seen in his wife's eyes when she became riled.

"Breckingridge is yours," Kwan growled, rising.

Iroquois war cries broke the night's silence as the Indians attacked the unsuspecting British troops.

As promised, the Cayugas returned Abbey to her village the next day. But something was happening in Kwan's village. There was no one at the gate when they got there, and they could hear the rhythmic tattoo of Indian drums and Iroquois voices raised in song.

"False Face," Black Crow said.

Abbey glanced at the Cayuga. "Someone is ill?"

Who? Spring Rain? O-wee-soo? *Kwan?*

The Indian shook his head. "Death chant. It is the song of sorrow. Someone is dead."

She paled, wondering whom. Abbey ran past the gate, anxious to learn if it was someone she knew well. She thought of all the people she'd befriended. There wasn't one she didn't care about.

The Onondagas had gathered in the village proper. They had formed a circle, and several masked figures danced and sang and shook turtle-shell and gourd rattles above their heads. The drums stopped. The Indians had detected their presence.

Silver Fox rose and came forward, his eyes bright. "Sun Daughter!" He gazed at the Cayuga brave, his face changing with recognition. "Black Crow."

Abbey studied the two men with surprise. "You know each other?"

Black Crow turned to her with a smile. "We are brothers of the same League."

"Oh." She blushed, feeling foolish. "Of course."

"You have come at a sad time, Black Crow," Silver Fox said. "We have lost a warrior. Big Turtle."

Recalling the brave, Abbey was saddened by the news. It dawned on her how the brave might have died. "Breckingridge," she breathed. The old man nodded, and her eyes stung.

"Kwan Kahaiska," the Cayuga said, "he is here?"

Silver Fox's face grew solemn. "He has not yet returned." He addressed his son's wife. "He is searching for you, Sun Daughter. His heart beat with worry when he saw you gone. His eyes told us that he would cry if he did not find you . . . if you did not return."

She felt her breath lodge in her throat. "He went looking for me?"

"He cares much for *Anikha Saghoa*." O-wee-soo, Kwan's grandmother, joined them.

"He loves me?"

The old matron stared at her. "More than shoe over a rough path . . . more than a morning flower."

Abbey's heart leapt. Kwan loved her more than the women who'd come before her? "How long have they been gone?" she asked.

"Since the morning of the last sun," Silver Fox said.

Yesterday morning, she thought. Kwan must have left shortly after he'd found her gone. "Will he be all right? He didn't go alone?"

O-wee-soo smiled. "He has five good warriors. He will return." She studied Abbey's appearance, noting with a frown her cut lip. "You were captured?"

Abbey shuddered with the memory, hugged herself her arms. "By the *Yen'-gees* colonel and his men."

"You have brought her back to us," Kwan's father said to Black Crow. *"Nee-yah-weh'-ha."*

The Cayuga acknowledged the old man's thanks with a dip of his head. "Sun Daughter escaped without Black Crow's help. We did not fight the *Yen'-gees*."

All gazes fastened on Abbey. She blushed. "I had help," she admitted. "A young man. I was ill, and he felt sorry for me."

"Ill?" O-wee-soo's eyes became sharp. "You are well now?"

"It comes and goes," Abbey mumbled, averting her gaze. She was unwilling to tell of the babe to anyone

371

but Kwan. The father should be the first one after the mother to know. *Please, Kwan, come back safe!*

"Come share our fire," O-wee-soo invited the Cayugas. "It is a sad time, but now it is a happy one, too. *Anikha Sagoha* has come home safely to her family."

Kwan arrived the next day, dispirited. He and the other Indians had searched for hours for Abbey, but there had been no sign of her anywhere. Finally, with his heart heavy, the sachem had given the order to head for home.

The British were dead. All but one—a young man. The lieutenant who'd apparently been the person responsible for allowing Abbey to escape. Kwan had his knife ready to kill him when he'd looked into the man's eyes and saw the fear, the innocence, the courage. He saw something in the young face that reminded him of himself. He recalled a time in his life when he'd suffered unjustly. He released the officer with a condition.

"You will go to your fort and tell your leader that the Onondagas are a peaceful people," he ordered the man. "Breckingridge killed many of our family. We attacked your fort to seek justice for his crimes. If the white man leaves us in peace, we will not kill." He had lowered his knife. "We are not killers. We kill only when we are forced to protect our own."

Nodding slowly, the young officer had stared at him, stunned. "You are Kwan Kahaiska."

"I am Great Arrow," Kwan confirmed. "Sachem of my village."

"Your woman . . . she was ill. I helped her. I hope she is all right."

Kwan nodded, hiding his sudden fear. Abbey was ill? "Go!" he commanded. "My braves will not harm you."

The Englishman fled. Kwan and the other Indians had continued their search.

Now as he entered the village, Kwan felt his heart thundering with anticipation. Was Abbey here? Had she somehow managed to return on her own? It was a slim hope, but he clung to it.

"Kwan!" Evening Sky, his wife's friend, hurried to meet him with a look of relief. "You are back. This is good. She will be pleased." She smiled. "May-be she will stop weeping all the time."

"Who?" he asked, afraid of the answer, afraid to hope.

"Sun Daughter."

He felt weak with joy. "She is here?" Abbey was home!

The Indian maiden grinned. "She came with Black Crow and his braves."

He glanced at White Bear. The brave had become his friend during the days of searching; a new bond had been formed between the Seneca and Onondaga tribes. Kwan saw the Seneca's eyes fill up with tears. "Your sister is safe," he said. "Ab-bey—she is in our house . . ."

"I will get her for you," Evening Sky offered.

But it wasn't necessary, they saw, for she came from inside the hut, her head bowed, her steps slow. She was obviously suffering as Kwan had suffered with concern for a missing loved one.

"Anikha!" Evening Sky called.

Abbey looked up, saw her friend, and then caught sight of her husband. She froze with shock. Her blue eyes brightened then, and her expression was the picture of happiness as she rushed forward. As she neared him, she slowed her steps. She seemed uncertain, and Kwan loved her for it.

"O-ka-o," he murmured, opening up his arms. She moved closer.

"Abbey!"

Her gaze swung to the man on Kwan's right. She stopped, her face paling. "Jamie?"

Kwan saw her changing expression . . . her doubt . . . her look of hope.

"Abbe!" her brother cried in a voice that sounded boyish, that made Kwan glance at the brave with surprise.

The woman ran then, flew into her brother's arms. They cried and held each other. It had been well over a year since they'd seen each other, but it could have been a decade for all that had transpired in their lives.

Kwan was happy for the two of them, but he was hurt that she had run to Jamie without greeting him first, that she ignored her husband that loved her more than life.

She has chosen, he thought. *She will go with her brother.*

He felt the agony of losing love. Kwan turned from the tender scene of brother and sister and left the village.

"Jamie?" Abbey gasped. She stood back to study his appearance. "My God, you've changed!"

He grinned. "So have you."

374

She glanced down at herself, seeing her tanned limbs and deerskin tunic . . . the moccasins on her feet. She returned his grin. "You're right!" Her expression became serious. "You're a warrior."

"Seneca."

"I saw you," she said, "in a canoe at Onondaga."

"It might have been me, but I think not. What made you believe it was me? My hair?" He grabbed his war lock, which was just a small clump of hair on the top of his head.

She smiled. "I see your point." Abbey's gaze moved about the compound. Where was Kwan? He had disappeared, she realized, and she hadn't had a chance to greet him! She felt her brother's gaze. "How did you come here?" she asked. She continued to search for signs of her husband, frowned when she couldn't find him.

"Your husband found me."

She blinked, looked at him. "Kwan sent for you?"

"He sent Crooked Ear. The brave told me that I had to be found, no matter what, because it was important to you." He lowered his voice. "He must love you very much." His blue eyes held a question.

"I love him," Abbey admitted. "More than I ever dreamed it was possible to love a man."

"Like Mother must have loved Father," Jamie said.

Abbey held his gaze. "Like Father loved Mother." Her eyes watered. "He's dead, Jamie. Father's dead."

His features contorted. "I'm sorry," he whispered sincerely.

"He wanted me to find you." She bit her lip. "I sold Mother's brooch to come."

Her brother smiled. "Always knew it would come in handy, Mother did." His eyes glistened with his own tears.

"He tried to save her, Jamie," she said. "Truly, he did."

"I know," he breathed.

"He wanted you to forgive him . . . for failing. He wanted you to understand."

Jamie broke down. "He wanted me to forgive him! My God, Abbe, I was the fool! Me and my rash tongue!" His voice cracked. "I'm the one who needs to be forgiven."

"No." She gave him a watery smile. "He understood that you were in pain . . . There was nothing to forgive. His words—not mine, but I agree with him."

Brother and sister hugged and sobbed quietly together. The Indians stayed away, allowing the two their private moment of shared grief.

"So, you're a Seneca warrior! Do you ever think of returning to Philadelphia to be a silversmith? What happened to Walt?"

Jamie wiped his eyes. "He went back to Philadelphia to be a silversmith. I convinced the Senecas to let him go."

"Then . . ." Abbey held her breath. Did that mean that Jamie was happy with the Indians? That he wouldn't expect her to return to Philadelphia with him?

"I'm happy with them, Abbe," he confirmed. "And I'm married—like you."

"You're married!" Her little brother? She studied him. He was a man. A married man! Abbey was ecstatic. Where was Kwan? She was restless to find him, to share the good news.

"I married the sachem's daughter," Jamie said. "Wind Singer." He watched her carefully. "She's different, Abbe, but I think you'll like her once you get past certain things . . ."

"Different?" Abbey echoed, but her attention was elsewhere . . . on her search for Kwan.

"She's dark," he said. "Her mother's a Negro."

"What?" He had gained her attention. "Did you say she's—"

Nodding, he said, "I love her."

Abbey thought of their parents, who had suffered from other's prejudice, but whose love was strong. "I'm happy for you," she said, meaning it. She looked for Kwan again.

"Damn!" Jamie exclaimed, drawing Abbey's glance. "Kwan! What a fool I am! The man's been worried half out of his mind and what do I do but take his wife away at a time when he needs to be with her!" His smile was apologetic. "Go, Sun Daughter. Find your husband."

Abbey grinned at the sudden change in her brother. He was White Bear once again. With a promise to talk more later, she left him to find Kwan.

She found her husband at the lake, gazing out over the moving water. Abbey paused several yards away. She felt her whole being swell with emotion . . . with love for this special man.

He had his back to her. She took a moment to run her gaze lovingly over his form . . . his broad shoulders and spine . . . his corded thighs, muscled calves . . . and his feet. Desire rose up to still her breathing. She moved forward, unable to bear the distance between them, for she had waited so long to be with him. *Forever*, she thought.

Her gaze blinded by tears, she traveled the remaining yards until she was a few feet away. Kwan looked dejected. Because of her? she wondered. Was it possible that he loved her and doubted her feelings for him?

"Kwan."

He spun as if shot. His silver gaze glowed with joy and then dimmed. "Ab-bey."

There was a long stretch of silence. Abbey felt an increasing tension, and she wondered how to banish the feeling, if there was hope or whether the relationship was one-sided. She recalled O-wee-soo's assurance that he cared.

Swallowing, she moved closer. "You looked for me." She saw that he was watching her closely, with an intensity that gave her renewed hope.

There was a pause, and then he inclined his head.

"It was the colonel," she said, needing to tell him that she hadn't left willingly, that she was kidnapped.

His lashes fluttered. He didn't speak, but seemed to be waiting.

"I . . ." She drew a breath, gathering the courage to confess her love. To do so would put her heart and her pride at great risk. She studied his handsome face, loving every rugged feature, and said, "I didn't leave you . . ." She felt wetness on her cheek—a teardrop.

"You came back," he finally said. His voice was husky.

"This is my home."

She saw a flash of joy light up his expression. "Your Jamie . . . ?"

Abbey smiled. "Thank you for finding him. I feel better now. He's happy. Do you know he's a Seneca warrior? And he's married to the chief's daughter!"

Kwan's lips curved in response to her happiness. "This is good then. I am happy if you are happy."

She froze. "Truly?"

He frowned, nodded. "You do not believe me?"

"No, it's not that. It's just that . . ." Her gaze clung to his, before she launched herself into his arms. "Kwan, I love you! Please let us be happy, too. Please love me back!"

She felt his muscles tense. He embraced her . . . slowly, gently.

"*O-ka-o,*" he whispered. Abbey looked up into his face and was surprised to see his silver eyes awash with tears.

"You are my sun, *O-ka-o* . . . my moon . . ." He place her hand on his chest over his beating heart. "The reason this body lives."

"Oh, Kwan," she cried, and he kissed her.

Abbey wrapped her arms about his waist and responded with all her passionate nature, holding onto him for dear life. They kissed in a ritual of mating mouths. They were both breathing hard when they broke apart.

Abbey studied his handsome, rugged features and thought of their child. Would it be a girl or a boy? Whatever it was, she wanted the babe to resemble Kwan. She thought of Atahkwa and wondered how Kwan would take the news. Would he be happy or merely concerned?

He was grinning from ear to ear. He had that look about him that promised her untold delights . . . a coming night of ecstasy . . . of love. They needed this time free from worry, from fear.

He bent his head. His lips met hers.

She would tell him about the babe tomorrow . . .

Epilogue

The little fair-haired girl ran to tickle her father's toes; and then when he roared teasingly with outrage, she raced back toward the edge of the lake. There, she hid behind her mother's legs, shrieking, until her father quieted and lay back on the grass shore.

Kwan closed his eyes, pretending to sleep. He waited, listening for his daughter's footsteps. He heard her approach and, sensing her near, he reached out to snatch hold of her leg, only to encounter not a child's leg, but a woman's. His wife's.

His eyelashes flickered open, and he grinned, studying her lovely face.

"Your daughter is gone," she said. Abbey saw his gaze flame with desire, felt an answering fire in her own body. Kwan's fingers were caressing her calf, making her pulse race and her knees feel weak. "O-wee-soo has taken her for a rest."

"You are tired?" he said, rising to lean on his elbows.

She shook her head. "Not a bit."

"That is too bad. I was to offer you my shoulder to lie on, but—"

She shushed him with her hand and pressed him backward. The scent of sweet grass rose up to tantalize the air. Abbey lay down, snuggling against him, placing her head on the offered shoulder.

They lay quietly together for a time, enjoying their moment of peace. It was a warm spring day, nearly summer. Birds chirped in the trees overhead. The sun beat down, heating the spot where they rested. Drowsy, Abbey studied the sky and listened to her husband's heartbeat.

She was content. Her husband was a wonderful man, gentle with their daughter, tender and lovingly passionate with herself. He had granted her wish and released her friend Rachel and the woman's daughter, Anna. The German mother and her baby had returned to the life of the white man, and Abbey was glad for them, pleased she had been able to keep her promise.

As for Jamie, he had chosen to remain White Bear. When Abbey had first met his wife, Wind Singer, she'd been startled by the woman's dark beauty. It had been easy to see that the two were deeply in love, and Abbey had been pleased for them.

She'd had her wish come true. She was happy here among the Onondagas; Jamie was with the Seneca and she got to see him several times a year—whenever she wished. Abbey smiled.

"You are happy?" Kwan said.

Abbey turned her head. "You know I am," she murmured, gazing at him with love. Who would have ever thought she'd love a savage? she thought with amusement.

They were alone where no one would disturb them. This was their own private place. Only O-wee-soo would dare to venture here and only when she knew that Little Sun, her great granddaughter, was with them.

Her husband stroked her arm, and Abbey enjoyed the contact. His hand wandered, slipping below to fondle her breast, and she sighed softly, closed her eyes.

"You are sleepy." Kwan's voice was husky with desire. He shifted, rising to his side so that he could caress and kiss her at will.

Heart thumping, he pulled up his wife's tunic, exposing her white breasts to the day's sun. She sat up to help. His gaze intense, he removed the garment, tossing it aside.

He touched first one and then the other full mound, watching with fascination the way her nipple responded to his fingers. The tiny tip pebbled, and he rubbed it before bending his head to suckle her.

Abbey didn't move, but she was only pretending indifference, he realized, noting her quickened breath. He kissed her belly, and it moved. He nuzzled his way upward, paying homage to her womanly curves, burrowing his face in her neck. He inhaled her sweet scent. She smelled like a warm breeze . . . like flowers and water . . . and clean outdoors.

He captured her mouth, deepening the intimacy

when she moaned softly and parted her lips.

"*O-ka-o* . . . it is hard not to touch you," he gasped. He felt his staff harden beneath his breechclout. He undid the tie, releasing the confining cloth.

"Then touch me, Kwan," she whispered, her eyes glazing with passion. "Touch me . . ."

"But if there's a child . . ."

Her mouth curved. "Then, he'll be born as easily as Little Sun." She stroked his jaw, his forehead, smoothing away the lines of worry. "Stop being concerned, husband. I am healthy and alive, and we're wasting time."

She grabbed and kissed him, and Kwan groaned, coming alive.

And the earth moved and the sky became even brighter . . . and this world ceased to exist for them as they soared to the heavens on the wings of love . . .